VESSELLESS

VESSELLESS

CORTNEY L. WINN

MAGPIE

Magpie Books
An imprint of HarperCollins*Publishers* Ltd
1 London Bridge Street
London SE1 9GF

www.harpercollins.co.uk

HarperCollins*Publishers*
Macken House,
39/40 Mayor Street Upper,
Dublin 1, D01 C9W8
Ireland

First published by HarperCollins*Publishers* Ltd 2025
1

Designed by Alison Bloomer
Map by Mike Hall

Cortney L. Winn asserts the moral right to
be identified as the author of this work.

A catalogue record for this book is available from the British Library.

ISBN: 978-0-00-876456-2 (HB)
ISBN: 978-0-00-876457-9 (TPB)

This novel is entirely a work of fiction.
The names, characters and incidents portrayed in it are
the work of the author's imagination. Any resemblance to
actual persons, living or dead, events or localities is
entirely coincidental.

Set in Garamond Premier Pro

Printed and bound in the UK using 100% renewable electricity by CPI Group (UK) Ltd

This book contains FSC™ certified paper and other controlled sources
to ensure responsible forest management.

For more information visit: www.harpercollins.co.uk/green

*For Mason, my best friend and
happily ever after every day*

VALZONN

BADDADWOM

LESSER DISTRICT

ZARR

ZARR CITY
(GOLD DISTRICT)

CALANTAZ MOUNTAIN RANGE

ZO

THARÉ

ZO CITY

NEUTRAL
GROUND

ZEM CITY

ZEM

VALOŃ

N

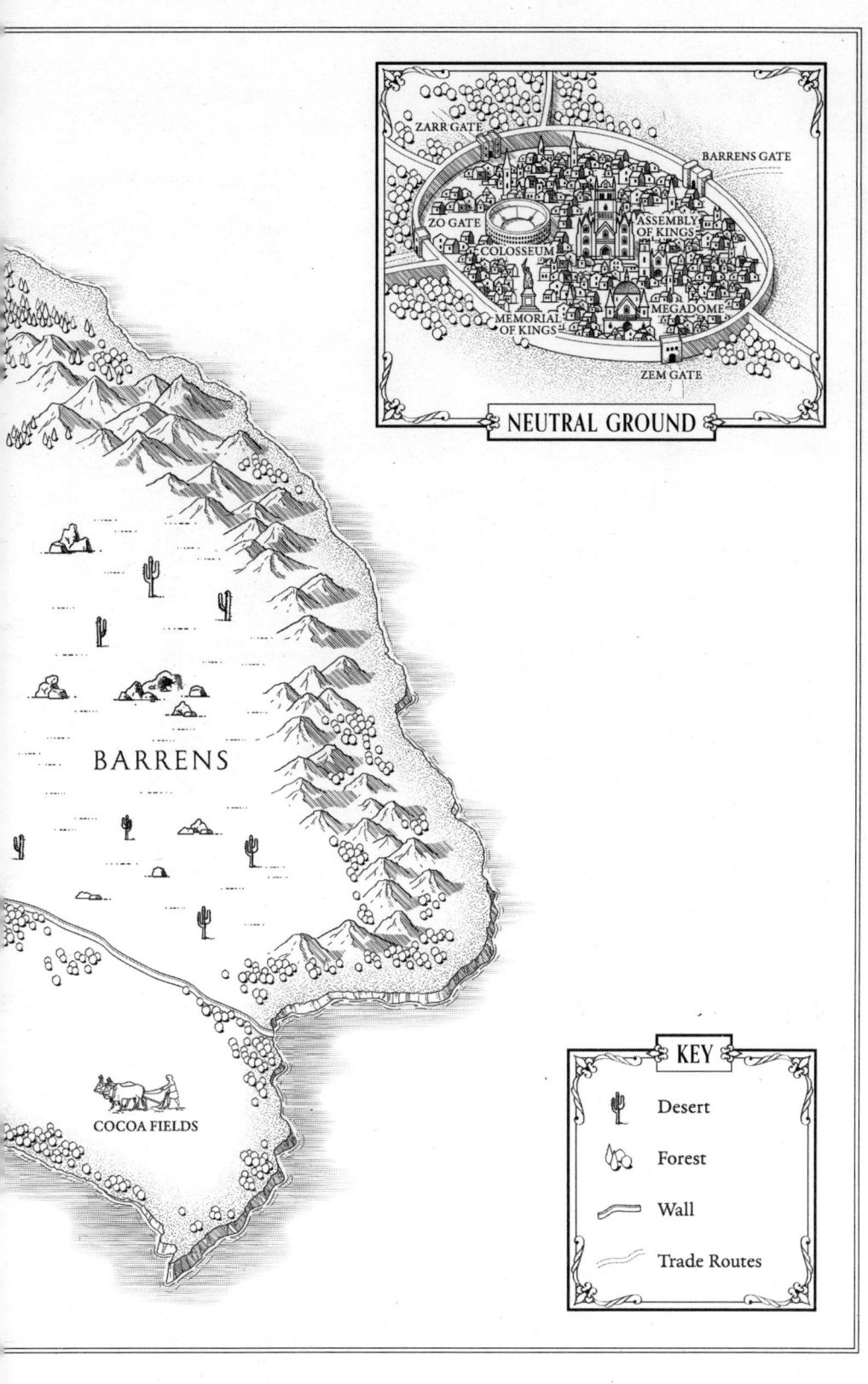

NEUTRAL GROUND

ZARR GATE

BARRENS GATE

ZO GATE

ASSEMBLY OF KINGS

COLOSSEUM

MEGADOME

MEMORIAL OF KINGS

ZEM GATE

BARRENS

COCOA FIELDS

KEY

Desert

Forest

Wall

Trade Routes

CHAPTER 1

NIZZARA

*To look upon the worst and see the best is true sight. To behold
the whole and find no flaw, only then can one be right.*
—*Love from a Blind Prince*

EVERYTHING HERE IS BLACK. BLACK WALLS, BLACK FLOORS,
and black furniture. It looks as if I'm standing in one of my nightmares.
But my new room is real, and it's furnished with the belongings of a
dead person. The ottomans were sat on and the vanities used mere days
ago. Shoving my storm of emotions down, I lean forward and glance
into the giant washroom—*pointedly* ignoring the hazy spirits floating
near the rafters.

Like everything else, the washroom is black. The only thing that
isn't are the white glo stones set into the massive chandeliers above,
which hang down in deadly, metal points.

My new maid, Preysee, follows me around the room with her
sharp gaze. I'm old enough to know that look. It's hatred. Hatred for
my father, and, therefore, me. I continue through the room, trying to
tamp my growing fear and anger. I hardly feel just one or the other,
especially when it comes to my father. Across the room, one of the tall
balcony doors is cracked open, allowing the winter chill in. I can't help
but wonder if the princess used it to escape when my father laid siege
to this castle.

With the walls slowly closing in on me—and Preysee watching my every move—I wander toward the balcony. Perhaps my fear of heights will be better than a roomful of spirits whispering about the darkness inside my soul. With shaky hands, I set my book down on an ottoman and heave the balcony door open wider, just enough for my little frame to fit through. I freeze as soon as I meet the night sky, realizing how high this balcony is.

"Don't black out," I beg myself as that darkness in my soul begins crawling through me.

My heartbeat thuds in my ears as I clutch the railing and peer over the edge. In the city far below, between tall, pointed buildings, the little red lights of glo-kars drift through cobblestoned streets.

They were, I remember now, one of the last inventions made by the fourth kingdom before it crumbled under warfare. I squint, looking over the long wall stretching toward the empty, inky horizon on my left, one of the few remnants of that time. On my right are city lights sprawling as far as I can see, lights of his kingdom and the other kingdoms, all meeting in the center of our continent—all pointing at our neutral ground.

Tears form and the skyline starts to blur. I wipe my cheeks and scan the glittering horizon, looking for my home—looking for some shred of comfort. When I see the white glow in the distance, my heart squeezes. The Zo kingdom.

I belong *there*. Not here in Zarr. It doesn't matter if my father is from here. I'm not.

Every fiber of my being yearns for the Zo palace, yearns to turn back time.

And then I feel it: my emotions have grown too strong; my world flickers into darkness, and power tingles in the air around me. Panicked, I dart back into the haunted room, nearly colliding with the maid. Preysee backs up, brushing her black uniform while I scoop my book up. Like everyone in this castle, she has an air of ruthlessness about her, with her pink scar reaching up her lip and her piercing gaze.

She glares down at me as I clutch my favorite book, *Love from a Blind Prince*, tighter against my chest. It's the only book I was allowed to bring from Zo. I held it the whole ride here.

"I do not blame you for what your father did, child." Preysee's voice is hard, but I hear the sadness hiding in it. She looks toward the bedroom door then back at me. "You don't have to fear me. Do you understand?"

I find her honey-brown gaze, and she conceals her flinch better than most who meet my pitch-black irises.

My father, still in his infantry general uniform, enters without knocking. Preysee stiffens, her expression turning even more piercing than before. When my father's heavy boots scuff the floor toward us, she leaves with a swish of her black maid's dress.

Father gestures to the bed draped in dark silks and velvets, adorned with more pillows than I could possibly use. "Do you like it?"

I don't say anything. He won't approve of my answer, not after he lost his temper with me yesterday. He kneels in front of me, his face a portrait of fatherly love. A portrait only shown to me when no one is around. When no goblet of wine is near.

When he holds out his palm to me, I freeze. A smooth golden ring rests in the crease of his hand. "You are my chosen heiress of the Zarr kingdom, my successor to the throne," he says. "It is time you take a vessel."

My voice is small but unafraid, despite the rising panic in my chest. "Most nobles wait until their teens."

He pushes the vessel ring closer. "Your mind is mature enough for this power, and so is your soul."

I swallow, doubtful anyone could be sure of that, let alone my father. I've witnessed his lust for vessel power grow over the last few months, changing him in ways . . . ways I refuse to acknowledge. "I don't want a vessel," I say, a sudden fire filling my chest. "I don't want to be the heiress of Zarr."

Simmering rage enters his gaze, and his mouth drops at the

corners. A flicker of the man he's been lately flashes in his eyes, and I catch the faint but sharp smell of wine lingering on his breath. When I step back, he snatches my hand.

"I don't care what you want," he says, fighting my small but determined arms. "I care about what's best for you."

He knocks my book to the stone floor and wrestles me to the ground, trying to jam the golden vessel onto my finger. I thrash against him, begging him not to force this on me.

But he ignores me, like I ignore the evil lurking in his gaze. Like I ignore a lot of truths. Truths I shouldn't know as someone so young.

As soon as he rams the vessel to the apex of my finger, intricate tendrils grow from the metal band, sinking into my flesh. I scream from the pain, and it echoes off black walls, dying in an empty castle still painted with fresh blood.

An invisible energy creeps from the vessel over my skin, humming in a near-silent frequency.

"There," he says, a smoothness reclaiming his face as he lifts me up and returns my book to my hand, an unspoken apology already lingering in the air between us. My chest is still heaving from panic and rage as the ring on my finger burns my skin. "We have many enemies. This will protect you, Nizzara."

I glare at him with every shred of hatred an eleven-year-old girl can muster as he continues. "I know spirits scare you, even if you don't admit it. You're right to be wary of them, but I've found one who will protect your soul."

From the rafters, a pinkish presence separates itself from other near-invisible orbs of energy. Everyone knows about spirits, but from conversations I've overheard, I realize I shouldn't be able to perceive them like I can. I don't know why I've always been more sensitive to their dimension, but I am.

"Her name is Liha," Father says. "Let her into the energy surrounding you now—your caster's shield." He clears his throat. A warmth enters his face as he gazes at me. "You are a caster now."

I feel Liha's presence, a more concentrated form of warm air nudging the caster's shield now clinging to my body like a glove.

"I don't want to be a caster," I say, clutching my book as if it can calm my racing heart. "I don't want power."

He bows his head. His voice trembles with so much emotion, I feel it clogging the space between us. "If you never trust me in any other matter, please trust me in this. Accept her into your shield."

My mind screams for me not to do it, but my soft heart wins, falling for his warm voice all over again.

I open my mind, energy, and soul to Liha.

She enters my shield, and her pink soul pushes away the darkness I feel inside.

CHAPTER 2

NIZZARA

TEN YEARS LATER

vessel/ves(ə)l/noun

1. An unremovable ring, capable of housing and
   protecting a bond between spirit and human
2. A conduit through which something flows
3. A binder of souls
   —FROM *THE ZO LEXICON*

ZARR INFANTRY SOLDIERS, ADORNED WITH MATTE-BLACK
armor and spiked shoulder plates, drag a beaten man up the dais steps
before dropping him at our feet with a thud. Somewhere in the crowd
of witnesses, a woman sobs. My knuckles turn white over gold armrests.

Another execution.

Liha isn't here. She used to calm me down, but lately, her bubbly
presence hasn't been enough. Now, when my emotions rise, so does the
darkness inside.

As the chosen heiress of Zarr, my throne sits between Father's on
my right and Mother's on my left, all of us towering over the assembled
court and witnesses below—tan faces against a sea of black stone.

I look to Mother at my side, wishing she'd offer me a loving glance or reassuring touch, like she always gives to my sister, but her face remains cold and regal, pointed away from me. My gaze flicks past the crumpled man before us to the assembled crowd, searching for the woman, her helpless whimper pulling tears to my eyes.

Father leans over to me. "Fix your face, Nizzara."

I arrange my face into the smile he's drilled into me despite the woman's cries trembling in the distance—he'll punish this poor man on the dais longer if I don't. I *will* fix what my father has done to this kingdom, but if there's one thing I've learned from him, it's the subtle art of timing.

The man in front of us staggers to his worn, bare feet. "Your Majesty, I swear on my family. I'm not a rebel—"

An infantry soldier punches the man's jaw, knocking him back down to the blood-speckled floor.

When the man dares to lift his head again, Father pushes up from his throne, a snarl curling his lips. "You housed rebels in your inn. That is punishable by death."

An infantry soldier yanks the innkeeper's head back by his hair and pulls him to his feet.

The innkeeper's stubbly throat bobs. "I didn't know they were rebels!"

Father prowls toward the innkeeper and snatches the man's throat, pulling him closer. Small black gems glisten on Father's glove as his hand flexes tighter and tighter around the innkeeper's thin neck.

"Then you will set an example to the rest of Zarr," Father proclaims, "for what happens when you don't make it your business to know."

The innkeeper's lips turn a subtle shade of blue, yet I smile, tension splintering my jaw as I do.

The throat. His new favorite spot.

Just before the innkeeper loses consciousness, Father releases him, dropping the bloody man to the onyx floor. When the man doesn't stir, Father returns to his throne, his cape unfurling over the armrest as he sits. I can tell by the angle of Father's brows, he's already bored.

Black smoke crawls from his gloved hand, and the room falls silent—everyone knows what's hidden beneath that glove. The First-Made vessel, a white ring bonded to his hand and the conduit of his spirit's power. The black smoke slithers toward the innkeeper, then takes hold of his thin body, as if he were a puppet whose master had just pulled the strings.

Sorren, Father's infantry general, draws his sword and holds it out for the innkeeper to take. Father's power forces the innkeeper to take it.

The innkeeper's shaking hands aim the sword at his own neck.

My face, still fixed into a splintering grin, matches everyone else's as they perk up in unfettered anticipation; the woman's cries are now screams scratching down the black walls.

The innkeeper stabs the sharp, gleaming blade through his own neck, and blood soaks his gray shirt. After he falls to the floor, a soft blue soul, that only I can see, departs from his body. It floats away as the woman screams.

Heat pricks my eyes, but for all the world, I *smile*.

A Zarr infantry soldier kicks the dead innkeeper for fun. I can't bring myself to watch. If I do, I'll likely ram my dagger up that soldier's ass, which would not end well for anyone. Angry tears rising, I study the vessel on my finger to distract myself from the sound of infantry boots kicking the dead man. I memorize all the places its gold tendrils sink into my skin. There are three kinds of vessels. Silver vessels, worn by Zarr infantry; golden vessels, worn by kings and nobility; and the white First-Made vessel.

My father's vessel.

A scream pierces my thoughts. A woman breaks through the arms of a young castle guard and runs toward the dead man, tears flowing down her face. When she hits the wall of infantry soldiers blocking the dais, my father waves his hand.

"Kill her too."

The woman screams and fights, but Zarr infantries silence her with a blade. I close my eyes, reminding myself that infantry soldiers and castle guards have no choice. Their silver, military vessels bow to the First-Made vessel—to my father. They follow every direct command, whether they want to or not. Infantries are supposed to defend the three kingdoms, but my father has tasked them with killing every rebel who remains loyal to the last Zarr king.

The young king my father overthrew.

Zarr people are known for their stubbornness. They never forget, never forgive. Their hatred for my father will last for generations, because their beloved king, Dagen Corvonna, is long dead.

CHAPTER 3

DAGEN

I TOUCH DOWN TO HARD GROUND PETRIFIED BY ICE AND wind, my thick winter boots offering little protection against the miles of ice beneath my feet. Phasing from my spirit form to my human form is always painful. The opposite of being ripped apart limb from limb, it's as if I'm being sewn together, piece by piece, with a needle of ice and a thread of misery.

Half alive, half dead.

The flat, icy ground crawls with snakes of snowy winds. Peaked glaciers jut skyward on the horizon, blocking what little light radiates from a waxy moon. Most souls who end up here call it Hell, but I call this realm by its true name.

Baratrum.

Shadows lurk and slither in the ice crags behind me, awaiting their next meal. They prefer souls who put up a fight, but they'll consume anything. One shadow curls around my boot, tugging—whispering, *"Come back, give in."*

I stand my ground against its pull and seal my mind off from everything. I feel a tiny piece of my soul harden just enough to fend them off. It's the only way to survive here.

The shadows hiss and dart away as Nil, the god of death, materializes onto the ice before me. His black mist converges into a blood barbarian with red, sawlike teeth and gray, leathery skin. It's not often he impersonates other creatures, but even this monstrous beast is one of his more pleasant forms, if only because he is solid—visible.

Nil's power weaves through my soul like invisible tethers, forcing me here. Normally, when he wants me to hunt, I'm pulled by those tethers. No formal meetings are needed. If my mind and soul had some warmth left, I might be curious why he's gracing me with his presence this time.

But they don't. And I'm not.

"You called, my liege?" I take a knee and bow my head, locking my gaze on my black, frayed boots that once bore magnificent gems up the shins.

"I have an . . . *opportunity* for you, Dagen." His voices echo, a compilation of souls he's consumed.

Souls I've hunted for him.

"Another blackened soul?" I ask.

They're my forte, it seems.

Nil's barbarian horns protrude from his head, their wide girth splitting the skin above pointed ears. "There is a soul I require," he says, his eyes alight with cunning. "A *pure* soul."

"A pure soul, my liege?"

Blackened souls, wretched souls, rotten souls—I've dealt with those. Never a *pure* soul.

The ice beneath us quakes as he stalks around me in a slow circle. Shadows jump and writhe at his presence.

"Yes, a *pure* soul. Deliver her to me, and I will grant you freedom."

I blink as if waking from a trance. I know not to think of such foolish, humanlike desires. Ten years here, and I've abandoned most humanlike things, but . . .

"Freedom?" I breathe.

Nil's smile is all wrong on the face of the blood barbarian, his expression too meticulous, too calculating for such a brute creature.

"*Some* freedom," he amends. "You will no longer be confined to this realm. I'll allow you to live where you wish, but you'll still be my deathwalker, bending to my will, a slave to the urges."

My fingers curl to fists at my sides when I'm reminded of the worst of the urges—the primal need to consume souls to sustain myself and the shadows inside.

"That does not sound like freedom."

He walks behind me, his voice dropping into the smooth, persuasive tones I've come to recognize as the calm before the conniving. "Just imagine," he says. "You could know the warmth of a bed again, the kiss of a lover . . ." His boots pause on the groaning ice. "Do we have a bargain?"

A *bargain*. I've seen souls bargain with him. It always ends the same.

Badly.

He circles me.

From the corners of my eyes, I watch him snatch up a shredded red soul with dark edges. He breathes it in with a long inhale. The soul screams, and when it dies its final death, it shatters, the sound like breaking glass.

Trails of red pigment disappear on his lips.

"I do not bargain with gods."

"Pure souls are quite powerful." He smiles, invigorated by the soul's fresh power now thrumming through his veins.

"So?" I ask. "You *own* my soul. Just order me to do this and be done."

I am not falling for the traps he calls bargains. If this soul is powerful enough to elicit coercion from Nil, it must be a specific breed of awful. Awful souls are his favorite. Like trophies.

His red, bone-like talons seem to lengthen as he inches one toward my chest. "Rules must be followed in the case of this soul." He smiles, red teeth glinting like razors in the moonlight.

He's being too patient, his voice too calm for my liking.

"No." My knee on the ice throbs from the unworldly cold.

"Then I shall sweeten my offer," he says. "Bring me the pure soul, and I will give you one hundred years of complete freedom from my will. You can reclaim your throne, help your people, and free those little slaves, like you were so set on doing before you died. That is my final offer. I cannot remove the shadows from your soul. You will still be what you are."

"How can I reclaim my throne? I am not powerful enough against the First-Made vessel—"

He snaps his fangs at me. "The pure soul has the power to kill your enemy. Convince her to help you before you bring her to me."

My throat tightens. I know better than to bargain, but . . . *freedom*. "Where is this pure soul?"

With a malicious grin he bends down, bringing the barbarian's bloodstained teeth and horns to my level. "She resides in the Zarr castle. Heiress to your throne." He tilts his head. "Daughter of your most hated enemy."

My half-dead heart hammers against my ribs. If I accept this bargain, I could find out if *she*'s still alive. My death was so violent, so sudden, I never found out what happened to—

"Do you accept?"

I have to know, and the chance of freedom . . .

"Free me of my bonds for the duration of this bargain, and I will accept."

A triumphant, bloody grin spreads across his gray skin. "Very well, but I require a soul to eat before you leave for your bargain." He waves his claws. "Fetch the one I marked."

I bow my head. An order.

"I suggest you eat a soul as well. You'll need your strength for this pure soul." He turns and walks a few thunderous steps before pausing. "Must I remind you what happens to those who fail to uphold my bargains?"

I bow again. "No, my liege."

His bottom half dissolves into shadow before he says with a knowing grin, "I almost forgot: You cannot shred her soul as you do others. She must *give* it to you."

There it is. The catch.

"Will she be marked?" I've never seen a pure soul before.

A bloody, cunning smile. "I cannot mark pure souls." He begins to disappear.

"Wait," I call. "How much time do I have to deliver on this bargain?"

"Until the final night of the King's Duel."

The words float in from a past life, long forgotten.

The King's Duel.

After Nil and his inky mist dissipate, I tear my pant leg from the ice and part of my flesh stays with it. I survey Baratrum in its empty, frigid expanse. I hope I don't see it again for a hundred years.

A sudden, insatiable hunger rips through my soul. Only the following of orders and the tearing of souls will satisfy it. I return to my spirit form and fly to fulfill my orders.

Nil's marked soul calls me to a different realm—a whole new dimension. The threads of space and time ripple around me as I navigate the magical realms woven through the air. The land of Heshena materializes beneath me in a matter of seconds, bringing forth pastel sands and giant trees with leaves larger than my face. This land is not like the dry deserts of the Yalk realm, nor the paved roads in the Tatum realm, and it's definitely not like my home, the Zarr realm. This realm, with its three suns and glittering air, is the prettiest realm I hunt in.

I drop low, my invisible soul weaving throughout the mossy trunks, unable to think or feel anything but the urge.

After miles of Shena trees, I arrive at the crater of Hesh—a bowl-shaped city nestled in a rocky depression. Dark-skinned fae, with hair of all colors, bustle up and down concave streets. As a ghost, I can hear their desires; as a deathwalker, I can see their memories. A cacophony of the two project through my mind without my consent as I pass soul after living soul.

I soar past the gold, sparkling palace, barely noticing the magnificent Sand Gladiators inside its walls below—rows and rows of statuesque men and women notorious for their physical acclimation and immunity to magic. They pass beneath me as I jet overhead and leave the city behind. The soul Nil marked pulls me past oceanic cliffs and pastel sands sprinkled with glassy stones and pale driftwood.

At last I come to a hut, modest and worn, carved out of a long-dead tree. The thin door hangs crooked, the windows fogged by years of sandstorms, and the roof has lost a shingle leaf or two. I don't have to be in my human form to harvest souls, but I prefer it. I materialize, dropping my boots to a shale pathway. The stones freeze and shatter beneath me on impact, and the windows ahead cloud up with ice. The marked soul's memories hit me before I see him, like the stink of rotting flesh wafting into my mind. His murders play out before my eyes, whether I want to watch or not. They're flashes.

Scents.

Emotions.

Brown pointed ears, studded with gold earrings covered in blood. Red luscious hair knotted in my—*his*—hands. Ice coats my tongue.

Their emotions are always so hard to distinguish from my own.

The door splinters in my wake, and the marked elf jolts away from a desk, dropping a pen and parchment. He's a normal Heshena elf, and I think that's what gets me the most. Monsters can hide in such humble, deceiving forms.

He creeps backward, his soul writhing around him with rotted darkness. "Who are you?"

The urge to rip into his soul suffocates me. The shadows inside claw and thrash to tear out his soul, whispering, *"Make him scream, yes, scream."*

But I call my sword of shadow.

"Fight or submit." I always grant them that much—a personal sentiment that's losing meaning to me.

He tries to bolt around me like a fucking coward. I snatch his leather vest in my fist, smash his skull against the mud wall, and sink my ghostly arm through his chest. He thrashes and screams as I clutch his darkened soul, pulling, tearing, *cracking*.

The shadows cackle at the sound.

No human feelings, I remind myself. His final breath is a shudder.

A yellow soul with a festered black center bleeds into the spirit dimension before it's sucked away to Baratrum.

I expect to feel Nil's will calling me back to Baratrum, but to my relief, there is nothing. The tethers recede from inside, allowing me to move as I wish.

Our bargain has begun.

I take flight and dissolve into the night skies of the Zarr realm. The world changes beneath me, trading the multiple suns of Heshena for dark, gloomy fog. As I soar above rock mills and infantry training grounds, a flicker of emotion trickles into my chest, and the sensation is so foreign, it takes me a moment to realize it's excitement.

I'm *home*.

The fog creeps across the sky in a slow-moving whirlpool, and I catch glimpses of the glowing kingdoms through the misty gaps. The four kingdoms stretch across the continent like walled-off pie slices meeting at the neutral ground in the center. Zarr, shaped like a giant sword, is the thinnest wedge. The Barrens (the remains of the fourth kingdom), the Zo, and the Zem kingdoms make up the rest of the pie. It's the same as I remember, except now, as a spirit, I see the ancient wards separating the kingdoms, like domes of swirling energy stretched over each—relics left behind by the fourth kingdom. I've always thought the inventions from the fourth kingdom were a magic of their own. Before its fall, the kingdom's inventors were masters of innovation, and especially so when their technology was combined with actual magic. These energy fields are one of the few inventions that are legally enchanted since they prevent bonded spirits from traversing the kingdoms without their caster. Because nobody in the kingdoms likes spying unless they are the one doing it.

I dip through the ancient dome of energy that protects Zarr, descending closer to the black, twisting spires that drill upward into the night sky.

Zarr castle.

My castle.

CHAPTER 4

NIZZARA

caster's shield/kastərs-SHēld/noun

1. An invisible force field surrounding a vesseled caster in which only a bonded spirit can enter
2. The place where a spirit and caster come together to draw upon their bonded power
3. A stabilizer of souls

—FROM *THE ZO LEXICON*

I PUNCH AND KICK A WHITE LEATHER BAG DANGLING FROM a chain until my knuckles are bloody. It won't help me win my last level-five duel in forty minutes, but it curbs my rage from today's execution, so I won't lose control of my temper in the ring.

Liha will be dropping in any minute. I have no doubt her little ball of energy is floating around the colosseum, taking note of all the new fashions sported by the wealthier spectators.

She'll be upset that I'm still in my black execution dress and it's torn up my leg now. She liked this one.

Another right hook sends a shudder through the white bag, smearing blood from my knuckles across it. I breathe in, ignoring my father's guards' ever-looming presence near the door of my royal dueler suite. Their gazes continually sweep the massive room full of weights and weapons on one side, and plush furniture, a dressing room, and a food table on the other.

I deliver a spray of punches as a flash of the innkeeper's execution burns through my mind again.

My arms are a blur in front of me when a young, spindly attendant opens the door to my suite, jolting my guards. All seven of them aim their swords for his neck, blocking the entrance. The attendant curses, pointing at his security badge on his colosseum uniform, before my guards recede. He hastens over to me, and my guards resume their statue-like positions. Every competitor suite comes with an attendant, but this suite apparently comes with a late one. Since this colosseum is on neutral ground in the middle of the kingdoms, anyone can work here. Compared to working in the Zem gem mines, it's a coveted job, so you'd think there'd be some sense of punctuality.

The blond attendant takes hold of the punching bag. I yell as I hit it, my knuckles painting more red blood across white leather.

"Are you nervous?" The attendant has a coy set to his lips, but his gaze remains cast down from mine. From that alone, I know he's familiar with my father's rules regarding me.

"No," I growl. My temper is still riding the edge of my control, and something about the snark in his voice tells me he enjoys goading competitors before they enter the ring. My fists continue to connect with the dense leather, and I throw in a spin kick.

The tear in my dress rips higher, revealing more of my leg, revealing the dagger I always keep strapped around my thigh. His gaze finds it between the torn strips of my dress, and he smirks.

"My brother doesn't think you'll last a single round in the level-six circuit *if* you win today."

I withdraw my dagger and deliver a punch-kick-slash combo. The bag vibrates and emits a satisfying ripping sound in the blade's wake.

He eyes the tear and readjusts his grip. "My brother would report you for that," he says, grinning like a cat.

I stab the bag close to his fingers. He jerks his hand away and waits for me to yank my dagger out before he resumes his grip on the bag.

"Your brother sounds like an arrogant Zem asshole," I say. If my attendant's blond hair and light skin weren't enough to tell me he's from the Zem kingdom, his red colosseum uniform with the Zem crest on the shoulder is.

"Oh, he *is* an asshole. That's why I bet against him. I put ten gold ren on your win today. I even bet him you'd last one full round in the King's Duel Tournament . . . if you enter." He says it like a question. He's prying.

The King's Duel Tournament is a bloodbath of elite duelers, all competing for the biggest prize in the dueling circuit. After I win today, I'll be in level six and eligible to enter the tournament's qualifying round. Since the tournament only comes on moonless winters, which can be sporadic, this year may be my only shot at the prize. If I want to rebuild trust with the rebels and end the senseless killing in this kingdom, I have to win the bestowment granted to the champion before my betrothal.

I deliver another punch-kick-dagger combo. If my father were here, he'd already have this attendant by the throat for simply speaking in a tone he deemed disrespectful.

The attendant opens his mouth as if to ask something but stops himself.

"Just ask," I snap, my rage still curling its fingers through me.

He hides more of his torso behind the bag. "You *are* going to enter the qualifier for the King's Duel, aren't you?"

Nosy Zem. I take a deep breath and count as I let it out, reminding myself that he is not the cause of my ill temper. "Yes."

I have no alternative. Since I'm the chosen heiress of Zarr, I'm subject to the betrothal law, which states my father must choose my suitor, and I must be married between the ages of twenty and thirty. My father has announced his plans to marry me off by spring, and winning the tournament is the only possible way for me to get out of it. The winner gets a gift of their choosing bestowed by the three kings, and I plan to use it to exempt myself from the betrothal law. My father hasn't announced my suitor yet, but whoever he chooses won't agree with what

I'm going to do when I'm queen. No one in the higher classes will, so I intend to rule alone. I may not have asked for this throne, but I will make the best of it.

Which begins with rebuilding trust with the rebels, among other risky things.

Dagger, spin, jump, kick.

"You better find another duel suite," I say upon landing. "My father doesn't tolerate chatty help, and he'll be here soon."

His eyes dart to the door, surrounded by my guards, then back to me. I sense an arrogant remark rising to his lips. "Your *father*—"

I throw my dagger at the hand gripping the bag. My blade lands true, slicing the skin that connects his pointer and middle fingers. He jumps back, yelping, before stalking toward the door, dripping blood as he goes. My guards part, allowing him to leave, and that's when my sister, Tarella, slips into the room. She watches the attendant storm out into the corridor. My guards allow her in without a word before slowly closing the suite door and sharing a quick glance, as if they're uneasy sealing off a room with the two of us in it. I don't blame them.

She tilts her head and her dark, straight hair glides away from her flawless ebony face. She's wearing black to signify her place in Zarr, but her dark skin and deep brown eyes clearly display her Zo lineage. I've always been jealous of that. With my snow-white hair and lighter brown skin, I clearly took after our father.

"Did the almighty heiress not like her attendant?" she asks. "Or did the attendant quit after realizing the almighty heiress is nothing more than a hotheaded temper tantrum in fancy clothes?"

I rip my dagger out of the bag and jam it back into its sheath on my thigh, so I'm less tempted to throw it at her too. I try to get along with Tarella, but with my raw emotions still coursing through me, I know it's not likely to happen today.

"What do you want, Tarella?"

Her dark eyes narrow. "I came to wish you luck on your last duel in level five." She saunters over to the table of meats with a malicious smile and pops a mini sausage into her mouth, chewing loudly. She knows the thought of meat makes me sick.

"Really," I say—not a question, just a response, one that's *not* hostile. I know she didn't come here for that.

"Okay," she says, taking another bite of sausage. "I'm not really here to wish you luck . . . more to say my goodbyes before you die in level six."

"Interesting," I say, "because the way you're attacking that piece of meat has me wondering if you came here looking for a sausage you haven't already put in your mouth." Her freedom to court whoever she wishes is yet another thing she always waves in my face, so I often resort to insults regarding her many, frequent partners.

She glares at me and licks her greasy fingers. "At least I know what it's like." She nods to the table of untouched meats. "The buffet table, I mean. Quite exquisite . . . and so many options to choose from." She offers a sweet smile as she wipes her fingers on a cloth napkin. "You should try one before you die."

My anger builds, and I clamp my mouth shut as my bloody fists tremble at my sides.

She glides to the door and waves her hand as the guards open it for her. "Goodbye, Nizzara."

LONG AFTER TARELLA LEAVES, AND I'VE PUSHED HER VISIT from my mind, Liha's invisible but palpable spirit feathers into the room. She settles into my caster's shield, humming around me like an invisible cloak of energy. I hurl my dagger through the air again, sinking it into the center of the punching bag.

"*Ready to warm up our power before your duel?*" she asks, her voice like tinkling bells inside my mind.

"*Father will force us to warm up when he gets here,*" I project through our bond and rip my dagger out of the bag.

Her little huff of annoyance doesn't sound surprised. She knows I never wanted to be a caster—unlike everyone else in the kingdoms.

Spirit magic is addictive, intoxicating, and runs the risk of accidental possession, but everyone in the three kingdoms sees nothing but prestige and power. They bond a ring and a spirit with so few questions.

I close my eyes, squeezing the hilt of my dagger tighter. Her soft, airy presence nudges my clenched fist like a warm draft, with slightly more substance than the rest of the air around me. It's her subtle way of calming me down, but it's becoming less and less effective.

Although I never wanted a bonded spirit, Liha's big heart—smothered beneath her fiery attitude—has grown on me over the years, and I've come to cherish her close friendship. Even if she was a snobby, prestige-seeking princess from the Heshena realm in her past life.

Oftentimes, she's all I have.

I'm taking aim at the bag again when a duel referee, sporting the colors of the three kingdoms—black, red, and white—knocks, opens the door, and peeks his head into our suite, holding up three fingers and a fist.

"Thirty minutes 'til go time," he says before bowing out again.

Within a few minutes, Father enters at last, and for once, his infantry general, Sorren, is not with him. He glances at the punctured, bloody bag, then at my torn execution dress.

"The innkeeper lied, you know." He walks over to the bag and runs a finger over the torn leather, looking amused. "He wasn't just housing rebels; he was trying to organize an attack on us. On *you*. He was hosting meetings for it."

Of course he knows why I'm so angry.

I throw my blade at the bag, sinking it into its ruined center before I stalk up to the thing and yank the knife out.

He smiles and for once, it touches his eyes. "The noblemen who fund this place don't like it when you put holes in their punching bags."

I scoff and slice another long tear into it. The noblemen are all greedy little worms.

He signals for his guards to leave the room and, once they're gone, he meets my gaze. His eyes are clear. I swallow against the tightness in my throat. It's such a rarity for him to be sober, but I know better than to fall for this ever-shrinking version of him. Sometimes I wonder if anyone else understands what it's like to feel both unconditional love and such deep hatred for the same person.

He reaches up to touch my face but when I flinch, he has the nerve to look *hurt*. He drops his hand away, and his voice is thicker when he says, "I hunt the rebels because they want to wipe our bloodline off the throne, and I will not pass that danger on to you. Everything I do is to protect you."

"Protect me?" I hiss. "Is that what you call it when you leave bruises around my neck?" The air zigzags in a warm pocket around me as Liha grows nervous in my shield.

Regret washes over my father's unnaturally youthful face—a side effect of his vessel, I theorize. I know it's regret because I see it every time his strange magic wipes away the scars he gives me. The cuts, the bruises, the black eyes . . . gone. They disappear with a wave of his First-Made power. But the pain always remains, even if no one can see it.

"I may not always show it, but I do care for you." He takes a steadying breath, and the dark circles beneath his eyes seem bigger, as if his sleep is as haunted as mine. "You're the only weakness I have, Nizzara."

"I didn't ask to be your weakness."

"But you are." His neck vein pops as he works to keep his voice level. "Caring for people is the biggest weakness one can have."

"Is that why you killed Tian? Because I cared for him?" I ask, angry tears threatening. Part of that memory is still gone—filled with darkness—but I'll never forget the moment my father's sword plunged into Tian's chest as he screamed.

Father stiffens. "Caring for people is unacceptable. It makes you vulnerable."

"Then you should rid me of yourself while you're at it."

He closes his eyes and balls his fists. Dark, oily power falls into the room like shadows, traversing the red floor beneath us. When he opens his eyes again, they're the hard, malevolent things I'm used to. He backs away, calls my guards in, and orders me to warm up my vessel power.

Ten minutes later, Father points at an eighty-pound weight and says, *"Again."*

Sweat rolls down my forehead, sticking white strands of loosened hair to my face.

"*Your faux-hawk braid is all messy now,*" Liha sniffs, her spirit filling my vesseled hand with pink smoke as she hovers at my shoulder.

"*Whatever will I do?*" I say wryly.

She flicks my nose, a quick puff of warm air against my skin before I release our power upon the eighty-pound weight. It lifts an inch into the air, hovering there for a full minute before I sense the darkness inside me, yearning to be tapped into. I cut off the power, and the iron metal clinks to the polished red floor. I sigh a breath of relief for how slow and controlled I kept the movement. It takes a lot of effort not to send it flying into the wall.

"*Your power is still growing,*" Liha whispers in my mind. "*That shouldn't be happening.*"

I scoff. "*I wouldn't know.*" Father has restricted my study on vessels. All I do know is that they were made by an inventor from the fourth kingdom long ago by the name of M. A. Kerm Rindola.

She makes a throat-clearing sound. "*I'm sure your father has good reasons for hiding the more detailed knowledge of vessels from you. Besides, knowing more than the basics makes you seem scholarly.*" Her invisible pocket of charged air shudders, as if appearing scholarly is worse than an unsightly nose.

"*The basics aren't enough. I want to know more than how to fling daggers around,*" I say, ignoring Father's pointed gaze. "*I want to know why they were made and how they're able to bond souls. I want to know what determines who gets a unique Mark like we have, what makes this power so addictive, and how possessions happen.*"

Her energy shudders above my head. "*Don't speak of nasty things like possessions.*"

I deliver a narrow side-eye toward her invisible presence. "*Why not? For all I know you're turning me into your mindless minion as we speak.*"

She sniffs. "*I'm not dignifying that accusation with a response.*"

It's not so much that I want to learn about vessels specifically. I want to learn about *everything*. Knowledge is an addiction, and books are my drug of choice.

"Next." Father points to the hundred-pound weight beside the one I just lifted.

I straighten, folding my arms. "That's too heavy."

He breathes through his nose before saying, "You won't survive level six if you don't bolster your training. Now, move the weight."

I swallow. Level-six competitors are drastically better than those at level five. Longswords are legal in level six, and so are death blows. It's only a matter of time until Father will break his silence on the topic and force me to fight with the longsword. I've avoided it this long because of what happened the last time we argued over it. I woke up in the infirmary, and I didn't see my father for a month afterward.

Father points to the heavy weight on the marbled floor. "*Now.*"

Liha musters up another wave of power. It builds inside my veins like too much energy trapped beneath a too-flimsy lid, waiting for me to release it into the world.

I breathe through the sensation, fully understanding why casters will bond a vessel and a spirit with so few questions. The feel of *power* inside my veins is an intoxicating high. I force myself to think about facts I've collected on vessels to keep my thoughts clear.

"*Casters wield moving power over lifeless objects but not living things,*" I say in my mind.

Liha's bubbly energy sparks through me as she lets me chant in my mind without interruption. I breathe again, working to remain grounded in my thoughts.

"*When a spirit and caster are compatible, a unique gift can surface between them, called a Mark. Liha and I have one, just a small trick of the light, and the possibilities of Marks are limitless.*"

"Nizzara," Father warns.

Liha's warm, tingling power begs for release, so I open my palm and direct it at the hundred-pound weight. Our power wobbles a corner up before I snuff it out, clinking the weight to the floor.

"*You're holding back,*" Liha says softly.

I'm sure if I can feel the vast expanse of power waiting to be tapped into, so can she.

"Unacceptable," Father says. "Do it again and do it better."

After fifteen minutes of me shirking my power, the duel ref returns with the five-minute signal. I reach for the fighting leathers draped over the velvet ottoman near the dressing room. Like with all my attire, Liha picked them out. Skintight leather, black spikes, gold stitching, and loaded with daggers.

I step toward the dressing curtain.

"Nizzara." Father signals for a guard to take my fighting leathers.

We've fought about this already. He wants me to showcase my dimensional ability, and much to Liha's excitement, Father believes an outfit swap will be the most memorable way to showcase it. There are three things that will always catch the attention of the dueling audience. Fashion, showmanship, and unseen power. His plan ticks all the boxes.

"Take her leathers and put them on the ottoman," Father instructs Brunar. Of course the head of my guard is quick to obey, avoiding my pointed stare as he tugs the material from my fingertips, his silver military vessel forcing him to obey my father's direct orders.

"You can't hide from your power any longer," Father says, a mix of fear and sadness in his hard expression. "Besides, after you demonstrate your dimensional ability, everyone will fear you for it." His jaw trembles before he adds, "You will not survive this tournament or anything else if people do not fear you." Father clears his throat and adjusts the cuff of his sleeve. "And make sure to use your vessel *after* the bell. We don't want a repeat of last year."

A bunch of cart cow shit. That was last year. Apparently, it's *actually* illegal to beat a dueler without using vessel power. I was knocked back thirty-two wins on my record.

My fists curl at my sides, and I take a calming breath like all my anger-management books are so keen to lecture on, but my response still comes through gritted teeth. "Fine."

The duel ref returns, signaling for me to follow.

My guards fall in around me as we walk through the stone halls lit with red glo stones. Levels above me, the voracious crowd screams and chants over angry music, thudding like the heartbeat of this blood-thirsty building.

We climb until the music and chanting are so loud, I can't hear the ref when he calls to me.

I read his lips, though: "The ring is ready."

He looks at my torn dress, opening his mouth to say something, but I push past him, and my guards block him out by their sheer size.

My opponent from the Zo kingdom, a nobleman, is already wait-ing for me, dressed in their customary white. Their symbol of purity and knowledge. This is the scene I've been entering repeatedly for years: a round duel ring centered on the floor and surrounded by spec-tators. Its posts are red, its ropes white and mat black, signifying the colors of the three remaining kingdoms in the alliance.

Chants fade to murmurs as fingers point at my gown from above. The music builds as I call Liha's charged energy. It fills my veins once again, and when I release it, pink smoke swirls high and thick around me. Under the cover of smoke, in a matter of seconds, our power moves my fighting leathers from their place in my dueler suite through a di-mensional portal, and replaces my dress with gold-tipped spikes.

As the beat drops, pink smoke falls away to reveal my fighting leathers. The Zo nobleman's jaw slackens, and the crowd explodes. The call to challenge buzzes throughout my entire body. I may be softer than my father, but I'm no less competitive.

I catch both my mother's and sister's hateful gazes narrowed on me from the royal box, and I'm surprised they're deigning to make eye contact with me. Side by side, and from this distance, they could pass for dark-haired twins.

Moments before the bell is about to ring, Father climbs up the ropes, eclipsing my glaring contest with my loving family. "If you don't duel like you're supposed to," he says, "you'll be punished. No more level-five shit."

My hands curl into dried, bloody fists as he detaches from the ropes and returns to our box, taking the seat farthest from my mother and sister. Punching the leather bag took the edge off, but my rage is potent, dark, and constant, just like his. I loathe myself for it.

The bell rings.

"Our outfit change doesn't count as a vessel move," Liha reminds me.

My opponent circles me, flipping long white daggers in showy spins before shooting one toward my chest with a puff of purple smoke from his golden vessel. I flip over it, an arc of pink smoke trailing me as I slice a portal in space and time, stealing the dagger from its spot midair beneath me and portal it across the ring, sinking it through the Zo's thigh instead of his carotid artery. The realization spreads across his face: my dimensional abilities are too fast for him, and he curses as blood blossoms to the surface of his leg.

"That language isn't very Zo-like," Liha says.

The corner of my lip twitches. *"No, it's not,"* I say, trying to breathe through the intoxicating mix of power and violence.

After regaining his ever-calm expression, unique to Zos, my opponent fires a spray of daggers laced in purple smoke. They fly at me in a V formation, just like the strange aircrafts I've read about from other realms. I find myself daydreaming of seeing the other worlds and all their strange inventions while I easily deflect his daggers with my own.

He throws his last dagger, and I catch it an inch from my nose, its blade slicing through my hand, wiggling as he drives it farther toward my face with his power. He's not allowed to use killing blows here in level five, but the refs will only penalize him after I die. I grip harder as the dagger slips farther toward me.

The bloodthirsty crowd is chanting for more as it slides again, blood slipping between my fingers.

"Just use our power so you don't die, or worse, scar your face," Liha scolds, pouring that addictive power into me as pressure builds against the blade.

Pitting my muscles against his magic, I angle the inching dagger toward the dome ceiling and duck beneath it as I let it fly. By the time his power sinks it into the duel post behind me, I'm already on top of my opponent, hooking my arm around his neck and using my body weight to slam him down.

My raw knuckles screech in pain as I reopen the fresh wounds with a rapid three-four punch combo to his face. Before I know it, I'm pulling my last dagger from my leather belt and plunging it into the crook of his elbow, earning a howl of pain.

He calls one of his fallen daggers from across the ring and his power sinks it into my shoulder from behind. Pain erupts down my back, and a shriek escapes my lips. He smiles up at me, grinning with bloody teeth, so I smash my fist into his face again, pulverizing his nose. He screams—a terrible, *beautiful* sound.

My opponent, thrashing and bleeding beneath me, calls another fallen dagger. Its white blade sinks into my side, twisting as it goes. Fiery pain ignites throughout my torso. His fist surges for my jaw. I dodge his blow, catch his arm, and wrench his shoulder into submission, forcing him to roll to his stomach. Jerking his arm into an unnatural angle over my thigh, I crank his elbow the wrong way.

"Tap," I growl.

His power yanks the dagger out of my shoulder only to slam it back in, inflaming the fire through my back. It takes all my control not to reach for power. If I touch that power with this much rage, I'll drive every last blade through his skull—just like my father would.

I wrench his arm harder. "Tap!"

"I do not submit to usurpers," he growls from under the bone-splitting tension I'm loading on his elbow.

"Have it your way." I break his arm over my knee with a sickening *crack*, and his eyes roll to the back of his head. I can't tell if the scream comes from him or the thousands of spectators.

The victory bell rings as the massive crowd chants my name.

CHAPTER 5

NIZZARA

Mark/mark/noun

1. A unique magical ability formed by a bonded spirit and
   caster whose souls are compatible

—FROM *THE ZO LEXICON*

❧

IT'S BEEN FIVE HOURS SINCE MY DUEL, AND EVEN THOUGH
Father erased my dagger wounds in my side and shoulder, making them
invisible, they're still *there*. They still hurt. Nevertheless, I enter the
level-six circuit in a week, so I'm in the training room of our castle instead of soaking in a hot bath like I wish I were. The walls of mirrors
around me catch every facet of the black room full of weights, weapons,
and duel rings.

My new, level-six coach sends a longsword at me from across the
ring with a puff of green smoke. A simple evasive roll allows me to
dodge it as it flies past me. He's not even trying.

With another wave of green smoke, he calls the fallen blade to his
hand and taps his arm to signal forfeit.

My father withers him with a glance from across the room. Level-
six coaches are rare. Not many former duelers were qualified to compete this high, and the few who were now tend to keep their techniques
to themselves. Whether this coach is stingy or incompetent doesn't
matter. He's ineffective.

And after the incident with the longsword, Father doesn't train me himself anymore.

When I glare at my coach, he averts his gaze, either because of my father's sporadic temper, the crazy celibacy law Father placed on me, or the blackness of my eyes, which makes everyone uneasy.

"Let's go again," my coach says, lifting his sword.

"No." Father signals for his guards. "You're dismissed."

Looking rather relieved, my coach bows to Father, then to me, before climbing out of the ring and allowing the guards to escort him out.

"You need a coach who'll teach you what a killing blow is." Father summons Sorren from his station beside the door.

Violence and shadows dance across Sorren's bronze face as he prowls forward, ducking through the black ropes. His boots jostle the hard mat beneath me, and I square myself up against his approaching, massive form. He surfaced nine years ago after one of my father's frequent trips to who knows where, and as the Zarr infantry general, he too is controlled through the silver vessel on his finger.

He stops in front of me, poised to slay the next thing that speaks, his demeanor exactly like my father's. I've never sparred with the infantry general, but I've watched him deliver countless executions, seen the way he handles his men, and noticed the way shadows seem to flicker when he's nearby.

I have no desire to spar with him.

"Since you always wish to fight without power," Father says, "I've decided to grant you what you want. No vessel training, just to prove you will not survive without using a fucking lot of it."

My mother and sister enter the room for Tarella's training. Like always, Father ignores their existence, like Mother ignores mine. They're on their way to the other training ring when my sister sees me in the ring with Sorren. She stops and sneers with delight.

I reach for the daggers sheathed at my thighs.

"No daggers." Sorren waves at a servant, who dismounts two massive swords off the wall and lugs them over before passing them through the thick, black ropes. "Lower-level duels are for daggers and child's play." His muscled jaw flexes as he shoves the longsword at me. "*This* is about killing."

"What are we killing, exactly?" I say to Sorren. "My time?"

I feel Father's attention combing over me, assessing every flicker of emotion on my face as I approach Sorren. I'll break jaws, smash noses, and even sever limbs if I have to, but I refuse to kill, and Father has every intention of changing that.

This weakness—as my father calls it—makes my plan to win the King's Duel much more difficult.

I've watched the King's Duel since I was old enough to know what a dagger was. No one has ever won it without at least one kill. The dueler who came the closest was King Dagen, who killed his opponent in the final round and went on to ask for mining rights and tunnels for his prize. It's not often a king enters the tournament, but in times of hardship or war, the people like to see the king in the ring—to see their military commander spill blood, symbolic of their enemies'—and I believe, in his case, he became king after he had entered the tournament.

Refusing to let Sorren see my hesitation, I grab the sword, and Liha takes her cue to leave. If I'm not allowed to use my vessel, she can't stand to watch bloodshed. There's a small *zing* when her spirit leaves my caster's shield. I always imagine it to be like a mini dimension meant only for us, since it hides her from other spirits. Like so many things, I find myself curious about why and how it was invented, or why she must be in it to offer me her power.

I heave the heavy sword upward and point it at Sorren's chest.

He looks down at the blade then at me. "Your form is pathetic."

This sword is all wrong in my hands—the exact reason I don't use one. "Then let me use my daggers."

"How are you going to block a longsword with an eight-inch dagger?"

"It's called *evasion*."

He pushes the shaft of the sword away with a gloved hand—my grip too weak to hold it in place. He scoffs at that and leans forward.

"Level-six duelers will wear you down and drive their sword through your unusually thick skull."

I swing the blade toward Sorren's flank. Before my sword is halfway there, Sorren's blade is at my open neck with speed and control I've never met in a duel ring; he slices my collarbone and a trickle of blood runs down my chest.

"Dead," he says flatly.

Tarella giggles, igniting my rage.

A familiar, golden spirit shimmers just beyond the ropes. It's appeared a few times throughout my life, but seems to prefer showing up when I'm about to lose my temper. As if it has nothing better to do in its afterlife than to watch my explosions.

It takes everything I have not to scream as I death-grip my sword and swing.

And swing.

And swing.

He blocks so easily. It's embarrassing.

He carves his sword through the air like it's an art form, landing blows with unmatched precision. I have no choice but to admire it, despite my mounting rage.

After countless, airy swipes of my sword, and even more elegant, bloody swipes of his, he fakes a swipe and blindsides me with a spiked fist to my face. Blood runs down my chin and heat climbs down my neck and chest, until darkness threatens to rise inside me. My control slips, and I begin screaming with my sloppy swings.

He slices for my torso.

I evade.

His green eyes flicker with something like amusement. He *let* me evade.

"Don't hold back!"

"You don't want that," he says with a breathy laugh.

"I do." I am a trained dueler, not some defenseless woman. I wipe blood from my mouth with the back of my hand. "Don't hold back."

Sorren looks to Father, and Father gives a curt nod as Mother and Tarella finally climb into their own ring.

Sorren unleashes his sword. Deep fiery gashes appear on my thigh, my calf, my shoulder, my cheek, leaving my blocks and dodges two full moves behind his. I'm used to having space and time to think in the level-five circuit, but this is too close, too *fast*. Where are the showy flips and spins? The pauses for dramatic effect the audience loves so much?

He slices up my thigh with his blade and slams my gut with the blunt end of his pommel in what feels like the same moment. His massive blow hurls me into a duel ring post, knocking the air from my lungs. I lurch forward onto my hands and knees, heaving for air. Sorren eyes me with clear disapproval as he walks over.

"Never," he says, stomping on my hand with a steel-enforced boot, "let anyone see your vulnerabilities in the ring." He grinds his boot down, cracking the bones in my hand before removing his boot. "If you can't breathe, pretend like you can." Once my lungs finally catch air, I cry out.

Not a cry of pain.

A cry of fury.

Father watches with a dark expression. "Get up, Nizzara."

My hand is broken, my fingers at unnatural angles, but I draw myself up and take the sword in my good hand, using my other forearm to brace against the weight of it. It feels even heavier now, but I grit my teeth and raise it. My hands shake, yearning to drive this sword through Sorren's snide grin.

He advances again.

And again.

And again.

An hour later, my arms can't hold their own weight. When I raise my sword, it trembles in my hand.

"Again," I say, wiping bloody sweat from my face.

"Sorren has real work to do." Father folds his arms over his chest, appearing unimpressed, except for the small lift at the corners of his lips. Pride. Almost like old times when he used to spar with me.

I let the thought go.

Sorren exits the ring and steps in line with Father.

I climb out of the ring and start to limp away, but Father says, "You are not leaving like that."

If my body wasn't wobbling, I'd argue the matter. I clench my teeth as Father's black tendrils of smoke roll toward me. They slink up my skin and wipe away each bloody wound.

He doesn't tolerate scars on me.

Especially with the Winter Rave coming up.

And certainly not when he's arranging my betrothal.

CHAPTER 6

DAGEN

I DESCEND INTO THE WALLS OF MY CASTLE, PASSING MAIDS, guards, and bondslaves as they bustle through wide stone hallways. As I float through the lounge on the ground floor, the fireplaces and dagger-like chandeliers greet me with a warm glow. It's as if the castle is whispering, "*Welcome home.*"

Except it's no longer my home. My mother is dead, my sister is *probably* dead, and my queen—

No human feelings, I remind myself. Especially feelings like the hatred and bitterness that suface when I think of my late wife, Kathreen. The shadows love those emotions.

I continue through thick, fortified walls until I find myself in the grand ballroom, hovering above a small army of servants busily moving about in all directions. When I spot servants carefully hauling in six sound amplifiers on rolling movers, I realize preparations for the Winter Rave are underway. The servants tilt the massive relics up, lining them around the perimeter of the giant room. A young maid climbs onstage and begins singing to test the red blare gems inside the amplifiers. As soon as her voice turns into a melody, four amplifiers wake up with a flare of red gem light, broadcasting her voice throughout the room. Two of the amplifiers don't light up at all. A loud hiss and a pop come from one of the lit amplifiers, and the black box goes up in sudden flames. Servants rush to put it out, holding void gems up to the flame. The black gems glisten as they siphon the flame into their centers, then crack and go dull in the servants' hands when they're full, unable to siphon anymore. The servants draw the flames away quickly, then tote a wagon of replacement gems over to the silent amplifiers and begin changing the gems inside. As I watch them go through the entire wagon of costly blare gems—and especially having glimpsed the Tatum realm's advanced technology—I'm reminded of how obtuse and inefficient gem power is.

I continue to hover throughout the room, watching bondslaves scrub the pillars with buckets of soapy water, maids hang silk streamers, and professional muralists glue colorful gems onto the biggest wall in the likeness of Rebelia, the goddess of . . .

What's she the goddess of? I used to care more about the gods before I died. Anything besides killing or consuming souls is hard to care about now, as if the shadows inside me have taken more space than I realized.

My own memories of the Winter Rave tickle the back of my consciousness. The biggest, showiest, drunken sex-fest to kick off the King's Duel Tournament. Each kingdom takes turns hosting the event. Preparations for it take weeks.

Two maids emerge from the grand archway, cradling another giant black streamer between them and discussing *rebels*. They tote the streamer to the tallest ladder, centered in the middle of the room, its apex directly under the curved ceiling.

"All I'm saying," the taller one whispers, grabbing a low rung and booting her foot up onto the ladder, "is the rebels are getting stronger. A group made it past the palace walls a few months back. With gem *guns.*"

The other maid holds the ladder while her friend climbs up, pulling the nose of the silk streamer toward the domed ceiling. Their memories poke at my mind, centering around manual labor, petty jealousies, and pining for Mazzar's favor. The shadows would devour these women in seconds.

"But what do the rebels want?" a maid asks.

The taller maid, peering down over her shoulder, pauses halfway up the ladder. "Rumors say they want revenge for King Dagen," she says before continuing toward the top.

Some long-forgotten sense of duty and pride flickers in my chest at the mention of rebels fighting in my name, but I quickly snuff it out.

Such dangerous things, feelings.

"*Still?*" the shorter one calls up the ladder, a giggle on her lips.

The taller maid reaches the top and fastens the acrobat streamer to the domed ceiling before shooting a look down. "You know the history of the Barrens," she calls. "If that wasteland doesn't speak of the Zarrs' ability to hold grudges, I don't know what does."

The short one smirks, waiting for her friend to climb back down before elbowing her in the side and saying, "How about your ability to never forgive your mother?"

The other maid scowls, adjusting the silky tail of the streamer now flirting with the black floor. "I have every right to hold that grudge. She spent my dowry on my sister's wedding gown!"

They drone on as they fetch the next streamer.

"*Feed us the short one first,*" the shadows inside me hiss, urging me to tear them apart and consume their meager souls, but with some effort I move to a corner and rest my ghostly boots on the ground, letting them live.

My invisible hand brushes the stone wall, and I close my eyes. There's no ice leaching into my skin or glaciers cracking in the distance. No screams and no bitter wind.

I can almost imagine it, almost taste the sweetness of it—*freedom.*

Whatever it takes, I will capture the pure soul. No force in existence is dragging me back to Baratrum in this century.

The room is full of busy castle staff, so I get to work investigating. Memories and desires flow through me from all directions.

So much life. So much *information.*

I see Mazzar, his wife, and their two daughters through their memories.

I see his chosen heiress, Nizzara, the one Nil asked for. In one memory she's threatening the slave master with a dagger, ordering him to send a bondslave to clean her rooms. In others, I see her fighting in duels, overseeing tax courts, and speaking to everyone with sharp, bratty snark.

"*What a little beast*," a shadow whispers with delight inside my soul, and for once, I agree.

I lift off the ground and soar through the hall, searching for her, when I'm surprised to see my portrait still hanging in its gem-studded frame, in line with all the Zarr kings before me.

I haven't aged since the portrait was made. I'm still twenty-six, but Baratrum has had its way with my appearance. My short beard is brittle, my lips cracked from cold winds, and death clings to me—as it does anyone who has faced the shadows.

Mazzar's frame proceeds mine as the next king of Zarr. He was my father's infantry general, then mine, up until he pointed a gem gun at my chest and pulled the trigger. The image of that gem-studded barrel pointing at my chest will forever be burned into my soul.

Ice breaks out in every direction from me, coating the walls in Baratrum frost. The icy, silver crystals crawling up the black wall is something only I can see, but the maids shiver when they pass it. I have to remember how thin the barrier between the spirit realm is, remember that my emotions can transcend it.

When I hear Mazzar's voice coming from behind a closed door, I condense my spirit form into a ball of energy, unrecognizable as myself in case any of his spirits decide to leave his caster's shield.

Another male voice comes from within the room. "Your Majesty," the stranger says in an Awom accent, "the workers in the Zem tunnels are growing suspicious of the missing void gems. They've increased security in the mines again."

"There's no other way, Alto. My gems are burning out and so are my coffers. Steal them."

"Yes, Your Majesty."

The door opens, and a tall Awom bondslave with snow-white hair and unnaturally youthful skin exits the room and hastens through me. He stops when he passes through my hovering essence, a crease forming between his white brows, before continuing on with purpose.

From the cracked-open door, I see Mazzar in my situation room, where he ended my rule.

I'd give anything to shred his soul now, but if I touched his caster's shield, it would solidify like a wall of stone, his First-Made vessel—*my vessel*—offering impenetrable protection against all spirits, even death-walkers.

But apparently not gem guns. Another unstable invention left behind by the fourth kingdom.

Mazzar steps into the hallway, his eyes narrowing in my direction. As a spirit, I can see his dark caster's shield sliding across the floor, a moving wall of hazy energy in sync with his step, making me wonder what spirit resides in it. I *feel* his magnitude of power intensifying as he nears me, so I retreat. For now.

I fly through room after room, each one stirring old, painful memories.

The foyer where I last celebrated the spring solstice.

The room where I kissed my first love, Emya.

The hall where I last spoke to my sister.

Lola.

Could she still be alive? It's foolish to hope, but with the Mark she wielded, she might have escaped Mazzar's attack that night.

I soar faster through halls and levels toward my sister's old tower until I smack against a wall of energy—a pink-hued caster's shield.

My gaze falls upon the caster behind the translucent shield, and for a second, I see nothing but black eyes on the face of—

The pure soul.

She's soaking in a bath of thick, concealing bubbles. Her white hair drapes over tan, wet shoulders, and her black gaze locks onto the wall behind me. She slowly lifts her hands out of the water and tucks a strand of hair behind her ear.

I saw her in countless memories on my way through the castle, saw exactly what she looked like, so I don't know why now suddenly feels different. Despite my hatred for her family—despite the shadows—a tiny surge of warmth ripples through part of my soul.

No human feelings, I growl at myself and focus on the task at hand. Taking her soul.

It's now, as I look for her "pure" soul, that I realize I can't even see it. Her faint caster's shield shimmers like a distortion of light, hiding it away.

Glancing at the golden vessel bonded to her hand, I wonder if it has something to do with her bonded spirit. Second-made vessels hide bonded spirits, not the wearer's soul. I should be able to see hers. Her bonded spirit is the only thing I can think of that would prevent me from seeing it. Sometimes spirits carry unique talents.

I stick my hand out, wanting to feel her shield again, but before I touch it, her memory flashes across my mind. I try to push it away, but I'm powerless to deny it. Her mind sucks me in without warning, devouring me.

The execution room wraps around me, consuming all my senses: the air like warm, soothing honey, the scent of roses, and the light shimmering with a golden color . . . and *blackness* edging the corners. I've never seen anything like it before.

A woman screams through the memory as a man is shoved to his knees in front of me. I'm in Nizzara's place, smiling down at the rebel. Her hatred and rage surge through me. I can't tell if it's aimed at her father or the rebel—or if it's simply my own rage, seeing her on my throne—but whatever it is, it takes over my mind.

Mazzar whispers at my side, *"Fix your face, Nizzara."*

Despite this bloody scene full of screams, I don't want to leave it, and when it ends, I'm thrust back into the cold, dull world like a beggar tossed from a palace in the dead of winter.

It takes restraint not to sift through all her memories, because suddenly, that warm light . . . her floral scent . . . It's all I want.

I do my best to shake the memory off, lending my mind over to the shadows as I reach for her soul again. As soon as my ghostly fingers touch her faint pink caster's shield, it turns to warm steel against my hand, and her bonded spirit juts out into the washroom, plowing into my condensed ball of energy.

"Who are you?" she hisses, darting around me.

"A spirit, like you," I say. *"I wish to serve the girl."*

Trust, I must gain her trust. How else will she hand over her soul willingly?

"*She already has a bonded spirit.*" The pink spirit twirls about me before slamming into me, our energies colliding with a zap. I reach out for the spirit's memories, trying to glean insight into Nizzara's abilities, but they're blocked. A spirit with a protective talent, I realize. *She* must be the reason I can't see Nizzara's soul.

"*Away,*" she hisses.

I float away, prepared to wait for the right opportunity, but when I move, Nizzara's eyes *follow me*, and they continue to follow me around the room as if she can see me. Her gaze bores into my soul until I dissolve into the wall on my way out of her chamber.

CHAPTER 7

NIZZARA

bonded spirit/bändəd-spirət/noun
1. A soul that a caster allows into their caster's shield
2. One half of a two-piece power system
3. A ghost who belongs to a vesseled human, capable of communicating through frequencies of the mind
—FROM *THE ZO LEXICON*

IF MY HANDS WEREN'T STILL TREMBLING FROM THE SPIRIT who just left my bathing chamber, I'd be annoyed that my bath is now ice cold. I stand up, sloshing the icy water over the black rim, and pull a robe over my dripping body as I step out of the large, round tub. The air is still cold too, even though Liha chased that spirit off minutes ago.

I shiver, tightening the fluffy, red robe around my waist, each stiff movement a blaring reminder of my training with Sorren. Thank the realms for my handmaid, Preysee, and her therapeutic oils.

"*What kind of spirit was that?*" I ask Liha.

His voice was so loud and clear, not like other passing spirits', his dark soul more pigmented . . .

And his power . . . I shiver again.

"*The kind that's gone, now.*" Liha sniffs.

"*Could you sense his desires?*"

"*No. Not all spirits can hear all desires, you know,*" she says.

"Every soul is unique, perceiving the world in different ways. Besides, some desires—like yours—are skilled at hiding when they want to."

I absorb the rare information Liha's willing to give on the subject and begin to ask more questions when she squeals, *"Oooooh, dresses!"*

As I step out of the bathing chamber, Preysee passes by, loading my expansive closet with countless new gowns and suits to try on for the Winter Rave. After Preysee empties her last armful of flashy fabrics, hanging them on a rack in my closet, she bustles out to clean the bathing chamber.

Liha yells, *"Come on!"* before darting out of my shield and into the freshly stocked closet.

I have to call out loud to Liha because she's not in my shield, "I'll be there in a moment," and I follow Preysee back into the bathing chamber to help her collect the oils.

"You don't need to help me," Preysee says in a stern voice as she tucks a stray tendril of dark hair behind her ear. It's the same shade as my mother's, her face just as hard as hers too, but Preysee has always been warmer than my mother. I think that's why I gravitated to her soon after moving into the Zarr castle.

I pick up two glass bottles. "I'd rather clean than listen to Liha go on about golden stitching and plunging necklines."

Liha flies back into my shield. *"You may not like to hear about it, but you always like to wear what I pick out."*

"Well then, go pick something out."

"You are not getting out of my very important fashion advice. I'll wait for you to procrastinate with Preysee before I resume."

Preysee dips her arm in the tub and unplugs the stopper. She yanks her hand back and shakes the water off.

"I'll never understand how you can tolerate it. If I took baths as hot as yours, I'd have no skin left," she clucks, and I'm left with chills crawling up my neck because she can't feel the spirit's icy draft that's still lingering like I can.

Preysee takes a glass bottle from my hand and says, "I still need to apply this one. It'll help you sleep," confirming that she knows about my nightmares. She motions for me to turn around, so I do. "It says to apply behind the ears and on the neck," she says, tilting my head and daubing the oil onto her fingers before massaging it into my skin.

"*Oooh, this reminds me*," Liha says, "*there's an enchanted oil on the dark market that makes the wearer irresistible. Tell Preysee to fetch it for us. It's sold in the golden district. Raven's Elixirs. Tell her.*"

"*I'm not—*"

"*Tell her!*"

I fold my arms. "*So, I'm not allowed to stay in the book coves past midnight, even though I'm a grown-ass adult, but an enchanted oil—an* illegally *enchanted oil—is okay?*"

She sniffs. "*It's called priorities. And the whole book thing is about beauty sleep. Your eyes look devilish when they're tired.*" She nudges my cheek. "*Which is often, lately.*"

I bat my hand through her airy presence. "*They always look devilish. And why bother with an enchanted oil when our Mark does nearly the same thing?*"

"*Our Mark is subtle. This oil is* not *subtle.*"

I peel the top of my robe back while Preysee rubs the oil farther down my neck and shoulders. Having worked around casters before, she's used to my frequent, unexplained snuffs, eye rolls, and random giggling, even if she doesn't have a vessel herself.

If I don't tell Preysee to fetch the oil, Liha will pester me about it until I do. So, I ask Preysee, and she promises to pick it up on her next trip into Zarr city.

Once the oil is massaged in, I ask her if she'll braid my hair before she leaves.

She nods and sits me down at my black marble vanity with metal roses climbing the edges of the mirror, and of course Liha uses the opportunity to summon our unique Mark, as she always does whenever I'm in front of a mirror. The filter falls into place, making me more desirable to the person who looks through it. It seems so laughable compared to my father's. His Mark is control over flesh, forcing his victims to move about like lucid puppets.

My Mark even works against my own eyes. In the reflection, my muscles are more defined than they really are, and the air about me is confident and calm.

"*You look like Afrina,*" Liha says. The Heshena goddess of lust.

I glare in her direction and wipe our Mark away with another wave of smoke. "*You say that every time.*"

"*I do not.*"

Preysee, unfazed by this ritual, shakes her head with a smile. "You always look younger when you do that."

She reaches for a towel to dry my dripping-wet hair.

Liha pools her power into my palm.

"*Liha,*" I scold.

"*We have dresses to go through!*"

Her popping energy fills my veins, and I practice *denying* it. But the feel of it is addictive, and I see how easily someone could become like Father.

"*Stop avoiding it. You need to learn how to manage the feel of power—allow it to flow through you—or you'll blow us both up,*" she says. "*Might even blow up the dresses,*" she mumbles.

I take a deep breath and release the pent-up power. One puff of our pink smoke removes every ounce of water from my hair and sends each drop back to the bathing tub, turning my hair to silk in Preysee's fingers.

"*Would it really blow us up?*" I feel dumb for not knowing the answer and angry—again—at my father for hiding it.

Liha sighs. "*No, but it's quite intense.*"

Preysee braids my hair down to the center of my back and excuses herself to her own chambers for the night.

I grab a book, *Discovery of the Seven Realms—an Autobiography,* from the sitting area in my chambers and follow Liha as she bounces through the air toward the closet. I got a new in-house scholar a few months ago, and he's given me books that even when I was in Zo, I wasn't allowed to read, so naturally, he's my favorite tutor. Once I'm in the closet, I change into a nightgown and strap my dagger to my thigh like I do every time I dress. I pull my legs up onto the ottoman and start reading the front matter notations:

"'M. A. Kerm Rindola, the greatest inventor from the fourth kingdom, who not only invented the vessels but discovered—and proved—the existence of the other six realms in 400 PA (Pre-Alliance). This book is the only surviving work of M.A.K.R. and is a translation and compilation of surviving journal remnants, as the rest of his works were lost in the fall of the fourth kingdom."

I wiggle down into a comfy reading position and take in the opening lines of the book:

"To step into another world doesn't require a step at all." That was the woman's response when I pressed her. She'd appeared out of thin air. Her skin glowed with an ethereal light; her eyes a brilliant color I'd never seen—a glowing mark on her palm. As she looked around my workspace, I pinched my cheek to make sure I was not dreaming her. Am I hallucinating? I asked myself. Could I be impaired?

But no, I looked at my glass of spicy rum. Only a few sips were missing. I gazed back at the beautiful creature before me, and that was the beginning of my insatiable obsession with the godlike people and the other realms—

The entry cuts off and jumps to another disjointed section of his writings.

The goddess-like woman returned again, her fascination with my gem inventions driving her to come back, and I couldn't lie to myself. I was inventing to impress her now. When I showed her my latest creation, her face lit with curiosity.

"It's a gem gun, or so I've named it."

She picked it up with rapt fascination. "What does it do?" she asked in my language.

"It kills anything with a soul," I told her.

She perked a brow. "Immortals have souls. Does it kill them?"

I point at the soft red glow emitting from the gun's center mechanism. "See the gem glowing in the center? It's cut in a specific pattern that makes its power resistant to any enchantment, any magic." I clear my throat. "Theoretically, of course."

She beheld the weapon like a treasure. "Can I keep it?"

How could I deny her, when she looked at me as if I were some sort of god?

When I nodded, she whisked it away from her hand, disappearing it into another dimension—another realm.

Liha's squeal interrupts my reading. *"Preysee outdid herself! Look at this stitching! You can always tell the quality of a garment by the stitching, you know."*

I snort with amusement. "No one gets close enough to see the stitching."

Her pink ball of light slowly rises above the rack of clothes, and I sense her little spirit eyes narrowing on me. *"The devil hides in the details, Nizzara."* She sniffs—a snooty Heshena sound I've learned means something to the effect of "your existence offends me."

I fight a smile and apologize for my obscene offense.

She mumbles something about dressing me in a rock-dust sack from the mineral factory, but quickly returns to her bubbly, bouncing tone as soon as she dives back into her selection process. First, she evaluates quality, color, then cut. After that, she considers current trends, automatically eliminating any dress style that is too popular or any outfit that's green. She hates green.

I go back to reading the disjointed compilation of M.A.K.R.'s autobiography as he begins to study the realms—driven by a desire to visit the unnamed woman. He writes,

After repeating the experiment and reaching the same result, I concluded that the realms are different dimensions, traversed only by magic. Theoretically, if I were a creature with the power to access that magic, I could stand in my workspace and enter a new realm without taking a step—just as the goddess described. The new realm would materialize around me. I theorize that the power to access this magic has something to do with souls as I've also concluded that spirits of all origins can also travel the realms.

Liha makes her little throat-clearing sound.

I lift my head to find her light pink ball hovering directly behind my book. "What?" I say.

She sniffs. "*I asked you if you have a preference for a floor-length skirt or a mini.*"

"Floor." I've learned her questions aren't actually about my preference. They are a test of my fashion sense. If it was a spring dagger tournament, the answer would've been mini.

I go back to reading the text, wishing I had a book written by another inventor who studied the realms since I've already read this one multiple times, and this one gets more and more disjointed as it goes on, since the majority of M.A.K.R.'s journals were destroyed. New books are especially effective at quieting my mind.

"*Intricate stitching or bold?*"

"Again with the stitching?" I mutter.

"*What was that?*" she says in a pointed tone.

"Intricate," I say, closing the book, suddenly craving my book on moon patterns because this one isn't enough to keep my mind away from what's been eating at me all day.

"Do you think my father will announce my betrothed soon?" I ask.

When she doesn't answer right away, I add, "And why do you think he's forced me into celibacy? No one else in the three kingdoms waits for marriage."

"*I'm sure we'll find out soon.*" She floats over to me, brushing near my shoulder like a draft of warm air. *"I just hope your betrothed is scandalously hot."* She giggles before darting back over to the giant rack of dresses. *"Now, shimmer or matte?"*

I sigh. "Shimmer."

She purrs with satisfaction. "You're learning."

CHAPTER 8

NIZZARA

Awoms value the life of all things and are rumored to have a connection with souls. They avoid violence at all costs, strive for peace, and harbor harmony within their habitats. In the eyes of the great continent, this is what makes them perfect for slavery.

—*Examinations of Economy and Trade*

❧

SOMETIME LATER, A SOFT KNOCK SOUNDS FROM THE TALL door of my room, and I can tell by the softness of it that it's not Brunar. I flip a page in my moon pattern book, and Liha flies through the door to see who it is.

"*It's Yisabell,*" she calls.

I close my book and stand up from my chair. "Enter."

Yisabell peeks inside, her white hair and ice-blue eyes bright against the blackness of the castle interior. Her twelve-year-old self beams at me.

"I"—she looks over her shoulder toward my guards stationed in the hall—"I came to empty your waste bins for the night."

I quickly wave her in.

She closes the heavy door behind her and runs to me, embracing me in a hug. I squeeze back tightly before letting go.

"Is your father gone again?" I say in Awom, her native tongue. She has that tightness in her shoulders that's only there when he's gone.

She nods.

Alto, my father's closest bondslave, has been gone more and more lately.

I take her hands. "He'll return. Just stick with Haren and you'll be fine."

"I know." She nods again, then says with a smile breaking through her lips, "I made something for you." She glances at the jewelry on my vanity and her smile fades. "But I understand if you don't want to wear it."

"Nonsense. Show me."

She retrieves a small metal ring from the worn pocket of her black slave garb.

"It's a snake," she says, holding the roughly forged strip of iron shaped into a serpent chasing its tail.

I take it from her palm. "The symbol of transformation and rebirth."

"You don't have to wear it," she says. "I know my beliefs are considered a weakness in your kingdom."

I hold the ring up between us. "Valuing life does not make you weak."

"Even smaller forms of life, like snakes or toads?" she asks.

I ruffle her hair. "Even those."

She beams up at me.

I swallow, a sudden tightness in my throat, and slide the metal snake onto my pinky. "I'll never take it off."

I long to give Yisabell a gift in return, but bondslaves are not allowed personal items. I vow, as I have silently vowed before, to free her and her people when I take the throne.

"Would you like me to tell you a story?" I offer.

She nods excitedly and takes a seat on my chair. "The answer to that question is always yes."

I chuckle and find a little detail about my life that I haven't told her, which is easy because we don't get much alone time together, and when we do, it's always rushed.

"I wasn't always heir to the Zarr throne," I say. "When I was younger than you, I lived with my mother in the Zo palace while my father was the Zarr infantry general."

She tilts her head. I almost expect her to ask about my parents separated living situation during that time, which always seems to provoke questions from other people, but she just waits for me to continue.

"The whole palace was gorgeous," I say. "But my favorite room was the library. They call it the Beacon of Zo because every surface—every spine of every book—is bathed in light. The ceiling rains down in thousands of glo gems strung at all lengths. And at night, after the library is closed, the ceiling has been enchanted by half-souls to mimic a night sky with twinkling stars. Not foggy and clouded like *our* night sky," I remind her. "But like the ones I've read to you about—the clear ones in other realms where you can see stars and galaxies."

She looks up into the rafters of the room as if she's imagining it. "Is that where you learned to speak my tongue? The Zo library?"

I nod, my throat tightening, "A friend of mine taught me there."

My heart gives a sharp tug when I think of Tian, and my thoughts of his death rush into my mind along with that dark, fuzzy spot in time—a trauma response, one healer suggested. But for Yisabell's sake, I keep my grief of losing him from showing and tap her nose while I hold back the sting behind my eyes.

"My story is about that friend, an Awom boy who was a little older than you are now. He told me legends of the first mother spider who was shunned from the world with nowhere to raise her children; how she created a home for them spun of silk."

Her brows furrow. "I know that story already."

I lean in closer. "But I didn't tell you *how* he told me the story. He traded his meals with some castle servants in exchange for a worn-out tablecloth. Deep in the library, he built a fort with it, draping it over a table. I snuck biscuits from the kitchens, and we ate them in the fort while he told me all about the mother spider."

I call for Liha's magic to fill my palm. She obliges, and pink smoke swirls from my hand, taking the shape of a great spider.

Yisabell giggles, her eyes so incredibly bright, as the smoke-spider skitters around her. She laughs and the sound is loud and beautiful, like harps during the summer solstice.

A pounding comes from my door and Brunar bellows, "Is the bondslave finished?"

Yisabell's laugh cuts off, her head snapping back and forth, looking for the waste bin that Preysee moved.

I point. "In my bathing chamber. Go grab it. I'll distract him."

If Brunar tells my father about Yisabell, she'd be punished at best. Or end up like Tian at worst. I tighten my robe and go out into the corridor, closing my chamber door behind me.

The spirit from earlier is here. His unworldly chill crawls through the air, and I find him lurking above my guards.

I'm used to seeing spirits, but not spirits like *him*. Most souls are barely perceivable. They're faded orbs of energy, unable to form words. But him . . . My palms go clammy at the amount of power radiating from him, as if the floor itself cracks in his presence.

Power like my father's.

I breathe, steadying myself, and focus on why I came out into the hall.

Withdrawing the dagger at my thigh, I snap it up to Brunar's neck. "Watch your voice," I hiss. "Because if I hear it after I return to my chambers—"

I pinch the blade tighter against his neck, testing the point of bloodshed. "I'll make sure no one hears it again. Understand?"

I would never kill him, but Brunar doesn't know that.

He swallows, his throat bobbing beneath my dagger. "Yes, Princess."

"Good. Now make yourself useful, and take the bondslave back to her quarters, where she belongs."

Yisabell is one of the bravest twelve-year-olds I've ever met, but being alone in the dark halls of this castle scares her.

One of Brunar's guards breaks formation to escort Yisabell, who has now come out into the corridor. He takes her arm, yanking it rougher than necessary, causing her to drop the bag of waste. Anger boils inside me, but I can't say anything without endangering her. He lets go and shoves her to the floor.

"Pick it up, slave."

She rushes to pick up the spilled waste, shooting me a look that says, "It's okay—I'm okay," before he leads her away.

The cold deepens behind me as the dark spirit growls, *"You cruel little beast."*

I shove my fear down and raise my dagger up, pointing its blade at where his frigid essence hovers above my guards.

"Say that again. I dare you."

His presence stiffens, but doesn't make another sound as I slip back into my rooms, trying and failing to tame my temper. Its depths are starting to feel bottomless.

I keep a level head just long enough for Liha to leave for her nightly entertainment. Her pink ball of energy disappears through my bedroom door, to float throughout the castle as she always does at this time of night, and darts off to eavesdrop on the gossipy maids. The moment she's gone, and no one is around to see, I kick the nearest thing to me: my reading chair.

When it only skids across the stone floor instead of a more satisfying catapult across the room, I take it by the backrest and throw it over with a scream, letting my never-ending, dark rage out.

A guard knocks on my door. "Everything all right, Princess?" I hear the hesitation in the guard's voice after he watched me threaten Brunar, and I know he's only doing his job.

My nails bite the inside of my palms as I count to three before saying, "I'm fine."

I slump down beside the upturned chair, every bit of black rage still coursing through me, and I hate that I'm no better at controlling my temper than my father. After deep-breathing exercises that don't work, I go to stand, but spot a little black diary lodged into the chair's underbelly. I tug it out and turn it over in my hand to find no name or marking on it. I bend the soft leather back and fan the pages with my thumb. Dust wafts from the book as I flip through pages of elegant handwriting. I turn to the first page and shamelessly dive in.

DIARY: PAGE 1

The power of manipulation really boils down to the understanding of three things: a person's strength, weakness, and motive. If you know any one of them, you have a serious weapon, because any seasoned manipulator knows: they all intertwine.

Strengths are also weaknesses.

Weaknesses are also strengths.

And motives drive every word and action.

Take this diary of mine.

As far as motives go, it's a place to unload my secrets—a strength because it contains documented evidence for me to piece together and analyze—but it's also my greatest vulnerability should someone find it.

That's why it's laced with poison and permanent, enchanted ink.

So, if I see you walking around my castle with inked hands, I'll kill you before the poison does.

—Lo

I drop the wretched book, kicking it away from me, but it's too late. My fingers are saturated in black ink. The room begins to spin, the poison already absorbing through my skin.

CHAPTER 9

DAGEN

SHE *HEARD* ME.

I'm positive I didn't project my voice. It takes a lot of energy to do so, like trying to push my words into the Heshena realm. Different dimensions, different frequencies.

The little beast returns to her room. After watching memories of her smiling gleefully at countless rebel executions, I wish I could just kill her with my sword of shadow. But no, I have to get close to her, earn her trust to gain her soul.

I have to bond with her vessel. That would certainly get me closer to her . . . We could even share a Mark.

I float down to the lower levels, listening to the conversations of castle staff as I go, trying to glean more information on Nizzara. I find more memories of rebels, and I can't help but wonder: If Lola escaped, could she be hiding with the rebels?

Flying through hallways, I catch Tarella, Mazzar's oldest daughter, walking toward the training room door. She pauses to look up and down the hallway before entering, appearing rather suspicious, so I follow her in.

Her memories swarm with Nizzara's fights, and I'd be lying if I didn't say the beast is downright captivating when she fights.

Tarella, it seems, has watched every single duel Nizzara has ever fought, and jealousy laces every memory. As each beautifully violent memory passes through me, I'm starting to wonder if Nizzara has ever lost a duel, because I can't find one. There's one where she didn't use her vessel in the ring, but damn, she managed to take down the other dueler without it.

I'm about to pull out of Tarella's memories when she lands on a recent one from just this afternoon.

Nizzara is in this training room, a longsword in her hand, fighting the infantry general. I can't even call it a fight. He's so above her level, he obliterates her. And I wonder what realm chewed him up and spit him out to be able to fight like that.

I keep expecting Nizzara to tap, or pass out, but each time she's knocked down, she gets up, more fire in her than before. Despite blood, broken fingers, and shaking arms, she fights.

And fights.

And fights.

Tarella's emotions flood my own. Admiration. Jealousy. Bitterness. She whips out her daggers and goes through firing drills with her vessel, shooting them into targets. She tries a backflip over a flying dagger, but spooks halfway through and lands on her shoulder. She sends daggers flying in all directions with a howl of frustration. They clink against the shatter-proof mirrors before she storms out of the training room.

After watching Nizzara through Tarella's memories, I find myself wondering again what exactly a pure soul is. Obviously, it isn't a *virtuous* soul because she's a violent little thing with a sharp tongue from what I've seen, but she doesn't exactly scream pure *evil* either.

Nil only sends me after *wretched* souls. My victims are traitors and murderers, like Mazzar, who is both.

Mazzar, who murdered me with one of my father's gem guns. I fly faster, passing long dark corridors, an idea forming.

If I can get my hands on a gem gun, I won't need to rely on the little beast to help me kill him. I could just shoot Mazzar point-blank, like he did to me.

I navigate the black halls until I reach the armory wing, where swords, axes, and a few gem guns should be stored. Six palace guards stand in formation beside the armory doors, four with their backs to the wall and the other two pacing up and down the long corridor.

I dissolve into the massive iron door, sliding past rows of swords, axes, and daggers before I halt midair.

The farthest black wall, once adorned with the gem guns my father bought from the Zo kingdom—who horded them after the fourth kingdom fell—is empty.

I double-check every row, every hook, chest, and blade. No gem guns.

I return to the hall and search through more memories to find what happened to those gem guns, sifting through as many accounts of Mazzar as I can handle. Executions. Starving people. Rabid conditions. Goblets of wine being emptied, and tables being overturned in his frequent rages. Until, finally, I find myself in a memory without Mazzar.

Jagged black buildings appear around me, mineral powder and the scent of dirt. The dust itself is so thick, it coats the inside of my nose through the memory. I'm in the body of a soldier, scurrying to the golden district, where the mineral dust doesn't coat the streets—closer to the castle. I'm in the soldier's point of view, but instead of wearing his uniform, I'm dressed as a commoner, ducking into a brothel near the outermost wall of Zarr city.

"I wish to get someone out," I say in the soldier's voice to a small, cloaked figure who sits across a marble table from me.

"Who?" the woman whispers from under her red hood, her face shaded.

I look over my shoulder and swallow, acting out the memory from the soldier's point of view. "My sister was maimed by her husband and can't find work."

The cloaked woman stiffens. "If she is maimed, I can't find her work here, but I will reach out to someone. I cannot guarantee the rebels will take her in, but I'll see what I can do. It *will* cost you."

I nod. "Anything."

"Bring her here. I'll do what I can, and we'll negotiate then."

I watch through the soldier's eyes as he makes his way back through the dancing bodies, and my heart jolts when I catch a flash of brown, wavy hair whipping around and darting through the crowd.

I could've sworn this woman looked *exactly* like Lo.

CHAPTER 10

DAGEN

I SOAR HIGH INTO THE NIGHT SKY, TURN INTO MY HUMAN form, and free-fall back down through icy wind, just to clear my mind. Everything about Nizzara still clings to me, the divine floral scent . . . and the warmth. Sifting through the guards' dry, tasteless memories has only made me want hers *more*.

Damn her.

Ice crystallizes in my hair as I plummet toward the streets skirting the lesser district. I shift back into my spirit form just before I would've crashed into an ice-packed road. Just because the impact couldn't *kill* me doesn't mean it wouldn't hurt.

Before I left my castle, I checked on the little beast to find her sick in her bathing chamber. As soon as she began to drift off to sleep, I decided to check out the brothel with ties to the rebels.

I float far above a small family as they huddle together, trudging past dark alleyways filled with lumps of garbage. After a few city blocks, the mother gathers her children to cross the cobbled street, and carriages, ranging from ones made of rusty metal to gem-studded gold, pass by. The faster carriages are powered by steam, but most are pulled by cart cows and king hogs, which hustle down the streets with surprising speed. When a gap comes in the traffic, the mother pulls her children toward the road, about to usher them across when a low growl rumbles toward them. An old glo-kar rolls past, splashing them with muddy slush.

The family barely reacts to being sprayed with road sludge.

I hover closer to them as they hurry across the cobbled street. Their skin is pale. Dark circles encase their empty eyes, and battered clothing hangs from their bony frames. Once they make it across, the mother gathers the three smaller figures, all without proper winter cloaks, and bustles them down the wintery streets of the lesser district. When one of the trash heaps on the walkway *moans*, I realize it's a person. Almost all the lumps leaning against glo poles and dark storefronts are homeless people.

My people are worse off than I feared.

I take to the sky, the weight of what's at stake pressing down even more on my shoulders. I have to win my freedom.

For my people.

After soaring through the tall, pointed buildings of the golden district I find the brothel from the guard's memory. The Red Mask, a suave black building, pinched between two of the nicest inns inside Zarr city. I keep the shivering family in my mind, a reminder of what's at stake if I fail, and stare down at the sleek brothel.

Right now, I owe it to Lo to find out what happened to her after my death.

The Red Mask is known for the most beautiful dancing women in Zarr.

As I enter the brothel, a dancer in a red, flashy outfit and matching mask walks through me on her way to deliver drinks to a table. She skillfully weaves through grabbing hands, dancing bodies, and stages until she's quickly eclipsed by the crowd. I shake off her memories of sex and parties and make my way through the wall of people in my spirit form, pausing by one of the stages. A masked dancer climbs a long taut rope while men and women dance around her platform, grinding against each other, lost in the loud music.

I don't think Lo is here, but with her Mark, and the sheer amount of people, there's no way to be certain. I scan the many faces, looking for her shrewd gaze, her wolfish presence. Luckily, only the dancers wear masks, which makes the impossible task slightly easier, but as I study each face and expression, no one fits the bill.

I reach the bar on the far wall to find a group of Zarr infantries leaned against the sleek, red counter. Their lethal size, the gleaming silver vessels on their hands, and the way people give them a wide berth make them stand out like beacons in the crowd. They're plastered, judging by the way their torsos drape over the polished bar top, probably celebrating a night off. After deciding they're far too drunk for me to catch any meaningful conversation, I open my mind to read their memories. Before I can latch on to one, a redheaded woman glides by, arm in arm with a crying dancer. Her high, sultry voice is the same as that of the cloaked rebel woman from the guard's memory. They disappear behind the main stage, so I follow.

The redhead scans the empty dressing room that they've entered before leaning closer to her crying friend and whispers, "I could get you to the rebels. Their numbers are growing, and they have a strong leader. It's a safe camp."

The distressed dancer sniffs and removes her mask to wipe the tears under it. She looks about the dressing room and whispers back, "I can't. I'm in debt here. My sister and her family live just a few blocks away. You know what Red would do to them if I left without settling it."

The redhead's caramel eyes harden. "I would not let that happen."

Before the other dancer can respond, more masked dancers file in to adjust their hair and makeup, ending the conversation. I try to reach out to the redhead's memories as she takes a seat in front of a vanity mirror and begins painting her lips red, but her mind is strange. Only some memories are available, as if she's censored them. Of course, the available ones are useless.

I'm about to leave for another room when a cane strikes the floor with a crisp *snap*, and the curtains part to reveal a tall man in a red mask. All the women go rigid. He strides among girls poised in front of mirrors, stopping behind the redhead. He bends down beside her, his mask even with hers in the reflection.

"My sweet Helina," he purrs.

She makes a fist in her lap beneath the vanity.

"Why are you dressed for the stage? Hmm?"

"I'm scheduled for the stage, Red."

He tsks and twirls one of her ruby curls around his finger. "I'm afraid I have you scheduled elsewhere. If you still want me to deliver on our agreement."

I reach out for their memories, but nothing comes from either of them, their minds blocked.

Helina tucks her face paint into a drawer on the vanity and mechanically rises, following him out of the room with her head bowed. I hover above them as they make their way to a backstage wall with a life-size painting of a dancer in a plume of red feathers.

A bouncer with a white piercing through his dark brow is stationed beside the giant picture frame. Armed with a gem gun and an entitled air about him, he instantly reminds me of someone from Zo. Their kingdom is the only one that prefers revolvers to swords, since their lands sit on the majority of metal core used for making the bullets. They are *not*, however, the only kingdom with entitlement issues.

The bouncer's jaw flexes as Red nears, but he pulls the painting open without a word; it swings out like a door into a hallway, revealing a secret maze of rooms and other halls.

Once Helina and Red are inside, the bouncer closes the painting. Red takes Helina's arm and yanks her down the low-lit hall and into a room with a large bed.

"Where's my shipment, Helina?"

She straightens, her arms stiff at her sides. "The supply carriages were attacked by Skeeves last night. We're cleaning up the mess before Mazzar's infantries find it. You'll have your guns by tomorrow."

He sets his gem gun on the nightstand, and her eyes narrow in on the movement.

"Where's the other First-Made vessel, Red? More guns for more information. That was the deal."

A sneering grin splits beneath his crimson mask. "It's not in the Barrens, where you and Jasper have been nosing around."

He unbuttons his collar, and Helina backs up a step.

"You agreed to give us the *exact* location by the end of this moon cycle."

"Well, Helina, you and Jasper teeter on the line of profitable and pain in my ass." He slips loose another button. "So, I'll be charging another late fee this week."

"We know you are not from Zarr. We'll report this business—"

He throws her onto the bed, grabbing at her red dancer's uniform. "See?" He grits his teeth as she fights beneath him. "Pain in my ass."

"Jasper will—"

He slaps her across the face. "He can't touch me with his mind tricks. I've had enough, Helina." He rips her strappy outfit from her, tearing it at the seams. "You're still my dancer, and I will treat you like—"

I materialize behind him, hooking my arm around his neck and crushing his airway before I consciously decide to do it.

His surprise catches in his throat as he claws and thrashes against me like a man beating against a closing coffin. He reaches toward the nightstand, his fingers grazing the barrel of his gem gun, just out of reach.

Not that it would help him.

Instead of killing him and letting his soul pass to wherever it will go, I sink my fist through his back and breathe in his dark, wretched soul, allowing its power to fill my limbs with a burst of strength and power. It shatters, and his final scream breaks free as his soul ceases to exist.

The shadows inside purr with excitement. "*So delicious. Give us more.*"

No matter how often I feed, they're never fully satiated. I drop his body to the floor, and it lands with a thud.

Helina pulls herself up and away onto the bed, looking at Red's lifeless body, then at me.

"You're—you're—"

I watch her most recent memory, making sure she didn't see the unnatural way I killed the man. From her perspective, I strangled him.

Mortals can't see or hear souls, but after Nizzara heard me, I have to be sure.

Leashing the shadows again is the hardest part. They growl for more.

"Look at those sweet parts of her soul."

I close my eyes, clench my fists, and rein them in. When I finally have some control again, I open my eyes. Her hands tremble as she scoots herself farther from me.

"I won't hurt you," I say.

"You're K-King Dagen—"

Well, I guess I take that back. My shadow blade materializes in my hand. If I let this woman live, her knowing who I am could cost me everything.

I raise the sword, every pathway of human emotion dull and frozen.

Helina yanks off a gold bracelet before tossing it to the floor. "I don't want blood on it when it's given to my daughter," she says, a tremble in her words, but I'm beyond hearing; my world goes still as I gaze down at the familiar gold chain.

"Where'd you get this?" I breathe, picking it up.

Helina's eyes harden as if I slapped her. "I didn't steal it, if that's what you're asking. I traded information for it."

It's Lo's.

Or it *was*.

I shove the gold chain up to her face. "Who gave this to you?" When she doesn't answer, I point my sword at her bare abdomen and the hiss of shadows comes through my voice when I ask again.

"Who gave this to you?"

"Some man! I don't know who he was—"

"Did he wear a golden vessel?" It could've been Lo using her Mark to disguise herself.

She shakes her head. "I don't remember."

I inch the sword closer, until the shadows on my blade writhe with excitement near her skin.

"More," they whisper to me. *"Feed us more."*

"Gloves!" Helina shouts. "He wore gloves!"

"What information did you trade for it?"

She leans farther from my blade. "He asked about the shipment schedule for the rebel camps."

"And you told him?"

She grits her teeth. "I told him a bullshit story."

"Like you're telling me?" I wedge my blade under her neck, severing a lock of red hair as it glides closer.

"No, I swear. I'm telling you the truth! I support the rebels! I support you!"

"Convince me," I growl.

She swallows, her neck bobbing so close to the flickering devil sword. "I have a daughter. She lives in the rebel camps. Six years old. I take supplies to them, send wages to them. I'd never give the shipment schedule to a stranger."

As if on cue, she thinks of the last time she saw her daughter, after delivering a sled of supplies. She has the same deep red hair as Helina. I look through her non-blocked memories and find the one with the man and the bracelet. Someone I don't recognize, and I can't tell if it's Lo using her Mark.

"I will kill you if you tell anyone who I am without my permission," I say before removing my sword from her neck.

She shakes her head, her arms still crossed over her bare chest. "I won't."

I whisk my shadow sword away, and it disappears into darkness. I shrug my long-sleeve shirt off and hand it to her, realizing it's the one I died in. She accepts it like I might kill her if she doesn't, and I turn away so she can put it on.

After a moment she says, "You can face me now."

I turn to see her bunching up the sleeves only to have them fall back down.

"I would thank you—I *do* thank you—but you've killed what I might call a very important business transaction." Her gaze keeps finding my bare chest then falling away as she begins rolling up the sleeves again.

"You wanted him to rape you, then?"

She flinches. "No. That wasn't part of—" She sighs. "He keeps this establishment running along with the shipments to the rebels, which keeps my daughter safe and fed."

I study the dead man whose hair is the same shade as mine, his body a similar build. If I could gain access to the rebels, I could not only find out if Lo is with them, but I could help my people.

"I have a proposition for you, Helina. I need help finding someone, and it seems you need a guy in a mask."

She scoots to the end of the bed and glances down at Red's dead body on the marble floor, then warily at me. "Find who?"

"The owner of that bracelet." I swallow. "You care for your daughter. I care for someone too."

She glances at the door, some deep emotion flitting across her face, but her desires and mind are suddenly blocked completely. Nodding, she says, "I'll help you."

I wish to help the rebellion, but I can't be seen as *myself*. I decide that even if I don't win this bargain or find my sister, using my time here to help my people is still worth it. And if there's any chance Lola made it to the rebels . . . I have to know.

I'm inspecting Red's gem gun, wondering if all people shot by one are sucked away to Baratrum, or if I was just an unfortunate exception, when she asks, "How much of that conversation did you hear?"

I peer down the barrel. "All of it." Fuck. It's out of bullets.

She pales. "Aren't you curious about the lost First-Made vessel?"

I scoff. "That legend is a lie. You're wasting your time looking for it." My great-grandfather went mad looking for it. He's the reason the Barrens are barren.

By the time we emerge from the room, I'm wearing Red's masked outfit—a deep red suit without a jacket—and Helina knows how I came to be here. She insisted trust was a two-way street, and she'd exchange hers for mine.

"I still can't believe how much you pass for him," she says, looking at the red mask over my eyes. "Except your beard is a tad longer . . . and I guess your voice, but still. The resemblance is unsettling."

"You're sure we can trust this bouncer? Jasper, was it?"

Her head bobs. "Don't worry, he does not support Mazzar. Besides, this plan won't work without him. Jasper is Red's second in command. He'll notice."

"But the others?" I ask.

"They won't notice, as long as you don't give them a reason to notice."

Our footsteps click on the polished stone floor as we near the painting. "Which one is Jasper?"

She peers up at me from the corner of her eye. "If you somehow miss the white bar through his brow, his skin is darker, his suits are pricier, and his words are always more compelling than those of the rest."

Helina knocks on the back of the picture and the bouncer with the eyebrow piercing—Jasper—opens it. His eyes harden when they register Helina in what's obviously a man's shirt, but he smooths the expression by the time his dark-brown gaze snaps to me.

I motion with my hand for him to come in. Jasper calls to another bouncer to take his place before stepping into the secret passage of halls and rooms.

Once the picture shuts us off from the rest of the club, I signal for him to follow. His black brows crunch together as he shoots Helina a tight glance.

She touches his fingers. "Come."

He stiffens for a split second before resuming his leisurely confidence. He reminds me of someone, but I can't quite place who.

I try to read his memories, but it's as if I'm blocked by a smooth wall with no give. My hackles rise. Trusting people is not what I do anymore.

Lo would've just killed both of them.

Jasper follows us to the room, brushing past me as he maneuvers the narrow doorway. He goes rigid when he sees Red's lifeless body on the rug and slowly turns to me.

"Helina tells me you support the rebels. Is that true?" I ask.

A glance in Helina's direction prompts Jasper to answer. "I don't mind their existence."

I tilt my head. "What do you remember of the late King Dagen?"

Another glance at Helina. She nods.

"He was known to be quite ruthless."

I had my younger years full of blood and wine. The rest was Lo.

Jasper's brown eyes begin calculating under dark brows. "But the last time my father and I paid taxes to him, we handed King Dagen the wrong bag of ren," he says, again looking at Helina then back at me. "King Dagen could've easily kept the extra ren, but he threw it back at us saying aloud to his noblemen that it was not nearly enough, even though it held thrice what we owed."

Jasper lifts his head.

That must be why he looks familiar. I remember this tax payment. His hair is much darker than in my memory, his face shape . . . different. But it was twelve years ago.

"Do you have any loyalty to Mazzar?"

His body goes rigid. "Only a debt to repay."

"A debt?"

His face hardens. "He took something from my family."

I debate on asking what, but the look on his face tells me it's not up for discussion, and I really don't care.

I remove Red's mask from my face. Shock then recognition fills his expression before he takes a knee in front of me.

"Your Majesty," he says.

For someone who doesn't trust people, I'm doing a lot of it so far.

CHAPTER 11

NIZZARA

DIARY: PAGE 2

My brother may be the chosen heir—his charisma and military skill set, lethal—but Father made it clear to me. Dagen is the face of Zarr, and I am the bloody, deceptive hand keeping him on the throne, because Father and I both know Dagen has too much of Mother in him.

—*Lo*

MY MIND RACES THROUGH EVERY FORM OF POISON I KNOW as I stumble into my bathing chamber. I barely make it to the latrine before I drop to my knees, retching. A cold sweat breaks across my forehead as I force myself to think through the stomach pain and heart palpitations. I quickly form a list in my mind, starting with the most likely poisons. Poppywart and boxelder vane are the two most likely. They're easy to find, effective, and versatile—any contact whatsoever with either one is fatal. Next on my list is devil's cap and lully nettle, which are rare. If it is devil's cap, there would have to be an obscene amount of it mixed into the ink to make it fatal to touch, since it's more effective as an ingestible poison. And lully nettle only grows in Badadwom. As I continue to retch, and my arms and legs go weak and shaky, I decide it has to be poppywart or boxelder vane. Neither has a cure, but they are very different types of poisons. Boxelder acts fast;

it's known to kill within minutes. Poppywart is slow, causing death by full-body paralysis. First the limbs go numb and immovable, then the facial muscles, then vital organs such as the lungs and heart. I think about yelling to my guards to fetch Preysee, but I struggle to breathe in between the violent convulsions, and no matter which poison it is, there's nothing she can do to help, so I let her sleep.

After thirty minutes of violent puking, I'm still able to move my limbs and thankfully rule out poppywart. My gut tells me it's box-elder vane, which is very deadly, but judging by the date in the diary, sixteen years of oxidation is enough time to dull its effects enough to not kill me.

I spend hours puking despite having nothing left in my body to spew, until finally I'm able to lie down on the cold stone floor, and slowly the bouts of retching begin to spread out, allowing me to find some small stretches of sleep. It's past midnight when I manage to crawl the long distance from the bathing chamber to my bed, and I'm so delirious, I can't decide if the cold, dark presence is the spirit from earlier or simply my subconscious reminding me how alone I am in this castle. My father would take one look at me and tell me I'm weak. My mother and Tarella might actually be entertained to know I was poisoned, and Liha, if she were here, would be more concerned with my sickly appearance than anything.

I curl into my sheets, grateful no one is here to see me.

A KNOCK SLAMS AGAINST MY DOOR HOURS LATER, JERKING me from sleep. I instinctively look for Preysee to answer it, but she won't be tending to me for another hour, which is inconvenient. I was really hoping she'd know of *something* to remove the black stain on my fingers, now that the poison has cleared my system. The poison was definitely meant to deter me from reading the blasted diary, but *Lo* doesn't know how I work. I'm invested now.

Invested, and determined to find a set of reading gloves.

The knock bangs again, demanding and rude. Luckily Liha is

inside my shield, so the moment I crawl out of bed, Liha summons an outfit from my closet. As I amble toward the door, a pink puff of smoke replaces my night gown with the comfortable red dress, and another stream of smoke twists my hair into a braid and applies a quick smear of khol around my eyes.

Another pounding knock comes from the door. If that's Brunar, I'll have him replaced for waking me up this early.

"*You look sickly,*" Liha says as I take my time walking to the door. I still feel a little sick, and I'm not in a hurry to talk to anyone. "*The red dress will help highlight what little color you have in your face.*" Liha nudges my cheek. "*Did you eat something bad last night?*" She pauses. "*Is that ink on your hands?*"

"Yeah," I say to both questions. Since she was away from me when I found the diary, I decide not to mention it. I'm angry that I was out-smarted by an inanimate object, so it's a pride thing.

I yank the door open to a pair of slicing green eyes burning down at me. Sorren.

"We're training." He turns and stalks away, adding over his shoulder, "Get changed into something other than a gods-damned dress."

"*Someone is obviously not a morning person,*" I say to Liha, grateful that the nausea in my stomach is slowly calming down the longer I'm up and moving. Liha surrounds me in smoke and summons another quick outfit change. I stir the pink clouds as I march down the hall after Sorren, now in a pair of fighting leathers.

"*His desires are always so silent,*" she mutters as Sorren stalks ahead of us.

"*I thought you can't hear desires.*"

"*They have to be very strong and loud for me to decode them, but I am always able to hear their noise. Sorren's are eerily silent. Not hard to understand, not protected, just silent.*"

"*What do you mean, protected?*"

"*I don't mean anything by it.*"

I know the difference in her tones, and right now she's using her very convenient I-don't-know-what-you're-talking-about tone that tells me she knows exactly what I'm talking about.

"*Liha*—"

"Your first level-six duel is in a week," Sorren says ahead, "and it will determine whether or not you make it into the King's Duel." He pushes through the doors to the training room. "The official start of the tournament, after preliminaries, is only a moon cycle—"

"Why don't you tell me things I don't already know?" I cut him off.

His face hardens. "Like how pathetic you are with a longsword? Or how the king has been too soft on you for not forcing you to learn it before now?" He shakes his head. "You're all fucking soft." He jabs my arm. "So, you'll be working on muscle growth."

"I have muscle," I snap. "And besides, muscle growth takes more than a week. Even a moon cycle—"

"Did I say *muscle growth*? I meant *discipline*."

I glare at him. "I have that too."

"Is that what you call your explosive, unplanned rages?"

I grit my teeth, ready to launch at him, but he turns his back to me and saunters over to a new piece of equipment I've never seen before. A rack holding a long metal bar.

"In order to grow muscle—I mean, *discipline*—you'll be pushed until failure."

As I grudgingly face the bar, he adjusts the height until it's level with my collarbone.

"Get under it."

"What?"

"I said, get under."

I look at the bar, then him, without moving.

He puffs a breath, as if I'm the most annoying thing on the planet. "Like this."

He ducks his head, steps under the bar, and rests it on the back of his shoulders, before surging up and away from the rack, his body a slab of muscle and intimidation.

"You will squat, lunge, rest, repeat."

He demonstrates, then re-racks the bar and backs away.

I'd rather lift weights with my muscles than with power, but I'm curious . . . "Why not vessel training?"

His face darkens. "Because your weakness isn't with your vessel. Because your father knows you hate using your vessel, and because your father has a soft spot for you. Get under the bar."

I stare into his eyes, which reveal nothing. "Where is my father, anyway?"

His jaw ticks. "Get. Under. The. Bar."

I clench my fists. "Fine."

Liha swirls around me as I obey and heave the bar up, its length testing my balance on both sides.

"How much does this thing weigh?" I gasp.

"One-fifty. Now squat."

"One-fifty is more than I weigh. That's not normal—"

"*You're* not normal. Now, squat."

My knees shake as I sink down.

"Lower."

"It'll crush me."

He points down at the metal bars on either side of my legs, running perpendicular to the bar across my shoulders. "It's called a safety bar, and I intend for you to use it."

I'm too burdened to glare at him, so I go as low as I can, determined *not* to use the safety bar.

"Now, back up."

My legs quiver, pushing my body up with the bar, and I'm barely able to get up. He adds ten pounds on both sides, then instructs me to do it again.

I drop into the squat with a whimper as my thighs give everything to then propel me up. Slowly, shakily, I rise and let out a breath when I reach the top.

He pushes me until my legs physically can't hold me or the bar. I'm about to fall beneath the weight when he takes the bar in his hands from behind me, assisting enough for me to shakily rise to my full height.

"Again."

He continues to spot me from behind, only helping when my muscles seize. When Liha tries to assist with magic, I don't have the capacity to stop the smoke from unfurling.

He stomps on my foot. "No vessel power. Squat again."

"I can't."

He slowly walks around to face me. "Pathetic."

My temper sparks, and the edges of my sight darken. "I will wipe the floor with you one day."

He tilts his head with the closest thing to a real smile I've ever seen on him and scoffs. "Not if you trained every day for the next twelve years, Princess."

He drops his hands on top of the bar, adding weight to it. "You're soft."

I yell from the added resistance, my knees about to buckle. "I'm not soft," I grind out. The gold spirit flutters in the distance.

He gets in my face, his hands still pressing down on my shoulders. "You're soft *and* afraid."

My knees crumble and I hit the ground, the safety guard catching the bar inches from my body. Stars dance across the ceiling as he bends over me.

"Time for arms."

"I hate you."

"No, you don't." His lips pull back from his teeth, the expression too dark for a smile. "But give it time."

He takes me through every muscle group until I can't hold myself upright. Until breathing is a workout in and of itself. Finally, he points to the rack where the weights go, and I wobble over to place them in their spot.

When I turn to find him holding a sword out to me, he has the nerve to say, "The next hour will be sparring."

Liha makes a squeak as I numbly take the sword. "You can't be serious."

He swings before I'm ready, slicing his blade into my arm. I swipe the sword into nothing but air, screaming from frustration.

"How do you expect to control an army," he says, cutting his sword across my chest when my evasion is too slow, "when you can't even control your emotions?"

My knees wobble as I try and fail to keep up with him, my anger rising, the darkness in my sight growing. His skill is not normal. It's beyond any I've seen, maybe even surpassing my father's.

"How will you do what needs to be done when your father gets worse if you're so damned afraid of your own power?"

"I don't know what you mean," I hiss, thrusting my sword forward and missing him again.

"You know exactly what I mean." He scoffs. "But you hide from the truths you don't want to see." He jabs his sword at my chest again with more speed. I stumble and fall backward, hitting the hard mat. Before I can jump up, his blade pricks the leather over my chest.

"You're explosive, undisciplined, and scared of what lurks inside you."

I glare up at him, my chest heaving and jaw clenched.

He presses down harder on his pommel, puncturing my leathers and cutting the skin beneath with the tip of his blade. "And all of those weaknesses will get the rest of us killed."

He withdraws his blade and walks away. The room seems to have its own pulse as I stagger up and unloose a swing. He spins and swipes my legs out from under me. I land flat on my back, and his blade finds my chest once more.

"Dead," he growls. "Get up. And if you have the nerve to try again, make it count."

Just to spite him, I don't stand when he lets up.

"Get. Up."

"Make me."

The look on his face immediately tells me I'm fucked. He stalks closer and presses his boot against my neck, applying more and more pressure until I cough. Darkness flares inside me, my anger fueling it.

"Fucking dead."

I yank my sword, slicing above his boot and into his calf. Blood spurts onto my leathers, but he doesn't flinch, and the gash doesn't stop him from *killing me* at least fifteen more times before he takes away my sword.

"Rest. Eat. Sleep. I'll see you in a few days." He hangs the swords on their racks. "Practice while I'm away."

I try to fold my arms, but even that is too much for these noodles attached at my sides. "Got somewhere important to be?"

He walks away from me. "I always have somewhere important to be."

YISABELL IS IN MY ROOM WHEN I RETURN, LYING UPSIDE down on my armchair. Her white hair tickles the ground as she giggles, and it's not the first time I've wondered how my father and I also share that rare, snowy shade that's unique to the Awoms.

She smiles up at me and speaks in her native tongue. "Finally! I've been waiting for you all morning."

I smile at her. "What are you doing?"

"Father helped me finish up my chores for the upcoming rave so I could come visit you."

I can't help my own giggle and the wince from my sore body that follows. "I meant, what are you doing upside down?"

Her whole face lights up. "Being silly. I don't get to be silly very often. It's good for the soul, you know."

Liha giggles. "*I think she wants you to be silly too.*"

I take my bloody gloves off, hobble to the armchair across from her, and manage to finagle my legs and body around until I'm upside down facing her, too tired to care about the drying blood smeared across my leathers.

"I don't get to be silly either," I say, fanning my hands on either side of my face, my arms feeling like dead weight.

Her eyes widen. "You're still wearing the ring I gave you."

"I told you. I'll always wear it."

She sits up. "I thought you were just saying that to be nice. It would be okay if you were."

I remain upside down, too drained to move. "It's special to me."

Her brows furrow. "Why? It's not worth anything."

"That's not true. It's"—I don't know the translation for the word, so I say it in my own language—"symbolic."

Her nose scrunches. "What is *symbolic*?"

"It's when something carries a deeper meaning."

Instead of trying to sit up, I slide to the floor in a heap of useless limbs. She laughs, which makes me smile.

"How much longer is your break?" I ask, managing to prop myself against the legs of the chair.

"I have to help prepare lunch soon." She frowns.

How's it lunch already? My stomach growls, completely empty. "Can you visit later?"

"No." She sighs. "I'm in the kitchens tonight, and after that, we've been ordered to ready the castle for your betrothed."

I freeze. *My betrothed.* Father hasn't told me who it is or when he'll be here.

"You didn't know he was coming?"

I shake my head, dread rising in me. "Not this soon."

My face must show exactly how I feel about that because Yisabell cocks her head. "You're not excited?"

"Would *you* be?"

She looks up into the air of my room as if studying something in it. "Maybe."

"Why?"

"The Awoms believe in pathways," she says, "and I am always curious to see why my path crosses with another's. There's always a reason, you know."

"What if it's a bad path to cross?"

"There's good inside every bad." She looks at me, her young eyes somehow flickering with ageless wisdom. "Like you. You are my good inside the bad." Her smile wobbles as she brushes her slave garb. "I'm really glad to have known you in this life."

Her world was broken and ripped apart in order for her to be here in my room, so it feels incredibly selfish for me to be glad she's here too, so I don't say it. But I am. I'm thankful for her.

She groans and slides out of her chair onto the floor like I did. "I have to go."

She helps me up and gives me a tight hug, holding it a second longer than usual. I've never told her that she's the only person who hugs me. I've never told her how she's the good in my bad.

"When I am queen, you will be free," I whisper, tears pricking my eyes.

She squeezes harder before letting go. "And when you're queen, you'll let me try chocolate too, right?"

"Obviously." I laugh. "We'll *both* try chocolate when I'm queen even if I have to order the infantry soldiers to bombard the trade routes to get it."

When she's gone my room feels empty. After I clean myself up, I fill the void with books.

CHAPTER 12

DAGEN

I'M FLOATING THROUGH THE SLEEPY WALLS OF MY CASTLE, reading memories of the few staff who are still awake at this hour. I'm just dipping into a guard's memory, when a scream reigns down from above.

"Stay in formation," a guard says to the others next to him. "I'll check on it."

The other guards nod and adjust their positions as he departs. I follow him down the hall and up the giant, circling staircase toward Nizzara's rooms.

"Another one of the princess's nightmares?" he asks once he reaches the top steps of the tower.

The high guard of Nizzara's night watch nods. "They're getting worse, I'm afraid."

The guard on the stairs dips his chin and turns back for his post.

I float through her door, the sense of intrusion creeping up on me.

Silver gloom trails in through the glass windows of the balcony doors. Nizzara is asleep, curled up on her side, and I'm taken aback by how soft her face is when it's not twisted into the sneer I've seen in so many memories of her.

I'm also stuck on what she's wearing. Or rather how *little* she's wearing. Her silky black nightgown is bunched up her legs, leaving her honey-toned thighs on display, where a midnight dagger catches my eye.

Sleeping with a dagger? Such a vicious little beast.

I find myself hovering closer until I catch the sheen of tears on her smooth cheeks and golden light—

Wait. Brilliant gold light edges her silhouette. My mouth goes dry. Her soul is . . .

I don't finish that thought.

Gorgeous.

Damn it. I finished the thought. If I can see her soul, her little pink spirit must be gone.

I hover closer, sure I'll find rotten edges on it somewhere.

Tears stream down her cheeks before disappearing into the black satin pillowcase.

I reach out for her soul, curious if—

The moment my fingers graze it, gold erupts in my vision, heating me from the inside out. I curl my hand deeper into her soul, hoping to find a weak, rotted part, but as I go deeper, my hand strikes—

Darkness like I've never known. An endless void takes hold of me, sucking me in. My shadows screech, an awful sound, and I yank my hand back, glaring at the little beast.

The blackness inside her is not like that of other souls. Not weak and rotted, but . . .

Smooth . . . Strong . . . Infinite.

I gaze into her sleeping face and decide it's time to get what I came for. Memories. If only to shake her soul from my mind. I open the door to her past and fall into another time and space.

Suddenly, I'm hunched against a wall, seeing through her eyes as her father throws a wine bottle at her in a drunken rage. It shatters against the wall above her. Her heartache punctures through me as she clutches her arms in front of herself. Mazzar kicks a fallen chair out of his way.

"She's fucking pregnant," he spits. "I can't . . ." His fists shake before he raises his hands and knots his fingers in his hair, nearly pulling it out. "I can't kill her." His voice cracks with rage and despair as his hands drop.

A silver military vessel gleams on his finger, in the blinding lights of the whitewashed room—the Zo castle, I realize.

He's wearing his Zarr infantry uniform, with the gold insignia of a skull on his arm. This has to be during Mazzar's first years of marriage to Soriah—while he was my general—meaning, Nizzara is only two or three years old. And Tarella would've already been born . . . So, I have to wonder. *Who* is pregnant?

He grabs Nizzara beneath the arms and holds her against the wall, his gaze softening when it focuses on her.

Tears stream down her face as if they're my own, and he wipes them away with his thumb. Her heart is full of fear, but also incredible, depthless love. I feel it all.

"Can you promise to be strong, Nizzara?" he asks, his black eyes boring into me with the look of a tortured father. "Promise to be brave?"

She raises her small chin. "I *am* strong and brave," she says, her voice too knowing for her age.

He closes his eyes. "Gods, so much like your mother. I will protect you. Do you hear me?"

She nods.

"You will not be as weak as I am." He curls his fist and punches the wall, splintering the stone beside her. "You will overcome pain!" He strikes again, deepening the fissure. "You will overcome fear!" He hits again, and again, and again until his fist sticks and his shoulders cave. "So when the world tries to hurt you," he says, sliding his fist down the white stone, "you will laugh in their face, Nizzara."

I yank myself out of the memory. No matter what scene plays out in her mind, the air in her memories is warm, and I've forgotten what warmth feels like.

When I leave the vision, Nizzara's black eyes are open and honed directly on me, and it's now that I see the golden strands of her soul tickling the air, singing her desires.

"*. . . to be calm . . .*"

"*. . . to win the King's Duel . . .*"

"*. . . to end my betrothal . . .*"

Her deeper desires are there too, but with the warmth of her memories still fogging my mind, I can't quite make them out.

CHAPTER 13

NIZZARA

DIARY: PAGE 3

There are levels of subterfuge between the kingdoms. On the surface, we mind our own business. The Zos and Zems don't ask why I'm trying to steal an illegally enchanted glo-kar, and I don't ask why the Zo king is hiding a son—not out loud, anyway. Beneath that are other levels of secrets not worth prodding at. Secrets about inter-realm smuggling, like how the Zems make their money selling void gem collars to creatures that can travel through the realms. Or long-dead secrets like how some inventors escaped the destruction of the fourth kingdom. The deepest level of subterfuge, however, is why the fourth kingdom no longer exists. Silent, deadly warfare among the allied kingdoms. It's also why I killed a sixteen-year-old Zem spy disguised as a weapons servant inside our barracks this morning. And it's also why I'm going out tonight, disguised as King Rajim's *favorite mistress*.

—*Lo*

❧

I WAKE, UNSURE OF WHAT PULLED ME FROM SLEEP, BESIDES, perhaps, the frigid draft. Dawn is still a few hours off and my cheeks are wet from crying through my dreams. Dreams about—

Wait. *He's* here. He's so pigmented, I can make out his tall, defined form leaning against the far wall, the air curling differently around his outline. Not a hovering ball like last time. *A man.*

He pushes from the wall and prowls to where I've propped myself up on my elbow. My nightgown has fallen off one shoulder, barely covering the more scandalizing parts of me, but I leave it because he's a realm's damned ghost.

"Spying on sleeping women in your afterlife?" I say. "You must've been one sick bastard when you were alive."

He slinks closer and I'm swallowed by his power, as if a vast, endless hole has taken root in my room, sucking everything into it.

He bends to my level, tilts that dark, airy head of his, and purrs, *"Hmm, such eloquent words for a princess."*

As much as I tried to forget his voice from the bathing chamber, I can't. It's a deep, velvet voice. The curling toes kind, that when whispered against one's ear—

"I want you to leave," I say.

A dark laugh slices the air around me. *"Your desires are quite mixed on that subject."*

Out of instinct, my fingers inch toward the dagger on my thigh. "You know nothing about my desires."

"Oh, but I do. You desire to win the King's Duel." He tilts his head to the other side. *"I'm very powerful. I could help you do that, Nizzara."*

Goose bumps trail up my neck as I grit my teeth. "I don't want more power."

"You will." He curls his black, ghostly hand beneath my chin. *"After you get a taste of level six . . . you will, and I'll be here when you beg for it."*

I punch my fist through his head, and he laughs as his presence vanishes from my room.

Not two seconds later, Liha's voice comes through my caster's shield. *"Oh, you're awake."*

"Where have you been?" I ask.

"Playing," she says in her snooty way, as if that answer is all I need

to know. A silence stretches between us before she adds, *"Why is your room like ice?"*

"That spirit passed through."

She stiffens in my shield. *"Stay away from that spirit,"* she says. *"He's a product of damnation."* Liha stays with me for the rest of the night, but I don't find sleep again.

CHAPTER 14

DAGEN

I WATCH THE LITTLE BEAST ON AND OFF FOR ALMOST A week, her days consisting of tutoring sessions, training with the infantry general, and reading. So much reading. Books about different realms, moon patterns, mythology, sciences, cultures, and lineages descended through the three kingdoms.

If I cared, I might think it was—

Nope, don't care.

Her eyes move up to me on occasion, but I don't speak.

She's nestled into a velvet chair, knees pulled up, a book perched between her fingers, and an onyx gaze that keeps rising above her pages.

Preysee, my old maid, appearing just as fortified as I remember, enters, announcing that the royal glo-kars are ready to trek to the Megadome. It's time for Nizzara's first duel in the level-six circuit. If she wins, she'll take the last spot in the King's Duel Tournament.

Nizzara blanches, and her hands shake as she slides her book onto the side table, but her desires are silent. The pink hue glowing around her means her protective spirit is in her shield, effectively blocking me out.

I dissolve into the balcony wall to find a rotted soul to end before returning for my shift at the Red Mask, but I find myself lingering by the two black glo-kars assembled in my courtyard. They're the same ones I had as king, and I idly wonder if the third one I owned broke down. After a moment spent circling the Zarr glo-kars, I decide to wait for the princess to come out. The little pink spirit leaves Nizzara often enough that I might get a chance to offer my assistance again before her duel.

As I wait for her to emerge from my castle, servants bring out buckets of blare gems to start the two royal glo-kars. Judging by the minimal rust on their squatty, boxlike frames, they've been well taken care of in my absence. The fresh gems ignite with a brilliant red light underneath the glo-kars, and their engines growl through the icy courtyard. I drift around their armored bodies, wondering if the enchanted glo-kar Lo found—and probably stole—for my birthday is still hidden beneath the castle. I kept it in the underground tunnel, driving it in the Barrens when I needed to get away from the castle and its politics.

When Nizzara and her guards cross the frosty courtyard, I fly over to her, pleased to see that her spirit is away.

"Begging for me yet?" I say, floating circles around her as she marches toward the glo-kars.

Her deadly gaze darts to me, and her desires begin whispering.

". . . desire to throw something at him . . ."

". . . desire to hear him speak . . ."

". . . desire to throw something at him . . ."

Her tan face goes pale when her guards open the door for her. She clenches her jaw, and her fists tighten. Her desires shift, not wanting to get into the glo-kar; nor do her swirling memories, which would feel trapped in the small space.

She faces the glo-kar, a cold resolve washing over her. "Get lost," she says, then ducks into the gem-powered contraption.

CHAPTER 15

NIZZARA

DIARY: PAGE 4

Dagen thinks he's in love with a bondslave, but he's not. I know everything there is to know about my brother, including his giant heart. He's still healing from the night Mother died. The Awoms have a way with healing souls. That's why Emya is good for him now, but once he grows through his grief, he'll need someone who fights as fiercely as she loves. I regret to say all the women in his pool of betrothals are beautiful, but otherwise disappointing.

Speaking of disappointing, I just returned from a visit with King Rajim in Zem. After his sleep elixir finally kicked in, I had a good look at his ledgers.

Someone is stealing void gems from his mines.

Ah, levels of subterfuge. What concerns me, however, is Rajim thinks it's my father who is stealing . . .

—*Lo*

THE MEGADOME COULD EAT THE COLOSSEUM FOR LUNCH. The ceiling rivals the height of the fog outside, supported by four giant pillars representing the original four kings in the alliance. Above that, on the highest floor, is the ballroom with its famous glass ceiling reserved for King's Duel after-parties.

The crowd encircles me in walls of yelling red faces, like tiny glinting blare gems in the distance. The dueler across the ring is murdering me with her eyes. We're competing for the same spot in the King's Duel Tournament, and she obviously wants it.

"*It's time*," Liha says, funneling her power into my hands.

I allow her power to run through me, compartmentalizing the fatigue weighing on me, my increasing nightmares making it hard to sleep lately.

Last night's nightmares were particularly bad, swarming with black, faceless creatures and poisoned diaries I can't seem to leave alone.

Then there's my other problem—the dark spirit who won't leave me alone either.

He's even here now.

But if Liha is content to ignore him, then so am I.

Pink smoke flashes around me and my black leathers snap on. This pair has red stitching and a sheer material down my sides, showing off skin. The crowd eats it up with roars of approval.

"*You look like a death god*," Liha purrs.

The bell in the Megadome is more like a siren. It blares overhead and my opponent from Zem lifts her gem-studded sword.

I call Liha's power, but my opponent's blue smoke is faster, yanking my daggers out of my sheaths and pinning them hilt-deep into the duel post behind me.

Fuck.

"Good luck, little princess." She smiles before charging, sword raised.

She swings. I dodge.

She cuts down. I spin to the side.

She thrusts. I jump back, taking a slice to my arm. She's fast, but luckily not *Sorren*-fast.

Six more desperate evasions, and a deep gash on my thigh later, my breathing is ragged.

Sorren was right. It's a different rhythm here.

"*Don't forget to use me*," Liha says as I evade the sword swinging for my abdomen.

The rules. They never cease to annoy me. I call her power to my palms, ready to pull my daggers out of the duel post, but Liha says, *"Vanish them into a different dimension, so she can't disarm you again."*

"Then what? Channel that power the entire duel? That's too long." Too intoxicating.

"If you don't keep your daggers away from her, she'll disarm you over and over again."

I take a deep breath and tuck my daggers away into a different time and space, holding them there.

My opponent jumps forward, slicing her blade toward my ribs.

I summon one of my far-off daggers to my hand and thrust it up in the tender part of her underarm, where her red leathers aren't reinforced. A yell of pain escapes her lips, and when her eyes refocus on me, they are like two blue stones in her sockets.

Her lips curl into a sneer. *"Kill her."* It's her voice, but not.

My blood turns cold. *"Liha—"*

"Possessed," she hisses.

My opponent's movements are suddenly different, belonging to her spirit. Her head tilts before she connects her boot to my chest. As I'm thrown backward, a wave of invisible force crashes down on me like an avalanche. My back and head hit the mat so hard my ears ring and the Megadome darkens.

For the first time, I'm witnessing the power of a possessed caster.

"Nizzara!" Liha's voice is distorted, as if I'm trapped beneath layers of invisible snow. *"Possessed casters are different! Their power is—"*

My opponent kicks the side of my head and bends down as I cry out from the pain. *"More of us are coming,"* she hisses. *"I'm doing you a favor by killing you now."*

My opponent raises her sword above my heart, and her eyes roll back in her head as if she's fighting for control over her body again as the audience screams, "Slow death! Slow death!"

"You have to kill her!" Liha yells through my shield.

"No." I lift my head, trying to stand up, but her power holds. *"I can't even move."*

"*Take her power and slice her head off!*" Liha hovers over my heart, as if her spirit could somehow stop the blade poised above me. "*It's the only way to kill a possessed caster.*"

The audience chants louder, "Slow death!"

"*I will not kill!*"

"*Nizzara—*"

"*I'll cut her vessel off.*"

"*That doesn't work if they are too far gone.*"

When the audience's cheers reach a riotous level, my opponent changes the course of her sword and buries it through my shoulder.

The fans scream as her blade slices and twists through sinew. Black, endless rage rises, darkening my vision.

My opponent withdraws her blade then stops, smiles, and thrusts it back into the same spot. Blinding pain erupts in my torso. I scream, and the strange, golden spirit flickers in the distance.

Darkness clouds my sight, and power seems to come toward me from everywhere. It doesn't belong to Liha. It's mine.

I can still see the bloody mat, the arena, my opponent, but I'm blinded by the intoxicating feel of this kind of power. Liha funnels her popping energy through my veins, and mine recoils from it.

Pink smoke with black edges erupts high and wide. I yank the sword from my shoulder and hurtle it through my opponent's body so hard and fast her feet fly off the ground.

When Liha's power releases from me, I rise to see my opponent impaled by her own sword, half of the hilt buried into her flank.

"*I knew you've been holding back, but . . .*" Liha says, her voice trailing off.

Self-loathing hits me in waves.

I succumb to the rage and power so easily.

I recall my daggers from their distant dimensions, sheathing all but one, allowing the last one to materialize in my hand. The intoxicating flow of power lessens, but the pain searing through my shoulder and torso does not.

I glide toward my opponent's half-conscious body and bend down to her level. I need to see her eyes. They flicker back and forth from stonelike orbs back to eyes. Back to stones.

She grabs my neck in a vise grip, nails digging through my skin. Blood pulses in my ears. The world opens for me, and I sense so much energy at my fingertips, energy I could simply breathe in. The golden spirit hovers toward my hand, as if offering power to me as well. I bury my knee into her gut and stab my black dagger into her kidney, knowing she only needs one. She crumples to the mat with a scream, her eyes going soft again.

Thousands of riotous fans scream as well.

I withdraw another blade, wrench her fingers backward, and slice her vessel off.

A screeching sound rips through the air as her spirit—writhing with shadows—slithers toward me.

"*You will pay for that*," it hisses. "*We will find you again and make you scream, yesss, scream.*" The soul shifts from cobalt blue to black—as if the spirit itself is possessed with shadows. It darts around me before spiraling out of the Megadome.

CHAPTER 16

DAGEN

IT'S OBVIOUS NIZZARA'S SOUL IS POWERFUL, JUST LIKE NIL promised. No wonder he's offering such a prize for her. After the duel, I could almost hear Lo's voice in my mind saying, "You need a fucking backup plan. Preferably one with poison." So here I am, honoring my sister's wisdom. Well, minus the poison.

A serving girl, wearing scant red leather across her torso and a matching feather mask, slides three glasses of amber rum across the polished table.

Jasper waits for her to leave through the red curtains separating us from the dancing bodies and strobing glo gems before sliding his dark gaze to Helina again, brushing his pinky finger against hers.

She takes a sip of her drink.

I lean back in my chair, taking in the scent of leather, cologne, and cigar smoke, about to bring up my situation with Nizzara, when I decide to get to know Jasper and Helina a little better first. "So, you two have been smuggling people to the rebel camps?"

Helina makes a face as if the drink is stronger than what she'd expected but swallows and shakes her head. "I don't think helping two or three strangers get in contact with the camps counts as 'smuggling.' We help deliver food and supplies to the rebels. Red helped with monetary donations."

Jasper leans forward. "Your Majesty—"

I wave my hand. "Just Dagen, or I guess *Red*, if others are around." The past week I've been filling in for him has been easier than I thought. Nobody here *likes* Red, so no one has noticed—or at least complained—that I let Jasper do most of the talking. I just loom in the distance and grunt the occasional order. Jasper seems to need Red's contacts. I find him asking them questions about the Zem mines.

Jasper nods. "I haven't smuggled anyone into the camps . . . but I have smuggled spies into Mazzar's infantry."

"Do explain," I say, lifting my glass to my lips. Realms, it tastes good.

"Last year, a small unit of Mazzar's infantry intercepted a rebel supply train in the Barrens led by my cousin and me." He takes a gulp of his rum. "We killed the Zarr soldiers, cut off their vessels, and stole their uniforms. Now, my cousin and two of his men are infantry soldiers—our eyes and ears—near Mazzar." He grins. "I thought you might find that information useful in your revenge against the king."

"As impressive as that is, Mazzar *controls* anyone who wears a military vessel," I say. Jasper's cousin would be useful to me if not for that glaring detail. Besides, the infantry soldiers are different from castle guards. They don't step foot in the castle often, aside from the general.

Jasper's grin deepens. "The military vessels," he says, raising his finger, "only bow to *explicit* commands. Since my cousin and his men were never properly inducted by Mazzar, they never received the direct order of complete, unwavering loyalty to Mazzar."

"Wouldn't someone recognize them as infiltrators?" I say.

Untamed mischief dances across his face. "That is where my expertise came into play."

"Which is?"

Helina looks over her shoulder, toward the thin slice of opening in the curtain, as if to make sure no one lingers outside.

Jasper tilts his head. "I can read minds and shape thoughts."

"Wouldn't someone notice you in their mind?"

He shrugs. "You didn't notice the other night."

My glass makes a *tap* as I set it down, and Helina flinches under my gaze.

"You looked like King Dagen, and your story was convincing, but I had to be sure," Jasper says, twirling his now empty cup. It's so mesmerizing to watch as he rolls it over and around his fingers that I don't realize his other hand is on my arm until he squeezes.

In my own head, in my own voice, I hear, "*I am a half-soul with the gift of reading and shaping conscious thoughts. I only have to be touching a person to enter their mind. The soldiers' thoughts were easy to shape. They all returned to the castle without a hiccup and none the wiser. Just like when I entered your mind the night you killed Red. Although your mind is too frozen for me to influence, I can see what I need to.*" He lets go of my arm and shrugs. "I had to know for certain you were who you claimed to be. You can't trust a soul these days."

I lean forward. "I thought half-souls only made potions. Potions that can cause a lot of trouble and often be mislabeled. That's why my great-grandfather executed them." I raise a brow.

The menacing smile returns as his hand continues to perform rolling tricks with his glass. "Oh, yes. Some of us are talented with potions, but those half-souls are gifted from Zathina's power."

"Who?"

"Zathina, the essence of Elixirs." He smirks. "I have a friend who could tell you all about it."

Helina's eyes narrow on him.

"The *essence* of Elixirs?" I ask. "You mean *goddess*?"

He chuckles under his breath. "I forgot. Your lot likes to call everything a god. For the sake of simplicity, I'll call her a god."

"So what god does *your* power come from?" I ask him.

"Scientia," he says, "the goddess of—"

"Life," I finish for him.

His eyes flick upward, not quite an eye roll. "No. You're confusing her with Wala. She holds the essence of Life. *Scientia*"—he points a finger at his temple—"holds the essence of Consciousness. That's where my gift comes from."

"There are too many realms-damned gods," I mumble.

Jasper's pierced brow rises. "Not all of us can be blessed with the patience to learn their intricacies." He scoffs. With a glance at Helina, his gaze softens, and he adds, "It took me a long time to straighten it all out." He wraps one arm around the back of Helina's chair and begins rolling his empty glass in the other hand. "There's a reason why many people use simple albeit *incorrect* terminology: everything involving souls and essences is vastly complex, discombobulated throughout history. I think the only people who truly understand all the facets of souls are the Awoms. And they like to keep that knowledge to themselves, which I respect them for—as frustrating as it is." He smirks. "The only term people use correctly is *half-souls*, even though you really have no idea what that term even means."

I absorb his words, which remind me of a Zo lecture—always served like an insult.

"Why reveal your powers to me?" I ask. "My father would've locked you up on sight."

Jasper stops his glass, balancing it on the precipice of his knuckle. "Because times have changed." He sets the glass down. "I've seen your mind, and I've chosen to serve you."

Helina straightens. "As have I."

I nod to them both. "If you have this power, then how did you end up under Red's thumb?"

Jasper's grip tightens around his glass before he slides it away. "Red learned to block my talent." He looks pointedly at Helina. "A very hard skill to learn. And even harder to maintain, isn't it, Helina?" He grins and turns back to face me. "She's been practicing. Anyone can do it if they have the resolve to commit to it." He motions to me with his empty glass. "Some people are lucky and their minds are naturally harder to mess with. Like yours. It's so cold and rigid. I can see your past and thoughts, learn from them, but I can't *shape* them like I can others'."

Helina clears her throat. "Red also has blackmailing, conniving scum everywhere."

I wave my finger between Jasper and Helina. "So, what did he have on you two to keep you here?"

Pain flashes on Helina's face. "My daughter. I"—her gaze finds Jasper then falls away—"I'm the most profitable dancer here, and he had a thing for me specifically, so he kept me on a tight leash."

I look at Jasper, waiting.

He gazes down at his empty glass then back at me. "He had Helina."

"This blocking technique"—I run my finger around the rim of my own crystal glass—"is it why I can't see *your* memories?"

Jasper shifts in his seat. "It's a dangerous world for half-souls. We're still hunted and executed for what we are. It's just done more quietly now. So, yes. I've held my mind's walls up for so long, it's a habit now, but I can let you in if you command it."

My father, like his father before him, executed many half-souls in his time as king.

"I won't command that." This small favor can be my repayment to his kind.

He dips his chin. "Thank you."

I take a breath, deciding now is as good a time as any to set up my backup plan, and since Jasper has a connection in the infantry . . . "Since your cousin has some freedom from Mazzar, can I ask for his help with something, if he's willing?"

Jasper smirks. "To help you capture the pure soul?" When my brows raise in question, he taps his temple. "I just read your thoughts, remember? He will, by the way. All I have to do is send him a message with your instructions." He sighs. "But messages between my cousin and I are delayed. It takes up to a moon cycle for him to receive them."

"As long as he's capable."

Jasper leans forward. "What exactly do you have in mind?"

I tap my finger against the table. "If I can't gain access to Nizzara's soul on my own, I'll need your cousin to get her out of the castle, away from her guards, so I can do this the hard way."

Jasper smirks. "I don't mind the hard way."

"What's the hard way?" Helina says.

"I'll have to remove her vessel." I draw a cutting line across my fingers. "I think the bonded spirit is the whole reason she has to give her soul willingly. The spirit is protecting her. That's why I can't rip it out like any other soul. If we can remove her vessel, strip her of that protection, I won't have to convince her to give it freely. I can just take it and deliver it to Nil."

It's a long shot. And awful. So I make a mental note to find someone she cares for enough to convince her—someone she might willingly and freely trade her soul for before I resort to chopping her vessel off.

Helina folds her arms and glares at me. "Why even bother trying to get into her shield to manipulate her if you already have such an easy solution?" Sarcasm drips from her voice. She doesn't believe it will work, and she's obviously not in favor of the brutality.

I glare back at her. "If I can get into her shield, I'd also have the power to fight Mazzar. I could free my people from his tyranny." After seeing a glimpse of her power, I know our bonded souls would be enough.

Helina slides her glass away, frowning.

Jasper pats her hand. "I'll arrange the capture with my cousin, but there's a small matter of gaining access to the castle. He lives in the barracks and has informed me that all castle entrances are heavily guarded."

I take a deep breath, trying to reel in the ice spreading through my chest.

"There's an access tunnel," I say. "Two miles past the gates, hidden in the barren rocks. It goes straight into the king's chambers."

Jasper perks up as I give him these explicit directions. "And it's unguarded?" he asks in disbelief.

I nod. "It's a tunnel reserved only for the king. My father told me of it on his deathbed. And I sure as hell didn't tell Mazzar about it on *my* deathbed."

The alcohol burns through my stomach, offering no sustenance other than taste as I drain the last bit. Rising from the table, I look at Helina, nodding toward the bracelet on her wrist. A silent question, asking if she's learned anything about Lo.

She shakes her head a fraction.

"Well then, time to get close to the princess."

CHAPTER 17

NIZZARA

DIARY: PAGE 5

I've never pretended to be soft. But, like subterfuge, callousness has its levels. I hope my brother never has to reach my level. My numbness has become a constant. I killed my lover tonight after learning she was a spy, sent to kill me . . .

Dagen's not afraid to deliver punishment to those who deserve it, but although I hope he never loses his big heart, he could use a little more callousness. If he gives one more extension to another struggling family in tax court, we'll go broke. Broke. As in unable to fund our infantry, who just fended off a Skeeve attack from the upper continent.

Where do we draw the line? Save one family from the dungeons or save thousands of families from all the wars raging down on us?

—*Lo*

PREYSEE NUDGES ME AWAKE. "NIZZARA, IT'S TIME TO GET UP."

I groan and roll over in my sheets, shooing her away. My nightmares are getting worse, which makes the mornings terrible. It seems like the moment my mind finally drifts past the dark creatures and settles into a deeper sleep, someone is already waking me up.

Preysee nudges me again. "Your father has announced his plans to depart soon. You'll be filling in for him today, so you need to get ready if you want to be able to fit your tutor session in before tax court."

I groan and pull my pillow over my head.

Today's the end of the quarter, which means tax court. My stomach slithers as if snakes roil inside.

I might as well waltz into our subjects' homes, beat them senseless, and empty their purses on my way out. At least that would save them travel time.

"Another departure?" I mumble from under my pillow. "Did he announce where this time?"

Preysee's silence tells me no.

Not surprising. He's probably dealing with the Skeeves that are strangulating our trade routes. Hence why Yisabell and I might never get to try chocolate.

"He'll return in time for the Winter Rave tonight," Preysee assures me.

After another failed attempt to shoo Preysee away, I relent and get out of bed with minimal wincing. Sorren insisted on training after my duel despite my obliterated shoulder. I gently touch the smooth skin where my father's power smoothed the wound after my duel, and I wince. The pain is still fresh.

If the dueler I defeated yesterday was the lowest rung of level six, how am I going to fight my way through the tournament without succumbing to the temptation of so much power at my fingertips?

"I have your oils ready," Preysee says, eyeing the grimace on my face. "I found stronger ones. They should dull the pain. Let's hope they kick in before tonight's festivities."

I meet her honey gaze. "I'm used to it."

"To what, my lady?"

I wobble on my sore legs. "Pain."

She swallows and walks beside me as I work my way to my bathing chamber. "That oil you requested from Raven's Elixirs should be delivered in a few days," she says, bunching her brows. "Unless their shipment is delayed through the trade routes again, then I guess it could take longer."

I'll pass the information along to Liha whenever she graces me with her presence again.

Preysee—realms bless her—has already drawn the bath. After dropping my nightgown, I dip into the hot water with an unintentional moan, the delicious heat melting away every stiff muscle from last night's training.

My bathwater hasn't even cooled before Preysee is telling me it's time to get out. I dress in a casual gown, since tax court isn't until later, and I refuse to wear that coffin of a dress required for it any longer than I have to.

Preysee zips up my red gown. It's a simple number, but I'm sure it cost Father a lot of ren. Thanks to our strangled trade routes, the price of this dress could rival that of smuggling a magic-powered aircraft from the Tatum realm. Okay, that's an exaggeration. I don't think even the Zem king has enough gold ren to smuggle something like that through the realms. I sigh and smooth the velvet dress over my abdomen. Father buys me things after his episodes. *This* dress was bought after the incident over the longsword. I wish I could make a point not to wear it just to spite him, but all my clothes are bought with his ren.

"Your father requested your presence at breakfast," Preysee says in her too casual tone as she turns me to face her.

"Why didn't you say that earlier?"

She shrugs. "I needed you to get out of bed."

I glower at her.

She smiles and ushers me out to my escorting guards, who lead me down the winding staircase of my tower and three more grand staircases to the main floor.

"Which duelers made it into the tournament?" I ask Brunar, who marches with his hand on his hilt beside me. The last round of duels went late into the night, finalizing all the King's Duel contestants, and I'm curious to know who my competition will be.

His gaze fixates on the polished floor ahead. "The Zem heir returned from his trip abroad and won his entry duel last night."

Kazem, the top dueler in level six. I swallow.

"Anyone else?"

"The Zem kingdom has four new duelers this year that made the tournament. Zo has three notable fighters, and the rest are barely ranked above you."

I'm the lowest-ranking dueler. That's why Father's been beating me to a pulp vicariously through Sorren.

Father is already eating breakfast when I arrive at the long onyx table, polished to reflect the menacing chandeliers above.

Tarella is in her place, sliding her fork around her plate, and Mother is mirroring her. With them sitting side by side, *they* look like the sisters here. Black hair, skin darker than mine, and rich, russet eyes. I've always wondered if I looked more like them if I would've been in their circle.

Father takes a gulp of wine despite the fact it's morning and watches me in a way that reminds me of a spider perching behind its prey—elegant and venomous with black, glassy eyes.

When I take my seat, the motion is stiff from sore muscles.

Father smiles. "Sorren knocked you down a peg, didn't he?"

My hands curl around the edges of my chair, tightening until I have to purposefully let one finger relax at a time.

Father sets his wine goblet down as a kitchen maid bustles out, placing a plate of greasy sausage before me that instantly turns my stomach.

"I'm ready to announce your betrothed," he says.

Both my and Tarella's heads snap up, and everyone in the room stiffens. Even my cold stalker-spirit seems to pause.

Father's grin is too sharp to be joyous. "You'll be marrying the second general of the Light Jaxelli."

Tarella's face pinches. "*Who?*"

My mind reels back through books and tutor sessions to teachings about other realms and dimensions. "They are a species of warriors from the Xoshbesh realm."

She glares at me for answering the question that was obviously pointed at Father. Tarella may not be as well-read in the sciences and the histories as I am, but that's because she has a singing voice that few can rival. All of her later studies were dedicated to vocal tutoring.

She whips her nose back to Father. "An inter-realm betrothal? How? Travel between realms is impossible."

Father waits for me to answer.

Tarella reluctantly slides her gaze to me. "Well?"

"A few species can travel between realms with ease, like the Jaxelli, Dwarf witches . . . and Guardians." I pointedly remind myself that Guardians are extinct.

Tarella huffs. "Get to the point."

My hands ball to fists in my lap. "Both Light and Dark Jaxelli Warriors can move through the realms at will." I point to Tarella's gold vessel on her left hand, and I feel my mind diving into textbook mode. "Their power is greater than spirit magic. They can influence elements, speak to the universe, shape-shift, and more."

"Well, if they are so damned powerful, why haven't they conquered all the realms already?" Tarella stabs a chunk of meat on her plate and tears it off her fork with her teeth.

I glance at Father, whose smug smile is pointed at Tarella.

"Very astute, Tarella."

She perks up at the compliment.

Father rests his elbows on either side of his gold breakfast plate, lacing his fingers over the top. "Because they do not have the temperament . . . yet."

I cut the oily meat on my plate into smaller and smaller pieces to give me something to do even though I won't eat it. My hands grow clammy around my knife and my muscles wind tighter by the second.

Betrothed.

Liha chooses now to enter my shield and zips around in a pattern I've learned is excitement.

"The Jaxelli men are quite delicious indeed!"

Father stabs the last piece of sausage on his plate with his knife. "Tarella, Soriah, you're both excused."

I look at Mother, silently begging her not to leave me alone with Father, but she doesn't even turn my way.

Tarella stops chewing and glares at me as she pushes up from her half-eaten plate and is escorted out by her two guards.

Father glances at my full plate, then at me.

"Why an inter-realm betrothal?" I shove my plate of meat away. "That goes against customs."

He chuffs. "I don't give a damn about customs."

"Why the Jaxelli?"

He balls his cloth napkin into his fist. "Because the Jaxelli are more powerful than casters and Zem princes. I will accept no less than what you deserve."

I set my fork down, a nauseating sensation taking root in my stomach. I know why any king would want an alliance with the Jaxelli. "You wish to absorb their warriors into our infantry lines, for their ability to move our armies through realms."

He drops his cloth napkin onto the plate. "Among other things."

A piece of the puzzle clicks into place. "The celibacy—"

"Yes." He shoves his plate away and takes his goblet. "Jaxelli are quite the snobbish prudes. They do not mingle before choosing a mate."

Raging darkness steals through my chest. I feel like I'm nothing more than a political pawn to be whored out as the *king* sees fit. "I will not have a betrothal," I say through gritted teeth.

Liha vibrates in my shield. She knows I'm toeing a line I shouldn't.

Father pushes up from the table, and I realize his goblet is now empty. "Say that again."

I shove up from the table just like he did and enunciate every word. "I will not have a betrothal," I say. "Because I don't *want* one."

When his eyes are this shade of black, when the room descends into a frequency that plucks the hairs on my neck, I know. It's too late to placate.

Liha shrieks with fear and juts out of my shield as soon as my father moves toward me.

He grabs my throat and lifts me off the ground.

My guards stiffen in my peripheral vision but do nothing as I struggle to breathe. *Cowards.*

"When will you realize?" Father growls. "In order to get what you *want*, you must be the most ruthless person in the room." A flicker of pain and regret shines deep in his eyes, but his hand squeezes tighter. "You have to *take* what you want." He tilts his head. "You don't *want* a betrothal?" He raises his chin, his voice turning sharper. "Then stop *hiding* from what you are."

Everything about him appears to be at war with himself, as if he is fighting not to be this way, until finally, he lowers me enough for my toes to touch down and his grip loosens. His face crumples. "The only way you'll truly get what you want, Nizzara, is over my dead body."

The set of his eyes, the distant pain behind them . . . It's almost as if he's begging me to end him.

Anger branches throughout my body.

He always does this.

He makes me feel bad for him. Anger builds and builds inside until the golden spirit flickers in the corner of the dining room, and power stirs deep inside me. But I ignore the rage, and I try like hell to ignore the power too. Because they are what ruined my father.

But just because I refuse to go down his path doesn't mean I'm spineless.

I spit in his face.

And he loses it.

CHAPTER 18

DAGEN

I'M ON THE TALLEST SPIRE OF MY CASTLE, LOOKING DOWN over my suffering kingdom, thinking about how I almost attacked Mazzar to *defend* the little beast. But I've made it a point not to feel sorry for the souls I hunt, and I don't plan on starting now.

In the distance, I make out the energy field glistening over the Zo kingdom. I wonder if Lo could be hiding there; after all, she spied on the Zos frequently. I need something else to focus on, so I spirit myself to the edge of my kingdom to where the Zarr force field ends and the Zo barrier begins. The force fields erase the memory of any bonded spirit who passes through without being inside their caster's shield. Spirits are free to dissolve into another realm, just not from kingdom to kingdom. Even the oldest generations in the alliance were concerned about spying, it seems. I materialize in the face of the stone wall, where the swirling force field meets the top of it, and climb up by hand, figuring it's safer for my memories to cross in my human form. When I reach the top of the thick wall, I can see all the way down it to the neutral ground, where the wall turns into a giant circle, wrapping around the dueling theaters and political buildings.

My father constantly lectured me about why we are structured this way. To share cultures and combine our strengths. Zarr holds the strongest infantries, which enforce the laws voted in by the three kings, Zem holds the wealth that pays for the neutral ground maintenance and stimulates foreign trade, which keeps our economies flowing. And Zo holds all the knowledge, histories, prophecies, and the power to veto laws in the annual congregations. I don't think the kingdoms in the alliance ever trusted each other, but after my great-grandfather destroyed the fourth kingdom, all technological advances came to a halt, and the silent warfare flared.

I step through the force field that runs along the top of the thick wall. Its energy washes over me, and to my relief, allows me through without wiping my memories. I climb down the other side and return to spirit form. I'm not sure if I was allowed through because I was in my human form or because I'm not bonded to a caster. Either way, I'm glad it worked.

Descending into the Zo castle, I'm reminded how self-righteous their style is. White and gold span every surface, symbolizing knowledge, purity, and refinement. As stated in the King's law, written upon the alliance's founding, there are three thrones in each kingdom. One for the king, the queen, and their chosen heir. And here, the three thrones are a web of gold over white stone, their backrests all dissolving upward into the ceiling of white glo gems. King Tigous perches on his throne, his face an emotionless mask as a servant informs him of a request from King Rajim. He wants to host the King's Duel preliminaries, despite it being the Zos' turn.

"Let the Zems spend their ren," Tigous drawls, his fourteen-year-old heir, Hollom, sitting on his own throne, the queen's throne empty beside him. "The cleanup after the drunken madness is insufferable anyway."

I wonder how many times Lo infiltrated this room, wonder what secrets she uncovered here. She never told me everything, but she did tell me that she always infiltrated the Zo castle disguised as a scholar because, next to King Tigous and his children, scholars have the most access to the libraries.

"I want to host!" Hollom folds his arms. "I'm always left out of the celebrations unless they're *here*."

"You will have your time, son," Tigous says.

The brown-haired boy, like all his siblings, looks just like Tigous. Dark skin, dark hair, and a strong jaw. He slams his small fist on the gold armrest. "You say that every year!" he yells.

I scoff out loud. Lo was right. Tigous's children are spoiled rotten brats who never grow out of their toddler-like tantrums.

Hollom jerks his head in my direction as if he heard me. "The only company I get are spirits! Do you know how dull they are? Be lucky you can't hear their droning, Father."

Tigous turns to his son. "This is exactly why I do not let you attend social events. You've not learned the art of tight lips, Hollom."

"If you'd let me bond with one, I'd stop hearing them all." Hollom slumps down in his chair while the guards in white, stuffy uniforms exchange eye rolls behind Tigous.

I look at Hollom's golden vessel on his hand and realize his caster's shield surrounding him is clear, without any tint to signify a bonded spirit. That's why he can hear me. Interesting. I remember when I bonded my first spirit. My golden vessel opened my senses for me to hear and perceive spirits long enough to select one, but once I bonded with Shena, the spirit dimension was closed off again. Tigous is keeping Hollom's senses open to spirits . . . *but why?*

Careful not to make a sound, I reach out for any memories in this room, but I find nothing but mind blocks.

I've only been gone ten years, but I've already forgotten how the Zos protect knowledge like the Zems protect their gems.

If any library contained the secrets of worlds—including mind guarding—it is here in the Beacon of Zo.

CHAPTER 19

NIZZARA

Diary: Page 6

Father's sick. His bones ache and I swear he's losing his grip on reality. At least he managed to separate the bondslave Emya from my brother.

Emya was sent to her homeland. That was Dagen's only stipulation to my father's request to end their relationship: Dagen promised to let her go if she could be free. He wants what's best for her, and they both knew they couldn't lawfully marry. Although he was heartbroken when Emya told him she'd never want to be the queen of Zarr, and that she longed to return home. Now, he's on date number six with his betrothed—the Zem princess, Kathreen. If there's one thing about Dagen that makes him fit to rule, it's his commitment to the King's law and our people. He's doing his duty and giving Kathreen a chance. He's far more optimistic than I am. I saw her kick a silver hound puppy at a tournament last year for slobbering on her gown, and I've hated her ever since. Once I hate someone, there's no redemption. Dagen says I'm too quick to judge, but I told him when someone's as talented at judging character as I am, I don't need years to decide if a person is worth my time.

—Lo

HIDING THE FACT THAT MY FATHER JUST STRANGLED ME IS a typical part of my life lately, and it feels like the worst kind of isolation. There's always an apology deep in Father's eyes when he hurts me, not that it makes it better.

Brunar leads me and my other guards through King's Hall on our way toward the eastern wing of the castle, where my tutor, Thaddeus, lives.

I never miss my studies. I need a place where my mind enters a book and ceases to exist outside of it.

Passing mural after mural of dead Zarr kings, my attention always gravitates to one portrait. King Dagen's. There's something about the small, menacing, round gouges pierced through his ears and the smirk in his hazel gaze that can distract me from almost anything, even the sore bruises I feel forming on my neck.

When Brunar clears his throat, I turn away and continue down the hallway. Thaddeus opens his door on the second knock. In his few months here, he's turned his room into a makeshift library with more lamps than any other room in the castle. All is neat and orderly.

Thaddeus leads me to a prepared study table where my new reading assignment sits.

"*The King of Kings?*" I ask, clearing my throat from the rasp my father left. "I've read that already. It's an eighth-year book." Everyone in the kingdoms are encouraged to read it because it's said to be written by divine power at the time of the alliance. It's a hodgepodge of King's laws, prophecies, and philosophies. Even Tarella has read it.

"You haven't read the *original*."

I fight the urge to roll my eyes. Zos are meticulous. The original will be the exact same as the one I read years ago. "I have all the King's laws memorized. I've already suffered through all the stuffy poems and laws—which lack rhetoric, by the way. Can't we learn something *new*?" I need the mental disconnect that comes with immersing myself in a new topic.

He pats the book in his calm way and motions for me to sit. His gaze lands on my fingers, which are still tinged with black ink, then up to me.

He scowls. "Clumsy with an inkpot, I see."

I fold my arms to hide the faded ink. All of Preysee's fancy soaps haven't rid me of it, and the Zos detest clumsiness, or messes, or anything that does not fit in a neat, little box of perfect, logical sense.

He runs his hand over the frayed, red cover. "This book is not just laws and stuffy poems. It's a riddle that's never been brought to light. A greater prophecy hidden among the smaller ones." He reverently scoops up the book, tucking it into his arm like a newborn baby, and stalks toward a shelf. "But if you are not up for that, I suppose I could teach you about the depleting energy gems inside the Zem mines. Quite interesting, those gems and all their undocumented and illegal uses."

I sigh, holding my hand out for the book. "What page?"

He sets it in front of me. "The cover. What can you glean from it?"

"The cover?" I run my fingers down the front of it.

"Yes, what do you see?"

"Just the title. *The King of Kings*."

He waits in silence.

"What?"

A puff of air escapes his nose. "Use the brain inside your skull. If the title is the name of the riddle, what is the riddle asking you to find?"

I trace the black letters, smooth with age. "The King of Kings," I say softly, "is a person? The riddle answers the question *who* is the king of all kings?"

The corners of his lips perk up before he pulls out three large, unfamiliar books. "I knew you were smarter than the average Zarr." He drops a stack of books beside the red one in front of me. "These are lineages and memoirs of royalty from each of the three families. They'll be your supplementary reading as you solve the riddle."

I fold my arms. The motion is stiff from my sore body, but notably less so than it was an hour ago. "How am I supposed to answer a riddle you claim has never been solved?"

He pats the stack of books. "I said it hasn't come to *light*."

"So, what if I solve this riddle? What's so special about the King of Kings?"

He cocks a silvered brow. "The King of Kings is prophesied to wield great power. Power that can return crops to our barren soil and unity to the kingdoms."

My fingers twitch, wanting to dive into the stack of books so hard I wake up with pages stuck to my face.

"How long did it take you to solve it?" I ask.

"Who says I have?"

I level a glare at him.

He grins. "Two moon cycles." He stands from his chair and brushes his white Zo robes. "We have an allotted time of two hours. I'm releasing you to read in your own chambers."

I take that as my dismissal, and my guards summon servants to haul the books that don't fit in my arms to my chambers. Since they're above helping me carry books with their own hands.

Useless cowards.

Once I reach my chambers, I clear my desk and read the first twenty pages of *The King of Kings*. I flip a thick, stale page. It does feel older than the edition I read, like Thaddeus promised.

I'm in the middle of a rather bland sentence when *he* enters my room, bringing the sensation of a cold, smooth abyss.

His dark velvet voice comes behind me. *"No quippy, insulting greetings today?"*

I turn another page, chills spreading down my neck. I swear, Zarr women would pay gold ren to listen to his voice.

"No responses for me either?" he purrs. *"Don't pretend you can't hear me, or that* The King of Kings *is so enthralling. I've read it."* His dark presence circles around the front of my desk to face me.

"Go. Away."

"Ah, the cruel thing speaks."

"Yeah, and I said go away."

He looms closer, the depth of his power tugging my neck hairs up. *"Why should I?"*

"My bonded spirit says you're dangerous."

"Does that make me dangerous? Just because others think I am?"

Tian flashes into my mind. He was big and intimidating for his young age, even for an Awom. Despite his peaceful, kind nature, the scholars still isolated him in the deeper levels of the library, fearing him for nothing more than his looks.

"No, it does not," I finally answer the spirit's question.

There's a long stretch of silence before he speaks again, his voice thicker than before. *"Then there's no harm in my visit. Is there?"*

My jaw tightens then releases, my body acclimating to the deepening cold in my room. "What do you want from me?"

His spirit gravitates closer, bringing his frigid lightning storm of power with him.

"I am alone," he whispers.

"That doesn't answer my question," I say, but my voice has already lost its harshness. He's alone. The memory of me and Tian deep in the Zo library flashes through my mind again. Me, crying because of something my father did, and Tian wrapping his arms around me. Tian was my best friend when I felt most alone. And he's gone.

The dark spirit falls silent.

His power consumes the room, saturating every corner with invisible pennants of deadly ice. I stiffen. Liha's warning about him courses through my mind, but what if this is how people feel when they see *me*? When those people are brought to the execution floor and look up at my smiling, ruthless face and see nothing but a monster.

I sigh. "You can stay if you just answer the question."

He looms forward until he's standing in the center of my desk, not the least bit distracting. *"Yes,"* he says. *"I'm very good in bed."*

I feel my cheeks flush red. "That is not the question—"

A dark, invisible laugh caresses the air. *"Isn't that always the question in Zarr?"*

I look down at my book, grumbling. "I suppose it is, spirit."

"Dae."

"What?"

"My name is Dae, not Spirit. If you call me Spirit, I will call you Human."

"Fine, *Dae*. I'll allow you to stay if you answer my question."

A smile curls in his voice. *"And how do you plan to get me out if I don't? Throw a shoe at me?"*

I lift my chin. "I'll pretend you do not exist for as long as I live. I'm very good at pretending."

"Are you, now?" I can almost hear an eyebrow raise.

"I am. And I'll let Liha chase you off every time you surface. I notice how you run off when she appears."

"I allow her to chase me off."

I turn the page. "The effect is the same."

"So much sass for such a cruel little beast."

I give up trying to read through him and look directly at where his dark air swirls in the middle of my desk. "Are you going to answer my question, or should I start ignoring you?"

"Fine, Nizzara. Ask your question again."

I try not to linger on the way my name sounds in his smooth voice, spoken in a dimension only I can hear. "What do you want from me if I cannot offer you a bond?"

"Can't? Or won't? Casters can *bond more than one spirit, you know."*

His response trips my thoughts. Father said my vessel can only bond one spirit. I wonder if this could be one of the details he's trying to hide from me. Rage pools in me, because he controls everything. I don't even know why he'd hide this kind of information. After he forced me to take one spirit, there's no way I would take another.

My teeth clench together. "Just answer the damn question before I start flinging shoes at spirits who I'm pretending don't exist."

A midnight laugh floats through the air. After a moment, he says, *"Today I only want someone to talk to. That's all I desire from you."*

I wave my hand. "Why don't you talk to other spirits?"

He pauses before saying, *"They fear me."*

I want to ask why, but the depthless cold of his presence tells me I don't want to know.

"So, you're saying I'm your only option."

If Liha knew I was entertaining this spirit, she wouldn't trust me to be alone ever again. A sting pricks my chest at my small betrayal.

But if I was in Dae's place, stuck in the spirit world with no one, I would wish to talk to someone too. I know what it's like to be alone.

Then there's the matter of his voice.

I like it.

He looks toward my bed draped in silk comforters. *"It is either you or a spoiled brat in the Zo kingdom."*

Does this mean there's another person who can hear spirits like I can? I think about asking, but when his ghostly outline leans closer, eliciting chills across my skin, I find myself saying, "What if I'm just a spoiled brat in the Zarr kingdom?"

"Then at least you are much more pleasing to look at."

I scoff. "As a Zarr man, I expected your flirting to be better." A smirk tugs at my lips. "It makes me question whether you are as good in bed as you claim."

There's a hint of delight in his tone when he says, *"What makes you certain I'm a Zarr man? As a spirit, I could be from any of the seven realms. We can travel through the different worlds, you know."*

I turn around in my chair. "Your accent is Zarr, and you've read *The King of Kings*. Don't insult me."

"I'd never." I can hear the mocking smirk in his tone as he tilts his dark, airy head. *"And just so we're clear—"* His velvet voice deepens. *"My claims are always accurate, Nizzara."*

I roll my eyes, ignoring the chill that just ran down my spine. "You can stay until Liha returns," I say, patting the open book. "But if you stay, then you have to be silent so I can read this blasted thing."

"That's an eighth-year book. Got held back in your studies, did you?"

I point to the door. "Be quiet or be gone."

He goes silent, hovering over my shoulder as I reread the same lines over and over again, flustered by his towering, bulky presence behind me, and when silence falls between us, his soul somehow whispers to me like a soft, familiar voice. Eventually, though, I slip into my book, and his presence that's impossible to ignore becomes the wall blocking out the rest of the world. He watches me for two hours, letting me read, and I swear I feel some emotion from his energy, something like intrigue.

I'm about to close the book when he disappears without warning, and the room is suddenly stifling in his absence.

A few moments later Liha returns.

She clucks. "*Ice in your room again.*"

"*He only passed through.*" I turn my attention back to my book.

"*Did the spirit speak?*"

I run my fingers over the page, noticing a misprint in the page numbers. The book has jumped from page thirty to page thirty-nine, then back to thirty-one. I flip the previous page back, then forward again.

"*Hmm?*"

"*I said*"—Liha's vibrant energy nudges my neck where the bruises from my father are blossoming—"*did the product of damnation speak to you?*"

I flip the page once more. "*Why do you call him that?*"

"*Because. That's what he is. He reeks of Baratrum.*"

I look up. "*The Lost Realm?*"

"*Precisely. Did he speak to you?*"

I consider telling Liha about our conversation, but if there's one thing I've learned about Liha these past ten years, it's that she is protective, snobbish, and jealous.

"*I told him if he didn't leave, then you would chase him off for me.*"

"*And he left?*"

"*Do you see him here?*"

A little flick comes from my caster's shield, as if to say *smart-ass*.

"*So, where have you been this morning?*"

She squeals with excitement. "*You don't think I would miss an opportunity to spy on your betrothed, do you?*"

A wave of panic washes through me. "*You saw him?*"

She purrs like a cat. "*I did, indeed. Just for a moment, but from what I saw, he is quite delicious.*"

"*You objectify men.*"

She sniffs. "*Let me live my death in peace.*"

My throat suddenly feels tight. "*Do you know when I'll meet him?*"

"*I don't. I've heard the staff say they've been asked to ready the castle for his arrival, only to have the date rescheduled more than once.*"

I study *The King of Kings* for another ten minutes until I can't put off dressing for tax court any longer.

"*Try not to think about it,*" Liha says as our power moves the formal black dress and a crown out of my closet.

"*That is impossible. I can't not think about it. Our people are suffering, and tax court only makes it worse.*"

"*Just do as your father commanded you.*"

The high collar of the stiff dress pulls tight, fastening around my throat, reminding me of my tender bruises. "*And further their suffering?*"

"*It will keep you safe from your father's temper,*" she says softly. "*He's been even more unstable lately.*"

My jaw tightens as the matte-black crown descends onto my white hair, the spires tipped with red, like bloody daggers.

CHAPTER 20

NIZZARA

Diary: Page 7

A nobleman insulted my preference for women at last night's feast. Dagen broke the man's jaw for it, then brought a pastry to my room afterward. I may not be all muscles like him, but I could've handled the nobleman just fine. When I told Dagen I could've dealt with the nobleman on my own, he laughed, saying a broken jaw was a lesser punishment than whatever I would've come up with. It made me smile. He's right. The noblemen and noblewomen only respond to bribes or violence, and I don't solve my problems with ren.

—Lo

THE COURT IS FULL OF MY FATHER'S SELECTED NOBLEMEN when I arrive, all sporting sleek, dark hair and matching coats. The richest among them—whose love of power and control rivals my father's—line each side of the dais with their own desks, counters, and ledgers. They stare at me in silence as I sit upon my father's throne, every action of mine being picked apart, sold to the highest bidder, reported to my father, and used to climb the social ladder. My Mark is, in effect, making everyone see the version of me they'll like most. Liha insists on using it in any formal situation like this, claiming it strengthens my ability to persuade.

I glance at the statue-like infantry soldiers stationed around the dais and nod to a castle guard. The guard opens the massive doors, emitting a loud creak throughout the room, and allows the first subjects inside. My gaze runs over the assembled crowd full of high-class townspeople and noblemen, and I can't help wondering which one is a spy.

Cloaked civilian in row one? Dark hair in row three?

Two rock-mill workers, husband and wife, approach the dais. Mineral dust falls from their tan garbs and black aprons as they walk.

The husband limps, and his wife assists him toward the dais. The lowest nobleman, Ropen, asks their names.

The husband answers, "Palko and Marina Everett."

Ropen's thin fingers ferret through the ledgers. "Ah, yes. Here to pay up two winter cycles of taxes." A sickening smile. "Either by ren or by blood."

Marina rushes toward me, jolting my guards. They step forward, their hands jumping to their pommels. I wave Brunar off, and when he falls back so do his men.

Palko stiffens and says, "Marina, don't—"

"Please, Princess." Marina clasps her hands together. "We have brought every ren to our name. The reason we are behind in taxes"—a sob breaks her voice—"is because we lost our son in the factory explosion two years ago. He became our primary breadwinner when Palko's legs started failing."

Ropen pushes up from his chair. "Money or blood, woman. Begging will do no good here. You owe upward of twelve thousand silver ren."

I raise my hand and silence Ropen with a look.

"*You've mastered that expression*," Liha coos.

Ropen has the good sense to sit back down, and I return my attention to Palko, careful not to soften my features even by a fraction.

I sense the prickle of my father's bonded spirit, playing overseer in the iron rafters far above. It's not often I sense her, so I assume she likes to stay in his shield, but I recognize the unbearable dread and hopelessness she spreads, like dripping, rotting decay.

"Why do your legs fail you? You do not look so old," I snap.

Palko is Zarr, so he lifts his chin, standing as straight as his body will allow. "It is a sickness of the bone," he says. "I have come to offer my blood as payment."

Marina shakes her head and scrambles toward him, tears streaming down her face. "No! You will not take him! I offer *my* blood as payment."

A twinge flicks in my chest. This isn't my first time in tax court, but this is the first time I cannot offer an extension. Two winter cycles past due is against the law. I take a deep breath and straighten my shoulders. If I'm to help, I have to do it later, without watching noblemen.

I stand up and the room goes still. "Bring me your coin, woman."

Marina shakily cups her drawstring bag and delivers it to my hands, a silent plea on her weathered face. I keep my breathing steady as I take the bag without counting it. I know it is not near enough and signal my guards to seize Palko. The debt is in Palko's name—by law, his blood must pay.

"You will pay your debt with blood, Palko Everett, and be delivered to the dungeons until the next execution day, or until your debt is paid in full."

Marina shrieks, trying to hold her husband, but the infantry soldiers rip them apart with unnecessary roughness, pulling them in opposite directions.

My stomach knots and twists throughout the rest of tax court. I'm unable to stop seeing that moment. It replays over and over in my mind, and it takes every shred of self-control I have to keep my face from showing my heartache—to keep tears from forming.

Mercifully, the remaining subjects bring their dues or qualify for extensions, but by the time court is finished, I am drained from the tone, expression, and intensity I'm forced to use. The noblemen wait for me to rise before they stand from their chairs. Ropen rakes in the pouches of rens to deliver to the royal coffers, but freezes mid-grab when I approach him.

"Princess." Ropen bows.

I flash a smile. "How much did Palko and Marina Everett owe to the crown?"

"I can't remember, Princess." His slimy grin tells me he's lying.

The first time I filled in for tax court, my father told me to manage the noblemen with an iron grip. He said they'd love to see us dead, because if there was no claim or heir to the throne, one of them could be voted in by the other kings in the alliance to rule Zarr. As I stare Ropen down, Lo's journal comes to mind. *Bribes or violence.* Since I prefer to keep violence in the duel rings, I drop Palko's bag of ren onto Ropen's table, feeling the stares of the other noblemen on me.

"A tip. For an afternoon's work," I say to Ropen.

"*What are you doing?*" Liha hisses.

I bat my hand through her floating presence by my ear.

He stares at the bag of ren. "It is a pleasure to serve, Princess."

When he reaches for it, I tug it away, tsking. "Tips are for noblemen who can remember things."

He sneers. "I remember that they owe far more than they can afford."

I focus on tempering my internal rage as I lift the bag from the table, feigning disappointment as I take a step toward the next nobleman. "Perhaps Percy here has a better recall. I saw him pull the Everetts' ledgers as well." I toss the bag of ren up and catch it. "Well, Percy, I want to know the *exact* amount. Is your memory better than Ropen's?"

Percy grins and opens his mouth to answer when Ropen calls out, "Twelve thousand six hundred and fifty-three silver ren," he says with forced politeness. "I just remembered, Princess."

"How convenient." I hold Ropen's gaze as I drop the bag on Percy's desk. "Next time, remember the first time I ask."

Percy smirks at Ropen as he tucks the bag of ren away in his pristine jacket.

My heart breaks as I watch, knowing from the weight, the pouch had to have held nearly a year's salary for them.

I will fix this.

I force a smile for each nobleman. "How tragic that their payment was lost in the commotion."

The devilish sneers on their faces tell me they are seeing what I want them to see. A cruel and ruthless ruler who can keep them in line.

When I turn to leave, a hand jolts toward me. "Princess, might I ask you to—"

I spin, catch Ropen's outstretched arm, and wrench his hand into a precarious, bone-snapping position. He yelps in pain and the room behind us falls silent. He probably meant to tap my shoulder, but it was too close to my bruised neck. Darkness rises in me.

Fear crawls over his pointed face as I crank his finger bones further and further.

"Don't. Touch. Me."

His knees bend to give more range for his fingers, but my grip is a vise, and his nasally voice begins to bleat as I wrench harder and harder.

He shakes his head. "I won't. I'm sorry. Please—"

I should let him go, but the darkness inside churns.

I snap his fingers. It takes all my self-control not to snap his wrist too. I breathe through the intoxicating rage and let go.

He wails in pain and drops to the floor, clutching his broken fingers. The other noblemen offer approving nods as I pass them, finally leaving this realms-damned place. The sounds of Ropen's whimpers and my heels clicking against the stone echo through the room as I walk away. I'm concentrated on my breathing, shoving that dark awful part of me away, when Liha says, "*So, are you going to tell me what that was about?*"

"*Later.*"

I'm not in the mood.

I can almost feel her annoyance, but she doesn't say another word.

CHAPTER 21

NIZZARA

DIARY: PAGE 8

Father's having manic episodes, and his legs are failing. Kathreen is here more often than not, doing things like taking food trays to Father and complimenting my "minimalistic" taste in dresses. Aside from hating her guts, I don't trust her either. Maybe it's because her lips twitch when she smiles. Or maybe it's because her father thinks we are stealing his void gems from his mines, which we aren't. Besides, I know Dagen isn't overly attracted to her because he hasn't run his hand through his hair—he does that when he gets flustered around a girl he likes. I've told him multiple times to work on his obvious tells. He has far too many.

—*Lo*

BY DUSK I'M WRAPPED IN MY FUZZIEST ROBE, READING *THE King of Kings*, when Preysee says, "I checked on that oil you requested. It's been delayed in the trade routes."

She straightens my stack of books beside me, eyeing my bruised neckline as I study.

"*Ooh, maybe we can use the oil on your betrothed when he arrives,*" Liha says, popping into my shield.

"*Yeah,*" I say, my mind still on tax court.

Frost clings to the glass of my balcony windows, and my heart wrenches for Palko. The dungeons are open to the winter air. Tonight will be my only window of opportunity because most of the perimeter guards will be inside, focused on security for the rave.

Liha bops around my shield with excitement for my betrothal, but I feel like shackles are slowly clamping down on my wrists. I want a choice.

"*Don't worry,*" she purrs. "*He is very handsome.*"

"*Yeah, because that's all that matters in a marriage,*" I say dryly.

She sniffs. "*Well, is it so terrible that he's delicious?*"

I roll my eyes.

Preysee lays the two dresses Liha picked out across my bed. "Did you make a final decision on which dress?" she asks. "The red one with the plunging neckline? Or the gold with the climbing leg slit?"

"Gold." The leg slit allows easy access to my dagger. Liha wanted me to take time to think on the decision, but I knew I'd be choosing the more practical dress.

Preysee holds the shimmering gown up to me, liquid gold cascading over her arms. "The color does create a striking contrast to your eyes, doesn't it?" She peers into them, then averts her gaze as everyone does.

"The Zem prince will be here tonight," Preysee says. "My niece tells me he is quite the dueler."

"He is." I remember watching his duels before he left for the third continent. Kazem is the only dueler with a no-loss record in the level-six circuit.

"Let's get you dressed," Liha says, pooling her power into my veins.

Pink smoke puffs from my vesseled hand, and my robe is replaced by the unforgiving dress along with my concealed dagger and sheath. The dagger's snug band is familiar and brings me comfort knowing I have it.

"*The second general does not know how lucky he is to have such a beautiful woman lined up for him,*" Liha says.

A sinking sensation settles in my stomach at the mention of my betrothed. "Why the frown, my lady?" Preysee asks.

"I'm just trying to decide how I should paint my face tonight."

"I see." Preysee gathers my hair into her hands and brushes the tangles from my strands. "If you want the opinion of a maid, I don't think it matters how you paint your face. You'll still be you underneath." She offers a soft smile through the mirror as if being myself is a good thing.

Preysee tugs my hair up, then down, then up again. "Up," she decides. "To show off the back of your dress."

"*Agreed.*" Liha swirls above, overseeing Preysee's work. If she finds any part lacking, she'll rearrange it, but as Preysee works, Liha purrs with satisfaction.

When Preysee is done, my white hair is pulled into a smooth, straight ponytail with a section wrapped around the hair tie. Tight, clean, powerful.

She reaches for the pallets of face paint and lipsticks, but Liha clicks her tongue. "*My turn.*"

"I can take it from here," I tell Preysee.

Preysee curtsies and takes her leave.

"*No red lips,*" Liha hisses, fluttering around me. "*Everyone and their mutty hounds will be wearing red lips.*" She circles me again. "*Silver will shame that wonderful gown, and pink is for helpless damsels. Not Zarr women.*"

I smile. "*Your favorite color is pink.*"

She sniffs. "*In Heshena, pink is the color of lust and passion. In Zarr it is frilly nonsense.*"

I lean back in the vanity chair. "*Then what color?*"

She pools her power into my palm, and I release it. Pink smoke falls around me.

"*Black,*" she whispers.

When her smoke fades, I see black lips and sharply winged eyeliner slicing above my cheekbones. Her power bubbles up as she throws our Mark on top of me to check the entire look.

Liha shivers in my shield. "*You look downright dangerous,*" she coos. But as I study my reflection, with my Mark in effect, I look the way I wish I did.

Unwaveringly calm, unafraid, and unbreakable.

There's a golden shimmer of dust high on my cheekbones and a shade of *pink* blended into my cheeks.

"I thought you said no pink."

"I do what I want."

The Winter Rave is coming to life far beneath my feet as people from all three kingdoms gather, but I wait until I'm summoned, opting to read a book. Liha, unable to wait any longer, buzzes out of my shield to enjoy the party below.

Soon, there's a knock on the door and Yisabell pops her head in. "I'm here to fetch you—Wow," she says in Awom so the guards in the hall won't understand her. "*That* is a dress."

Her smile turns dubious as she slips in and closes the door. Her hand dives into her pocket and pulls out two wrapped pieces of chocolate.

I gasp. "Where did you get those?"

"The Zems brought chocolates as their gift to the host." She crinkles her nose. "The Zos brought *paper*."

"Yisabell. You could be punished for this." By *punished*, I mean *killed*.

She skips over to the chair next to me and sits. "I could be punished for any number of things. Chocolate"—she holds the candies up between us—"might be one of the few things actually worth the punishment, or so people say."

"Then you better fully enjoy them," I reply, unable to tame my smile.

Her lips fall. "I brought one for you. So we could share." She perches one of the little chocolates on my armrest.

My heart clenches. I look toward my closed door. "Okay, then we better hurry."

She wiggles in the seat next to me. "I've waited my whole life to try chocolate," she says. "I've heard it is the dessert of gods."

For as long as I can remember, all people have talked about is how the crops throughout our lands continue to die, including cocoa bean plantations in the south. Since the trade routes are still riddled with Skeeves, chocolate is definitely a luxury, even among royalty.

Together, we unwrap the small parcels and look at the wonderful velvety brown squares. "On the count of three?" Yisabell asks.

"The whole thing? Or do you want to savor it in small bites?"

She shakes her head. "Nope. I want the whole thing."

"Good. Me too."

She smiles wider and begins counting. On three we both shove the chocolates in.

Realms. It melts immediately, coating my tongue in the most decadent taste I've ever experienced.

Yisabell turns to a boneless lump in her chair, slumping down with a groan. "It tastes like—like a hug from my mother. Instant comfort." Her eyes close as she swallows. "Definitely worth it. Even if I knew I was going to get caught, I'd do it again." She peeks an eye open. "As long as I still got to eat it, of course." She giggles.

"Here, give me your wrapper," I say so she doesn't get caught with it.

She hands me her wrapper, then sighs as if she's completely content with the world. "I'd better get back to work." Her lips perk up on one side. "I'm in the kitchens tonight."

She likes kitchen duty the most. That's why I threatened the slave master with his life if he didn't put Yisabell in there as often as possible.

I follow Yisabell to the door, clutching the two silver wrappers in my hand, and decide I want a taste of something else forbidden before the shackles of my betrothal slam shut completely. When Brunar's guards fall in around me, a plan unfolds. It's possibly the worst stunt I could ever pull, but as we pass the top-floor windows, holding back winter winds, I smile.

Because this plan hits every point I need it to, including Palko Everett.

CHAPTER 22

NIZZARA

DIARY: PAGE 9

I've been undercover for weeks. Coco is drained from using our Mark for such long periods, but it paid off this time. We discovered a secret library hidden behind King Tigous's throne during one of the Zos' parties. It's warded with ancient magic from the time the four kingdoms were founded. Only the king of Zo and his bloodline can open it. After failing to get through the wards, I returned to the festivities to ask drunken scholars about the secret library. Apparently, Rebelia made an appearance tonight. That goddess must be as pretty as the stories claim because she was the only thing anyone would talk about—except the scholars called her a Guardian, not a goddess, so naturally, I went to the library to see why. How the scholars love to let the world live in ignorance.

—Lo

I'M STANDING UNDER THE BLACK ARCHWAY, CLOSEST TO the dais, where my family reigns over the crowd. I linger here in the shadows, not wanting to be spotted as I take in the intensity of the Winter Rave. A strobe of red gem light swings across the floor, almost hitting my heels as I lean out to see the musicians onstage. Their music pulsates through the amplifiers stationed around the ballroom, and the

crowd sways in their red glow. Noblemen and ladies toy with their partners on the dance floor, spinning, dipping, and grinding as acrobats
roll and slide up and down fifty-foot streamers.

When I look up above the glare of lights, I find Dae swirling
high in the shadows of the domed ceiling. I'm thinking about our last
conversation—when Father spots me.

Liha feathers into my shield and immediately funnels her power
into me.

"*Really?*" I ask.

"*Use it to hide the bruises on your neck.*"

I sigh and allow our Mark to wash over me.

Father halts the music with a wave toward the stage and sends an
announcer in a crisp Zarr uniform to escort me across the dais. When
the music stops, the dancing crowd falls still.

"Nizzara Glindella, the chosen heiress to the Zarr kingdom," the
servant proclaims in a loud voice, and the sound of my heels clicking
across the stone echoes through the suddenly silent room.

The crowd bows as one. Even King Tigous and King Rajim,
brooding in their roped-off lounge areas, dip their chins in acknowl-
edgment. I keep my head high as I walk, ignoring the hateful gazes
lurking beneath the exaggerated bows and curtsies.

Tarella stands beside Mother's throne, pointedly eyeing me as I
take my seat. As soon as the crowd rises from its bow and the music
starts again, she leaves the dais, making her way toward a group of rich
noblemen mingling on the outskirts of the dance floor.

Mother's attention follows Tarella while I look at her. My mother
wears a white gown that represents her Zo heritage, and I can't help
but notice how beautiful she is in it. The stiff dress comes to a dangerous angle on one shoulder, leaving her other side bare. I've always
thought she makes a striking queen, not just because of her appearance,
but because of her mind. She's truly brilliant. I remember watching her
compete in the scholar debates long ago. No scholar could recall lines
or absorb information as fast as her. I wish she still competed in the
debates because she was fascinating to watch.

"You look beautiful, Mother."

When she peels her gaze away from Tarella, a flash of hatred blazes across her face. "Beauty is one thing that hasn't been stolen from me," she says, narrowing her eyes at me. "And it will be stolen by time eventually, if not by anyone else." She returns her attention back to the dance floor.

I'm fumbling for a response, smothering the sting welling in my chest and wondering what she meant, when Father leans over to me.

"You are free to roam as long as you follow the rules," he says. I turn to face him, just as a red glo light hits the black spikes on his shoulder, giving the illusion of blood running down the sharp points. "And I will know if they are being followed."

My gaze flicks to the infantry general standing behind my father, then to all his men stationed throughout the room. They tower above everyone else as if they're a different breed of man. I look back at my father, and Sorren lurking nearby, and I see why people fear them. Even among monsters, they are striking.

My father signals to a servant for another goblet of wine, and for once I'm happy he's drinking. Because if he's drunk, he'll be quicker to anger and even quicker to banish me from the ballroom once he sees me breaking his rules.

When the music changes to a slower song, I look out at the dance floor and find Tarella already dancing with a Zo nobleman. She drapes her arms over his shoulders, grinding her hips in sync with the demanding music. Her partner lifts her in a sensual glide and spin, her leg artfully wrapped around him.

Father takes a sip from his goblet, then says, "Watch your face, Nizzara."

I scowl.

"Much better."

Tarella and the nobleman slip farther and farther into the dancing crowd, spinning around other couples, until I lose sight of them.

I take a deep breath, working up the courage to leave the dais, then rise from my throne. When my stilettos hit the dance floor, the crowd breaks apart.

Liha's essence brushes against my arm. *"Look how they respect you. Especially now as a level-six dueler."*

I barely hear her, my mind already focused on the only person here that my plan will work with—the prince of Zem—because the King's law prevents my father from executing him.

Slowly the sea of people falls in around me, and bodies begin twirling again.

I've only danced with a partner twice in my life. The first time, a nobleman—liberated by wine—touched me *too* much and found himself with my father's sword protruding from his chest. The next nobleman I danced with refused to touch me at all.

A break comes in the music so the musicians can enjoy a goblet of wine and guests can mingle before the next song. And by *mingle*, I mean find a partner and a dim alcove.

Conversations begin to bubble as I move through the crowd, and I can't help but listen in, vaguely aware of Dae following me high above the revelers. Some guests flaunt their money, status, or lineage, but I've learned a lot by sticking to the sidelines.

I pass by a brunette with a lip ring who watches me run my hand along the back of Kazem's red uniform. His head turns, but I'm already walking away. He breaks away from a group of women who all glare at me as he dismisses himself, falling in lazily behind me. I continue toward the back of the ballroom, where Father won't see until I want him to.

"Oooh!" Liha purrs. *"Finally we get to have some fun! Look at that jawline . . . and those arms!"* She bounces around my shield with excitement. *"Mmm. He'll be fun to play with."*

"He will be," I agree.

She sighs, obvious disappointment bleeding into her voice. *"Just remember your father's rules."* I think my father's celibacy rule actually causes her pain.

I slip around a massive black column, disappearing into a dark alcove where a couple is getting handsy against the recessed wall. Nearby, another pair whispers flirtatiously, but their heated gazes tell me they will be getting closer soon. Kazem slowly rounds the pillar behind me. A stream of red smoke falls from his golden vessel, as he calls a set of goblets to him on a phantom wind, both brimming with wine. He takes one in each hand.

"You better be careful with those eyes of yours." He saunters toward me. "Someone might think you're a menacing goddess, attending the party to wreak havoc and stir trouble."

I scoff. "No *goddess* has been spotted at one of our parties in over a decade." I don't bother telling him that *goddess* is an ignorant term for what he's referring to. Looking Kazem up and down, I add, "They must've grown bored with our selection of men."

Liha snickers.

"I doubt that." He catches the gaze of a woman speaking to a Zarr nobleman and winks at her. She blushes and stifles a giggle, her attention suddenly fixed on the heir prince in front of me instead of her nobleman.

Kazem slides his attention back to me. "I have it on good authority that the men at this party are quite desirable."

He lifts one of his goblets to his lips, his muscled arms straining against his burgundy uniform as he does.

I glance at the woman whose attention is still on Kazem. "Just because you made a mortal woman giggle," I say, "doesn't mean you know what a goddess would find desirable."

He raises a brow at me and skillfully levitates his second goblet of wine over to the only other woman in the alcove without spilling a drop. His red vessel smoke curls around the woman until she breaks her kiss with a nobleman to see a goblet of wine floating next to her. She eyes the goblet, and when her gaze rises to Kazem, her breath hitches, and she tucks a strand of her hair behind her ear before taking the goblet.

Kazem's smile is nothing short of dubious when his blue gaze returns to me and flicks over my body. "I know what all women find desirable."

I pull my hand up to study my nails. "That's not what I've heard."

"*Oooh, what have you heard?*" Liha asks. "*You are not allowed to hide the juicy gossip from me! I neeeeed it.*"

Kazem closes the rest of the distance between us. "And what have you heard?"

"*Realms, he's hot,*" Liha pants.

I shrug, deigning to meet his gaze. "I've heard your family is disappointing in bedroom matters."

Liha gasps. "*Nooo. That's worse than being scholarly!*"

He watches me above his goblet as he swirls his wine. "Is that why you tapped my shoulder on the dance floor? Because you think I'd be disappointing?" He tilts his head. "I don't think so."

"*Look at the way his eyes are undressing you,*" Liha says. "*There is no way he isn't good in bed.*" She pauses. "*Unless you are just saying—*"

She gasps. "*Oh, you hound!*"

I go back to studying my nails. "I believe you're confusing me for a brunette with a lip ring." I nod toward the dance floor. "She went that way."

His eyes simmer. "She'll find me later."

I push a finger into his firm chest, right above his black Zem crest in the shape of a dragon. "You should go find her now."

He looks down at my chest, which is rising a little too quickly for me to feign nonchalance, and whispers, "You know, I have a theory." He tilts his head toward mine.

"And that is?" I lean closer, trying to ignore the scent of wine, which I've come to hate so much.

"*I'm all for toeing the line, but if your father sees you this close, he'll lose control again,*" Liha warns.

I bat her away.

A kiss. That's all I want. A single, blissful moment before I belong to someone else. And a reason to get sent to my rooms for the night.

A song starts, sensual with a demanding beat.

Kazem passes his goblet back to a server and tugs my waist, pulling me tight against him. That's when I notice Dae feather down from the ceiling until he's hovering behind me, turning colder by the second.

"I think your father has declared you off-limits," Kazem says, his breath hot in my ear, "to weed out the cowards."

I tilt my head up to him. "Hmm. Are you brave enough to test that theory?"

"Nizzara! You will be punished—"

"If you don't want to watch, go away."

She hums nervously before she leaves my shield.

A devilish grin splits Kazem's lips before he dips his head toward mine.

I'm leaning in to kiss him when the music stops, and a giant hand of black smoke rounds the pillar. It takes hold of Kazem, and his hands go rigid around my waist.

My father's power yanks him back, walking him out from behind the giant pillar and into the gasping crowd. My father floats his sword over the guests' heads on black vessel smoke and lowers it in front of Kazem.

Kazem fights my father's power, his neck veins bulging as he tries to keep his arms down, but slowly, they rise until he's gripping the black pommel. His hands shake as he points the sword's razor-sharp tip at his own crotch.

Father's arrival parts the crowd, his fur cape—and Brunar, the big snitch—trailing behind him earlier than I planned.

Father clasps his hands behind his back as he paces around Kazem, his jaw working. When his gaze finds mine, the promise of a later punishment is clear.

King Rajim and his trail of Zem guards break through the murmuring crowd. His face flushes red as he points a crooked finger at my father. "Release my heir."

My father's dark gaze remains on me as he answers, "Your son tried to kiss my daughter—an act I've declared punishable by death." His attention drops to the sword shaking in Kazem's hands, and the tiniest curve ticks up his lips. "A rather agonizing and embarrassing death, I'm afraid."

King Rajim's beady blue eyes narrow on me. "What is so special about your heiress that she cannot mingle with my son?"

"If I were a guest in your home," my father says, patting Kazem's reddening cheek, "I'd follow your decrees, Rajim."

Father raises his fist, increasing the force on the blade against Kazem's balls, and Kazem *squeaks*. His bladder releases, and darkness spreads down his pants. A few people in the crowd snicker.

Rajim stiffens. "Kazem is my heir. He's protected by the King's law, which states you can't harm him outside of a duel ring."

Kazem glares at me as if I planned this whole thing.

I lurch forward, shaking my head. "Kazem, I didn't—"

"It seems Nizzara wants me to kill the heir prince quicker." Father smiles at me—a silent command to fix my face.

My nails bite into my palms as I take a step back and smile.

"Bitch." Kazem barely gets the word out before my father raises his fist again—nothing but murder on his face—and Kazem squawks out an apology.

Father whistles and a swarm of infantry soldiers falls in around us. "I have broken the King's law before," my father reminds Rajim. "It does not pain me to do it again."

Rajim's face pales as countless infantry soldiers corral the room tighter by a few feet. He looks at his son and clears his throat before returning his gaze to my father. "Then, I ask you to consider a stand-in for my son, one who will receive his punishment for him."

Everyone's eyes are on Kazem, but his gaze is still on me, simmering with newfound hatred and silently promising retribution for his public embarrassment.

Father's attention glides back to me. "I hope this warning is very clear, Rajim. My rules are to be followed." Father tilts his head. "A bondslave. That is who I will accept as a stand-in." I try to breathe, but my lungs can't find air, as if it were knocked out of me.

The entire Zem party nearly sags with relief when Rajim agrees without hesitation and sends for one of their royal, Awom chauffeurs.

The bondslave arrives, his white hair and sheer size marking him as Awom. My chest fractures when he is informed of his duty.

Without flinching, the bondslave steps in between the two kings and faces my father. He speaks in Awom as his gaze trails the air around my father. "To save a soul is an honorable end to this life."

Tears prick in my eyes. I wonder if anyone besides me can understand him, if anyone besides me has taken the time to learn their beautiful language.

The Awom man could tear my father apart, limb by limb, if the Awoms weren't so peaceful. If the First-Made vessel wasn't involved.

Father gives the order.

Sorren pushes the bondslave onto his knees in front of me.

The Awom looks up at me with something like forgiveness in his expression, as Father passes his only gem gun, which he keeps hidden in his uniform, to Sorren, since his sword is busy.

"Make it quick," Father orders. "This is a party, after all."

Sorren wedges the gem-studded barrel beneath the Awom's jaw.

Angry tears blur my vision, and darkness rises in me. My heart pounds inside my chest like a vicious animal clawing to be free—thrashing with the desire to end them all. The golden spirit appears above the crowd. I feel its immense power without glancing at it. Too much power. Power I want nothing to do with—because I do want it. I pinch my eyes shut.

I jump at the sound of gunfire. Loud and final. Gun smoke clings to the fallen bondslave. The Awom's white, brilliant soul leaves his body, swirling about my father before disappearing from the room.

I want to scream. At my father. At Sorren. At myself for being so naive—so stupid. There were other ways to get sent away from the party, but I chose the one that would anger my father the most.

The crowd whispers, shooting fearful glances at my father, and the few people standing closest to me take a step away for good measure.

As the Awom's body is dragged away, I swallow a cry.

"Release my son," King Rajim growls.

Father releases Kazem.

The prince falls to his knees, his chest heaving.

I take a step toward him to ask if he is harmed but stop. Father's pointed gaze is boring into me, saying *fix your fucking face*.

I raise my chin.

Kazem points a shaky finger at me. "You're fucking dead."

I open my mouth to explain I didn't mean for my father to—

"Nizzara. Do we tolerate threats?" My father toys with the cuffs on his uniform. His body language is relaxed, exuding the calm that only comes from being the most powerful man in the room. He nods toward Kazem. "Go on. Teach him a second lesson this evening."

Rajim stiffens, glaring at my father, but doesn't protest.

I approach Kazem and slide my dagger out from the sheath on my leg. "Say it again."

His nose wrinkles, and his lips pull back with rage."I said you're fucking dead. As dead as that bondslave. I hope they dump your body in the trash next to his after I'm done with you."

I kick him in the balls so hard his eyes roll in their sockets and all the air leaves his lungs. He lurches forward. Black, endless rage spreads throughout my chest, and I use the point of my dagger to lift his head up. To face me. "You're quite cocky for someone who just pissed himself."

He speaks through clenched teeth. "We'll finish this in the ring."

"We will," I say, my voice cold. "And you'll be in the same position you are now. On your knees."

CHAPTER 23

DAGEN

I'M ABOUT TO CUT DOWN ALL THE BODIES IN THIS ROOM like fodder.

"*Do it,*" the shadows inside me whisper. "*Drain them all.*"

I try to block out their hcinous voices, forcing myself to look at each face around me—reminding myself these are people with children and loved ones waiting for them to return home—but the Awom's death flashes through my mind again, and the growl that erupts in my chest is straight from Baratrum.

I sift through the memories of the guests to distract myself.

And of course, they all linger on *her.*

Nizzara gliding into the ballroom in that sinful golden dress, her chin high and expression fierce.

Nizzara walking through the crowd, with every gaze pinned on her.

Nizzara as the Awom man was shot and killed. I try to skip over those memories, but her face—There are *tears* in her eyes as she beholds the Awom on his knees, and after her memories of the Awom boy in the library, I can't help but wonder if the tears are real.

For some reason, she appears noticeably *different* in each perspective. Bigger breasts in one memory, fuller lips in another—

"I want to know who designs her gowns," a loud brunette with a lip ring says beside me, interrupting my thoughts.

One of her tipsy friends snorts into her black goblet. "*I* want to know who actually believes she's a virgin." The woman's memories flash to Nizzara's entrance, lingering on every inch of her body. Her drunken desire pools into me. "She's twenty-one . . . And with those curves?" She shakes her head. "It's obviously a ruse, but damn, the ruse is working on me."

The brunette giggles. "Maybe tonight I'll pretend I'm off-limits too."

They laugh and sway before passing their empty goblets to a server and disappearing toward the darker corners writhing with entangled couples.

Shadows continue to curl through me, still whispering, when Tarella tugs a Zo man in a white suit toward my corner, and her memories of Nizzara flood into my mind. They drip with jealousy, of both Nizzara's betrothal and her Mark.

Her Mark.

I see it in Tarella's memories. Nizzara can alter her appearance. Is that why her beauty is so intoxicating to me?

It can't be. Every time I've talked to her, she's been without her spirit, which means—

There's no magic behind it. I find her unbearably attractive as she is. *Fuck.*

Not wanting to think any further about Nizzara or the Awom's death, I leave, fading through the gem-studded wall. I emerge into the dark winter fog outside, where my once father-in-law, King Rajim, and his royal party are piling into their squatty glo-kars, parked among steam-powered carriages.

His memories fill my head. He's not remembering Nizzara, but suddenly I wish he were. His memories swirl around my late wife, Kathreen. My soul turns to ice at the thought of that bitch, and the shadows inside me hiss into an excited frenzy, wanting again to devour every soul in sight when they sense my hatred.

The shadows whisper louder, *"Drink their souls . . ."*

I take a deep breath, blocking them out, and fly away.

I jet past seven infantries patrolling around the gem-studded carriages, but other than that, the exterior walls of the castle are bare of guards. All of Mazzar's infantry are inside the castle, since that is where the enemies are tonight.

CHAPTER 24

NIZZARA

Father passed away this morning. As tradition goes, my brother inherited the First-Made vessel as it fell from Father's lifeless hand, and Dagen's Second-Made fell off as soon as he put the white ring on. He is now the king of Zarr, the married king of Zarr. He's falling for Kathreen, but only because she is his wife, and if I know my brother—which I do—he's taking his duties as husband and now king seriously. But not only is Kathreen so wrong for him, I believe she's the one who poisoned Father. His illness started after King Rajim suspected us of stealing—and after Kathreen started visiting. Needless to say, I've ordered Preysee to replace every food item that goes to Dagen's rooms. I don't trust anyone in this castle, but if I did, it would be Preysee.

P.S. I tried looking for information on Guardians, but it turns out all the books about them are locked away in Tigous's private library.

—*Lo*

***

MY GUARDS BLAZE A TRAIL UP THE GIANT SPIRAL STAIRcase to my chambers, visibly sour at the sudden absence of short skirts and deep necklines.

"I will be reading the rest of the night if you wish to go enjoy the rave,"

I say to Liha as she fades into my shield. She will try to talk me out of what I'm about to do, and I don't have time or patience for it tonight.

She nudges me. *"Are you sure?"*

Her voice is light and energetic, as if the Awom's death never happened.

I walk to my desk and flip open *The King of Kings.* *"I'm sure. Have fun."*

"Oh, I always do. Tonight I might catch one of my little boyfriends doing something scrumptious."

"Oh, for the love of—"

She giggles and the small tug on my shield tells me she's gone, off to spy on the living.

Preysee arrives and ushers me into my closet. Once inside, she turns me to face the giant mirror, and I watch her face fall as she unzips my dress and sees the purple finger marks around my neck. They've deepened in color.

Her voice is thick. "My lady—"

I wave her off. "It looks worse than it feels."

Her lips press into a firm line.

"Preysee."

She looks up from my neck, and I hate what I'm about to involve her in, but I can't do it without her knowing. "I'm going to sneak out, and I need you to cover for me."

Her expression sharpens. "Why?"

I step out of the golden dress and reach for a pair of matte-black fighting leathers.

"There's something I have to fix."

After sliding my legs and arms into my suit, Preysee pauses at my zipper, holding it. "This has to do with tax court, doesn't it?"

"How did you know?"

Our eyes meet in the reflection, and she slowly zips up my suit. "I've been your maid for ten years, my lady. I know what happened in tax court, and I know you." A small smile tugs on her lips but falls again when she zips up the back of my neck, over the bruises. "I will help however I can."

I walk deeper into my closet and grab a plain golden necklace with a small blue gem strung from it. It's not a notable piece, but it is worth a small fortune to a mill worker. "I will be back in three hours, realms willing."

Her brows pull together, giving a hard cast to her face. "That's too long. Your father gave Brunar specific orders after what happened tonight. He's to check on you in an hour and report back."

I look down at the necklace in my palm and feel my shoulders drop. There's no way I can deliver it. With only an hour, I'd barely have time to help Palko in the dungeons.

Preysee takes my hand in hers. "Let me help."

I shake my head. "No. It's too dangerous."

"My lady," she says, her voice stern. "I want to help. Tell me what needs to be done, and I will do it."

Something flickers in her gaze as she beholds my pained expression and I relent.

"It needs to be delivered to someone." I pour the gold chain and pendant into her palm and give her the name of the mill worker's wife along with the district she belongs to.

She takes the necklace with reverence. "I will do this. I can't make it out of the castle tonight, but as soon as I'm able to leave without raising suspicion, I will."

I nod, reminding myself that Preysee goes into Zarr city all the time. She will be fine, I tell myself, but it doesn't calm the fear coursing through me. If she's caught with my necklace—helping the Everett family—she'll be executed . . . I shove the thought far away, knowing neither of us can afford for me to be afraid. I pull down two of my warmest winter cloaks, one for me and one for Palko. I layer one on top of the other, fastening them both around my shoulders, and go to the balcony doors.

Her fingers clasp tighter around the necklace as she follows. "I will run your bath. For as often as you get in the tub, no one will suspect otherwise." She almost smirks. "If Brunar knocks before then, I'll tell him you're not decent yet."

I look out the glass panes toward the wind and fog. "I'll be back within the hour."

When I open the balcony doors, high above the castle grounds, the cold cuts through my two cloaks like they're nothing.

I roll my shoulders as I mentally talk myself through my plan, but when I look down at the ground so far below, the fear and vertigo set in. My heartbeat hammers in my chest, and blackness fills my vision—*fills me*. The panic deepens as a far-off memory scratches at my consciousness, clawing to get through. A memory. Tian's face . . . In pain . . . Before my father ended him. Then, darkness. It sweeps through the memory and then myself as I grip the stone railing. It has stolen my memories before—leaving glaring holes in my past—always triggered by immense fear or rage. In my gut, I know I can't afford to succumb to my emotions.

I force my eyes to focus on the ground so far below.

Of all the things.

Heights.

Maybe that's why Father stuck me up here in the first place—he knows I hate heights.

That little thought propels me over the edge as I grab hold of the slick stones and swing my legs over. The icy cold bleeds through my gloves as I navigate the angles and spikes of my turret while the wind whips my cloaks around.

Fast. The key is to move fast, before my hands become too numb. I risk a glance down and swallow.

My fingers slip in a few places, slick from ice, but I'm able to catch myself on nearby ledges and crevasses as I descend.

After a shoulder-wrenching twenty minutes, my feet smack the icy ground.

That's when *his* velvet voice sounds at my shoulder. "*Sneaking out? So naughty.*"

CHAPTER 25

DAGEN

NIZZARA GASPS AND WHIRLS TOWARD THE DIRECTION OF my voice, her eyes landing directly on me.

I swallow the melee of confusion that hits me when I look at her— ignore the tug I feel toward her—as I try to connect the girl with the daggers and threats to the one curled up with an Awom boy in her memories.

I forget the human things and focus on what I have to do. Gain her trust and find out who she cares about. Between playing my role as Red and waiting for her pink spirit to leave her unattended, I haven't been able to spy on her as much as I need. This opportunity has to count.

"*Out to see a lover?*" I taunt. "*Your betrothed Jaxelli Warrior will be so put out.*"

Her eyes narrow as she pulls the hood of her cloak up over her white hair, still in the ponytail and draped over her shoulder. "How do you know who my betrothed is?"

When my only answer is a soft chuckle, she hisses, "Why don't you go haunt someone else?"

"*And miss the fun?*" I say at her shoulder.

The icy wind whips her gathered, white strands out of her hood, bringing a few across her mouth. They tease her lips, sticking to the black lipstick, a color that only adds menace to the full curve of them.

Damn those lips.

"I bet you're sneaking off to see someone tall and dark, with hazel eyes—"

She scoffs and takes off running.

What *is* the cruel thing up to at this hour in the cold? Parts of her gold-and-black soul whisper her desires to me as she sprints away,

"*... Earn Palko's forgiveness ...*"

"*... Win the King's Duel ...*"

"*... End the betrothal ...*"

"*... Dae's voice ...*"

I ignore the fact that I'm in her desires and focus on the one about Palko. Could Palko be the name of a lover? But wasn't she just trying to kiss the Zem prince?

The shadows whisper deep in my mind, "*She's a cheater, just like your late wife ... All souls are wretched ... They all deserve to die ... Feed us, Dagen ...*"

I close my mind to them, and they fall silent.

I follow, careful not to touch her memories. The ones of her and the Awom boy still won't leave me alone.

I can't have that.

She clings to the darkest shadows along the base of the black castle wall. The only thing giving her away is that hair of hers, the ends of which keep dancing off her shoulder from the wind.

I hate that I'm curious, hate that I'm itching to delve into those honeyed memories and see exactly why she's out here sneaking around—why she pulled the stunt with Kazem when her desires don't whisper for him ... but I refrain.

Again.

Even though it's only a matter of time until she actively recalls a memory, and I won't be able to stop myself from watching it. My traitorous self buzzes with anticipation, waiting for it.

Those memories are part of her soul, and they are a drug to me.

She turns the corner. Her steps are quick, precise, and silent across the icy ground.

The length of the castle's monstrous back wall appears never-ending as she runs, brushing her hand against it as she goes. When she touches the bars of the dungeon cells, she skids to a stop and crouches, cupping her hands to peer down inside.

"A thing for bad boys, I see."

Her soul pulls on me, the soft gold with smooth obsidian edges flaring around her. She turns to face me, and I don't even notice the way those full lips are parted just so, breathing heavily from her run.

Nope. Don't notice.

She points *at* me, those black, devilish eyes boring through me. "New rule. If you are here, you help. Find a man in one of the cells. Brown hair, has a limp."

"So I was right about the dark hair," I tease.

Maybe this will be the person I can use as leverage against her. I slink down into the dungeons, which have drastically suffered in my absence. They are a filthy, uninhabitable maze of stone walls.

Fortunately—or unfortunately—they are almost all empty. I'm able to quickly find the man and return.

"Thirty-second cell from this window."

She takes off running again, counting softly as she passes each half-sunken, barred window.

"So, why am I helping instead of your bonded spirit?"

"Because she's gone, and you can't seem to leave me alone." She stops at the thirty-second window. "Palko?" she whispers. Time seemingly stops when I'm catapulted into her memory.

Golden light and black swirls explode in my vision as I look out from her eyes, ordering the death sentence of Palko Everett, sending him to await execution in the dungeons.

Rage fills my every pore; the shadows claw and thrash through me, begging me to *kill*.

I watch as guards tear Palko from his wife, wrenching his weak and twisted leg. Anger and immense heartbreak suffocate me, but I can't tell which emotion is mine and which is hers. I close my eyes, fighting the memory, fighting off the shadows that don't see reason—

Until the vision shifts, and I'm handing over Palko's bag of ren with her hand to a nobleman of the Zarr court.

The shadows grow louder, their words bleeding into my thoughts.

"*Kill her . . . Look at what she did to your people . . . She stole from them . . . Just like your late wife did . . . She deserves to die . . .*"

Suddenly, I don't care about my freedom or that I won't gain her soul this way. I only want to end her. I materialize behind her and call the black, flickering blade to my hand. My muscles coil, about to surge my blade forward until—

Another memory. I'm in her room, facing Preysee, handing a necklace to her, and instructing her to deliver it to Palko's wife so she can use its worth to free him. My blade halts inches from her back.

A strained cough floats up from the dungeon. "Who's there?"

Nizzara unbuttons her top cloak and drops it through the freezing bars. "Here, take this and keep it hidden under your mat when the guards pass." She shivers as a gust of snowy wind whips at her, then unbuttons the second one and drops it too.

Palko's voice is raspy and weak, but I hear the hitch in his words. "Thank you."

She sinks to her knees, her back still to me. "I'm so sorry." Her voice cracks. "Keep holding on. Your wife is coming with payment."

"Thank you," Palko says. "Realms, thank you."

"I'm sorry," she says again, too soft for Palko to hear over the wind.

"*Kill her!*" the shadows screech, but in the face of her, their words fade.

I jet back into my spirit form, knowing she'll undoubtedly recognize me if she so much as turns her head.

She stands up and turns back the way we came. For a fleeting moment, tears glisten down her flawless cheeks until the wind steals them away.

I can't help it.

I have to know.

I dive into her memories.

Gold and onyx. Everywhere. Her memories pull me in, and I swear they grow more intoxicating and addictive each time I enter them. I see her left alone, cross-legged on the floor, while her mother reads to her sister but not to her.

I see the Awom from the library helping her learn his language, his hand reaching for hers.

I see Mazzar hugging her and telling her stories of far-off lands. I've never, in my whole life, witnessed that look on Mazzar's face, but it's here in the memory when he beholds Nizzara.

Multiple images pass by of him smiling *softly* at her, followed by his backhanded slaps to her face.

Glimpses fly by, of her first duel, her father watching as close to the ropes as possible. He cheers as she lands her first pink-puffed dagger, like an infantry general claiming the sweetest victory, but when she goes to find him afterward, he's gone.

More memories pass of them training together, him teaching her moves and techniques I've never seen before, all of varying degrees of brutality.

Sprinkled through her past, I see his descent. More goblets of wine and less life in his gaze, until the first time his hand finds her throat. Until he can't control his temper enough to train with her, until his punishments turn to whips.

Her memories flood through my cold center and it takes monumental effort to close the gate again. Suddenly, the world around me is dust compared to the intensity of her soul.

A pure soul.

Without a rotten edge to be found.

CHAPTER 26

NIZZARA

Diary: Page 11

Just as I'm sure my brother has fallen for his wife, I find her in bed with a Zem nobleman. Dagen's out leading our army against the horde of Skeeves breaking through our continent's borders, and it's taking all my self-control not to kill her while he's away. It's going to tear him apart, but I've got to tell him. He's due back for the King's Duel in a month, which I'm worried about. He's a badass in the duel ring, but I know how dirty the other kingdoms fight.

—Lo

⌒⌒⌒

THE IMAGE OF PALKO AND HIS WIFE BEING SEPARATED AT my command burns behind my eyes, and I let the tears fall as I run back to my tower. No one is here to see. At least, no one who'll punish me for it.

Dae is utterly silent behind me. His presence grows colder and darker around me. I slink in and out of shadows and past waterless fountains. I dart behind a single line of perimeter guards, a fraction of what normally patrols here because of the rave.

"You're lucky the visibility is shit tonight, otherwise those guards by the royal carriages would've spotted you."

I scoff. "Because you'd be so torn up if something happened to me?" I slip around the corner and press my shoulders against the black stone on the other side.

"*Yeah, because then I'd be stuck with the brat from Zo.*"

I stifle a snort. "You could always pretend she's me." I jump, catching a spike on the turret, and begin scaling my way back up my tower.

"*He's a young boy, so I'd rather not.*"

My fingers, so raw from the cold, are too stiff to bend properly. Looking up at the mile-high tower above me, the panic hits. I squeeze my eyes shut and breathe through the fear, reminding myself that Preysee is up there, risking her life to cover for me. The frigid wind bites into my skin as I start moving again. As I climb, the stiffness only worsens. I slip and catch myself many times, and try to reason with my hands, begging them not to shake.

They tremble harder the higher I go, and I don't look down. I will not hand my fear over to this tower so easily. It's just a tower. Lifeless. Unmoving. I reach for a ledge near the top, but my fingers are useless, and the ledge has grown an extra layer of ice in my absence. My hand slips and I fall, sliding down the wall until my arm hooks around a spike, jerking me to a stop and slamming my body into the cold, hard wall.

A growl comes from Dae. Or up here, it might just be the wind.

I compartmentalize, saving my emotions for the top. Forcing my throbbing arm to stay locked around the spike, I look up—

A big, black bird with green-slivered wings watches from my balcony. It tilts its head as if it's somehow annoyed with *me*. It's dark and hard to tell for sure, but I swear it's not any species of bird I've seen before. When my arm starts to ache, I take hold of a ledge and make my way back to the top.

Finally, my fingers curl around the top edge, and when I heave myself over, the bird is gone. Part of me wonders if I hallucinated the damn thing.

I heave out the breath I've been holding and punch the black stone of my balcony much harder than I should. Tears stream down from the delayed fear and also the blinding sting now climbing up my knuckles and arm.

I hate heights.

The first time my father lost control of his anger—the first time I ever felt truly endangered by him—was on top of a Zo turret so many years ago. The image of my father holding me at arm's length toward the edge is littered with dark spots, as if my mind doesn't wish to remember it, but I distinctly recall the pain of his fingers digging into my arm. I swallow that memory and lock it away—deep down with other dark and fuzzy memories.

Dae's spirit shifts, spreading. Darkening. The temperature drops around me, and I swear ice cracks up the tower walls.

His voice is strained in the air. *"What makes you happy, Nizzara?"*

"What?"

His words are tortured. Desperate. *"Give me a happy memory."*

I swear I hear whispers coming from his presence. This might be the danger Liha warned me of, so I give him what he asks for.

A happy memory.

I tug my gloves off and look down to the small ring on my finger in the shape of a snake. "I have a friend. I don't get to see her often, but she makes me happy."

The longer I think of Yisabell and all the little stories I tell her, the more my breathing calms.

Exhaustion hits me. I take one more breath of the winter air and return to the warmth of my chambers, heaving the thick balcony doors shut and relatching them.

Preysee looks relieved to see me. Through the archway of my closet, I see she has a nightgown waiting on the ottoman. She looks me over from head to toe, making sure I'm whole, before she informs me that she's been asked to return to the main floor. I thank her and she offers a meaningful nod before she slips out. Not a minute later, Brunar pounds on my door, checking on me.

After calling back to him, I take off toward my closet, having to undress the old-fashioned way without Liha. My fingers are still numb as I try to work the main zipper, and I make a mental note to thank Liha for her outfit changes.

Dae lingers, silent, but close behind me at the edge of my caster's shield, which clings like a second skin—its own mini dimension, according to some books I've found. He doesn't come close enough to touch it like he did in the bathing chamber. But I haven't forgotten the current that ran through me at his touch.

I remove each ice-cold dagger from my fighting leathers and place them on black velvet pads formed to fit each one, then unbuckle my now empty knife belt and roll it before placing it on its own cushion. I reach for the small black zipper at my neck, pulling it down the front of me, and that's when Dae disappears. I unclip my bodice and sigh with the release before finding the red silk nightgown Preysee picked out.

I'm surprised when I leave my closet and find Dae is still in my room. "So, you can spy on me when I sleep but not undress?"

"Those are two very different things."

Does his voice sound tighter?

"Not for spirits." I point to my walk-in closet. "There were about ten in there just now." Although most of them weren't whole spirits, just leftover shreds of souls.

"It's different for me."

I climb into bed, sighing with undiluted pleasure as my bare feet slide through the silk sheets.

"Does Liha leave you alone a lot?"

I close my eyes, my body feeling heavy. "She likes to go play."

"So, she's off playing while you risk your life helping your people?" The space Dae hovers in—just beside my bed—turns to ice.

"She was a princess in Heshena about a thousand years ago." I yawn. "Only sixteen when she was captured sneaking out to see her lover. It was forbidden love. From what I gathered she was tortured in a slow, terrible way before she was killed. So, she can't stand to see me in danger, can't watch anything that involves pain or blood. She will duel with me, but even that is hard for her."

"Why not bond with a spirit that has a stronger stomach? Who will stay at your side, especially during those times?"

I peek my eyes open to glare at him. His presence now hulks at the side of my bed, no longer a floating ball. His outline, with wide shoulders and tapered hips, is almost as bad as his damn voice.

I deepen my glare. "I do not fault her for her traumas, and she doesn't fault me for mine."

His voice sounds pained, almost guilty when he asks, *"What are your traumas?"*

"None of your business," I snap, but they flash through my mind.

Watching my father slowly lose his grip on his temper, taking it out on me. And me, born with that same dark, endless rage that never leaves.

His anger.

My anger.

His violence.

My violence.

Dae's voice is almost a whisper. *"Why risk your life for Palko?"*

My whole life plays across my mind in answer, the things I've seen, things I've experienced, but ultimately, at my core, this is who I am. I've known for a long time this softness in my heart is a weakness. Father has proven that much. A weakness I shouldn't show to anyone.

I roll away from Dae. "Because those cloaks were last year's fashion, and they deserved the dungeon."

CHAPTER 27

DAGEN

I PACE UP AND DOWN THE EMPTY CORRIDOR BEHIND THE
secret painting until Jasper slips in, the thumping music growing piercingly loud as he opens the painting, then muting to a dull thudding as
it latches shut.

Jasper grins, rubbing his hands together. "I sent the message to my
cousin," he says.

I stiffen. "Now what?"

"We wait for a response and take care of our end in the meantime.
How are you doing with the princess? Did you discover any information we can use against her once we've captured her?"

"*If* we capture her. That's the backup plan," I remind him.

"Yes, of course. Did you find anyone she cares for?"

She cares for the bondslave. I imagined her sister or mother, maybe
even a secret lover, but she has no one like that little bondslave.

I swore after my first love, Emya, I would protect the Awoms. I
dedicated my entire four years of rule to liberating them.

To threaten the bondslave . . . I won't do it. I'll find someone else
she cares for, but not a bondslave and certainly not a bondslave *child*.

"I haven't, but I will."

An ounce of guilt worms into my chest, but I remind myself this is
only a backup plan. Remind myself, *no human feelings*.

Helina's red curls appear in one of the hallway doors and she joins
us. "Another supply train is ready to be delivered to the rebel camps."

Jasper's gaze locks onto her. "I have meetings scheduled with our rum supplier tonight which I have to attend, or we won't have a business here. Not to mention the bouncers are getting restless now that Red has taken a more hands-off approach." Jasper points a look in my direction. "Don't forget. You'll need to meet with Red's noblewomen who fund these supply trains soon."

Helina scoffs. "He'll need a bath and a haircut for that."

I roll my eyes. "I apologize. The grooming standards in Baratrum are subpar." I turn to Jasper. "The supplies are more important. They need to get to the camp."

"I told you I can't take the shipment tonight—"

"I'll take it," I tell him. "The club isn't busy, and I have nothing else to do."

"But you don't know where to go."

"I'll go with," Helina says, stepping in between us.

He glares at her. "It's dangerous, Helina."

"I know," she says. "I've gone before."

"That was before the Skeeves showed up."

I stiffen. "Skeeves? In the Barrens? That's so much closer than—"

"A lot has changed since you died," he says, as if that is explanation enough.

"I can handle myself," she says, her gaze stern. "My daughter needs food."

He puffs air through his nose and fidgets as if he wants to bridge the gap between him and Helina, but he doesn't. "If they spot you without protection, they'll eat you alive while you scream."

"You promised the supply trains would not be interrupted," she says, her gaze flicking to Jasper's balled fists. "If you're going to keep that promise, we need to go now." A memory of her daughter playing inside a cave-like structure flashes through her mind, nothing but anxiety in the vision.

Jasper takes a breath, his jaw flexing, before he points a gloved finger at me. "Don't you dare let anything happen to her."

"I'll protect her," I say. "I've handled Skeeves before."

Helina breathes a sigh of relief.

After a stretch of silence, Jasper finally nods and steps aside, but when I go for the door, he grabs my shoulder. "The Skeeves are far stronger than you remember." He seems to fight for the right words. "They share a collective mind. You can't kill the essence that lurks within them, but you can sever the connection from their master by beheading." His grip tightens. "And even then, they can rise again if their master is close enough . . ."

"I will protect her," I promise again.

He seems to believe me this time, and he lets go.

CHAPTER 28

NIZZARA

DIARY: PAGE 12

My brother dominated this tournament until last night. He almost died in his final duel, and it was the worst twelve minutes of my life. After digging around, I found out the Zem dueler was using blare gems under his fighting leathers. Fucking cheaters. As for the thing about Kathreen, I decided to wait until the tournament is finished to tell him so he could focus on not dying. And now I'm being followed. Okay, five minutes ago, I was being followed. Every time I glanced over my shoulder, a man in white was there. If there's one thing I've learned, nothing is ever a coincidence. I'd bet gold rens Kathreen doesn't want me to tell my brother about her sleeping around. She's probably sending assassins after me and having them dress up as Zos so I don't put two and two together.

—*Lo*

WITH THE PRELIMINARY DUELS—WHERE I'LL BE GIVEN A rank for the tournament—happening tomorrow, and my first official tournament duel only three weeks away, I *should* be on my way to the training room to work with Sorren—even though he's been mysteriously unavailable more often than not lately. I wonder if the Skeeves are what's pulling him away. As I trail my guards, I find myself *wishing*

I were on my way to get my bones crushed by Sorren because instead, I'm on my way to face punishment for the stunt I pulled at last night's rave. My guards lead me down to Father's chambers.

I knew this would be the cost, but since he didn't call on me first thing this morning or later this afternoon, I'd hoped . . .

My breathing becomes shallow. He only summons me here for *whipping* punishments.

Those started last year.

As I descend these stairs to the tunnel hidden beneath his chambers, I promise myself this time will be different. This time, I will not feel so broken. At the bottom of the stone stairwell, lit with white glo stones, there's a hallway full of closed doors with no end in sight. The hall simply gives itself over to the darkness.

"Be strong," Liha whispers, then leaves my shield.

I try not to feel so alone when she does that.

My racing pulse is the only thing I can hear as I face the door closest to the stairs. Every fiber of my body wishes to stall, to remain outside for as long as possible, but I enter.

Father is already there, sitting on an iron stool. Glo stones are arranged in a circle on the ceiling and torture devices of varying shapes are attached to the walls. Father frowns at me, his face contorting into the one I hate most: vein-popping tension through his neck, slicing disappointment in his gaze, and an unmistakable, wine-induced flush in his face. He taps down his goblet on the blood-smeared floor before standing up.

"I don't like to punish you."

I clench my fists. "Then why do it?"

Before I can blink, he's off his seat, his hand smacking across my face. A fierce sting radiates from my cheek. He's every bit as fast as Sorren.

"You know why."

I grit my teeth and turn my head back to face him. "Because you're a drunk."

He slaps me harder this time and I resist the urge to touch the burning fire where his gloved hand hit. The gold spirit bleeds into the room, and darkness rises inside me.

Father takes a deep breath. The gems on his gloves and boots twinkle, and the golden light around me dulls.

He arranges his face into his "execution floor" smile. "I've told you, Nizzara. I am preparing you for the real world and all its realms. I promise, they're more ruthless than I."

I clench my jaw shut, fighting the anger rising in me.

"I know you don't want a betrothal," he continues. "I know your little stunt with Kazem was to spite it." The vein in his neck pops. "But I'm giving you what you deserve to have, Nizzara."

I lift my chin. "I *deserve* to make my own choices."

My hand brushes over my thigh where the edge of my dagger pokes my dress, but my stupid heart won't let me touch it. Because if I do, I will be no different than him. Because the darkness inside wants me to. Once I have a dagger in my hand, in conditions like this, I won't be able to stop. My vision will go black, and I'll be lost to the ugliness inside. He and I are the same that way.

"I deserve to marry who *I* choose," I say.

He hits my face again. The sound of his leather glove smacking my cheek is just as sharp as the sting.

His chest heaves. His fists curl, and his eyes—

He's teetering on the edge of his control, which only pushes me to the edge of mine. He's the reason I'm so angry all the time. This depthless pit of hatred and rage never leaves.

And I loathe it.

"I deserve a better father," I say, angry tears forming.

If he was balancing on the edge, I just shoved him off. His hand shoots out, crushing my throat.

"You are so young, and it takes time and pain to see yourself for what you *are* instead of what you wish to be. But you'll see it much faster than I did, won't you?"

I grit my teeth and raise my jaw, not answering. Not breathing.

His hand tightens around my throat. "Won't you?"

I mouth the word no.

His eyes shift, a flash of regret, but he does not release me; he squeezes harder. I pushed him too far. He's killing—

Spots begin forming in my vision. I claw at his hand. He lets go.

Air surges into my lungs.

My knees buckle and my sore muscles don't respond in time. I drop to the cold floor.

I hate how I refuse to hurt him, even though he hurts me.

He takes a deep breath through his nose, his eyes flickering between black and blacker, before he snaps a whip off the wall. He cracks it on the floor at my feet.

"Remove your dress, Nizzara. It is a fine dress, and it doesn't deserve your punishment."

I curse my hands for shaking as I remove my dress, leaving my silk underdress with its open back. My foot slips on the floor. Fresh blood. Someone else's.

He jerks his chin toward a hook across the room, and I hang the dress on it before returning to the place at his feet where he is pointing. "On the ground, Nizzara."

I drop where I am, letting my knees meet cold stone with a hard thud, my leg muscles unable to slow the descent.

"Hug your knees on the floor. You know how."

I lean over my bent knees, allowing my forehead to graze the floor and exposing my back.

"Twenty lashes for trying to ruin your betrothal."

He releases the whip, cracking it over and over again. I stifle a cry—more from the reality of what my father has become than the physical pain.

The fiery sting buries itself into my skin, deeper with each strike. Lash after lash hits the same spot, slicing further.

Darkness continues to rise inside, and the golden spirit spills toward me again. I feel its power beckoning to me—as if I can simply drink it in. As I breathe in, a wisp of its power absorbs into my bones.

I squeeze my eyes shut, holding my breath, resisting all of it. Agony spreads through me, and I do the thing I've always done—escape into my books, reciting one of my favorite lines.

Power over the mind can only be taken when it is given.

It's the only thought that keeps my lips from tearing open in cries. I will not give him power over me, even as small as a cry. I will not give power to the darkness in me either.

Finally, he stops, well after twenty lashes, and he waves his hand. Black tendrils of his power crawl toward me, about to wipe my skin clean, but stops mid-reach.

"Actually," he says, exasperation clear in his voice, "since you are so afraid of power, I'm going to make you use your own Mark to cover them."

My fists tighten as I rasp, "I hate you." It's a lie, as much as I wish it weren't.

He looks away. "Not as much as you need to."

I brace my hand on the sticky, bloody floor and stagger to my feet.

A deep sadness enters his voice. "There's no stopping your power, Nizzara—believe me, I've tried. It grows every day, and the harder you run from it . . ." He closes his eyes. "The faster it will take over your soul."

When he glances at the tears on my face, his black eyes are tortured—a mix of unspeakable evil and depthless love. I loathe it.

He looks at me as if he longs to say something more, but instead, he *disappears.*

Gone.

Sucked away into nothing.

Is this a dream? No, the slashes in my back are excruciating enough to know this is all real.

He is powerful. I've always known that. But I've never seen him—or anyone—*vanish.*

I hurry to dress despite the agony in my back and my trembling hands.

When I emerge into the hall, my guards fall behind me, unaware—

or maybe completely aware—of what has transpired while they waited for me outside my father's chamber door.

Preysee's salves she's been applying daily must be enchanted, because the pain in my back is much more manageable by the time I reach the book coves.

CHAPTER 29

DAGEN

HELINA LEADS ME OUT THE BACK ENTRANCE OF THE CLUB, lighting our way through the cold alleyway with a glo lantern to a mining sled full of excavation tools, medical supplies, and food.

"What? No supply carriage?"

She motions for me to take hold of the sled ropes. "Where we are taking it, the boulders are too close together for anything wider than this to pass through."

I grab the ropes and follow her lead along the city wall, which skirts a string of rock mills that are closed for the night. We travel about five miles until we near a perimeter gate.

Helina's gaze scans the wall in the glow of her lantern. "Once a week, Jasper's cousin has control over the guards here. He has them disappear for an hour."

Sure enough, when we reach the gate, it's unguarded. She waves for me to hurry, and we pull the lever that raises the portcullis.

Once outside of the city wall, I peer out to the dark, flat ground of the Barrens—as far as the glo lantern reaches.

An eeriness fills the air on this side of the wall. Even more so without the light of a moon. This entire land is a burial site—a whole kingdom disintegrated in an explosion of gem power. As we walk, the rocks and boulders, lodged into the ground like fallen projectiles, grow bigger and closer together. Each one casts long shadows that dance as Helina's glo lantern sways. I flinch at the sight of the dark smears, even though they're not the whispering kind. Our boots pad against barren soil and snow, until I can't help but notice a tingle in the air, as if power lingers here. It seems to be the *only* thing lingering here. There's no ruins. Thousands of buildings, homes, markets—gone without a trace. And the spirits . . . there are none.

Helina's eyes keep finding me, her mouth opening as if to say something before closing again.

She does this a few times until she finally says, "Jasper is overprotective sometimes. Out of the countless runs we've made, we've only had one encounter with Skeeves."

I turn toward her, watching fear settle on her face.

"I watched them kill," she whispers. "The woman's screams were awful."

I tighten my grip on the sled ropes and settle into a steady pace, listening.

"I know they feed on souls," she says. "But I think they gain sustenance from misery and pain too. That's why they drag the end out."

"Did the Skeeves attack your group?" I ask. "Did Jasper fight them off?" The black, faceless creatures I used to fight on the borders were slow and fairly easy to kill, as far as monsters go.

"No." She looks at me. "We let them be." After a minute, she adds, "The Skeeves are stronger than they were years ago. Back when you ruled, they were easily stunned."

"Stunned? No, we slayed them." I painted battlefields black with their blood. Their faceless bodies lay dead in heaps.

She shakes her head. "*Stunned*. They always rise again. The same ones you fought years ago are the same ones hunting our lands now— but stronger. They've been feeding on souls for ten years, *growing*, Dagen." Helina's voice hardens. "The only way to stun them now is by chopping their heads off. If you can't stun them, they'll devour your soul—" She closes her eyes. "Or possess it." Taking a steadying breath, she opens her eyes again and looks at me. "Together, the First-Made vessels are rumored to have some effect on them, but the only thing they fear—the only thing that can truly kill them—is the essence of Death itself."

I scoff. "If by Death you mean Nil, we're all fucked." A sinking feeling takes root in my stomach. I remember seeing my men die, witnessed the jolt of power a Skeeve received after it killed a man. And the only time I ever revisited a battlefield—marching back through it days later—the fallen Skeeves were gone. I'd just assumed their bodies disintegrated like some magical creatures do when they die. "Do you know where the Skeeves came from?"

"The essence of Evil is like the essence of air or the essence of stone. It simply exists. It never *didn't* exist." She scans the dark horizon. "But I've heard stories . . . about how it showed up on our doorstep in the shape of Skeeves."

"Stories?" I ask, sliding the sled between two large boulders.

Her brow raises, visible in the light of her glo lantern. "I once had a friend—a half-soul—who would get visions of the past."

"And what did your friend say about Skeeves?"

After a long pause she says, "Nothing my friend told me makes a lick of sense if you don't know what an essence is, but it's complicated to explain." She smirks. "It could take a while for your frozen mind to absorb it."

I roll my eyes. "I've got time."

"Fine, but if you don't understand the first time, I'm not repeating it."

I huff a laugh. "I'll try to keep up."

Her gaze rises toward the foggy sky. "Everything in our world has an *essence*. Some people confuse essences with *souls* because they move about our world like spirits, and some confuse them with *gods* because they have immense power, but they're neither. They are the purest embodiment of a thing." She looks back at my confused face and snorts. "Think of *love*. It has an essence—Love in its purest form. People can feel love because the essence of Love exists in the world. Now, when the essence of Love actually *touches* a soul—that soul becomes a *half-soul* with power derived from Love itself."

I raise my brow. "You mean to tell me there is an essence for everything?"

She nods. "Not all essences are as big and as powerful as Love." She twists the bracelet on her arm. "Take the essence of Elixirs."

"Elixirs?"

She huffs. "How else do you think enchanted potions exist? It takes a soul—touched by the essence of Elixirs—to make them enchanted, otherwise the concoction of liquids is just like any other ordinary tonic."

I try to wrap my mind around what she's saying. "So a half-soul with the power to see the past was touched by the essence of History? And a half-soul with the power to influence thoughts was touched by the essence of Consciousness?"

She nods. "More or less. The essences were given actual names, Like Zathina, Scientia, and Nil . . ."

"So a pure soul is . . . ?"

"When an essence *bonds* to a soul as the soul is forming . . . *in the womb*. The essence *lives* in that soul." She pauses, then adds, "You call them *gods*, because they have so much power, but my friend says they've been called many things throughout the eons. Some called them Guardians. Some call them pure souls." She points her gaze to the dark, foggy sky as she walks beside me. "It's said that a pure soul lives more than one life." She glances at me again. "I don't know if that means an abnormally long life, or if they actually live *multiple* lives. But when a pure soul dies their final death, they are absorbed into the essence, and the essence lives on to bond another soul they find worthy of all its power."

A scratching sound comes behind us. I jump to find an armored snake slithering around the base of a boulder.

Helina giggles.

I disappear my shadow sword and clear my throat. "So, what did your friend say about Skeeves, then?"

"He said there used to be a prison where all the dark essences were locked away. Forbidden essences like Death, Greed, Evil . . . The prison was created by the Guardians," she says, pulling her cloak tighter around her arm holding the lantern. "They deprived the forbidden essences of any contact with living souls—so they could not bond with anyone—and it remained that way for thousands of years. Until the essence of Evil escaped."

"How?" I ask.

"I don't know," she says. "My friend couldn't see. But when Evil escaped it found a way to bond itself to *many* souls."

"Skeeves," I mutter, then realize . . . "The essence of Death escaped too."

She nods.

"So Nil is the essence of Death?"

She shrugs. "Nil is the name given to the essence of Death. It means '*to take from life.*'"

I replay her words, trying to wrap my brain around it all. We walk another mile into the thick maze of odd-shaped rocks, until we reach a boulder that has a tunnel hollowed out into it. "Hide the sled in there," she says. "The rebels will retrieve it from here."

I slide the sled into the small alcove. Once it's fully hidden from the elements, I drop the ropes and turn back for the city wall.

"Can I ask you something?" Helina asks, gripping her fur cloak tighter.

When I nod, she says, "How did you end up in Baratrum?"

The memory is slow to come, and when it does, it's hazy. "One minute I was staring down the barrel of Mazzar's gem gun," I say, "then after he shot the bullet through my chest, I was swarmed by shadows . . ." I still feel their claws inside, still hear their awful whispers and feel their coldness . . . Such terrible coldness.

"When the shadows receded and I regained consciousness, I was in Baratrum, and Nil had control over my soul."

After a stretch of silence, she asks, "What's it like?"

"What? Being controlled by Nil?"

"Everything," she says. "Nil, Baratrum . . . your last ten years."

"I rarely see Nil, and I've spent the majority of my last ten years in isolation. I've only seen two others like me." I look up at the sky and just talk. "Nil controls me as if I'm merely an extension of himself. If he wants me to hunt souls, which he does often, I simply get the urge to do it—and I can't resist. If he wants me to stay put in Baratrum for days at a time, I do. Sometimes he orders me to hunt for myself. I'd rather wither away into nonexistence, but the shadows still lurk inside me . . . and they always crave souls. They're hard to resist."

"Is that how he controls you? The shadows?"

"Honestly, I don't know how he does." A chill runs down my spine as the shadows curl inside my soul. "The shadows seem more like his pets . . ."

She tilts her head. "And Baratrum?"

"Cold," I say.

"Colder than this?"

I brush my hand through the air. "This cold is nothing. It remains outside of your body. The cold in Baratrum sinks through you as if its sole purpose is to torture."

She shivers.

I look at her. Her soul is a deep red, just like her hair, with the tiniest of dark spots. Most of her memories are blocked, but the ones I can see are of hardship after hardship. Abuse after abuse. "How about you? How long have you been with Jasper?"

She shivers from a draft of icy wind. "A year." After a moment, she looks to the horizon. "He takes care of my daughter and he's . . . very attentive to me."

After a long awkward silence with still a mile left to walk, I ask, "How'd you meet?"

"He saw me dancing and decided I was his." She huffs a laugh. "When he wants something, he gets it."

After another long silence she asks, "What does Nil plan to do to the princess if you deliver her soul?"

A surge of guilt clenches my stomach. *No human feelings*, I remind myself, but the lurch doesn't go away. "I'm sure Nil will want to own her soul like he does mine. He said she has power. He likely wants it for himself." But now that I know what a pure soul is, I wonder . . . what kind of power.

She frowns. "You mentioned that Jasper's cousin is your backup plan. What is your current plan?"

I kick a pebble across the barren dirt, and it skips onto a patch of snow. "I've seen some of her desires," I say. "She doesn't let on, but she longs for companionship."

Her brows pinch, and something like compassion enters her honey gaze. "So, you plan to exploit that?"

"I have no choice."

As we near the Zarr wall, I ask again if she's seen my sister in the camps.

Her memories flash by of the times she's visited her daughter, but I don't see Lo in them. They stop on a woman who I don't recognize, before she says, "I haven't. But I know someone who might know more."

CHAPTER 30

NIZZARA

DIARY: PAGE 13

Normally, I could catch an infantry general punching a stone wall and carry on about my day, except Mazzar cracked said wall. And I swear, his hair flickered from his usual, exotic white to a depthless black. So, I did some digging. Turns out he's not from Zarr. It also turns out he took a fleet of Zarr infantry somewhere very far away without my brother's orders. And by very far away, I mean another realm. Few creatures can travel the realms, and even fewer can alter their appearance.

    I think I know what Mazzar is—if that's even his real name.

—*Lo*

MY GUARDS REMAIN OUTSIDE THE BOOK COVE DOOR. A door that's different from the rest of the castle.

Older.

The designs etched in the black iron are symbols in another language from another time. The door's heavy weight glides shut behind me, and I descend between two walls of books that grow taller as the spiraling stairs sink downward. With each step, I become more and more grateful for Preysee's salves. They siphon much of my pain away, even my sore muscles from training feel better.

Liha floats in and out of my shield as she does after my punishments, with too much nervous energy to stay put.

Mother sits beside a fireplace with a stack of Zo books at the base of her chair. Her legs are tucked beneath her, and she's leaning one arm over the armrest, the other hand clutching a small book. Sometimes I wonder if she goaded Father into sending her to live down here because she prefers books to people.

"Nizzara." Her eyes rise above the rim of the book. Like always, there's an additional level of hatred when they're aimed at me. I breathe in the smell of books to ebb the familiar ache of loneliness coursing through me.

Mother drapes her book over the armrest. "What can I do for you?"

I'm surprised she's talking to me. Then again, she is the acting librarian, since the last was executed for aiding rebel supply chains, and I think Father ordered her to locate books for me when I visit.

"I need a book about the Jaxelli, a book on gems, and one of the usual." My insatiable brain still hasn't let go of Thaddeus's mention of energy gems. I know the red blare gems amplify energy, and the black void gems *siphon* energy, but what did he mean about their illegal uses?

Mother raises a sleek brow. "The first one belongs to my private stack, the second is on the third level, and scholars frown on the last."

"That's why I asked for a two-to-one ratio. Two educational books to one romance novel." I meet her gaze, silently begging her to lend me the book from her collection.

"Ha," she says. It's the closest thing to a laugh I've ever heard from her. "That's what I'll tell the scholars next time they look at my stack of books." She picks up her book again as if she's fulfilled her duty to help me by telling me their location. I look out over the iron railing into nothing but darkness. Most of the glo gems have slowly died out down here, and Father still hasn't had them replaced. After my stunt with the Zem heir, though, I'm sure the glo gems from the Zem mines will cost extra.

"Can you lead me to them? I might get turned around in the dark."

She glares at me, her jaw working until the tiniest flash of regret—or perhaps guilt—flickers in her gaze. "Fine."

She rises to her feet, and purple smoke falls from her golden vessel. It summons the glo lantern from the nearby desk through the air, until it's levitating above her head.

She waves for me to follow, the glo lantern hovering behind her as she leads me to the stairs. I peer over the railing to the dark levels below, thinking how small this library is compared to the one in Zo. Mother's living quarters are on the top level, and below are ten floors of books, but the Beacon of Zo has towers with bridges between them and hundreds of levels.

The darkness gets oilier the farther we dip.

We reach the landing, and Mother silently leads me through dusty, squat shelves. Here, alone with her in the depths of the library, I finally build the courage to ask something I've been mulling over since I arrived.

"The preliminaries have a warm-up duel before the festivities begin," I say, a pinch forming in my chest. "Would you be my partner for it?" Mother was a good dueler in her younger years, and I'd love to spar with her just once.

"No. I'm practicing with Tarella while you're gone."

The pinch sharpens. "You're not coming to the preliminaries?"

"Tarella has a level-three duel she needs to prepare for."

Liha's feathery being brushes my cheek as if she senses my growing heartache.

I take a steadying breath. "The preliminaries aren't until late evening. Couldn't you practice with her earlier? So you could be there for both of us?"

Her shoulders stiffen as she walks ahead of me. "I can't. She has a concert in the afternoon."

"And you're attending it?"

Her voice sharpens, but she doesn't so much as look over her shoulder. "Yes."

"*Let it go, Nizzara,*" Liha whispers in a soft voice. "*You don't need her there anyway.*" I feel a wave of Liha's power slip into me, but it's so subtle I almost don't notice.

I ignore Liha, pushing past the undeniable feeling that my mother just doesn't want to come. "What about practicing with her tonight instead?"

"I am. We have the training room scheduled for later this evening." Her voice hardens. "I'm not coming to your duel."

And there it is.

"Why do you detest me so much?" It comes out a whisper, but darkness begins to fester deep inside, and my rage builds. Years of similar conversations boil through my mind. It's always Tarella first, and Tarella only. Every time I try to connect with her, it's like this. Cold, hurtful responses.

"*Nizzara, calm down,*" Liha says. "*Breathe.*"

Mother halts in front of me with her back to me still and says, "No more questions."

She resumes her brisk pace, fists clenched, but I stomp after her, following down the dark alcoves full of dusty books that get shabbier the farther we go.

"Just tell me why," I say, my voice breaking from pain and loneliness and rage—always rage—until black spots appear in my vision.

I love books like she does, love angry music like she does. We have the same taste in desserts, the same desire for scholarly conversations. Tarella shares none of that.

"Why do you love her more?"

She stops in front of a decaying shelf but still does not face me, so I round on her to force the issue.

"Why?" I plant myself there, ready to hear about my anger issues, my lack of political tact, or how I disgrace my Zo heritage with my white hair and lighter skin, but she says nothing. Things around me begin to change as the darkness continues to grow—I sense Liha's power, but also my mother's . . . and the power of the glo lantern above. They all feel ripe and available . . .

"Nizzara! Go back to the top level and calm down."

Mother goes to step around me, her jaw clenched shut, but I step in front of her.

"Answer me."

She grits her teeth. "We are here to get books, not discuss *feelings.*"

She's not even denying it. I try to talk myself back from that black endless abyss threatening to suck me in. "Is it because I look like Father? I know you hate him, but I—"

"We're *not* discussing this."

She attempts to push past, but I need to know, and my rage winds tighter and tighter inside me, until blackness bleeds further into my vision, and instead of blocking her path, I shove her back.

"Why! Why do you treat me like I am nothing to you?" Tears break free.

"Breathe, Nizzara," Liha pleads, but her voice is distant.

Mother jolts away from me, her balled fists shaking at her sides, and a heady concoction of rage and fear on her face. "Because you are not mine!" she shouts.

The dark tunnels around us absorb her words faster than I do. But when they sink in, they cut—slicing into a layer of hope I didn't realize I was clinging to.

"What?"

She shoves me back. "Before I was *forced* to marry your father," she says, tears welling, "I was in love with a servant, and I fell pregnant with his child."

"Tarella," I whisper.

She backs away from me, her lips pressed into a hard line. "I was the second chosen heir to the Zo kingdom until my father found out I carried a servant's child. He killed Jock when I was barely ten weeks along and arranged the marriage to your father, who was the Zarr infantry general at the time.

"I wanted nothing to do with your father, so I stayed in Zo during the first years of our marriage while he led the Zarr infantry. He didn't care about me either, so it worked. After I had Tarella, I struggled to recover. I locked myself in my own wing with only one servant. Nine months went by, and that's when your father brought you to me. He told me if I wanted Tarella to live, then I would claim you as my own."

Her face tightens. "Then he killed the only witness who knew you were not mine." Her steel-hard gaze bores through me. "I can't help my resentment of being forced to raise someone like you. You drained me and everyone who tended you."

I swallow, my throat tightening. "Then who is my real moth—"

She points her finger at me. "If you care about my life, this conversation has to be over."

Did my real mother leave me? Does *no one* want me? Am I that awful?

Her face hardens in the white light of her glo lantern floating above, and when I don't fill the silence, she says, tears still glistening, "It is time to find your books."

With a jolt of Liha's power, the darkness recedes from my sight.

SORIAH LEADS ME AS WE PASS ROWS OF SHELVES IN SILENCE. I battle against myself, controlling my expression despite the fiery sting of her words and the lingering throb from Father's whip. With every step I take, it becomes harder to see through my tears.

"Here," she says, pulling the spine of a thick book. "A book on gem theory." She turns back to the stairs. I follow as she weaves deftly between the maze of shelving until she finds the wall of books she was looking for. "A romance novel," she says. "And the other one is up top on my stack."

When we return to the top, I follow her to her living quarters. Soriah pushes the iron door inward, and it swings open.

I step through the doorway and into a study with a hallway leading to more rooms. The room is old but ornately decorated. The glo gems still work in this room, so she rests the lantern on a luxurious black desk with a wave of purple smoke and plucks a book from her private bookshelf beside her fireplace.

"A book about the Jaxelli."

I take it from her, but she doesn't let go. "I have plans to leave, Nizzara."

My hand freezes on the binding. "What?"

Liha fades from my shield for the umpteenth time, my emotions probably too intense for her.

Soriah looks at the open door behind me. "I cannot stay here much longer. You are betrothed now, accepted into society as my legitimate, royal heir, because I've repeatedly claimed you through every political dinner, ball, court, and duel. This will be solidified when you marry. Your father will have no more use for me, and that's a very dangerous thing."

"But—"

"I plan to take Tarella with me."

"Of course you do."

Alone. I will be alone. Even though I am not close with them . . . I want them to stay.

Liha bops in and out, too anxious from the tension, but returns to say, "*You will have me.*"

She nudges me with her warm pocket of air, her voice seeming distant as my world continues to crumble.

"Will you take me?" My voice cracks. I know I'm not perfect. That I have a temper and say things I don't mean, but I'm trying—

"Even if I *wanted* to take you, your father would hunt me down and kill me for it."

There it is. She doesn't want me either. I have nowhere to look but the ceiling as more tears betray me. "Where will you go?"

"Nowhere that concerns you."

When she looks at my face, a flash of pity crosses her expression. She makes to touch my shoulder, but before she does, her fingers ball to a fist and she drops her arm away.

She pulls one more book off her shelf. "Raising you . . . There were signs of what you are." She shakes her head. "Since everyone is too scared of what you'll become to tell you, I will leave this for you to learn it yourself. You can come back for it after I leave. If your father sees—"

"Soriah!" Father's voice booms from a distance.

Soriah shoves the book back onto her shelf and ushers me out of the hidden room, closing the door behind us. "Fix your face, Nizzara," she orders as she stalks past me.

For once, I can't *fix* my damned face, so I call on our Mark to filter out my unwanted emotions as I follow.

"Do not ignore me, Soriah!"

"We're here," she calls to him.

Another two bookshelves and we are back at the staircase that leads up into the castle. Father's expression lightens some when he sees me with her. I've always wondered how my Mark makes me look in Father's eyes, much more ruthless, no doubt.

"Nizzara," he says as if he is pleased to see me, as if he wasn't just whipping my back thirty minutes ago. The way he'd disappeared surges into my mind again. I make a mental note to analyze it later, when I have a moment to think.

"Mother curated some books for me."

He looks at Soriah as he motions me to come with a flick of his fingers. "Show me."

"A history of the Jaxelli Warriors," he says, approval clear in his tone, before snatching the next one. "Gem theory." His brows tighten. "And—"

He takes the last one. "A romantic novel. What rubbish." He hands them back to me then says, "Go to the training room and practice for your preliminaries tomorrow. Sorren is gone, but you know what you should be doing."

I glance at Soriah before leaving, wondering if this will be the last time I see her, but she doesn't look at me, not even to say goodbye.

CHAPTER 31

NIZZARA

DIARY: PAGE 14

I know what else lies in Tigous's private library behind the Zo throne. Prophecies. In my time impersonating a scholar, I've learned there are many creatures who can see futures. Like the notorious goddess of life, Wala. She sees the future in pathways and can see all possibilities stemming from one point in time. I can only imagine the size of her books.

—*Lo*

WHEN I EMERGE FROM THE COVE DOOR, BRUNAR SUMMONS a maid for my books and leads me toward the training room, even though it's the last place I want to go.

Liha whispers, *"I don't think you should read that book Soriah left. At least for a while."*

There's only one reason Liha ever keeps me from doing anything. To protect me. I don't have it in me to argue with her about it.

"Why don't you go play?" My emotional state is probably wearing on her. In fact, I'm surprised she's still here.

"But we're supposed to train for tomorrow."

"I'm not in the mood."

She nudges me with her warm pocket of air. *"Let's practice, like we're supposed to."*

I grit my teeth. *"Liha, I'm sore, tired, and hungry. I may be going to the training room, but I'm not moving a realms-damned thing."*

"But the preliminaries—"

"Don't mean anything. No killing blows are allowed, and losses don't count. It doesn't matter if I rank last. I'll just get a shitty tournament schedule, and I'll manage it."

She sniffs. *"Very well."* And she leaves.

My guards perform a sweep through the weights and weapons, then station themselves outside the only door.

I find the squat bar and sit in front of it. No one is around. The weights are racked. The lights are dimmed. The silence and darkness seem to grow the longer I sit, staring up at the bar, trying to breathe. All I can think about are the countless times I convinced myself that deep down, she loved me.

A cool, velvet sensation brushes my shoulders like a cloak of night. *"In the middle of a demanding workout, I see."*

"I don't want company."

Dae's darkness envelops my senses, tucking me away into a precious cloud of *him*.

"Hmm, then why do your desires ask me to stay?"

I scoff. "Because I'm weak." Apparently, my desires do not hide from him as easily as they do from Liha.

"I doubt that very much."

His presence brushes near my cheek, sending a jolt of icy fire through my caster's shield, like lightning in a winter storm. I close my eyes, savoring it because somehow, it soothes the churning in my chest.

There's a stretch of silence and my stomach takes the opportunity to growl.

His cold air stirs around me. *"It sounds like you need to eat."*

As if on cue, a bout of lightheadedness hits me. Did I even have breakfast today? I lean back against the padded bench behind me and wince from the concealed lashes on my back, still tender but not excruciating, thanks to the salve.

"I can't eat."

"Don't tell me you are on one of those diets—"

"All that's ever served is meat." Tears break free. "Have you ever watched a man's head be severed from its body?" I ask. "Do you know what it looks like? *Raw. Meat.*" My father's executions surge into my mind, making my hands shake. "He forces me to eat meat, sometimes. Just to prove that he can."

The temperature around me drops until my breath clouds in front of me.

"So you starve?"

My fists curl, the cold air biting into my fingers as they bend. "It's my only way of making a point."

"What is your point? How long you can go without passing out?"

"That I'll be able to rule without killing," I say, glaring at where his condensed ball of swirling air hovers above. "That control, power, and ruthlessness can exist *without* killing!" My fists tremble in my lap, from anger or the growing cold, I'm not sure. Images of heads rolling, blood spurting, and the sounds of loved ones screaming take over my thoughts.

His voice sharpens. *"Speak of something else."*

"Like what?" Like how half of my family tree just disappeared?

"Tell me about your friend who gave you the snake ring," he whispers.

"Yisabell?" I rest my chin on top of my knees, curling my hand with the ring closer to my cheek. "She's from Badadwom. In the far north, like all Awoms."

When I don't say anything else, he settles beside me, taking his full, human shape as if he too is leaning against the bench beside me. *"Go on,"* he says.

Tension releases from my shoulders. "She was brought here when she was five. Even then, she was too intelligent for her age." A hint of a smile tugs my lips. "She's like a wise, old protector mashed with the silly desires of a twelve-year-old girl."

The cold air softens around me, becomes more fluid, calming, even. *"You know, it's said that the Awoms were once protectors of the realms."*

"I know. That's why they worship the—Wait. You're speaking Awom?" I turn to face him.

He continues in Awom, his pronunciation perfect. "*I am skilled in many things, Nizzara.*"

Despite the cold, my skin heats when he says my name like that.

I clear my throat. "I told you about Yisabell. Now tell me something about you."

There's a pause. "*What do you wish to know?*"

"Something real," I say.

I'm surrounded by false faces.

False emotions.

False *family members*.

"I need something real."

After an even longer pause he says, "*My mother passed away during childbirth when I was seven.*" His spirit swirls in a more frenzied pattern as he speaks. "*The day before she passed, I threw a tantrum over some stupid toy, mad she wouldn't buy it from this peddler on the road. We had the money for it, and I knew my father would've bought it, but she said I should buy it for another child who needed a toy, since I had plenty. After an hour of my kicking fit, pushing her to the end of her patience, she told me she'd sooner die than raise a selfish, spoiled son. Later that night, she kissed me good night, told me she loved me, and died a few hours later, having gone into premature labor while I slept. My little brother passed too.*"

"I'm sorry," I say.

The chill through the air is heavy and sad as he faces me, his misty head inches from mine. Lifting my hand, I reach out toward him. He stiffens, or at least his dark air stops swirling. I place my hand where his wide chest should be. My vessel hums on my finger as I brush through cold air, and I wonder if our desires align—I've read that can be important in bonding with spirits. That has to be the reason for this undeniable current coursing through me when he's near.

"What is it you desire?" I ask.

He takes a long time to answer. The air shifts from cold to colder around my hand. "*Honestly,*" he says, leaning closer, "*I desire you.*"

My throat dries. "You wish to bond with me?"

"*Among other things.*"

Heat blossoms in my cheeks. He must be like Liha, a shameless flirt in his afterlife.

"I'm already bonded. And I will not abandon Liha."

"*Even if it meant winning the King's Duel?*"

I drop my hand from him. "No, not even if it meant winning."

There's a pause before he says, "*You wouldn't have to abandon Liha. You can take multiple spirits into your shield, remember.*"

It doesn't matter. I could never do that to Liha. I know how her mind works, and she would see that as a betrayal.

Dae is silent, letting me work through my thoughts as I imagine two spirits in my shield. I think of Liha's babbling, about fashions and nonstop gossip, but also the amount of power . . .

"Two bonded spirits sounds like a headache," I say.

"*Do you have a headache now, talking to me?*"

"No."

He tilts his head, and I imagine some sort of smirk on his face. "*See, you'd do fine. You'd have more power—*"

"I don't *want* more power."

Does no one get it?

"Power corrupts those who touch it, especially people like me."

"*Nizzara,*" he purrs. "*I assure you, just because I am older, more experienced, and all around devilishly handsome, I would only corrupt you if you verbally consented to my corrupting.*"

He is definitely a shameless flirt and undeniably Zarr. A smile breaks through my lips, but the weight of what we're really talking about pulls it back down. I stand up and go to the smooth black bar, racked at the same height I last used it.

"I'm serious," I say. "I don't want to become a monster, brimming with power and no control over it."

A flash of my father's descent into madness takes over my thoughts.

The night he came home drunk in the most violent rage over something I was too young to grasp . . . He got better for a time, but then he stole the throne and the First-Made vessel. The rages, punishments, and executions followed. It isn't like he was a *model* person before, but he wasn't the person he is now.

At least, not with me.

A tongue of ice writhes through the air and I shiver. Dae's presence glides over to face me, opposite the bar.

"You can choose not to be a monster."

A humorless laugh puffs from my lips. "Can such things be chosen?"

I think of my rage that's always near the surface. It is not my choice, and when that rage gets within reach of power . . .

"I've seen monsters, Nizzara, and you are not one of them. A little beast, maybe, but not a monster."

I huff, shoving down the sensation that tightens through my abdomen when his outline towers this close in front of me. "You must've won many ladies with that *exact* compliment." I allow myself to imagine what his voice would sound like whispering sweet nothings—or just my name—in my ear. Allow myself to admit I want that more than I let on.

"Oh, absolutely, I did." He leans down until his airy head is right beside my ear. *"The women loved it when I'd whisper sweet nothings, but they went feral when I'd call them by name, Nizzara."* That invisible smile seeps into his voice.

How does he know—

"You stay out of my traitorous desires. They don't know a damned thing about me."

A deep, midnight laugh rumbles through the air, intensifying the heat through my cheeks and neck. I shove off the bar and walk around to where the big round plates hang on the wall. I grab the twenty-fives, load one on each side—ten more pounds than Sorren pushed on me.

"Aren't you tired?" he says, a smirk still obvious in his tone.

"I am. In every possible way. I'm tired." I adjust my dress and kick off my shoes.

"And lifting weights will make you less tired . . . ?"

I get under the bar and heave with everything I have. My sore, tortured legs tremble. My back throbs, but I manage one full squat, crying out at the weight of everything on my shoulders.

"How I *feel* does not dictate what I do." Re-racking the bar with a satisfying *clang*, I lay my head against the solid bar and close my eyes to block out the *spinning*. "At least, I want that to be true."

My stomach offers a hollow, nauseating grumble. I'm glad Sorren is not here to wipe the floor with me tonight.

"You know you can't keep up with your training without enough food." Is that a growl in his voice?

I look at the empty room behind me in the mirror. "'One does not become resilient under ideal conditions.'"

"Are you quoting Marko's works to me?" A smirk curls in his voice and, realms, I wish I could see it. It sounds dazzling, if that's possible. To hear a smirk and know it's dazzling. *"You'll have to try much harder to stump me."*

I smile and think of a harder line. One of my favorites. "'To look upon the worst and see the best is true sight.'"

Dae goes stone still before he whispers, "'*To behold the whole and find no flaws, only then can one be right.*'" He whispers, "Love from a Blind Prince."

"My old tutor said nobody in the three kingdoms should read that book because it's too *soft*."

"But you've read it."

I shrug, sliding my gaze toward his presence, which is now leaned up against the far mirror. "Tell me not to do something, and I can't resist."

His presence jets past my legs, under the bar, and re-forms into his full height behind me.

"In that case, never kiss a spirit," he says at the base of my ear. *"It might set the bar too high for poor mortal men."*

I laugh. Actually laugh. "Kissing a ghost"—I struggle to get the words out—"I might as well kiss the wind from a cart cow's ass."

I remember the day our court comedian told me that cart cow joke. It's still the funniest joke I've ever heard. I giggle harder, tears breaking free. I think I might be delusional from hunger, or emotional trauma, but I don't care because, realms, it feels good to laugh.

Dae's dark laugh rumbles around me, eclipsing all else. We laugh together until happy tears run down my cheeks. Slowly our laughter ebbs until it settles into a charged silence between us.

"*The funniest jokes always have a thread of truth, you know,*" he says.

There *has* to be a smirk on that ghostly face of his.

"Are you referring to your joke about kissing spirits? Or my joke about cart cows?"

"*Wouldn't you like to know.*"

I roll my eyes. "You are a shameless flirt."

He chuckles. "*Perhaps.*"

I turn my head over my shoulder, looking to where his wall of a presence guards my back. "Thank you," I whisper.

He moves closer, until my shield hums across my back, his chest brushing against it. "*For what?*"

I turn to fully face him, studying the outline of his head, wishing I could see the color of his hair or the shape of his lips. "For making me laugh."

The air around us thaws, a silent current humming between us until the door to the training room barrels open. I jump.

"Your time is up," Tarella says. "I have the next hour in here."

Dae disappears, taking his addictive current with him.

I re-rack my weights. Thanks to Dae, I'm in good enough spirits to say, "Do you want me to stay? I can help you with your flips if—" I look around for Soriah, and my chest tightens all over again. "If Mother is late."

Her nose wrinkles. "I don't need your help." She points at the bruises on my neck. "By the way, your necklace is a beautiful shade of green."

The light feeling Dae left me with boils away. I try breathing through it, try not to say it, but my vision darkens and I find my voice slipping into a cold, lifeless tone. "If you like it so much, I'll give you a matching one."

She gasps and swings her fist up to hit my face. My fist connects before hers, snapping her head to the side. My body stays in motion, all muscle memory and reflexes. I tackle her to the ground and drive my fist again when she flinches away. My hands shake but I get off her and stand up.

Two deep breaths.

I point at her. "That right there is why you can't duel worth a shit. You're a coward. Face your fear," I say. "Or it will own you."

I want to walk away.

Actually, if I'm really being honest, I still want to punch her. Our entire relationship is nothing but snide comments and forced niceties.

And jealousy.

She can be with anyone she wants because she's not the chosen heiress. She's never met a whip or my father's hand. *She has a mother.* But I still don't want us to be this way.

I offer her my hand. It feels equivalent to lending my flesh over to a rabid dog. She stares at it, then takes it, and I silently pull her up, not trusting my mouth or my fist. I leave before I can change my mind.

PREYSEE BALKS AS I ENTER MY ROOM. "YOU LOOK HAGGARD."

I can't even bring myself to shrug.

She looks around, then lowers her voice. "I'm going to the lesser district tonight." Her hand goes to her neck, where a gleam of metal peeks out from her maid uniform.

My heart lurches for Palko, who will have to spend another night in the dungeon.

I nod. "Go."

Preysee's gaze lingers on my bruises. "Are you sure you don't need me—"

"I'm sure. Go."

She nods and leaves my room.

CHAPTER 32

DAGEN

WHY DO HER MEMORIES HAVE TO CRUSH MY DEAD HEART in a vise?

I slipped.

I looked through them, and it was a big mistake. I try tossing her memories out of my mind like a sinking seaman bailing out his boat.

My mother. I told her about my mother.

The wind catches my collar as I grip the tallest spire of the castle. The guards march across the rooftop, far enough below to resemble rolling pebbles. Back and forth.

My mother.

It was because of Nizzara's memory, deep in the coves, following Soriah. I felt her heart break when she realized she truly has no one.

I would've refrained from telling her about my mother, if not for the rest of her memories, ones with her father forcing her to eat meat, getting beaten to a realms-damned pulp by Sorren, protecting Yisabell. I think back to one of the first memories of hers—remember her threatening Brunar ...

It was to protect Yisabell.

I saw the snake ring on her finger and heard how she told Yisabell she'd never take it off ...

I should be inside the castle, giving her compliments, making her laugh, offering to help her win the King's Duel. Doing everything to earn her trust.

The only problem with that—the biggest fucking problem here—is that the smiles, the compliments, the laughs are *real*.

All because I can't stay out of her memories. Those sinfully addictive, warm memories.

One thing is certain.

My mother would've liked her.

I knew it the moment she dropped the second cloak to Palko.

My mother would've liked her very much.

I wish that was enough to change things, to deny Nil, but I am a deathwalker. My *feelings* don't mean anything.

I think of the Skeeves outside the city wall. The starvation, the executions, and the terrible living conditions in Zarr.

My people need me.

I let go of the spire and free-fall toward the pebble-size guards in black uniforms. I fall until the icy wind coaxes tears from my eyes, until the guards are the size of guards. They don't look up, and at the last possible second, I dissipate.

I'M ONLY DOING THIS TO GAIN NIZZARA'S TRUST.

Not because she was swaying on her feet in the training room.

Gaining her trust. That's the reason I'm in my physical form, rummaging through the kitchens. I find mineral biscuits in the pantry, a plate in the black cabinets, and some cheese in the cooling locker. Manipulating her is wrong, but I lost the chance of being a decent human when I was sucked away to Baratrum.

A scuff comes from outside the kitchen doors. My head snaps in that direction, listening.

I can only imagine the look on the chef's face if he stumbled in here at this hour to see me, the deceased king dressed in Red's suit and tie, looking for *cheese*. Another muffled scuff comes.

After straining to listen again, I decide it's just the guards stationed outside the double doors. I'm about to quietly close the door to the cooling locker when I see a glass pitcher of cart cow milk. I can't help it. I am doomed to smile every time I see *anything* to do with a cart cow. That joke in Nizzara's memory was the funniest damn joke I've ever heard.

I go to close the big steel door again when it dawns on me. Cart cow milk has a lot of protein, which she needs. Especially for her training sessions with Sorren. I try not to think about that memory of her sparring with him.

Because, realms. I felt so much of *her* in it. How much pain she can take. How she does not quit, even when she is so incredibly outmatched, without the use of her vessel.

I pour a glass of milk and, out of habit, try to spirit to her room, but I can't. I curse the delicate laws of spirit magic. The clothing I'm wearing is fine, but not a fucking dinner plate? I try to spirit away again, but I remain in my physical form as long as I'm holding the plate.

How convenient.

I survey the servant tunnels, just beyond the pantry, then glance back to the plate. This is the most idiotic plan, but I sip the milk down from the rim, so it doesn't spill on my way. And realms-damn it, I almost choke laughing because it's *cart cow* milk.

I wonder how long it will take the shadows inside to dull this joke in my mind like they do everything else.

Slinking to the other side of the kitchen, I realize Nizzara made me laugh, something I haven't done in ten years. Maybe longer.

I also realize I'm risking a *lot* to bring her a plate of food.

No, no, no—not bringing her food.

Gaining her trust.

After climbing into the servants tunnel, something else dawns on me. I can't *tell* her the food is from me unless I also plan on telling her how I was able to carry it. Something like, *"I'm a demon from Baratrum who is here to steal your soul, who also tried to run you through with a shadow blade two nights ago, and who still plans on killing you at some point in the near future."*

Hmm. Could use work.

I turn back for the kitchen, abandoning this stupid idea, only to stop when I think of her white ponytail whipping in the winter wind as she dropped her last cloak between Palko's cell bars.

So cruel of her to steal my thoughts this way. A *thank-you*. That's all this is.

For a kindness done to one of my subjects . . . and for reminding me what it feels like to laugh.

I add this to my list of reasons and continue back up the dim tunnel. The dark servants tunnels are a maze behind the walls of the castle with guards positioned near every entrance and exit.

The trek through the arched tunnels is the easy part. Most of the servants are asleep, making it quick work up to the fourth floor. But that's where the tunnels end and all the castle guards begin.

As I near the final length of the tunnel, I set the plate and cup on the ground and turn to spirit. I map out the remaining distance to Nizzara's tower. One long corridor, a right, another long corridor, then the climb to her tower, where her guards wait.

Including Nizzara's seven guards, there's fourteen guards between me and her door. The shadows slither inside. *"Let her starve."*

But the old me, buried under the shadows, whispers, *"Keep going."*

I find a hallway away from my route and touch down, materializing onto the plush black and gold runner in front of a row of massive paintings, one of which is a portrait of Mazzar. It doesn't take me long to choose which painting to smash on the ground. A loud crash throughout the corridor. Who knew terrorizing things could be so satisfying?

Footsteps stampede down the corridors, racing toward me. I turn to spirit and soar over the heads of five guards as they round the corner.

I solidify, grab the food, and run it through the first corridor, which is now empty. When I reach the next hallway, I set the plate and cup down again to peek around the corner. Two more guards stand at the base of Nizzara's circling staircase, and I know her seven personal guards are at the top.

After turning to spirit, I fly to another hall for another distraction.

Two guards march down this hall, but the walls are bare, no picture frames.

I look up. A giant, intricate chandelier dangles halfway down the stretch of hallway, hanging by an iron chain. I soar toward the chain, materialize midair, slice with my blade mid-flip, and phase back to spirit.

The chandelier takes three whole seconds to plummet before thundering against the marble floor. The black and gold rug does little to soften the sound as black shards of crystal gems, spikes, and chains explode at the point of impact. Brunar and five of his guards come running, meaning he left one at Nizzara's door.

I make another run with the food and hide it at the base of the steps before turning to spirit to deal with the last guard. I'm about to materialize behind him and land a blow to his temple when a guard calls for him below. He grips his sword and stalks down the steps.

Lucky him.

I return for the plate and am darting up the last stretch of stairs toward Nizzara's door when the air freezes around me.

Baratrum ice creeps along the walls, pooling into an empty space beside me. I set the plate and glass down with a soft *tap* on the marble floor, and my shadow blade is in my hand before I'm fully turned to the source.

"You always did make a good delivery boy." The figure emerges from the dark corner of the dead-end hall.

"Fen," I say, ice rolling through my dead veins. "What do you want?"

"What? No warm greeting for your brother-in-arms?"

He swings his shadow blade like a pendulum at his side as he strides toward me, shadows clinging to his frost-burned fingers. His blackish-blue hair is ice-blown from the winds of Baratrum, and his deadly gaze pierces through me.

When I tighten my grip on my hilt, he smiles. "I'm just here to bring you a message from our handler."

Footsteps begin trodding up the base of the stairs. Nizzara's guards. "Say your message, then."

His gaze pointedly falls to the plate of food outside Nizzara's door, then back to me, still smiling. "I came to remind you what will happen if you fail your bargain."

Ice crawls down my arms as I step toward him, the tip of my shadow blade edging closer to his uniform.

"I know what will happen."

The climbing footsteps grow closer.

He grins, looking every bit the ruthless, pillaging war general from his past life. "I also came to inform you that *I* will be your replacement if you fuck up." He leans his shoulder against Nizzara's door. "Considering how delicious she looks through your memories, I really hope you fuck up."

My jaw tightens. "You can tell Nil I received his message."

Fen flashes a memory into his thoughts, knowing I will see it. It's him, seducing a woman before tearing her soul from her flesh.

"I bet the princess will moan for me like a—"

I plunge my blade toward his chest, but he vanishes into inky mist before contact, only to materialize behind me. I can't kill him with my blade, but damn, it would be satisfying to bury it through his flesh. It would still be every bit as painful for him.

"You're down to two moon cycles," he taunts before returning to spirit once more and leaving the castle.

I knock on the door before disappearing. The guards round the corner and Nizzara opens the door, dressed in a long bathrobe, her hair wet.

She looks at the plate of food then directly at me in my spirit form, and her brow raises.

"Halt," Brunar says to her, noticing the plate.

Nizzara goes to pick up the plate, but Brunar points his finger at her. "I said halt!"

She pins him with a glare worthy of the shadows in Baratrum, and he sputters an apology.

"There were two disturbances on the lower level," he explains.

She lifts the plate. "They weren't caused by a plate of biscuits, were they?"

"They could be poisoned, a trap—"

When her deadly black gaze bores through him, he flinches and averts his gaze.

Suddenly, a memory of hers flashes into my mind. The dining room snaps into place around me. I'm in Nizzara's point of view and—

I can't *breathe*. Mazzar's hand crushes my neck. Fear, pain, rage—and darkness—slash through me as Brunar and his men stand idle at my side, doing *nothing* to protect her.

Nizzara's thumping pulse thuds slower and slower beneath Mazzar's viselike fingers. Her vision darkens, fading in and out through the memory until Mazzar releases her. I catapult from the memory, gasping for my own air.

She shoves a biscuit up to Brunar's nose. "Are you willing to test them for me?"

He closes his eyes.

"That's what I thought," she says, and takes a bite of the biscuit herself, and I know it's just to spite him. Poison or no.

With the shadows still scraping their icy claws up my throat, longing to slay her guards, I decide to wait until the melee of anger and self-hatred calms before following Nizzara into her room. Because I'd been there too, hovering idly in the rafters as her father hurt her.

CHAPTER 33

NIZZARA

DIARY: PAGE 15

Coco and I hit a roadblock in the Zo library. I'm working it out, but it means we have some extra time at home, so I checked in on a little experiment of mine. As I've instructed, Preysee has been dropping off my brother's food trays to our live-in Zo scholar— who I've learned has been informing Zo about our military movements. And guess who has started limping. I checked the infirmary and found out he is complaining of bone pain too. Just like Father. Thankfully, Dagen hasn't shown any signs of poison, so Preysee has been doing her job. I'm going to have to properly thank her with a visit to Zem to see her niece. I don't know what I'd do without Dagen. He found me on the roof tonight. He knows if he finds me up there, I'm not okay. He sat by me, put his arm around my shoulder, and didn't say a word.

—Lo

AS SOON AS I SHUT MY GUARDS OUT OF MY ROOM, I CRUMPLE to the floor.

My body shakes from fatigue, hunger, and the hole Soriah punched through me.

I need food to calm my roiling stomach and trembling hands. Whether or not it's poisoned is a secondary concern.

The milk is cold, condensation gathering on the outside of the goblet.

My thoughts go to Dae. He was there outside my room, and I can't help but wonder if he had something to do with this plate of food. Preysee is gone, and Yisabell, along with all the bondslaves, is scrubbing the palace in preparation for my betrothed's arrival.

I skip over *that* thought.

I close my eyes and chew with my back against the door, grateful again for the numbing salve that still seems to be working. I plan to ask Dae about the plate of food when I see him again, and the thought of talking to him loosens something in my chest. It's a little thing, but it helps me breathe easier, until my mind wanders back to the book Soriah left in the coves—her words.

As much as I long to know what's in that book, I'm terrified to have my worst fear confirmed. That something *does* lurk inside me. That the darkness I feel is more than just my temper.

As if the darkness hears my thoughts, a tendril of it rises. My vision flickers, my worldview tilts, and my thoughts and emotions dip into a pool of cold, endless hatred. My thoughts spiral. *Pain, revenge, isolation, death—*

I jolt from the trance, my heartbeat racing and warmth returning to my mind. I stand up, brushing my shaking hands down my robe, chastising myself for letting my thoughts slip directly toward that darkness.

I know better than to think about it. It *likes* to be acknowledged.

I take deep breaths and push it far from my mind.

Once my plate is clean, I hobble to my closet and change into the sleeping gown Preysee left for me before facing my stack of books. I pluck the Jaxelli book out of my stack and climb onto my bed. I begin reading the history of the Jaxelli Warriors, pretending this is just another book recommended by my tutor, Thaddeus. *Not* a history of my betrothed's lineage.

I read, ignoring the subtle but nagging sensation of being shoved toward a deadly, jagged cliff inside myself. I feel my mind sliding closer and closer to the edge, overlooking an endless pit of darkness, knowing if I slip, there will be no returning. No coming back.

I'm reading about the unnaturally long lives of the Jaxelli when Dae's velvet voice caresses my senses. *"And you call me the flirt? What kind of sleeping attire is that?"*

I look up at the ceiling where he just feathered in above my bed.

I take the silky, midnight-blue material in my fingers. "The comfortable kind." My eyes dart back to him.

"Comfort is big and fluffy. That nightgown barely covers you."

My father's whip snaps in my mind, slashing through the skin on my back. "That's what makes it comfortable." The open back allows me to move without fabric rubbing against my wounds.

Ice coats the air, and his words come out clipped and angry. *"Let's talk about something else."*

"Like how you delivered food to my door?" My logical mind balks at the accusation, but my gut tells me I'm right. He knew I was hungry, knows I don't eat meat, and as he touches down to the floor taking his human silhouette, I'm also reminded he's not like other spirits.

"What makes you think it was me?"

It's not a denial, and I wonder if this is another thing Father doesn't want me to know about spirits.

"Just tell me how you did it."

His spirit drifts over to my bookshelves, a taunt in his voice when he says, *"How about you tell me why you almost kissed the Zem prince?"*

I glare at him. "Don't change the subject."

He stops eyeing my shelves and prowls toward me until he's at my bedside. Bending down and placing his ghostly arms on the edge of my bed—leaving no impression—he leans forward.

"Come on, Nizzara."

I sense his exact outline, the air swirling in different patterns where *he* begins. And his broad-shouldered outline is very close.

I think of my near-kiss with Kazem and shake my head. It was so stupid. So girlish.

The air moves as if he is reaching out his hand to brush his fingers across my caster's shield, over my shoulder. The cold storm of lightning sets my skin on fire. For a split second, I sense his desire. Desire, and frustration. Then it's gone.

"What will it take for you to trust me?" he says, his velvet tone slightly tortured.

I bite my lip. Damn that voice of his. "Tell me how you got a plate of food to my door. Are you bonded to someone else?"

Dae is silent for so long, I fold my arms, trying to smother my sudden, irrational jealousy. "So, you *are* bonded to someone."

He sighs. *"No, I am not bonded to anyone."*

"Then how are you capable of moving things on your own?"

His words are quiet. *"If I told you what things I'm capable of, you would run from me, Nizzara."*

A shiver works its way down my spine. I remember how he claimed to be alone before. How spirits steer clear of him . . . But I know what that feels like, to be alone.

As if he knows exactly what his voice does to me, he makes a low, rumbling sound. Ever since he made the comment about kissing spirits, I find myself imagining him. Alive and touchable, whispering in my ear, his lips brushing my—

"What exactly are you thinking about right now to make your desires so terribly scandalous?"

Damning heat floods to my cheeks. I swallow. "How about an exchange. I'll tell you what I was thinking, if you tell me how you moved a solid plate of biscuits on your own."

I convince myself—barely—that it will be worth the embarrassment to know; to have some insight into what kinds of dangerous things he's capable of. Plus, he's a spirit.

Embarrassment doesn't count with spirits, right?

"You are a cruel little beast," he says, and it has the tiniest hint of fondness in it. *"But I will take that deal. You go first."*

"I was thinking—" I clear my throat. "About your voice." My gaze falls to my fingers as I play with the edge of my nightgown. My vivid imagination replays the daydream for me in even steamier detail than before, and I bite my lip from the sudden heat rising through my center.

"*And?*" he prompts, a hint of desperation in his voice.

"And I was imagining what it would be like if you were alive—if I could touch you—while you told me exactly how you liked to be touched."

My heartbeat hammers in the silence.

Complete, unbreathing silence, until he says, "*You can tell me that, but you won't tell me about the almost-kiss?*" His voice suddenly sounds tighter.

I force my gaze up to him, arrange my lips into a smirk, and pretend my heart isn't beating just as hard as when I'm in the duel ring. "Try bringing chocolate next time. See what information that gets you."

"*Chocolate. That's the key to all your secrets?*"

I hold up my finger. "We aren't talking about me anymore. Now, tell me how you moved the plate."

"*I carried it,*" he says. "*In my hands.*"

I drop my brows flat. "But *how?* What power allows you to do that?"

"*You did not ask what power I have, just how I moved it. And I have told you.*"

I point directly at him. "Sometimes, I wish I could see your smug smirk just so I could wipe it off your face."

He laughs, and just like in the training room, its sound is wonderful.

I bite my lip to keep from smiling.

His laughter settles and his cold presence feels lighter. "*Be careful what you wish for, Nizzara. Many women have faced my smug smirk—as you call it—only to be dazzled by it.*"

I roll my eyes. "No one likes a cocky flirt."

"*Hmm,*" he purrs. "*Your desires say otherwise.*"

My throat goes dry. "What I desire"—I hold up my book—"is to read."

A soft chuckle. *"Not* The King of Kings *tonight?"*

"No. Not tonight." My mind is in knots from that book, trying to see meaning in every ink blotch.

"Ah, reading up on your betrothed, are we?"

I dip my chin and run my finger along a book corner.

"Find anything interesting?"

"It's pretty much the same as any other history of peoples. War, oppression, power, feuds."

"It troubles you?"

I close the book. "Have you read any of their history?"

"I know a little about the Light and Dark Jaxelli."

"The Light Warriors *tortured* the Dark ones for thousands of years, because they were afraid of their power."

The Awoms come to mind. Yisabell and her people have been hunted and feared long before my time. Even though they are a peaceful people, they're believed to harbor ancient magic regarding souls.

"It's not right."

"Just because your betrothed is Light doesn't mean he tortures his Dark siblings."

I trace my finger over a chapter heading. "Do you know anything about the Dark Jaxelli?"

"The Dark Jaxelli are very powerful. That's all I know."

My mind lingers on the torture devices used to restrain the Dark Jaxelli. "What if the Dark ones are just misunderstood?"

"Most people are," he says softly.

CHAPTER 34

DAGEN

NIZZARA PLACES THE JAXELLI BOOK ON HER NIGHTSTAND next to *The King of Kings* and three other books she appears to be working her way through.

I don't understand. Nil sends me to steal darkened souls. Murderers. Thieves. Traitors. Nothing about Nizzara is fitting that mold.

I mentally prepare myself to dive into her memories—again. There has to be something she did to deserve Nil's attention, something cruel and awful. The anticipation bubbles in my chest for her euphoric memories, but also dread. Because if I find nothing, I am doomed to wreck an innocent woman.

And if I do find something cruel and awful . . . A twinge sours my gut.

"Thank you for the food," she says, exhaustion clinging to her.

She lays her head down, a far-off gaze in those black eyes. A memory—the same one that has popped into her current thoughts at least four times tonight—surges into my mind again.

I'm there, in the coves surrounded by ancient books and shelves . . . and immense darkness. Soriah clenches her fists, her gaze hardening as she yells, *"Because you are not mine!"*

A crack splits straight through my chest. Every emotion Nizzara felt in that moment becomes mine. It hits me the same as it did last time, and the time before that.

Fucking hard.

I take a deep breath and take the plunge. Memories wash over me in a fury of blinding gold light and shimmering onyx. Emotions and images so strong my breath is sucked away. A lifetime of memories to sort through. They pulse past me, one after the other, like priceless fortunes flying by—too many to gather them all.

At a party at Zo castle, she shares her food with a bondslave, then bests a fifth-tier scholar at a trivial debate about the velocity needed to break a jawbone.

In the Zo library, a sixth-tier scholar tells her she can't read the Bible of Kiya in a day, so she does.

At a dress shop in Zarr city, she leaves gold ren for a pregnant woman to buy dresses.

In her room, crying.

In the training room, beating a punching bag until her knuckles are bloody.

In a room full of people, no one looking her in the eyes.

Her father slapping her for defending a bondslave. He recoils and apologizes to her before leaving, his fists trembling.

In the training room with her level-four duel coach, learning a standing backflip combined with a three-dagger throw. She watches it once and masters it on her first try.

Listening to Tarella sing at a spring concert.

Liha gossiping about the Zem queen.

Alone, standing over a hot bubble bath. So much physical pain. Pain in her back, like razors sawing back and forth across her skin, but her body is not visibly injured. Nothing but smooth, glistening skin when her robe falls—

I shut the memories down immediately and gasp from the weight of her emotions still flooding through me. When I finally regain my wits, I peer over to find her curled on her side, fast asleep, her long, smooth leg peeking out of that nightgown. Her hands clench the black satin sheets as she lets out a soft whimper.

A nightmare.

I tell myself it's because I need to gain her trust. That's why I do it. My ghost of a hand reaches out, brushing her fist that's balled in the sheets. When her fingers relax and the angle of her brows soften at my touch, I tell myself it's a coincidence.

Until her eyes flutter, and a memory pops into her sleepy consciousness.

She's in the training room, sitting on the floor, staring at the long, weighted bar.

She's in pain, on the verge of tears . . .

Until she hears my voice.

Until she feels my cool presence embrace her. And I *feel* the twinge in her chest, like a weight being removed in my presence.

The memory fades away as she's pulled into a deeper sleep.

I take her hand.

After she's long asleep, I materialize to turn off the chandelier lights, but when I reach the gem switch mounted on the wall, I find myself staring at her, not wanting to lose this view to darkness. Even in her sleep, she is regal and polished, her expression both soft and hard; her body is the same. If I didn't know a thing about her, I'd say she's the portrait of a natural-born ruler. But I do know things about her, and she is someone I'd choose to rule in my stead. I glance at her manicured nails and supple, soft skin, then down at myself. For the first time in ten years, I care about my appearance. I need a bath and a shave.

I shake my head. It doesn't matter what I look like.

I reach for the gem switch again but stop once more when I see her stack of books.

The Written History of the Jaxelli Warriors sits on top of *The King of Kings.*

Another glance at her sleeping face goads me into opening the Jaxelli book. A bookmark with notes scribbled on it falls out. I pick it up and read, smirking at her sharp, hurried handwriting.

The note has many points of their history, including their war between Light and Dark Warriors—along with an ancient feud with their cousin species, the Guardians. I read all her notes to the bottom of the bookmark, where she's mapped out the Jaxellis' six elemental powers:

Fire, Water, and Earth gifts are common to the Light Jaxelli.
Blood, mystic, and sky are more common for the Dark Jaxelli.

I slide the bookmark back in and stack it onto *The King of Kings*. I'm about to turn the light off when I spot a romance novel, and curiosity gets the better of me.

I slip it from the pile and flip through its pages until I reach her bookmarked page:

Together they laid in the wild grass, watching the stars. Her family hunted demons like him. She should let him go back to where he came from, and she'd return to the ball still raging in the distance. She was about to do just that for his sake when his fingers grazed hers.

First a graze, then a weaving and pulling. Gently, he tugged her closer, until their noses were a breath apart.

"I don't want you to get captured," she whispered.

He leaned closer, until his lips brushed hers. "You've already captured me." And he kissed her—

My eyes find Nizzara, roaming the smooth plains of her face, and her lips forming that sensual curve.

I run my thumb over the gem switch, turning the light off, and spirit away from her.

I don't even know where I'm going until the icy wind hits, sinking into my soul. I touch down and take a knee, bowing.

Nil forms in front of me. My shiver is not from the cold. It's from his shadow form.

"Why do you return empty-handed?" Nil's voice is a hiss of many souls.

"Why do you seek her?" I ask.

His pet shadows snap at me as if they know my question angers him. "That is not your concern."

"I will pay for the answers to my questions," I say before I come to my senses and change my mind.

A long dark shadow plunges through my chest. Unworldly pain erupts in every corner of my being as the shadow takes part of my soul, consuming a small shred of my being. When it is done, I feel the difference. If I could see my own soul, I know it'd be darker. My thoughts are sharper, warped in a way that allows less light in.

"I have paid," I say through clenched teeth.

"There is a war, and her power will become a very important piece in it."

"So, she has done nothing to *deserve* her capture?"

Nil hisses. "It's not what she's done. It's what she is."

His shadows crawl over me, nipping.

"What is she?" I grind out. "What is a pure soul?"

"Your little redheaded friend told you enough of pure souls," he says, his voices coming from all directions. "She is like me. Born of high power."

"That's why I cannot tear her soul? That's why she must give it to me?"

"Yes."

I clench my fists. "What will you do to her?"

"Many seek her. I am the lesser evil, I assure you."

My jaw tightens as I remain on my knee, unable to move until I'm released.

"If you fail, I will send another." Nil clips his words. "If you *fail*, you will cease to exist, and your kingdom will fall to ruin, Dagen Corvonna."

CHAPTER 35

DAGEN

WHEN I GET TO THE RED MASK, THE PATRONS ARE GONE, and the normally pristine club is a disaster. Dancers limp toward their living quarters above the bar—barefoot and dangling red heels at their sides. Blood and broken glass cover the floor, and almost every person is injured. I float past cleanup crews scrubbing floors and sweeping up the broken glass. Tired bouncers, with fresh cuts on their cheeks, lock the outside doors—which are also broken and hanging crooked. And weary bartenders with bloodstains on their white undershirts pick up knocked-over barstools.

I'm hovering near the stage, eyeing a giant blood splatter, when Jasper steps out from a private room. A cloaked individual in white slinks out behind him and disappears down the hall leading to the back exit. The rebel contact he's kept in his pocket, no doubt.

When I near him, he stiffens, goose bumps rising on his arms.

"It's been a long night," he groans, but returns to the private room, waving for me to follow.

"What happened?" I ask as he takes a seat.

His face remains blank, waiting, and not even pointed in my direction. After a moment, he says, "I'm not a realms-damned ghost talker, so if you want to speak to me, you'll have to put feet on the ground or project your voice."

I materialize, forgetting that others cannot hear me like Nizzara. "You have power like Nizzara. Can't you hear me?"

His bloodshot eyes raise to mine. "I'm a *half-soul*. Big difference from your girl."

I open my mouth to say she's not my girl, but notice his hair is disheveled, and his bouncer's uniform is torn. "What happened?" I ask again.

His jaw tightens. "Mazzar's infantry soldiers plowed through here searching for rebels. And by *searching*, I mean drinking, hitting, and tearing through the place." He looks down at his hands. "Helina got a nasty gash up her arm. Some of the dancers were . . ." His fists clench, and he takes a breath, releasing his fists. "And they took a mill worker who was delivering salt. He's to be executed for rebel association." He keeps staring down at his open hands, hatred contorting his face. "I couldn't stop them—not without a First-Made vessel. I couldn't get close enough to touch one. There were too many, half tearing the place apart, and half keeping us at a sword's point."

He falls back against his chair and pinches the bridge of his nose. "I'm sorry, Your Majesty. I tried to protect the man, but I failed."

This wouldn't be happening if I hadn't lost my crown in the first place. The rebels, the executions, the starving people—none of it. Ice spreads from my feet, crawling along the floor and up the legs of the table.

"No. *I* failed. And I will not fail again."

If I accomplish nothing else, I must end Mazzar's rule. That means using Nizzara. Something inside me whispers that she's on the verge of trusting me. And it feels as wonderful as it does terrible.

The curtains shift surrounding the private room, and Helina enters. Blood is beginning to blossom through the layers of white bandage wrapping up her arm and shoulder.

"Oh," she says, her gaze falling to the ice-covered floor then to me. "I'm sorry about the rebel. I hope for his sake they kill him swiftly." She glances over her shoulder toward the closed curtain. "The girls are shook up," she says. "Between the infantry tonight and the growing roughness of the bouncers in Red's more frequent absences . . . They don't feel safe."

Another sense of failure plummets through my chest. I curl and uncurl my fingers before turning to Helina. "I need a room with a bath." I've made appearances in meetings, grunted the occasional order, and kept a distance from the bouncers, but it's time to take a more hands-on approach.

Jasper raises a brow and Helina folds her arms. "It's about time," she says.

They lead me to Red's chambers below the bar.

Once I'm alone, and my bath is drawn, I get in. My skin stings as hot bathwater climbs my chest, and the sensation doesn't leave until I'm washed and out. I force myself to look in the mirror for the first time in ten years. The shadows hiding in my eyes, just beneath their hazel coloring, are worse than I thought they would be.

I shave my beard, trimming it to the clean Zarr length I used to wear.

I find a fresh suit in Red's closet. When I step into the empty bar to meet with Jasper and Helina, I tap Red's sharp, pointed cane to the hard floor, and Helina drops her broom.

"Give me a heart attack, why don't you," she hisses, before retrieving her broom from the floor. "You look just like him."

I lean the cane against a table and straighten my red suit jacket. "Jasper, gather Red's bouncers."

Jasper folds his arms and leans against the bar, grinning at me. I ask him to fetch the men, and when he leaves, I turn to Helina.

She flinches. "Sorry. You look too much like him with the mask and the cane."

"I don't have to use the cane, I just—"

She shakes her head. "No, if you're going to get up close and personal with the bouncers, you'll need it. He used it for beatings." She flicks the cane with her red nails. "As much as I'd like to see it snapped in two."

I chuckle. "I can arrange that later." When I smile at her, she clears her throat and goes back to sweeping.

"Any news on my sister?" I ask.

"No one has seen her in the rebel camps," she says, bending down to scoop up a pile of glass into a waste bin. "But I have a few more contacts I can reach out to."

"Thanks." If my sister is in the camps, she could be using her Mark to hide. Simply asking around is a slim bet. I watch as Helina begins sweeping behind the bar, favoring her bandaged arm. "How are the dancers?"

She presses her lips together then says, "The infantry soldiers had their way with two of us, but it's nothing new. Red's bouncers do the same thing on a weekly basis. Job hazard."

"Are there any who want to leave?"

She sighs and takes a seat on a shiny red stool. "I'm not sure. Since Red has been . . . absent more frequently, they've been on edge. A lot of the girls need the money, and some have family to consider." She toys with the bracelet around her wrist, and I can't help the ache it sparks. I want to know if she's alive. "Some owe the club a lot of money."

I tilt my head to meet her honey gaze. "Anyone who wishes to leave can go. Tell them I forgive their debts, and any dancer who stays will not be forced to do anything they don't want to."

She blinks. "You'd free them all of their debts? What if they all leave? You will have no establishment to supply your rebels through."

"I will not exploit them. They are free to decide."

She's quiet for a long time before saying, "What about the princess? Is it okay to exploit her?"

Ice breaks out across my knuckles, and Helina notices it.

"I have orders," I say.

She folds her arms, hiding a tremble in her hands. "I thought kings did not take orders."

I point at her. "From gods, they do."

Her jaw works. "I guess you have to draw the line somewhere, huh?"

"Why do you even care about Nizzara?"

She leans forward on her stool and answers with a memory. It flashes across her mind as if she's showing it to me on purpose. I'm in Helina's place, looking through a high-end dress shop window.

Helina wraps her arms over her growing stomach, her fear and morning sickness slicing through the memory as she watches a younger Nizzara inside, wearing an extravagant red gown. Her face is warm, and the shop owner's smile seems genuine. Not like Nizarra's guards lining the street, whose faces are cold and hard.

Helina looks down at the few copper rens in her hand. Her own dress is ripping at the seams, over her pregnant belly. A sharp bell rings from the shop door as Nizzara leaves, and when she passes by Helina, Nizzara locks eyes with her.

Helina drops her hands away from her abdomen and turns to leave.

"Miss," Nizzara says.

A wave of fear washes through the memory as Helina slowly turns back to the princess. "Your Highness?" She curtsies, triggering another wave of nausea.

Nizzara smiles at her. "The shopkeeper has something for you."

My knees become weak as the memory withdraws itself. "You're the woman from the dress shop," I mutter. From Nizzara's memories . . .

Helina looks at the door Jasper left through before saying, "I don't know her personally, but I can't imagine she's so cruel if she can leave *two hundred* gold ren for a homeless pregnant woman."

It becomes hard to breathe.

"Do you think being a deathwalker is so simple? That I can pick and choose which souls I'm ordered to tear apart? Do you know the real price it takes to seize a kingdom?" Mazzar does. Not that it bothers him to pay it.

Ice spreads across the floor and the shadows begin to whisper for Helina's soul.

She flinches away from me.

"This kingdom is worth more than a single life," I say, my hands balling into icy fists. The words taste like ash.

Helina's red lips press into a firm line. "Is it?" She stands up from her stool. "Is that how you will rule?"

The back door swings open and Jasper emerges, leading eleven large men in red suits. They file into the room, lining up and clasping their hands behind them as if they've done this before. Their suits are unwrinkled, their hair untouched, not a single cut or scrape on them.

"Take your masks off," I say, mimicking Red's voice and stance the best I can from their memories. "And explain why you allowed my establishment to be ransacked by infantry soldiers."

The bouncers stiffen and slowly remove their masks. I see how Red treats them from inside their memories.

I approach the big brute in the middle, who has the most rancid soul and most twisted memories. I grab his jacket and throw him to the floor, careful not to use my full strength. I see his name inside his memories—Garret. They spiral into images of violence involving women inside the establishment and young girls outside the establishment.

The shadows inside me hiss excitedly, starved and demanding to be fed. It doesn't matter how often I feed them. They're never satiated. It would be so easy to bury my hand into his chest and rip his soul from him. My hand moves on its own, rising above him to plunge.

"*Break him*," they hiss. "*Make him scream.*"

"They were infantry soldiers, sir," Jasper says, as if he knows I'm about to lose control.

"That's no excuse," I grind out. My arm inches toward Garret's chest. I have to stop. I'm begging my hand to stop, until a speck of yellow flashes through Garret's mucky soul, and for a second, it looks . . . gold.

Like Nizzara's soul.

Like her memories.

A breath shudders through me as the shadows slither back toward their depths. Instead of burying my hand in Garret's chest, I rise, and thrust the pointed cane into his gut, holding him in place and using more strength than I should.

He throws his head back against the red, marble floor, howling in pain.

"How about it, Garret? What's your excuse for letting other men into my territory to take what is mine?"

From the corner of my eye, I notice an approving nod from Jasper and a shudder from Helina.

Garret sputters under the cane as I press my full weight into it. "They wore vessels," he says. "They moved under orders from the king."

"Jasper," I call. "Assist me."

Jasper approaches, a smile flitting across his face as if dishing out torture is a leisurely activity.

Garret sneers back at Jasper, despite the cane pressing above his large intestine.

"Get creative," I tell Jasper, releasing the cane from Garret's gut.

Jasper slams his boot down over Garret's crotch. Another screeching howl breaks from Garret, but Jasper only presses his foot down harder, twisting.

I tap the cane in sync with my right step as I pass by each guard. They squirm, watching Garret scream.

"Let this be a warning to each of you," I say. "I don't care who comes in here. They do not touch the dancers or the patrons."

I allow Jasper a few more moments before calling him off.

Garret staggers to his feet and gets back in line, hunched from his bleeding abdomen.

"You don't think I know what you did during tonight's chaos?" I turn to walk back down the line, reading each of their memories as I go. "Some of you took the opportunity to steal my booze, steal my money, and—"

I stop in front of a guard. "Take advantage of my dancers," I say, keeping my gaze pointed ahead and my ice to a minimum.

His eyes bulge.

I pass by one bouncer—Liam—whose memories and soul are lighter than the others'. "While some of you"—I tap his shoulder and nod for him to step out of line—"some of you hid two dancers from the infantry soldiers."

He stiffens, and I send him to stand beside Jasper.

I pass another guard. "And some of you protected the bar staff." I send him over to Jasper as well.

Jasper nods as if to say, *Yes, these men will follow.*

I face the remaining lot of rotten souls that tempt the shadows inside me. "Things are going to change around here. Starting with authority." I point at Jasper and the two other guards. "Liam, Jasper, and Kile now have authority over you. You will do as they say, and you'll answer to me if you don't."

All their eyes slide to the three of them, obvious loathing in them.

"And the dancers are off-limits."

Liam stiffens behind me, and I see his memories of him and his girlfriend—one of the dancers.

"Unless," I clarify, "it is consensual."

He lets out a breath while the remaining guards simmer, their jaws tightening.

I point to the door. "You are all excused."

Garret straightens his jacket. "What about the job you gave us last moon cycle? Where's our perks for that?"

The surrounding guards nod as if they want to know too.

In his memories, Red is instructing them to scout for new dancers, promising prizes for the best girls, and Garret, I see, has provided many by using coercion. Coercion being a kind word for it.

"No perks," I say. "Now, get out."

Before Liam and Kile follow the others out, I pull them aside, telling them to keep tabs on the others and report to Jasper if anything troublesome arises.

After they leave, I turn toward Jasper, who is leaning against the bar, his eyes heavy. Helina also looks exhausted. I miss that feeling. What I feel now is a never-ending kind of tiredness.

"Cancel the message to your cousin," I say.

This seems to wake Jasper. "Why?"

"I've decided to handle the princess myself."

"I'll try to get word to him, but like I told you, the process is long," he says, and Helina shoots a piercing glance at Jasper, who adds, "But I'll do what I can."

There should be plenty of time, since Jasper's cousin was instructed to wait until the King's Final Duel, which is still two moon cycles away.

"I also need to get in contact with the rebels," I say.

If there's any chance Lo's still alive, I have to know. And besides that, they are my people, fighting in my name.

Jasper scratches his head. "They aren't in the best position to help you fight against Mazzar," he says. "They're recovering from Skeeve raids, they don't have notable numbers, and they don't like visitors."

"I need to meet them."

"I'll arrange a meeting between you and the rebel leader tomorrow," he says, eyeing Helina as if I'm no longer in the room.

Helina yawns. "I need beauty sleep if I'm covering for the injured tomorrow." She passes Jasper, and he takes her hand. They wish me a good night before leaving.

In the empty silence of the bar, I pour myself a glass of honey-colored rum. I've never considered disobeying Nil because it's impossible.

When he orders, I obey.

The threads of my soul belong to him.

I can't help but imagine my mother here in the room with me, like I used to do when I needed to talk to her. In my head, she's sitting on the stool next to me, a chocolate-spiced rum in her hand. Her golden-brown hair tied up in flawless braids.

"It won't make a difference, you know." She raises an eyebrow like she used to do when she knew she was right about something. "If you don't take Nizzara's soul, Nil will only send someone else to do it."

I rub my thumb along the side of my glass. "But I don't want to be the one to do it."

I imagine Mother taking a sip of her drink. "'A soft heart makes a short rule.' That's what your father always said."

I scoff. "Turns out he was right, wasn't he?"

"*But*," she prompts.

I sigh. "You would disagree with him."

She flashes me her coy smile, the one mine was so often compared to. "Would I, now? Why is that?"

A soft smile tugs up my lips. "You said a soft heart is only a liability when the mind is soft too."

"Oh." She smiles, her eyes sparkling. "I sound like a brilliant woman."

An ache climbs my chest. "You were."

"So, are you afraid to die? Is that what holds you in this bargain?"

I shake my head. I don't fear a final death. "It's my people. They're suffering."

"Hmm. If only there were a way to rid the throne of Mazzar and protect your girl."

I stiffen. "She's not my girl."

"Right. So," she says, leaning over to nudge me with her shoulder. "Tell me this joke about cart cows."

I look down into my drink, smiling.

When I tell her, she laughs so hard tears form in her eyes. "I like this girl," she says.

"She's betrothed."

She sets her cup down. "Is it finalized?"

"No."

"Since when have you backed down from a challenge?"

A hopeless dread slithers through my stomach. "Since now. There's no happy ending here." When I look back to the barstool next to me, it's empty.

CHAPTER 36

NIZZARA

DIARY: PAGE 16

After two weeks of being trapped in the castle with Kathreen, I've resorted to spying on her squawking handmaid for entertainment, because it's not safe to continue spying on the other kingdoms yet. After watching Kathreen and said handmaid, I'm positive Kathreen is not the one poisoning Dagen's food, but that doesn't mean she isn't bribing someone else to do it. High-maintenance women prefer clean hands. It could be any of the kitchen staff. And so commences experiment number two. If Dagen wasn't the way he was, I'd simply kill the entire kitchen staff and hire a new one. But it would take a long time for him to forgive me for that. I'll have to do it the hard way.

—Lo

WHEN I WAKE EARLY THE NEXT MORNING, LIHA IS BUZZING around as if she just ate an entire bag of Zem pastries. My body, however, still throbs from my punishment, rendering me unlikely to move without major motivation.

"Are you ready to play?"

"It's too early," I groan and stiffly roll over to tug the pillow over my ears, but her voice is just as clear in my head.

I'm meeting my betrothed today; in a few hours, actually.

"I spent all night watching your betrothed. He is quite the hunter. Come on, we haven't played in so long."

I peek an eye open. *"Fine."*

"Okay. Blond, brunette, or redhead?"

I sit up in the same manner I imagine a corpse might, rigid and grumpy for not being left in peace.

"He's obviously blond if you have this much excitement over him. Not stark blond. You like that in-between color."

She giggles, and I know I got it right.

"What color are his glyphs?"

I can't help my smile at her palpable glee. She loves this game. I recall my studies on the Jaxelli Warriors, remembering the strange light markings that cover their bodies.

"Red? No, wait. That's a Dark Jaxelli color. Hmm." I try to think of the Light gifts. *"Orange?"*

"They are a dark orange, almost red." She squeals. *"Why do you even need me to spy?"*

I raise my hand for her to nudge against. *"Because it makes you happy."*

For a second, I feel a swell of emotion from Liha, a clump of confusing sentiments all jumbled together. I take a breath, and it disappears.

"What do you think of him?" I ask. *"What's his personality like?"*

Liha purrs beside me as other spirits outside my shield hover in and out of focus. *"Very delicious,"* she says. *"Not like a Zarr man, who relies on fancy suits and jeweled collars."*

"I meant . . . is he good?"

A pause. *"I believe he desires to be. I've only seen snippets of him when he leaves their blue dimension. Did you know they are living in a dimension inside another realm?"*

"Be careful, Liha. You're starting to sound scholarly."

She sniffs. *"Why don't you just call me an ugly old hag? It would hurt less."*

I chuckle until I try moving. My entire body aches as I stretch. The salve helped tremendously, but I'm still sore. Preysee enters in time to witness my hobble. She readies the bath with a concoction of therapeutic scented oils.

After dipping into the steaming water, I massage my favorite oil over my skin, one that smells of rose petal and sultry cologne.

Liha continues to hum on about my betrothed. *"He reminds me of the Sand Gladiators from Heshena."* She rolls and twirls beside me, making feather-like waves in my shield. *"Strong chest. Intense gaze. I know you have a weakness for dark hair, but I think he may be an exception."*

"I do not have a weakness for dark hair," I say.

She floats around, giggling. *"Don't think I've forgotten about your infatuation with a certain painting in King's Hall."*

I glare in her direction. *"I was twelve."*

"You may not lean up and kiss him anymore, but I notice your steps slowing down when you pass his frame."

Heat floods my face.

Preysee returns after I'm thoroughly bathed and pulls down a black robe from the far wall.

I climb out and she drapes it over my shoulders. "I got a fair price for the necklace," she says. "And Palko's wife wished to thank the donor." She looks out of the bathing chamber windows that overlook the kingdom. "I hope she hurries. It's an awful winter this year."

"You told her the donation was anonymous, right?" I double-check. "You weren't in your uniform or anything?"

Preysee dips her chin. "I did, and I wore common clothes, my lady."

I nod. "Thank you, Preysee."

She smiles and leads me to the vanity.

"Your father has excused you from training today," she says, taking a brush to my wet hair.

I slump with relief. Good. I don't know if I could last five minutes with Sorren today, which doesn't boost my confidence for the tournament. I've managed to keep up a cocky front, but I'm the lowest-ranking dueler in the tournament, and my skill with a sword hasn't improved as much as I'd like.

"*It took you years to master the daggers,*" Liha says.

My desire to be efficient with a sword must be loud and desperate for her to pick up on it.

"*That's why I should've taken up the sword years ago like Father told me to.*" It's just . . . I always associated them with level-six duels and killing. Daggers have always been more for show. For some reason, the golden spirit chooses now to appear. It lingers above, its power pooling near the ceiling, offering itself to me.

Preysee combs my hair in long slow strokes, her face taking on a practiced, neutral expression, with her pink scar reaching up her lip. I've always wondered about it, but now hoping to distract myself from the churning power above, I work up the courage to ask her.

"Where did you get your scar?" I look at the barely visible line extending from her lips.

The brush pauses in my hair and her expression turns distant. "My late husband."

Her face moves through a span of emotions, landing on something that resembles regret. "I married young, trying to prove I was more desirable than my older sisters. He was handsome and his family was from the wealthier district, so my parents didn't object." She frowns.

I turn in my seat.

"The scar," she says, "is from when I finally fought back."

Anger sweeps through me for her, and the golden power turns fluid and accessible. Suddenly Preysee's smooth scar paints a lucid picture. I see her husband pinning her to the ground, a blade in his fist. In a flash, the image is gone, and wisps of gold surround me.

I raise my chin to keep the tears and panic from rising. "I'm sorry." I pinch my eyes shut and mentally beg the spirit to leave.

"He paid for it," Preysee says. When I open my eyes again, the golden spirit is gone, and Liha is vibrating through my shield—anxious.

Preysee sets the brush down and asks me if she can help me into my dress. She knows Liha can cast it on, but there's a maternal gleam in her eye.

After my flowing black gown is fastened, Liha nudges me, wanting to help, so I allow her to have her way with my face and hair.

The pink smoke fades away from my face, and Preysee gasps. I look at my reflection. Besides my black eyes, which are just plain devilish, Liha has casted me with an extremely soft look. My makeup is so natural it's almost bare. No black lipstick, no winged eyeliner. None of my usual favorites. And my hair is *down*.

"*I don't like it*," I say to Liha.

"*Your betrothed will like it*," she says, floating around me.

"*I look like I just rolled out of bed.*"

She purrs, "*I know. Isn't it scandalous?*"

As I leave my chambers, I sense Dae's presence. It helps me breathe a little easier, but he remains distant, hovering far ahead.

"*Your guards keep glancing at you*," Liha's smug voice bubbles from all around my shield.

"*Probably because my face is naked.*"

She giggles. "*Like I said, scandalous.*"

Dae's cold spirit fades as we descend the stairs and I try to ignore the pang of loneliness that hits me when he disappears.

When I enter the throne room, my father is sitting on his throne, unnaturally stiff. Soriah's throne is empty, and Tarella is standing in her assigned spot on the dais, tapping her foot—probably impatient to get to her voice performance today.

"Leave us," Father commands my guards.

They bow and recede into the shadows of the room.

The apex of winter has settled outside, bringing three more moon cycles of gloom. Glo stones buzz overhead, all three fireplaces dance with flames, and red, glowing gem heaters hum along the walls, but it doesn't bring much light or warmth to the giant room, as if the castle's corners bleed darkness.

Liha slinks off, out of my shield, and past the reach of my senses.

I expect my father to make a comment on my bare appearance, but after he surveys me, he says, "When the second general arrives, and you are alone with him, you will invite him to stay for dinner as well as the preliminaries. He will attend both."

There's the slightest slur behind his voice, a very bad sign. I wonder if there's a fully sober day for him anymore, but slur or no slur, the threat in his voice is clear.

A knock sounds from the exterior doors.

Father holds a gloved hand up, and the single crease between his brows tells me he's talking with his spirit, no doubt asking who stands on the other side of the doors.

Father's dark, oily spirit leaves his shield only to return a second later before disappearing again, most likely back into Father's shield.

"It's the second general of the Light Jaxelli," he says. "Open the doors."

Liha flutters back into my shield. *"Ooooh. Just in time."*

"Where'd you run off to?"

"Playing," she says.

The doors open and for the first time, I lay eyes on a being from another realm. Lekk Rexion, a Light Jaxelli Warrior.

CHAPTER 37

DAGEN

I SPIRIT TO THE RED MASK, NOT SURE WHY I THOUGHT IT'D be a good idea to see Nizzara on her way to meet her betrothed, or why I thought her little bonded spirit would allow me a window of time with her. It's been a challenge, finding those windows while remaining distant enough not to raise suspicion.

I materialize across from Jasper as he readies a pack of food and replaces the energy gem in his gun.

"Blasted gems," he mutters. "Seems like I'm replacing them daily now. At this rate I'll be returning to a sword like everyone else." He fiddles with the tiny, burned-out gems until they've all popped out, then deftly replaces them with new ones. "At least this one didn't catch fire. I hate when they do that." The gem gun glows back to life, and he loads it full of expensive bullets. If not for the delicate laws of my ghostly condition, I would've asked Jasper to borrow his gun to kill Mazzar when I first came to Zaar, but I can't carry objects in my spirit form, and I wouldn't make it far into the castle in my physical form before the guards overwhelmed me. I could fight them, but with that much warning, Mazzar would be able to control me with his Mark.

"I have no sway over the rebel leader," Jasper says as he swings the pack over his shoulder. "His mind is fortified. So, I can't influence him to meet with you or believe you. We also have to walk"—he grimaces—"a ways."

I chuckle. "You mean, *you* have to walk."

His brows flatten over tired eyes. "Right.

"Remember," Jasper says, opening the back door to the morning gloom. "The Skeeves are different from years ago. They're faster, stronger, and they re-spawn in a matter of hours." He glances at me. "I know you're already . . . dead, but their power is like Nil's. They can easily consume your soul, or possess it if they choose." He steps out into the brisk air. "And they've gotten sneaky about it. It's not always obvious someone is possessed. Someone can look and act normal ninety-five percent of the time and still be a Skeeve." He starts walking toward the Zarr wall. "If we come across any, the only way to stun them now is by chopping off their heads."

Jasper leads us past trash bins and through a few alleyways before stopping at the perimeter wall of Zarr city. He starts to climb.

"No gate today?" I fly over the wall and return to a solid being on the other side.

"Nope." He drops the ten feet to the ground. "No sled, no gate. This is faster than walking all the way to the gate. Besides, my cousin isn't stationed at the wall today."

Jasper brushes the red dirt off his black pant legs. "So." He straightens his pack on his shoulder and starts walking. "Are you going to tell me why we have to meet with the rebel leader?"

"You haven't already read my mind?" I don't *think* he's touched me, but I've watched him use his gift on other bouncers and suppliers in the club. No one ever notices when he does because he's very skilled at distraction.

He sighs. "I get tired of touching people. Besides, this morning I have a slicing headache."

"They want Mazzar dead." I shrug. "So do I."

Half an answer. I want to help them more than just making supply drops, and I need to look for Lo myself, before my time is up.

He raises a brow. "I told you; they aren't a raging army ready to tear down walls. They are mill workers, miners, and families who are trying to survive."

I straighten my shoulders. "They're my people. I will help them however I can while I'm here."

By late morning, the wind's icy barbs whip against us as we walk deeper through orange boulders capped with snow.

"Wouldn't it be more comfortable in your spirit form?" Jasper yells over the wind.

The wind shrieks through the rocky formations, too loud to answer. I wouldn't ask him to trek all the way out here if I wasn't willing to do it myself. Besides, this is nothing compared to Baratrum.

After a few more hours, Jasper swivels his head east then west, assessing our location.

"This is as good a spot as any." He drops the pack and hunkers down against a large boulder to block the wind. He reaches into his packed lunch and tosses a mineral roll at me. I catch it and turn it around in my fingers.

He shrugs. "You drink rum, so I figured you might like to eat too."

"I don't need food. I'm dead." I toss it back to him and take a seat on the ground, waiting for him to finish. I pinch the dry, cold dirt, rubbing it in my fingers.

"The soil is darker out here."

"It's the Skeeves. Their presence turns everything darker—and colder," he says through a mouth full of jerky.

"The prophecies," I whisper.

Kingdoms will fall to beasts of nightmare
In shadows they hide, keeping prey unaware
As the world turns darker, and realms get colder,
The beasts do not die but grow older and older.
—*The King of Kings*

I've been reading Nizzara's copy while she sleeps. There are so many passages I don't remember from my eighth-year studies.

"What?" he calls over a gust of wind.

I shake my head. "Nothing."

He plops the rest of a butter curd into his mouth and brushes his hands off. "I'm ready. Let's go."

Before Jasper can grab the pack, I swing it over my shoulder, taking my turn.

After another twenty minutes, we find human bones littering the ground under patches of snow.

Jasper squats down to examine one of the bones. "Left behind by Skeeves." He points at a femur and shudders. "See how shadows still flicker around it?"

He quickly rises and waves for me to keep going, but I kneel, inspecting the bundle of bones—the remains of a small child. Grief fills my chest.

I step around the bones, careful not to disrupt them. If the ground weren't frozen, I'd give them a proper resting place.

In the late afternoon, we reach the center of the Barrens flats, where the boulders range in size from glo-kars to small hills. They're so close together and some piled on top of another, it's no wonder carriages can't get through here.

"We wait here," Jasper says.

The sound of boots scuffing on rock comes from all around, but no one emerges.

Jasper pulls his glowing gem gun out from under his jacket and lays it on a dry section of dirt. He nods at me to do the same with my weapon.

I summon my shadow blade. Its black, gleaming steel materializes in my hand, and I toss it to the ground beside the gem gun.

"I'm an illiterate swine," Jasper says and gestures to me.

"And I'm an ugly celibate." It's the perfect code to keep anyone in the kingdoms out, since I've never heard anyone openly insult themselves willingly.

A big man wearing a thick winter coat and holding a battle axe emerges from his hiding place, and three others fall in behind him.

The man points his axe at me. "What is your business?"

"We've come to speak with the leader," Jasper says.

"Why?"

I step forward, looking directly at the man. I see his memories. His name is Hoack. He's young, but old enough to remember me.

"Because," I say, "I am King Dagen, here to serve your cause."

His axe creeps forward, and the other axes follow suit from all around us. "King Dagen is dead," he says.

I turn to spirit in a splash of black mist and witness the shock on his face when I change my frequency to speak only to him. "Oh, yes. I am quite dead."

His memories spiral deeper and deeper into hardship. The loss of his wife to Skeeves, then his son to poor living conditions. The shadows inside me churn. They enjoy bad memories that roll in hate and despair. I shove them down and return to my solid form. "I am Dagen Corvonna, son of Queen Maven and King Gorrik, born on the sixth moon of the year 3039."

After a long moment, he says, "I'll take you to Reb." His voice has a hardness to it that seems permanent. "Follow me."

I see the rebel leader through his memories as well. They all call him Reb, short for "Rebel leader," since no one knows his real name.

The guards surround us, and one stoops to gather our weapons.

"I wouldn't touch that blade if I were you," I warn him.

He looks up at me, his grip tightening on his axe as if I meant it as a threat.

"It will hurt you whether I'm holding it or not. Just leave it."

He backs away from the sword and opts to leave it in the red, snowy dirt, taking only Jasper's gun.

Hoack and his guards lead us through narrow passageways, and under boulders wedged above, until we come to a cave leading underground.

"Wait here," Hoack says.

After disappearing into the cave, he returns minutes later with a tall, broad man. The man's black hair seems abnormally dark—as if it sucks light from the world—and his eyes seem too bright, an unnatural shade of purple. Unnatural for the Zarr realm, anyway. My time as a deathwalker has introduced me to many walks of life in many realms, although I can't quite place which realm he's from. The guard hands him Jasper's gun, and he takes it, nodding his thanks.

The rebel leader is shirtless, as if the cold doesn't affect him, and he stalks with the prowess of a trained warrior, scars on every surface of his tan skin, minus his missing left hand.

His eyes fall on me, gleaming, but his mind is silent. No memories surge from him.

"I had a feeling," he says with an expression that feels much too old, much too experienced for his young face. "Come. Let us speak out of the wind."

He leads us into the cave, lit by lines of glowing, multicolored strata flowing through the rock. The farther we walk, the more glowing strata blossom from the walls of solid stone, and the warmer it gets.

We pass many small alcoves in the wall, carved to form makeshift rooms. Men, women, and children bustle about, carrying buckets of packed snow and mineral rocks. They stop to watch us as Reb leads us. I study each woman we pass, searching for Lola's dark waves or green-eyed smirk, but no one I pass is her, and even if she were in disguise, she'd make herself known if she saw me. Jasper follows in silence next to me, his gaze wandering as if this is his first time inside the cave too.

Reb leads us to one of many small alcoves, identical to all the others we passed, where a bundle of burgundy rocks are piled into a small cutout in the wall. Reb follows my gaze to the piled stones and returns Jasper's gem gun to him before plucking one of the roughly cut stones from its place. "You might not recognize them in this state," he says, "but blare gems are more stable and more useful when they aren't cut and polished to look pretty. They hold their energy much longer this way. And they're safer too. When their outer layer is left on, they don't combust into flame without warning." He nods toward Jasper's gem gun with its glowing blare gem. He turns the stone over in his one hand before handing it to me. I take the jagged, dull stone. It's almost too hot to hold comfortably. But it feels good to hold, as it staves off my never-ending chill. "In their raw form, blare gems radiate much more energy, but at a slower, steadier rate, making for a sustainable source of heat down here, and the cave walls trap the warmth in nicely." Reb tilts his head. "You can keep it if you like."

A woman carries in a platter made of stone with extra lumpy biscuits on top. "You traveled a good distance through the cold. Care for a mineral biscuit? Or some heated water?"

"I'll have a water," Jasper says, and Reb nods to the woman, who hurries out and quickly returns with a cup carved of stone. Jasper takes it, his pierced brow bunching when he looks inside. "There's pebbles in it."

Reb eyes Jasper, a flicker of something like tolerance on his face. "If you were not privileged enough to import wood for burning," he raises his arm toward the solid rock ceiling, "and let's forget the lack of ventilation down here needed for flame anyway—how else would you heat water in a cave?"

Jasper grumbles something into his cup before eyeing the bottom of it again.

Reb turns back to me. "I have done my best to protect your people, King Dagen."

"You believe I am who I say?" I ask as we sit on roughly carved rock benches.

Reb smiles. "I do. I've been waiting for you, actually. Now that you're here, it's yours."

I open my mouth, but nothing comes out.

"Feel free to speak your mind, Your Majesty."

"I just . . . I was expecting a power struggle: proving my identity, promising titles and rewards . . ." I expected just about anything other than this.

Reb smiles. "I knew you'd be back. I also knew you'd take care of them when you came."

"How could you possibly know that?"

His eyes glint with purple light. "Call it intuition."

I look around to see if this is somehow an ambush or trap, but everyone's expression seems just as surprised as mine, even Hoack's.

"But why?" I ask, trying to understand what could possibly motivate him to do this.

"If I took the time to explain, we'd be here for a long while. So I'll summarize by saying that I know when and where I am needed." His face falls slightly. "And now, it seems I'm needed elsewhere." He turns to Hoack. "This is my second-in-command. He will serve you well if you decide to take over things here." Another gleam flashes in his eyes. "Which my intuition tells me you will."

Hoack bows his head to Reb, and I see in his memories that Reb has prepared him and the people here for this day, telling them that their king would return, but I also feel the blatant disbelief in Hoack's memories. I see all he has sacrificed to protect the people here, risking his life to trek back and forth between the city, smuggling people out, toting sleds, grinding mineral dust, and carving new alcoves.

Hoack takes a knee before me in the same fashion that I am forced to do to Nil. "I cannot offer land or money, but I can offer my loyalty and servitude," he says.

His mouth gapes when I take a knee in front of him and clasp his shoulder. "I offer the same."

Reb's eyes light up with some hidden source as he says, "I apologize for such an abrupt meeting, but I'm afraid my time here must end." He offers a sad grin. "I have nothing but time, and yet, it still evades me."

He takes a deep breath. On his exhale, black energy washes over his skin, and like his hair, he suddenly seems to absorb light. He becomes taller, and bigger. Black and purple cosmic tattoos of light appear on his skin, swirling as if they are alive. He is . . .

A Dark Jaxelli.

He sighs a giant release of air, as if he's shed a heavy burden. "You'll see me again, but in the meantime, keep your wits about you, focus on securing the First-Made vessels, and trust that everything will make sense in time." Then, he disappears into time and space, vanishing into nothing, and I find myself wondering what he meant.

The room feels vastly empty in his sudden absence, and it is a long stretch of silence before Jasper blurts, "What in the actual hell?" He sets down his cup on the stone bench and surges to his feet. "What did -he mean about the vessels?"

I climb to my feet, still processing what just happened.

Hoack rises and says in a voice filled with disbelief, "He told me how it would happen, but I didn't think it'd be so—" He shakes his head. "I didn't think it would actually happen."

"You have no idea who he is?" Jasper asks, his gaze still fixed on where Reb once stood.

"No. He saved our lives on more than one occasion, so we just followed him and respected his wish to stay anonymous."

Hoack takes me through the tunnels, showing me around and introducing me to the other guards, who appear to be just as much mill workers as guards.

Hoack gives me the reports, and I can tell he did this often for Reb. Number of guards, number of new arrivals, water levels, food stores, recent Skeeve attacks, and reports of the Zarr infantry movements through the Barrens, looking for the rebel groups.

We spend the day learning everything about the rebel camps before Jasper reminds me that we have to return to the club before the trek back becomes too dark, running the risk of a snowstorm or Skeeves.

Leaving Hoack to run things, I clutch the raw blare gem in my hand, promising to find a way to return these people to homes within the city—away from the Skeeves—before we head back.

CHAPTER 38

NIZZARA

Diary: Page 17

I captured the head chef, blindfolded him, and dumped him in a dungeon cell. Then I really wanted to have Preysee deliver Dagen's food to Kathreen, let her own poison kill her, but Dagen has been trying to work things out with her. Sometimes that honorable heart of his is wildly inconvenient. He doesn't know about the poison for two reasons: 1. I'm not 100 percent sure Kathreen is involved, and I will only deliver that kind of accusation if I'm positive. 2. It's not my job to tell Dagen. It's to fix it. Dagen's meals are being fed to one of five nasty prisoners that deserve bone problems. The head chef has been locked away for three days, and the first prisoner I fed the meat and biscuits to foamed at the mouth and died in less than five minutes. Whoever's poisoning the food is getting a bit impatient, it seems.

—Lo

MY HANDS GO CLAMMY OVER THE GOLD ARMRESTS AS THE second general of the Light Jaxelli approaches me. He simply is power. Silent, undeniable power. His power is different, though. It doesn't derive from spirits, nor is it possessive and addictive like mine.

I take in his appearance, from the angle of his defined jaw and the warm lines of his face to the curves of his supple, rolling muscles beneath his leather plates and straps. And his glyphs—blazing orange markings swirling across his skin, so dark they could almost pass for red.

"*I told you*," Liha purrs. "*Mouthwatering.*"

He and his two warriors stop at the foot of the dais. One warrior behind him has light blue glyphs, the other has green. Even Tarella's jaw is still open. Liha is right. The second general has a presence about him that does not exist in this realm. They all do.

Lekk's fiery gaze brushes over me slowly, warm but calculating.

My father's smooth voice booms through the throne room, speaking a language I've never heard.

"*How does he know their language?*" I ask Liha.

"*Spirits who've been around for a long time usually pick up on multiple languages,*" she says. "*His spirit is probably translating what he wishes to say.*"

"*Can you understand it?*"

"*If I say yes, will you tell me I sound scholarly?*" she snips.

I roll my eyes. "*Can you?*"

"*He welcomed Lekk to Zarr.*"

I glare at the spot she hovers at my shoulder. It's just like her to withhold such fascinating knowledge from me. How many languages is she fluent in? What lore does she know from other realms besides her home in Heshena—which she never talks about either?

Lekk does not bow but instead brings a strong fist to his chest, and Liha translates as the conversation goes on, after a profuse apology from me for my scholarly comment from earlier.

"Let's make the arrangements for the betrothal," my father says. "A date for the ceremony."

Lekk drops his hand to his side, bringing my attention to the leather straps encasing his muscled thighs.

"The Jaxelli do not mate for political reasons," he says in his tongue. "I request time to court your daughter, to see if she speaks to my heart."

"This is a betrothal, not a courting service," Father says, leaning forward on his throne. "How do I know you will not take advantage of her?"

Lekk's whole body tenses and the patterns on his skin flare into a deep orange. "You insult my honor."

Liha giggles. *"Lekk's desires are very strong and loud right now. He wants to lunge across this dais and blacken your father's eye for insulting his honor. Honor is a very strong desire for him."*

Lekk's jaw tightens. "Will you accept my request to court in the presence of a chaperone?"

"I will accept a chaperone *and* collateral," Father says. "If you hurt my daughter, I will hurt your collateral."

This is one of those moments I want to believe my father is still there beneath the power—the man who was so quick to protect me. Like the night a group of rebels tried to kidnap me. He killed all twelve men in my room before they could touch me and he stroked my hair until I fell asleep. Brunar and his men were assigned to me the next day.

He does just enough to hold a place in my heart. My anger rises inside me.

Lekk's head snaps in my direction, and I suddenly remember the chapter from the Jaxelli book on their ability to sense emotions.

His head tilts slightly. Is he still reading my emotions?

Father's eyes find mine, and I know what they are silently saying. I fix my face.

Lekk unsheathes a mighty sword from across his back strap, its deep red hue fading to orange near the tip. He reverently touches the sword's tip to the ground and takes a step back from it, leaving it balanced without his hand. Its power thrums throughout the room.

Father chuffs. "A noble gesture. I understand the Jaxelli blade to have nothing of equal value across all the realms, but I also know that I can do no harm to your sword. I cannot even keep it against your will, Second General. I've heard you can beckon it from across lands and it will come. I deny this collateral."

"I carry nothing else with me, King."

My father points. "You have brought two very acceptable collaterals. They stand silent behind you."

Lekk's markings again plunge into a deep, angry amber—almost red. His energy is palpable.

"You think it's fair to claim two of my best warriors as a matter of insurance? I will not order their obedience to satisfy your insecurities, King."

Father pushes up from his throne and raises a gloved hand, ladened with glistening black gems. "It is more than fair. Nizzara is my heir should death fall on me. She is also physically weaker than you. Neither of your warriors are heir to your monarchy, nor are they as defenseless or as tempting as my daughter."

A warrior with blue glyphs and a long white scar over his eye clasps Lekk's shoulder and whispers to him.

"*What are they saying?*" I ask Liha, and she darts over to listen before snapping back into my shield.

"*The warrior with the scar insists he finds honor in the task. The other warrior with him agrees. They wish to serve. Very deep loyalty.*"

She continues to translate for me as the warrior with the white scar over his light blue eye steps forward. "My name is Korin, Light-born Son of Water. I accept your terms."

The redheaded warrior with green glyphs steps in line with Korin. "My name is Solis, Light-born Son of Earth. I accept your terms."

Father smiles and waves for them to approach. "I assure you, Lekk, I will treat them as well as you treat my daughter. Now, it seems there's one final matter to settle. *Time.* You'll be given until the end of the King's Duel tournament, almost two full moon cycles from now." He glances at me. "After my daughter wins, we can announce your betrothal."

Lekk stiffens. "Two moon cycles?" He appears to count under his breath. "That's only sixty days. The Jaxelli take years before selecting a—"

"A king does not wait on other men. Two moon cycles. You can come and go as you wish, so long as your presence is announced to me and a chaperone of my approval escorts you alongside my daughter at all times."

In fear of my father selecting Sorren for a chaperone, I blurt, "I want Preysee to be our chaperone."

"Preysee is a helpless maid. She can't protect you," Father retorts in our own language.

I flick my hand to where all seven of my personal guards stand at attention near the fireplaces. "Isn't that what my guards are for?"

I meet his gaze, and something tiny softens in him. "Very well."

He turns his attention back to Lekk. "If you could not call your sword, I'd insist on keeping it, but since that would be moot, I warn you not to reach for it or your collateral will suffer."

Lekk's neck muscles tighten. "I have one more matter to settle."

Father raises a brow. "Speak, Son of Keirmon."

Lekk's glyphs swirl faster. "Eighteen years ago, you aligned with our greatest enemy, the Dark Jaxelli Warriors. Your infantry aided our Dark siblings in the murder of our Light king," Lekk says. "Are you still allies with the Dark Jaxelli?"

Eighteen years ago. Could this be the unauthorized mission Lo mentioned in the journal? Before he stole the throne?

My father's neck vein pokes out—he's trying to manage his temper. "I have no more business in your realm."

"If I accept this betrothal, you'll help my warriors reclaim our land in Xoshbesh?" Lekk asks.

Father goes still. "If you marry my daughter, you'll inherit my infantry soldiers as the future king of Zarr."

Lekk opens his mouth as if to ask another question, but Father waves his hand. "I've settled your matter. You're dismissed."

I come to my feet. "Brunar," I call. "Fetch Preysee."

Brunar waits for a nod from my father then says, "Yes, my lady."

When he returns, Preysee is with him, and she comes to my side silently. Tarella asks if she can be excused for her concert, and Father dismisses her. Part of me wishes I could go and support her—a small goodbye gesture before Soriah takes her away, but her concert is in Zo, and Father has never let me return to that kingdom since we left.

I descend the dais toward Lekk and ask Liha to help me translate what I wish to say. She offers me the translation, but when I try to speak his language, it comes out awkwardly. "May I show you the castle?" I say.

Lekk looks at his warriors, who stand at attention before my father, then offers me a stiff nod before joining my side opposite Preysee. My guards fall in behind us, and we leave the throne room.

Lekk is taller than I, with muscles wrapping every facet of his body, most of which are on display. Heat radiates from his glowing-orange markings, which move and swirl like veins of lava. But the most striking thing about him is his bright, fiery gaze.

"Can you sense his desires?"

"Mmm. Barely. He desires the safety of his friends."

I turn us toward King's Hall.

Lekk's quick steps outpace mine two to one. Multiple times he notices his speed and slows back to my pace.

"What should I know about you, Lekk? Besides your hurry to walk?" I say, butchering the pronunciation.

He halts amid the portraits in King's Hall, a soft smile on his face. "I am sorry, Daughter of Zarr. My mind races, so my feet follow. It's my mother in me."

His smile widens to show straight, white teeth. I idly wonder what a sensuous bite from his pointed canines would feel like.

Liha giggles in my shield. *"You're ogling him. And here I thought you didn't want a betrothal."*

I huff. *"I don't. But I'm not blind."*

Lekk's nostrils flare, and I remember that he can sense my emotions—my attraction.

Heat floods my neck and cheeks. I ask Liha to translate what I wish to say through our bond and try to match her pronunciations. "Your mother," I say. "What is she like?"

A sad smile pulls on his lips as he studies a portrait. "She was vibrant, with one speed and one direction—as fast as possible and straight ahead." His smile fades. "But she is no longer with us." After a stretch of silence he asks, "What of your mother? She was not in the throne room."

"I'm sorry for your loss." I start walking again. "My mother," I say, rolling various answers around in my mind, ignoring the fresh stab deep in my chest. "My mother spends her days in the book coves. Her knowledge is on par with the best scholars in our realm." I leave out the fact she actually lives in the coves.

"What of your father?" Lekk asks.

My body goes rigid. "What of him?"

His brows furrow as if trying to find words in the air. "What kind of relationship do you have?"

I look up at him. "A complicated one."

"How so?"

I stop and face him, opting to be as honest as I can. "My father is not a soft man. He's quick to anger and is vastly powerful," I say. "But when he cares for something—which isn't often—it runs extremely deep."

"So, he treats you well?"

My jaw flexes. "That is not what I said."

Before he can ask more questions, I turn toward the king's balcony. "Come see the view. The fog is thinnest in the morning."

Brunar and two other guards haul the giant doors made of black glass open, inviting the icy-gray sky into the hall.

He strides onto the balcony that's warmed by a large gem heater and approaches the smooth black railing slowly.

"There are a lot of buildings," he says, looking out at Zarr city. "And a lot of gloom."

I tilt my head up. The sky is a silty gray, despite the early hour. "It is the winter cycle. Today is a rather good one. The wind is barely noticeable."

I admire the visibility. Beyond the castle walls, yellow glo light shines from the countless small windows, stacked six and seven levels high. The black buildings lean at slight angles, poised to represent swords at the ready, their roofs pointed and some painted red.

I glance up at Lekk, who appears every bit a general, his expression stoic—and as much as I hate to admit it, beautiful. The power clinging to him takes up the entire balcony, and just by looking at him, I know he's skilled in battle. Like Sorren and my father, his balance is centered, his movements are precise, and his eyes are ever-calculating.

Liha funnels her magic into my body.

"*Really?*"

She sniffs. "*Yes, really. Have some fun with me.*"

Pink smoke drips from my fingers, and our Mark settles over my face.

Preysee is unfazed, but Lekk notices the small zap of pink smoke and takes a step back. He looks down at himself, searching for the repercussions of the cast.

A half smile tugs at my lips. "I didn't cast on you."

His gaze falls on my face, and he swallows. He traces my cheeks with those russet orbs and a zing of excitement flutters through me because he doesn't shy away from my eyes like everyone else.

"Freckles." He smiles and clears his throat. "I didn't notice them earlier. They are pretty, Daughter of Zarr."

I can't keep my smile from falling. Tarella has made comments about my Mark in the past, enough to know she's jealous of it. But all my Mark does is point out the ways I am not enough in the eyes of others. Lekk sees freckles because he'd find me more attractive if I had them. No one has looked through my Mark and found me perfect as I am.

Lekk looks down at the golden vessel on my hand.

"*I think he desires to know its workings,*" Liha purrs.

I meet his fiery gaze. "How about we make a deal, Lekk?"

His jaw tightens. "The last deal I made put two of my lifelong friends in harm's way."

"I am not my father," I say, my dark anger curling inside as if to laugh at that statement. "I think you'll find my deal much more palatable."

His eyes continue to search my face, lingering on my fake, freckled cheeks, before he says, "What deal do you wish of me?"

Liha feeds me the words. A few are hard to pronounce because of the odd syllables placed so close together, but I manage to get out, "When you visit, I'll answer one question you have with full honesty, if you agree to do the same in return."

His brows furrow, adding intensity to his continually brooding expression. "No questions that could endanger the position of my people."

"Agreed. You ask first."

He leans his back against the balcony's railing.

It's a moment before he finds his question. "What do you desire from me?" he asks. "Do you wish for this betrothal?"

I nearly snort. "That's two questions, and I don't know if you'll like my answers."

He folds his arms, waiting, so I answer both. "I am competitive. Part of me enjoys the challenge you pose by requesting to court me. Any Zarr man would accept my hand in a matter of a heartbeat." I leave out the detail that their fear of my father would be half the reason. "But I don't like being told what to do, and my father is forcing this betrothal on me, so naturally, I don't want to bow down to it."

He shifts his feet. I might be making him uncomfortable, but I'm used to having that effect on people.

"As far as my desires are concerned, physical relationships are a part of Zarr culture. All women my age have had lovers—as many as they wish—before they marry. But I've been placed in a cage of celibacy because of this betrothal. Your body does call to me. I desire to know what it's like."

His markings flush with a wave of orange red, and I swear the air thickens around us. "I believe you've answered in full honesty," he says, his voice tight.

"Are you born with those markings?" I ask.

He glances down at his glowing orange-red swirls. "Is that your question?"

"No," I say, mesmerized by the bold strokes of light over his tan chest. "But I am curious." I find my head tilting as I say, "And why are your marks bigger than your friends'?"

He studies my face—the *freckles* on my face. "No, we are not born with them. They find us in our early years of life. Glyphs are sacred and unique. No two patterns are alike, and they appear in their own time, in their own way."

When I continue to stare, he clears his throat and says, "You may ask your real question, Daughter of Zarr."

So many more questions surge to my mind. *What is it like to travel to any realm? What realms have you seen? How old are you? What's your entire history? What's the history of the Dark Warriors?* But I rein in my insatiable curiosity and keep it relevant to the question he asked me.

"I told you a little bit about Zarr courting. What is the courting culture of your people?"

A soft smile takes his lips, showing those white teeth, and my stomach does a little flip. "Quite the opposite of Zarr," he says. "I am in my hundred and seventy-sixth year and am only now entering the time to find a mate."

I gasp. I did not make it to that chapter. I knew Jaxelli lived long lives and were on the prudish side of things, but *a hundred and seventy-six years?*

"No one has called to you in all that time?"

He chuckles. "Nature isn't so cruel as to tempt us for so long. The Jaxelli do not have the urge to mate until we near our second century of life." He leans his lower back against the black balcony railing. "Some discover the urge as early as a hundred and seventy or as late as two hundred and thirty." His gaze finds the neckline of my dress and falls to my abdomen. "Although I do not know if this would be true for our offspring. Half Jaxelli . . ." He frowns. "That is a discussion for a different day."

I nod, glad to skip the topic of children today. "How about you? Has the urge found you?"

He makes a face. "The urge found me last year, and it makes me want to take back what I said about nature and its kindness."

A laugh slips out. "So, you've acted upon it, then? The urge?"

His brows furrow. "No. Taking a mate is a sacred process among our people. We don't choose a mate for a night, or a few years, but a life of near millennia. We exchange these rings to announce our chosen mate." He unwinds a sleek band from his wrist that holds two smooth bands of stone and places them in my palm.

I rub my thumb against the foreign stone. Of all the minerals, stones, and gems in our realm, I have not seen this. Their white surfaces gleam, reflecting the nearby glow of the gem heater as I turn them over in my fingers. They have a *feeling* to them.

An energy.

I swallow my spitefulness toward my father and this betrothal, trying to let go of my pride. Perhaps I should give him a chance. "What attributes have called to you in the past?"

His orange glyphs intensify across his muscular chest under his brown leather plates and straps. "You are asking more than your allotted questions, Daughter of Zarr." He studies my freckles once more. "But if we only have two moon cycles to navigate our courtship, then I suppose more questions are best."

I fold my arms and wait.

"Many things have called to me, Daughter of Zarr, such as a female's full lips or the angle of her hips against her waist. Some things, more important, such as a female's ability to bring peace into a room, or a female who demonstrates humility and tranquility."

Humility? Peace? The two things I don't have a drop of.

"Worthy attributes," I say.

We talk around a few awkward silences before my curiosity gets the best of me. "I read that your kind is related to another species—the Guardians," I say. "Is that true?"

Liha stops moving about my shield.

His face turns contemplative. "The Guardians and the Jaxelli are not related by blood but are similar in many ways." He purses his lips, thinking. "We have six essences who bonded to our species as a whole—"

"Essences?" I ask.

He pauses as if looking for the right words. "I believe your people call them *gods*." He holds out his arm to me, and his orange glyphs illuminate the space between us. "I was gifted by Ignis, born with his essence of Fire in my blood, as are some other Jaxelli. That's why my glyphs are the color of flame." He smiles, "I can show you my gift if you'd like?"

I find myself biting my lip as I try to rein in my excitement to learn. "Show me."

He raises his hand toward me, and heat begins flooding throughout my entire body, growing until I'm uncomfortably hot—until it starts to burn.

I gasp from the intensity, and my guards palm their swords.

Wary of Brunar's pointed gaze boring through him from the balcony doorway, Lekk withdraws his power from me before the heat becomes unbearable, and my internal temperature drops back to normal.

"I can't produce actual flames, like other Jaxelli with the essence of Fire, but I can make my enemies feel as if they are burning alive. The manifestation of each essence varies from warrior to warrior."

"How does the essence of Blood manifest in your kind?"

"Blood?" His nose wrinkles. "It is more commonly a Dark gift. Some can change their appearance, heal wounds, and control others."

I nod as if confirming it to myself. "What about the warriors you brought with you? What essences do they wield? I mean, I know they announced it in the throne room, but how do their gifts manifest?"

Raising a brow, he says, "Korin, the warrior with blue glyphs, wields the essence of Water. Like me, he can't summon water, but he can make you feel as if you are moving *through* water." He chuckles. "Many warriors made fun of him for that gift, until he started blowing them off the ground with the power of a massive, invisible flood."

I smile at the thought. "And Solis?"

A grin creeps on his lips, as if remembering a funny memory about Solis. "He is gifted with the essence of Earth. He can manipulate creatures, snakes, ants, birds, and such." He tries to fight the smile, but it only grows bigger. "We were discussing his gift before we came here. Korin was harassing him about—" He stops mid-sentence and shakes his head. "Actually, that's not the most appropriate topic of conversation."

I scowl. "Why not? I want to know."

The smile finds his lips again, until it turns into a chuckle. "Korin's jokes are rather crude for a princess."

"It won't offend me," I say.

He glances at my lips, which are set into a stubborn line, then relents. "Solis has a mating ceremony coming up, and as I mentioned before, our mating culture is quite different from Zarr's. We aren't intimate with our chosen mates until after the ceremony, and his energy has been nervous for days. Well, Korin was harassing Solis about his gift, telling him it's a shame that he's not an animal-shifter so he could change into something with a bigger . . ." He shakes his head, chuckling. "I'm sorry, my mother would have my hide for a rug if she heard me say that word to you, but let's just say I have no doubt, Korin's bed will be ridden with fire ants by morning, knowing Solis."

"Poor Korin." I laugh—and grimace—imagining a small army of insects attacking him in his sleep.

He nods. "Poor Korin."

"So how do your gifts differ from the Guardians'?" I ask, noticing Liha's stiffer movements and uncharacteristically flat tones.

"Jaxelli bloodlines are bonded to six different essences," he says. "Many warriors share a sliver of an essence, which gives us great power." His brows pinch and his face turns serious. "But with Guardians . . . An essence would choose a Guardian and bond with that soul only." He frowns. "Too much power for one soul to handle, if you ask me."

My curious brain swirls with more and more questions. "Did they live longer lives like your kind? What happened to them?"

"My ancestors didn't discuss them because, frankly, they flaunted about the realms, accepting worship like gods. Our kinds hated each other, but from what I know, Guardians lived more than one life . . . A sort of reincarnation cycle, I think. And no one knows what happened to them. They simply vanished."

As Lekk finishes his answer, his gaze wanders from the balcony back to the hall where he left his friends, and I get the impression he wants to return home—if only because he worries for their safety.

Grudgingly, I do the thing my father ordered and ask him to stay for dinner and the preliminaries.

CHAPTER 39

DAGEN

ONCE JASPER AND I MAKE IT BACK TO THE RED MASK, WE find Helina serving drinks to the growing crowd. Jasper asks me to linger in view tonight, since one of Red's donors might stop by.

So I do. I'm dressed in one of Red's slick black suits with black gems sewn at the cuffs and a red mask like the dancers.

I sit at the table I usually do, where people expect to see Red, with a view of the entire room and all the red-suited dancers. After Helina told them their debts would be forgiven, enough left to leave the stages looking sparse.

A woman delivers a glass of honey rum to my table and taps it down in front of me. She leans forward, showing cleavage. "Helina said I'd find you over here." I can see in her memories that she is one of Red's girlfriends who often offer donations in exchange for Red's attention. I find it hard to think there's not some kind of threat or coercion behind these *girlfriends*.

My gaze finds Helina, who's now dancing with elegant but fierce grace on one of the stages. I see why Red kept her around. The entire room is throwing money at her.

I nod my thanks and the woman lingers, her gaze trailing my chest and jaw before she says, "You seem different tonight, Red."

I tip the glass and roll it back and forth, sloshing the liquid from one side to the other. "Good," I say.

She bites her lip, and it instantly makes me think of Nizzara biting her lip in her room—wearing that barely there nightgown—as she confessed to imagining her hands on me.

Fuck, I was so close to materializing in front of her right then.

That damn lip-bite nearly undid me. As I try—and fail—to shove that memory to the back of my mind, where I've been trying to keep it, I can't.

The woman leans against my table. "You haven't called on me for a while, Red. I have a donation waiting in your bedroom."

I throw back the liquid, trying to ignore the tightness I feel through my core when I replay any interaction I have with Nizzara.

I smile politely at the woman. "I have somewhere else to be tonight."

CHAPTER 40

NIZZARA

DIARY: PAGE 18
After holding half of the kitchen staff hostage, I discovered it was one of the dishwashers. She wouldn't name the person supplying the poison. So, I ended her slowly.
—Lo

✎

DINNER WAS FUN. LEKK DIDN'T STAY. FATHER PROMISED punishment because of it. For that reason, I'm glad to be standing in a duel ring.

The Zems have always been the pinnacle of excess, but they've surpassed my expectations this year, and it's obvious by the gem murals plastered on the walls that they've been planning on hosting the preliminaries for a few moon cycles, even though the Zo king officially relinquished their turn to host two weeks ago.

But calling the Zems presumptuous is like calling this winter black.

King Rajim rises on a gem-powered platform among the sixteen duel rings. At its highest, the platform is still hundreds of feet beneath the red dome ceiling sparkling with gems. I can't fully appreciate the gem mural, because there are gems *everywhere*.

Gems on the walls.

Gems on the hanging chandeliers.

Gems on the duel rings.

Even the small device in Rajim's hand is powered by bright red gems. Blare gems that amplify whatever they're melded to.

For preliminaries, the duel rings are four rows of four, and two referees are stationed at each one, including mine.

So many spirits jut around, and the ceiling is so tall I can't be sure if the dark one high in the rafters is Dae.

I pretend it's not and move on; Liha can sniff out attraction easier than other desires.

"Welcome," King Rajim's voice echoes and bounces off every vast corner of the Zem arena, "to the hundredth King's Duel in our history!"

Spectators, from the wealthier districts, rage and cheer in the thousands of seats around us. And yet, this is nothing compared to the King's First Duel, which will take place in the Megadome three weeks from now.

"This year's competitors will compete in the four-duel method to rank the duelers," he announces.

I flip my dagger in my hand to keep me from lingering on my opponent—one of Sorren's infantry soldiers. If he wins against me—a chosen heir—he will be legendary. If I win against one of my own infantry soldiers, I will be seen as a *rightfully* chosen heir, solidifying my rule.

"Duelers who win all four rounds will receive the highest rank of four," Rajim says, his voice booming. "Duelers who win no rounds will be given a rank of zero, determining the fight schedule for the tournament."

The infantry soldier glances at the dagger in my hand and smiles. I am still not skilled enough with a sword.

"Tonight's preliminaries will commence with level-five rules. No killing," King Rajim says. The audience boos.

"Don't worry." He smiles at the crowd. "Killing blows will be permitted next week, in the King's First Duel. Now, let's meet this year's duelers!"

Columns of light from giant, overhead glo stones sweep across all sixteen duel rings and the audience cheers. Duelers who rank high in the preliminaries get a schedule advantage, not to mention preferential treatment like better healers and more attentive weapon servants.

Two rings over is Kazem, whose eyes are murdering me from across the arena. I swallow, tightening my grip on my daggers. I know what I said at the rave was bold, but seeing him ready his sword, knowing he is the most skilled dueler in the tournament . . . well, I'm not feeling so bold now.

A few more announcements are made before the refs close in and the sound of drums floods the cavernous room. The infantry soldier across the ring is as chill as the air outside, and when the siren sounds, he lazily draws his sword.

My leathers have red spikes on the shoulders and calves. No outfit swap tonight. With fifteen other duels going on simultaneously around me, it won't even be noticed.

I portal a dagger toward his left shoulder with a puff of pink smoke, but he catches it and hurls it out of bounds.

"That's why he's infantry," Liha says.

I palm my next dagger and run to attack, but his sword slices into my left flank before I can get close enough to stab. His cut is deep, and blood spills down my side. He retracts—no spins, no frills—and thrusts again, nicking my shoulder as I spin away.

I throw a dagger at his leg. He flicks it away with silver smoke. I grit my teeth and throw another, but he sidesteps away, moving fast. Not as fast as Sorren, but it's obvious who trained him.

Liha funnels power into me, but I don't release an ounce of it as I charge.

"You are not going to win if you don't use our power."

I drop mid-sprint and slide between his wide stance, dragging my last two daggers along with me.

I slash his calves and blood spurts on my face. A deep growl erupts above.

I'm skidding, jumping up behind him, when his giant fist snatches the leather over my chest. My world tilts as he body-slams me down onto the mat.

Stars break out in my vision, and his massive knee crushes into my abdomen.

I kick, claw, punch, and bite, trying to get out from his pin, but he's too big and—

He grabs my wrist mid-punch and pins it to the mat. The gold spirit falls around me, and Liha pools her power into me.

I spit on my opponent's face, and he turns red with rage. He punches my jaw. Black spots bleed into my vision—but not from the impact.

"Move your daggers!" Liha yells, but her voice sounds muffled, underwater, distant.

Darkness grows inside me. Liha's power spreads and builds through every inch of me, but it's not cutting through the darkness. It's only being sucked into it.

The gold spirit floats closer to me, its power about to be sucked into the darkness too.

I grit my teeth, mentally clawing my way through the power drowning me from the inside as my opponent squeezes the pressure point in my wrist, releasing my fingers' death grip on my dagger.

Another burst of Liha's power, and the darkness I feel recedes from my mind. I need to end this duel quickly, since the darkness seems to love violence so much.

If only my opponent's head were closer . . .

"I bet this is the closest you've ever been," I grunt to the soldier, meeting his gaze.

A snide smirk pulls up his lips. "Closest to what? Beating a cocky, shit-brawling princess?"

I shift underneath him, forcing myself to relax. Forcing myself to ignore this unignorable power within my grasp.

I tilt my chin up. "To a woman, you ugly fuck."

He bends closer, his lips curling back farther. "I'm going to wipe the floor with—"

I headbutt him so hard his growling mug is the last thing I see.

CHAPTER 41

NIZZARA

DIARY: PAGE 19

It finally happened. Kathreen's little assassin tried to kill me tonight. He almost succeeded too. He caught me crossing the border into Zo after I managed to steal a book about Guardians and soul magic. He ran me through with a dagger before slinking off into the night. Dagen is gone, out defending our borders. As I bled out, the only available person I trusted was Preysee. Coco found her and projected her voice to her. Preysee helped me back to the infirmary. Guess I'm stuck here until my abdomen is healed. I'm sure Kathreen will be delighted to know I made it home safely.

—Lo

MY EYES OPEN TO BRIGHT WHITE GLO STONES DANGLING from the ceiling, red walls, and the smell of antiseptic—the Zem infirmary. My head feels like it met the sharp end of a mining axe. I know I won't get an enchanted salve here. The Zems would never waste something like that on me.

"This proves my theory about how thick your skull is." Sorren's deep voice comes from behind me.

I sit up and turn until I see Sorren, in his spiked armor, leaning against the red wall.

"You headbutted my infantry soldier."

"Yeah, I did. And I hope his head feels worse than mine."

His jaw flexes. "You held back."

"You think I *like* losing?" I grip the edge of the cot.

"You didn't lose. You *tied*. It knocked both of you out."

"Same thing."

"You're hiding from your power like a coward." He points at me. "Pretending it doesn't even exist. But I promise, the longer you hide from it, the faster it'll devour you."

I swing my legs over the side of the cot. "You should leave. Only family is allowed in here."

Rage ignites in his gaze. He bridges the distance between us in two quick strides and slams his fist down on my metal cot. "Face what's in fucking front of you! Your father—" His jaw works. "Your father is *possessed*." His gaze bores into me. "And once he's fully gone, you'll be the only one who can end him."

I swallow, the room around me suddenly feeling too small. "I don't know what you're talking about."

"Don't. Fucking. Lie."

But it feels so much better to lie. To blame my father's violence on the wine and lust for power. Those are normal things. Fixable things. Things that don't require the unspeakable monster I feel lurking in the depths of my soul.

I meet Sorren's deadly gaze, my knuckles turning white over the edge of the cot. I say again, "I don't know what you're talking abo—"

He grabs my neck, crushing my airway, and raises me off the cot with one arm.

Instant. Fucking. Rage.

And unspeakable darkness.

I kick my feet, but they meet only air. I claw at his arm, but it doesn't faze the death sentence on his face.

"I do this for your own good," he says as the darkness sweeps through me. A river of deep, sad resolve runs behind his eyes. "Use your power or die, because you'll die anyway if you can't face who you are."

I reach for my daggers, but they're gone. The darkness closes in around me until only parts of Sorren's elegant, violent face waver in sight. I feel *it* assessing Sorren, ready to drain—

Gold trickles into my sight, among the black. The golden spirit descends, it's power spilling over . . . filling my body with a sense of healing and—

A vision surges into my mind like warm, golden liquid, pouring into my consciousness like it did when I listened to Preysee tell the story of her husband giving her her scar. The scene shimmers in my mind. I see a glimpse of Sorren and a woman. Somehow, I know this vision is in the future—somehow, I know its meaning. I claw at his grip, rasping out the nearly soundless words: "She will love you anyway."

Somewhere behind his hard expression, something cracks.

His hand trembles around my throat before he drops me to the floor beside the cot.

I mentally scream at the spirit to go away. When it does, the vision disappears, and my pain returns with full force.

As his jaw works, he visibly tries to calm himself and says, "See. Power."

I glare at him, wincing from the sudden return of pain. "Just because I said some words that apparently struck a chord doesn't mean I have power."

He crouches next to me on the floor, his eyes a green, murderous flame. "Yes, you do. So much power even *I* will tremble when it fully wakes, Nizzara." He rises and strides for the doorway.

"Some power shouldn't be woken," I mutter, careful with my thoughts. Careful not to go to that dark place.

He stops under the archway. "It's already peeking its eyes open, watching," he says. "And the longer you run from it, the longer its leash gets."

WHEN I RETURN HOME TO ZARR, I GO TO MY ROOM, STILL caked with dried blood. Preysee isn't waiting for me, which isn't like her. I decide she probably ran into the city. She mentioned she'd be making a trip soon. I strip down and turn on the bathwater. While the water crashes into the bottom of the deep tub, I walk back into my room and grab the closest book I can find—*The King of Kings*—and hold it to my chest with both hands while I step into the filling tub. As the soothing sound of splashing fills the room, I sit in the water, perch the book on the tray poised across the tub, and open it, trying to forget Sorren's words. Nothing good can come from thinking about what lurks deep inside me.

The monster inside is dark.

It's angry.

And it takes things.

As if on cue, an image of Tian's tan face flashes into my mind—as if the monster is taunting me with the memory it stole from me. I see a giant grin on Tian's face before the memory fades to black.

As if I had just opened the door for it, its darkness leaves my thoughts and crawls into my view. Across the windows, up the walls, on the ceiling of my bathing chamber, until I can't see the room I'm in.

Breathe, I chant. *Breathe.*

It's in my head. I know that, but it's fighting to get *out*. I squeeze my eyes shut, steady my breaths, and slowly—grudgingly—it recedes back into the depths of my mind.

Each time it rises, it becomes harder to shove away again.

I wonder if this is how my father felt in the beginning, wonder if this is what casters feel like when they become possessed.

The logical part of my mind whispers, *You felt the darkness before you became a caster.* And when I shove that thought down, it fires back with *It's always been a part of you.*

I'm not possessed by a monster.

I was born one.

That single thought is enough to steer my mind far away. I only know one thing: the less I acknowledge the dark, terrible *thing*, the less it stirs. I focus on the light—the good inside me. It's there too, and just as strong. That's what I wish to be—what I will be.

I won't become my father.

And with that, I nestle into the bubbly bathwater, focus on the *The King of Kings*, and stare at the same passage for who knows how long, unable to process the words in front of me. My eyelids are heavy. I'm utterly spent, but I can't bring myself to go to bed. My nightmares are getting worse, and my thoughts begin spiraling toward their slithering shadows when *his* cool voice seeps into the chamber.

"Unless things have changed drastically since I died, you have to turn pages to read books."

I rub my eyes, trying to refocus. "What if my Mark is osmosis?"

He hovers over to my priceless perfumes, lined up on my black vanity. *"It's not. Besides, your bonded spirit isn't here to use your Mark anyway."*

I turn the page and take a deep breath. It should scare me that he's been watching me so closely, but it doesn't.

"Although, I am curious as to why your Mark doesn't work on me. You used it at the Winter Rave, but you looked the same to me as you do right now."

I lift my gaze to him. He knows what my Mark is. "Maybe it doesn't work on spirits."

"Then why does it work on Liha?" A soft chuckle. *"When she looks through your filter she says you look like the Heshena goddess of lust. Hmm,"* he purrs, tilting his head. As if he's imagining me more . . . lusty.

I glare at him. "How do you know that?"

"I have my ways." I hear the smile in his voice.

If my Mark doesn't alter my appearance for him . . . Heat flushes through my cheeks. It must mean he can't find me more desirable in any way.

"How did you know I was using my Mark at the rave if it didn't work on you?" I breathe.

"I told you." He hovers to the side of the tub. *"I have my ways."*

"You're really good at avoiding direct questions, you know."

My Mark has never *not* worked on anyone.

Another dark chuckle. There's a heavy pause and when he speaks again his voice has an edge to it. *"Are we going to talk about you head-butting an infantry soldier?"*

"No." I glare at him. "I'm not in the mood."

I adjust myself, sliding deeper into the bubbles, and pain surges from everywhere. I hiss and, in a dark surge of irony, find myself comparing this pain to my father's punishments, and I don't know what's worse: having so many lashes in the same spot or having every inch of me sliced to ribbons. The whip replays over in my mind . . . The whip is worse, maybe less painful than this, but worse.

Ice crackles in the distance, and the temperature in my bathing chamber drops. *"I would not allow you to be whipped,"* he growls. *"And even if I was powerless to stop it, I'd never let you face it alone."*

When I don't say anything, still stunned by his intensity and sudden change in topic—which happens to be the topic I was just thinking about—he says, *"I can protect you if you let me in, Nizzara."*

I don't want any more power at my fingertips. But that's not the only thing stopping me. "I will not betray Liha."

No matter how much I enjoy Dae's company, that's what it would be. A betrayal.

When I sit up out of the thick, cooled bubbles to pull myself out, he groans and disappears.

I'm tugging a robe down off the wall hook when Preysee rushes in, apologizing profusely for being late. I wave off her apologies, assuring her I can draw my own bath.

She gasps at the red slices all over my skin and rushes to grab the enchanted healing salve.

"Any word from Palko's wife?"

Preysee bows her head. "No, my lady."

I frown.

She opens the salve jar and begins tending to my sliced flesh. How has his wife not come with the money to free him yet? It's nearing the date for executions. Liha pops into my shield.

"Where have you been?"

"The usual." Her voice sounds tired.

The darkness stirs inside me, unprovoked. Panic sweeps through me. I don't want to know what's in the book Soriah left, but . . .

What if the book has ways to ebb my power? A way to suppress it?

I stop Preysee from grabbing my hairbrush and surprise Liha by summoning a dress onto me, flicking the water from my hair, and pinning it up into a bun before I leave for the coves.

"*Where are you going?*" Liha flutters in my shield.

"The coves," I say out loud, as if saying it out loud will keep me from changing my mind.

Liha pops out of my shield and plants herself in front of me. "*I wouldn't go to the coves tonight.*"

Yes, her voice sounds exhausted, so she won't fight me too hard.

I walk through her, swirling her pink soul. "It's not a discussion." If I let her, she'll talk me out of it.

For once, she seems too tired to argue.

I open my door, and my night guards pave the way toward the coves until we reach the main floor. I find my father pacing at the base of the stairs. He looks normal. I think that's why it's so easy to lie to myself. The change was so subtle. But if I had a picture book of him, one portrait for each day over the years, and I flipped through it, I wouldn't be able to deny it. The evil that clings to him is beginning to bleed through the cracks. It's in the angle of his brows, pinched down in the center, the emptiness behind his gaze . . . the way his hands twitch as if looking for something to strangle . . .

My throat tightens. It's so much easier to believe he's drunk. I take the final step, my slippers making a soft tap on the floor behind him.

His head snaps to me. "Nizzara. Go back to your room." His eyes turn glassy, and his hands tremble at his sides.

I square my shoulders. "I am going to the coves."

My guards stiffen behind me.

"Take her back," he instructs them, and my heart tugs when they hesitate. I always liked my night guards best, but their silver vessels kick in and they begin to shuffle into a reverse formation.

"No," I say.

"Turn around"—he grits his teeth, and I swear shadows fly behind his eyes—"and run."

I shrug off the nudge from a guard. "No."

This word seems to snap some layer of his control, and an eerie calm settles around him. "Very well." His lips curve into a plastic-looking smile. "Guards," he snaps, tilting his head, until his glassy eyes bore through mine, narrowing as if something about me perplexes the evil lurking inside him. "Lead her to my chambers for punishment." Turning away he adds, "With force."

"*Be strong, my Nizzara,*" Liha whispers before fading out of my shield.

A tightness climbs my throat. She's leaving me again.

My night guards lightly tug me through King's Hall when Dae brushes my shield. "*You don't have to go alone,*" he says.

I pinch my eyes closed. "I do," I whisper, low enough the guards won't notice, or if they do, might think I'm praying.

"*Liha leaves you while you suffer—when you need her most. What kind of friendship is that?*" he growls.

I open my eyes. He's in a more fluid state, his cold encasing me like a blanket wrapped around me. Possessed casters have powers beyond what they should. Could my father hurt Dae too?

"I won't betray her." *I won't let my father hurt your soul.*

My answer stuns him.

We approach Father's doors to his bedchamber when he adds, "*I cannot go past this point unless I'm in your shield—*" His voice cracks.

"I know."

Without another word, his icy darkness rages through the castle behind me as I descend into the secret dungeons beneath Father's chambers.

Without another word, his icy darkness rages through the castle behind me as I descend into the secret dungeons beneath Father's chambers.

CHAPTER 42

DAGEN

I'D GIVE ANYTHING TO HAVE SUBSTANCE TO MY HAND right now so I could punch the solid black wall and without it sinking through, but there are guards around.

I watched her memories in the bathing room, felt the loneliness and fear she feels when Mazzar punishes her like a fucking child.

I will not leave her, even if she doesn't know I'm here, waiting for her outside Mazzar's chambers.

The worst part is I can't even fault her.

She refuses me out of loyalty—and for my safety.

That kernel of truth hits my stomach like a shot of fire whiskey, warm and buzzing.

She's loyal. Not just when it is easy, or convenient, or when Liha is near, but fiercely, unconditionally loyal.

And good.

A flame sparks somewhere inside me, hissing, snapping, and *hot*. Just like it had when the refs hauled her unconscious body out of the preliminary duels.

I replay that duel over and over in my mind. She *headbutted* an infantry soldier so hard she knocked him out too.

Awe and ice sweep around me. Nizzara's spiteful grit—no matter how impressive—won't be enough to survive King's Duel if she doesn't learn to wield a sword or use more than a puff of vessel power.

And I fucking care.

A guard leaves Mazzar's room and hurries down the hall, his eyes darting around like he's searching for someone. He disappears around a corner, and not five minutes later, Sorren appears at the end of the corridor. "Hurry, slave," he says.

Yisabell rounds the corner behind him. "Yes, sir." She hastens to keep up with his brisk walk as they approach Nizzara's guards.

"Move," he barks at them, and they part from Mazzar's door immediately.

Yisabell slows when her feet cross my line of invisible ice. Tilting her head in my direction, a knowing sparkle enters her gaze, and a depth of knowledge fills her face, as if she can sense everything about me.

She smiles, and her memories fan out before me as if she's playing all of the ones with Nizzara on purpose.

The first time she and her father arrived here in a cage, and Nizzara sent her a trail of pink smoke in the shape of a hunter bee, the Awom symbol of small but courageous strength.

The first time Yisabell scrubbed floors, and Nizzara found her, knelt beside her, and started scrubbing too, asking her to tell her stories of the Mother Awom.

Images of Nizzara smiling, laughing, and warmth beaming from her.

Images of hugs, and tears, and jokes.

A tightening sensation cranks in my chest until I can't breathe. I've fallen for the little beast.

"Slave," Sorren barks, turning back to Yisabell, who's stopped in the midst of my invisible ice.

She turns away from me, a soft smile still on her face, and continues through the massive black door.

CHAPTER 43

NIZZARA

Diary: Page 20
When Kathreen looked all shocked asking what happened to me, I told her I was fighting in the infantry pits. She must've written to Dagen, because in his letter he called me a little shit for fighting in the pits, claiming I'd be safer jumping off the castle's tallest spire. He told me I'm not allowed to die. Ever. Because I'm all he's got. He had Preysee pick up a box of my favorite pastries. Not from our kitchens, but from Zem. He also informed me the next time I endanger my life I do NOT get expensive pastries. Maybe I did get a little bit of our mother, because I kept his stupid letter. The past few days I've been holed up in my room reading the books I stole from Zo while I recover. I've determined half-souls with foresight are jerks, especially when the prophecy is cryptic and unclear, like this one: "The King of Kings will begin his reign, with two First-Mades and the blood of Zo, whether the blood is shed or bred will remain a future still unknown." And don't get me started on what the half-souls had to say about Skeeves.

Okay, no. I'm already started on Skeeves.

The book says the black, faceless creatures plaguing our borders . . . are Guardians.

Possessed by what, you ask?

The fucking essence of Evil.

God? Guardians? Essences? All the books I read interchange
those terms, and it's confusing—which brings me back to my
point about half-souls being jerks. A glossary would be nice.
—*Lo*

⁓

FATHER MUTTERS AN ORDER TO A GUARD, WHO HURRIES
off as the door shuts. When he turns to face me, his gaze is empty,
not a flicker of regret or pain to be seen. He's a degree worse than
yesterday, but compared to years ago, there's hardly a degree of him
left. The shadows beneath his eyes never leave anymore. In fact, as he
stalks closer, the dark circles look permanent, as if his skin is turning
into something else.

He reaches beneath his stool and clutches two black bolts of fabric. When he unfurls them, blood drips from their edges, and—

They're my cloaks, the ones I gave to Palko. My stomach drops.

A malicious crook bends in Father's smile—as if the presence inside him takes immense pleasure hiding in plain sight.

Toying with the threads of our relationship.

Reveling in my slow, prolonged misery.

Father hangs the bloody cloaks on a hook, and the quiet room fills
with the sound of *drip . . . drip . . . drip.*

He tilts his head, watching my fear-riddled face, but he just smiles
at me, not telling me to fix it at all.

"Where is your necklace?" he asks. "The one with the little blue
pendant?"

I freeze. The cloaks are one thing, but the necklace . . . How does
he know about that?

"Hmm," he says, a hint of glee hidden in the deep baritone of his
voice. "I distinctly remember warning you, Nizzara." He picks up a
goblet of wine and smiles at me from above its rim as if the thing inside
him *wants* me to blame the wine, as if it thoroughly enjoys my denial.
"Caring for others is a weakness—a deliciously tender spot to exploit.

Tender spots," he drawls. "Make it so easy to punish someone . . . when they *misbehave.*"

The words sink through me: the presence inside my father has been punishing him . . . by hurting *me*. My fists clench at my sides as the cloaks continue to drip on the stone floor. "Caring is not a weakness."

Drip . . . drip . . . drip.

"It is," he says. "And I'm going to show you exactly *why* it is."

A small knock comes from the door. Father opens it with a puff of black smoke.

The door swings open to—

Yisabell.

"Enter and kneel," he orders, and she does.

I throw myself between them. "No! She's done nothing wrong. *I* took the cloaks to Palko. Punish *me*."

"Oh, Nizzara." His evil smile deepens. "I am punishing you."

I square my shoulders, the sting of his last punishment still slicing through my back. "I won't let you hurt her."

Yisabell studies my father then reaches up and brushes my hand with the snake ring.

"I will take this pain for you, my friend," she says in Awom. "I will be okay."

I shield her with my body, but Father's black tendrils reach out from his hand, curling around my feet, threatening to move me out of his way. He's never used that power on me, but it climbs up my legs just like it did with the innkeeper, just like it did Kazem.

I raise my chin. He'll have to use it. I'm not budging. His smoke halts, swirling, and a whisper of softness enters my father's gaze as if he's still in there fighting—but losing. He sends his smoke away from me, out the door, and it returns with someone in tow.

"Sorren," Father says when the door opens to his tall, muscled form in the doorway. "Restrain my daughter."

Sorren's in a tunic and pants, as if he was off duty until moments ago. He glances down at the silver vessel on his hand before he stalks forward and hauls me against his chest.

"No!" I scream and fight him, but he cranks my arms back in a bone-crushing hold, pulling me away from Yisabell as if I'm nothing—his strength surpassing that of anyone I've met.

As soon as I'm out of the way, Father takes a whip from the wall and releases it on Yisabell. She cries out as it cracks. I throw my head back, trying to dislodge Sorren, but it thuds uselessly against his chest. Tears stream from my cheeks as I thrash and kick and bite . . . But he's a statue locked around me, despite bloody teeth marks on his arm.

Another whip crack, and another cry pierces the air. Darkness like I've never known pools inside me, and the golden spirit enters the room. Its power trickles into my senses. *Everyone's* power trickles into my senses like orbs of energy. I sense Yisabell, like an icy blue energy source ready and open for me to pull from—to drink in. And my father . . . A beautiful red soul diseased with black, rotting spots.

And the golden spirit . . .

All offering power. As if I could drain them all with half a thought. A slip of control. That's how simple, how easy it would be.

If this darkness inside is what I think it is . . . I'm worse than the Evil lurking inside my father. I *feel* it. Cold, emotionless, and exacting. I sense the way it sees the world—remorseless and unfeeling. When it looks at my father, the monster feels nothing; at Yisabell . . . nothing.

I don't trust it.

Yisabell stiffens with each crack of the whip, her cries building each time, and I'm breaking apart. Anger, misery, pain . . . they bury me with each whimper. And the darkness spreads through me so potent, I can almost feel its mind as my own.

I could end them all, it thinks. *And afterward, you'd feel nothing . . . It is power, to feel nothing.*

If I slip, if I linger near it for too long . . . I will feel nothing as I drain the entirety of this room. I would do *anything* to protect Yisabell. I'd lose myself to this darkness a hundred times if I knew she wouldn't be sucked away with me.

But I know one thing for certain.

If I touch that darkness . . . *I* will become the monster in this room. Bad things happen when I see black.

I bite into the skin of Sorren's forearm and squeeze my eyes shut, willing the monster back into the depths of my being, until it no longer peers out of my eyes with me. The icy blue color surrounding Yisabell disappears as the darkness relents with a vengeful growl.

I scream with each crack of the whip, uncontrollable tears streaming down my face as I continue to fight . . . but Sorren adjusts his stance and grip to restrain me more each time.

I never stop fighting.

When Yisabell rises from the floor, her back a bloody mess, Father sends her to clean the dungeons.

She makes eye contact with me as she leaves, and I swear that is love in her gaze. Father orders Sorren to release me and he does.

Father discards the whip and tugs a black glove on with void gems that no longer glisten. "I've told Sorren to place guards at the bottom of your tower and throughout the dungeons. So, no sneaking off to visit your Awom friend or the prisoners. Not that there are any prisoners left to visit now."

My fists curl at my sides.

"I think I'm beginning to get my point across." A sad smile takes over his face, as if there's no clear line between where my father ends and his possession begins, as if some words and expressions belong to him . . . and others don't. "Stop caring for her, Nizzara, and I will have no power over you." He gazes at me as if to say *Stop caring for me too.*

Father finishes pulling on his second glove. "As for Lekk, stop messing around and gain his hand. He is good for you."

Before I can scream at him, he disappears into a spray of darkness, into nothing. He's gone, just like before.

Sorren nudges me out the door and guides me up the steps. The world tilts and wobbles around me, my knees trembling as I follow, my mind numb. His voice is gruff when he says, "And the leash lengthens."

CHAPTER 44

NIZZARA

Diary: Page 21

Dagen returned home. He looked awful. I would've chalked it up to the fact that he's been at war with the possessed demons at our borders, but I found him in the memorial room. Sitting by Mother's statue. He let me sit with him. After a while, I asked what was wrong. He told me Kathreen really wants children, but a healer confirmed he isn't capable of making them, not even with an enchanted potion—apparently even magic has its limits, and producing the ability to create life is one of them. Of all the problems I'm capable of fixing, I really wish I could fix this one. If anyone deserves to be a father, it's my brother. He would make such a good one.

—Lo

I CLIMB THE STEPS OF THE TOWER, AND LIHA SURFACES AS I reach my door. My cheeks sting from my tears. My limbs hurt from fighting against Sorren for so long and hard. His blood still tastes bitter in my mouth.

She nudges my cheek as I close myself inside my chambers.

Numb, empty, I say, *"How did my father know about the necklace?"*

She halts midair.

The only person who knew about it was Preysee.

Until Preysee mentioned it in the bathing chamber . . . when Liha was with me. If Preysee was so loyal to King Dagen and his people, I can't believe she'd tell my father.

"How did he know about the necklace, Liha?"

She darts around me, nervous.

The day I bonded with her feathers into my mind. It was Father who suggested her.

Then, I remember being on the dance floor with Kazem. She left my shield right before Father stormed through the crowd.

"You"—I fall to my knees—*"you are his spy."*

She doesn't speak, and it is confirmation enough. My hand shakes as I point to the door. *"Leave."*

"You don't understand—"

"Leave!" My anger rises, stealing away what little other emotions I have left. My voice is cold . . . *empty*, when I say, *"And don't come back."*

She zigzags through my shield. *"I can't leave you, or you'll be in danger from his other spirit . . . And yourself."*

My hand goes to my dagger—a stress reflex. The golden spirit descends, bringing trails of light that move through the room like rivers, and I can't bring myself to care. *"You leave me all the time."*

"I can leave you, but I will not unbond you."

I look down at my vessel. *"I don't want you anymore."*

I feel her hurt surge through our bond at my words, but that means she feels mine—how deep it goes. She lied. She betrayed me.

"I have the gift of protection." She pauses. *"I know you feel the darkness inside you. I've been shielding you from it . . . and your father from his. Trying to save you both—"* Her voice cracks. *"But both of your darknesses grow. And I . . . shrink."*

She funnels a zing of her power into me, and it warms the numbness throughout my soul. The colors brighten around me, and my emotions surge back to the surface as if yanking me out of a cold pool.

"Is our darkness the same?"

"No," she says. *"Your father has an enemy—"* She stops herself. *"Enemy is too light of a word for what Nexia is. She is the Dark queen of the*

Jaxelli, and your father killed her soul's mate—the person her soul was bonded to." Liha hums in a nervous tone and flutters about my shield as if trying to decide what information she's allowed to give me. *"Nexia is not a half-soul with special gifts. She is a pure soul, born with the entire essence of Evil inside her. She's the creator of Skeeves, and she's taking a very long time turning your father into one, torturing him over the course of years, for killing her mate, Nizzara."* After a very long pause she adds, *"You . . . you are a pure soul like her, born harboring a dark essence. Not the essence of Evil, but . . . something else. And I'm trying to protect you from it, but I'm losing power . . . I know you've felt it. If it takes over—"*

"That's not going to happen."

"It might," she says softly. *"If it does, gods, creatures, and souls will fear you like they've feared nothing else."*

Tears fall down my cheeks. I don't want to be what I am. I don't want to fear my own hands. If I had any energy left, I'd scream. All I can do is say, *"You are his."*

She nudges me, and I stiffen at the contact.

"I've been his from the beginning." She pauses. *"I made the mistake of leaving him once, a long time ago, and he bonded another . . . and now they're both . . . I'll never forgive myself for it. I won't abandon him again. Or you."*

"You told him about Palko."

"I did, but it was the darkness within him that killed Palko, not your father. He's fighting a losing battle, Nizzara. Him and his other spirit."

Something clicks, knowing Liha has listened to almost all my conversations. *"Where is Soriah? Did he do something to her?"*

"I cannot tell you that."

"Why? Because you're more his than mine?" I snap.

"Because I don't want you to get any dangerous ideas. My whole purpose is to protect you. Even from yourself, Nizzara."

I stand up and swipe the tears from my cheeks, deadly anger rolling through me as I try to breathe through it. *"I want you to unbond me."*

"You may hate me. You may never love me as you did, but I will not leave you unprotected."

I jerk my vesseled hand out in front of me and try to claw the wretched thing off, despite how useless it is to try. It's burned into my flesh. The only thing that will sever it is—

I yank my dagger out from my leg sheath and snap it to my middle finger, pressing its razor edge against my skin.

"*No! Nizzara, please. I'm begging you. I am only here to protect you.*" Her voice breaks like panes of glass. I feel her agony and love bleeding through our bond.

My hand trembles, poised to slice my vessel off.

"*Please don't lose your soul out of spite. I'll give you space. I will not bother you, but please allow me to continue protecting you. Despite what you think of me, I love you, Nizzara.*"

My heart cracks because I feel it in our bond. My rage is building, that familiar darkness rises, filling my ears, my chest, my hands. I throw the dagger so hard it buries itself hilt-deep into the solid wood post of my bed, chipping the black paint.

"*I only have to be in your shield for a few hours to weave the protection.*"

"*How could you do this to me?*" I ask, because, deep down, that's what's really breaking me. She lied. She was in his shield while he hurt me every single time. I thought I was protecting her from her traumas by facing my father alone, but she was on the other side of it, helping him deliver my own traumas to me instead.

She's quiet before saying, "*You do not understand the battle he fights every minute.*"

I slump to the floor, my knees giving out beneath me. "*You said you'd give me space. I need you to do that.*"

A crack breaks through me—through my soul—and in the span of a breath, I am alone.

CHAPTER 45

NIZZARA

Diary: Page 22

I'm done reading my stolen books. I figured out all these lesser prophecies are fragments, taken from one original source. *The King of Kings.* But the copy we own conveniently leaves out a lot of important tidbits. I know exactly where the original is, but it might cost me my life to get it. So instead of trying to get myself killed today, I spent time with my brother. We played a round of Kaji. Dagen accused me of cheating because his blare gems kept landing on the "miss a turn" space. I informed him, in between bites of pastry, that it's impossible to cheat at Kaji. He grumbled through his defeat.

Dear diary, I totally cheated at Kaji.

—*Lo*

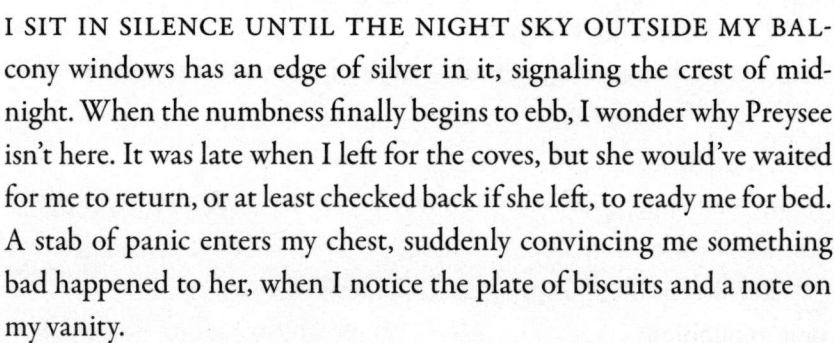

I SIT IN SILENCE UNTIL THE NIGHT SKY OUTSIDE MY BAL-cony windows has an edge of silver in it, signaling the crest of midnight. When the numbness finally begins to ebb, I wonder why Preysee isn't here. It was late when I left for the coves, but she would've waited for me to return, or at least checked back if she left, to ready me for bed. A stab of panic enters my chest, suddenly convincing me something bad happened to her, when I notice the plate of biscuits and a note on my vanity.

She took her alotted night off. Good. She deserves it. I quickly read her note informing me of bath oils that were delivered and restocked in my bathing chamber and how she laid out a nightgown for me. After my heart rate returns to normal, I stuff a biscuit in my mouth and shed my dress for a bath.

Preysee is definitely more skilled at mixing fragrances and oils. The concoction I'm dumping in is as thoughtless as my mind.

I dip my toes into the scalding heat and release a sigh, absorbing the security I feel when I'm here: floral scents in a blood-ridden castle, encasing warmth in a cold, neglectful home, and the solitude that is chosen, not forced. The sudsy water climbs my torso as I sit, and another sigh breaks from my lips when it covers my breasts.

I'm so broken, so empty, and this warmth feels so healing, I keep lowering myself, down, down, down. As if the water will hold me until I'm okay.

I'm fully submerged, head and all, noting how my concoction of oils is making my skin tingly, when I sense *his* darkness above, calm and soothing and cool.

I remain in my watery cocoon until my lungs are bursting. When I sit up, sloshing water, he doesn't say anything, but he's here.

"It's not polite to lurk." Water runs down my face, dripping from my lashes as I stare at him.

An edge cuts through his voice. *"I'm just making sure you're okay."*

"Why do you care?" I'm relieved when my voice is more normal, not as empty or as cold as before.

A pause. *"I find it hard not to."*

I ignore the tug I feel at his words and the increasing tingle on my skin.

"Why?" I bite out. My voice might sound calmer, but I'm still drowning inside, unable to breathe.

A moment passes before he whispers, *"I see your memories, Nizzara. I see what Liha, and Soriah, and your father have done to you."*

His words bring a tremble to my hands, and I'm glad they are hidden by bubbles.

My insides teeter between two extremes: a cold, angry monster and a scared, lonely girl. I bend my knees in the water and clutch my arms around them.

"*So, yes,*" he says. "*I care, and I want to make sure you're okay.*"

The tingle on my skin grows to a nearly unbearable level. Something about the scent of the oil overrides my mind—filling it with sudden color and life. Heat begins unfurling throughout my abdomen, and his voice—always smooth and delectable—is suddenly *sultry*, and all those things combined have me overheating.

"What do you want from me, Dae?" I try to keep my voice normal, but it comes out breathy and slow. Something strange is going on, and I can't figure out what. But at the same time, it is the kind of distraction I need. Is this somehow his doing?

"*Besides fewer bubbles?*" he says, and I swear if *tortured longing* had a sound, it would be his voice.

Damn his voice.

I try to dampen the sudden heat surging through my thoughts. "Does it suck having an urge you can't act on?"

The water is stifling, my body tingling everywhere it touches my skin, so I lean back and kick my legs out to rest on the opposite rim, trying to find some sort of reprieve from the building heat.

Somehow, I feel his gaze lingering on my legs. "*I'm not like other spirits, Nizzara.*"

I gaze up at him and swallow. "Always avoiding direct questions."

"*Among other things.*"

"If your only desire is fewer bubbles," I say, "then I'm afraid you're too late since I'm betrothed and all." My mind, which was so empty and cold minutes ago, is suddenly finding very creative ways to fill itself, starting with wondering what he meant when he said he's not like other spirits . . . He *did* manage to carry a plate of food to my room. What else could he do with his hands? I reach for one of the calming oils I used in my water and begin massaging it into my neck and shoulders, giving my hands something to do other than twitch from this building tension. As soon as I get to my arms, I stop, realizing with sudden clarity that this is *not* a calming oil.

Preysee's note.

This is the enchanted oil that Liha insisted I order. The one that makes the wearer irresistible—she didn't mention that it would make *him* irresistible too. The scent alone fills my mind with extremely vivid daydreams. I curse Liha under my breath because *of course* the oil she had ordered would do . . . *this.*

Dae stalks closer, and my thighs press tighter against each other in response. Even the way he walks is coy, and something tells me he fucking knows it.

"*I want you, Nizzara.*" He pauses. "*I mean I want to be inside you—I mean your shield.*" His dark outline of a hand finds his ghostly hair. "*Fuck,*" he says. "*What in the realms is that scent?*"

This blasted oil. It's already in full effect, making his voice feel like a trail of soft kisses up my neck to my ear. Even the dull pain from my wounds are more like sensual tugs on my skin now.

It takes everything I have to ignore the way my nipples hardened and the sudden need that surged through me when he said those words in that order.

"Why do you wish to be in my shield?" I close my eyes and take a breath. "So you can spy on me and report back to my father?"

"*I am no spy of your father's,*" he snarls, but realms. That sound just sent waves of pleasure through me. "*I already told you. I can see your memories. I wouldn't need to be in your shield to report things.*"

"Prove it." I bite my lip, satisfying the need to be touched by slowly trailing my foot higher up my leg. I will be throwing this damned oil away the moment I have my wits returned to me. But for now, it's so much better than what I felt before.

Dae clears his throat. "*I see memories of men too afraid to look you in the eyes. I see your memory of your betrothed, how he insults you by seeing you differently through your Mark. I see your Awom friend in the Zo palace bringing you books—*"

"Stop. I know my own memories. Prove to me that you do not serve my father. Make me believe you."

There's a long stretch of silence filled only by my heartbeat, frantic from the oil.

"*You wish me to prove it?*" he whispers, and I swear his lips are by my ear.

"Yes."

"*That fucking lip you're biting is responsible for this,*" he says before his presence moves around the onyx tub, toward the gloom-filled windows that look out above the fog.

He materializes.

Into a fucking man.

A beautifully dark-haired, hazel-eyed, smirking—

I gasp.

Dae.

Short for Dagen.

King Dagen.

I glance over toward my dress, piled on the floor where my dagger lies beneath it. Even though he is a *spirit*. He's dead. I can't do anything to him with a dagger, can I? I open my mouth. Maybe to scream for my guards or Liha, I don't know.

He must be here to kill me—he has to hate me. Cold plunges through me—this was a ruse to—

He places a finger to his lips, then speaks out loud. Not in the dimension of spirits, but *out loud.*

"I won't harm you, Nizzara."

"Do not lie to me."

I've been lied to enough. I can't take any—damn this oil! Now that I can fully see Dae—Dagen—I see it's affecting him too. His hazel eyes burn with desire every time they find me. And they keep finding me. They're even more mesmerizing than in his portrait.

"I swear on my soul, Nizzara. I am not lying to you. At first, I planned to hurt you, but I—it's not my plan anymore. You're not the one who wronged me." He sighs and it produces goose bumps up my neck. "But now you have to believe me when I say I'd never serve your father." He walks to me, crouches down, and takes the oil from the rim of the tub.

A devilish grin splits his lips. His smirk definitely isn't portrayed accurately in King's Hall, not even close.

"An enchanted aphrodisiac," he tsks, his eyes still ablaze. "How naughty of you. I hope you didn't plan to use this on your betrothed. I don't think his poor prudish soul could withstand such torture." He tilts his head, nothing but untamed mischief in the set of his lips. "Unless this is intended for personal use—"

"I used it by mistake." I surge forward, sloshing bubbles, and snatch for it, but he moves it out of my reach.

"Hmmm." He sets the small vial back down. "I like my version of the story better."

"This conversation is over," I say.

He smirks. "Not in my head, it's not."

The bubbles are beginning to thin, and the water is no longer hot. When I stand up to reach for my towel, Dagen turns his back to me.

"You're a spirit, are you not? What does it matter if you see me naked?"

He folds his arms, accentuating the broad shape of his shoulders that are very noticeable beneath his snug, black shirt.

"I still have a tiny shred of decency left. Let me use it in peace."

I tug on my nightgown, then bend down to strap my dagger onto my leg. The movement pulls at a wound that hasn't healed as quickly as the others. I hiss.

"I will not tolerate him hurting you," Dae says.

I half laugh. "Who?"

His shoulders tighten. "Anyone."

It dawns on me. I haven't told him I'm covered now, probably because I'm still tracing the lines from his wide shoulders down to his waist, like a V. There *has* to be some kind of lingering effect from the oil.

"I don't need a knight in shining armor. You can turn around now."

He turns around, his arms still folded. "I'm not going to fight your battles for you, but I won't let you sit idle, being less than what you are. That won't help you win your tournament or help my people who are suffering."

My fingers curl into my palms, digging nails into my skin. "You know what I am?"

His gaze trails my wet legs and scarlet nightgown, and his throat tightens. "I know exactly what you are."

"What am I *exactly*?"

His smirk is easy and sinful, beneath eyes that are still on fire. "You are a cruel little beast."

CHAPTER 46

DAGEN

"I MAY BE CRUEL, BUT YOU ARE NAIVE IF YOU THINK I'M LET-ting you in my shield now."

She flicks her dagger from the sheath on her leg and points it at me, drawing a lazy circle in the air.

Nizzara in her fighting leathers making a man scream on the mat is one sight, but in her barely there gown with wet, glistening skin, dripping hair, and a dagger pointed at me is quite another.

I shrug. "I've never backed down from a challenge before and I don't plan on starting now. I'll earn your trust somehow."

Her face does that thing when she's purposefully keeping some emotion from showing. Her expression hardens. Her shoulders square up, and her lips relax into an unimpressed pout. Damn those lips.

"This isn't a *challenge*. It's a rejection."

"Let's make it a challenge, then." I step directly in front of her dagger, pinching its sharp point against my chest. Her eyes widen when the blade meets substance.

I refrain from smiling at that and tilt my head to catch her gaze. "Tell me how to gain your trust, and I'll do it. Or don't tell me, and I'll still do it."

Her eyes narrow. "Brutal fucking honesty. Nothing less." She twists the dagger, deepening the pressure. "And yes, lying by omission is still lying. If you can do that, I will consider trusting you."

Something in her gaze tells me it will take more than honesty to gain her trust, but it's a start. "Done."

"The story about your mother passing away with your little brother," she says, still applying pressure. "Was it true?"

Air turns cold around me. "I never lie about my mother."

Her chest rises and falls more rapidly now, and I'm curious if it has anything to do with the way her eyes keep roaming mine.

"You said you planned to hurt me." She swallows. "Elaborate."

I lean forward, pinching the dagger harder against my chest. "I was sent here to steal your soul by the god of death in exchange for my freedom. I have until the King's Final Duel to deliver it."

"The god of death," she says slowly, almost disbelieving. "You mean Nil?"

I nod.

I can almost see her mind working, jumping from one piece of information to the other, until she says, "Freedom from what?"

That mind of hers reminds me of Lo, jumping straight to my motive. "Freedom from Baratrum, where I've been the last ten years."

"And you expect me to believe you'd ever give your freedom up for my benefit?"

I shrug. "I can only take your soul if you freely give it to me, so I guess that means you're in control here."

She deepens the pressure of the blade, until I'm sure if I were fully alive, there'd be blood. "Why would you tell me that?"

"Because it's the brutal fucking honest truth."

I glance down where her lacy nightgown clings to her wet, toned thighs. "Do you usually assault men with daggers while wearing racy nightgowns? Because if so, I've been hanging out in the wrong social circles."

She rolls her eyes, but when her gaze finds my lips, pink flushes across her cheeks.

"I told you my smirk is dazzling." I dip my head. "Are you going to wipe it off my face like you promised?"

She does the thing with her face again, and I'm met with stone-cold Nizzara once more. "You are even more cocky as a—" She pokes me harder with her gleaming black dagger. "What *are* you? How can I do *this*?"

"I'm a deathwalker, caught between life and death." I tuck my icy hands into my pockets. "And yes, considerably more cocky in my human form. So, how about it? Was I honest enough for you?"

She flips her dagger before sliding it into the sheath at her leg. "For now. We'll see if you can keep it up."

She leaves the bathing chamber.

I lean in the archway and watch her glistening legs walk away. "I'll keep it up."

She grabs a book from her nightstand and tosses a glance back at me. "Doubtful."

I fold my arms, grinning.

CHAPTER 47

NIZZARA

DIARY: PAGE 23

Kathreen told my brother that his infertility is the reason she's cheating. He'd never admit it, but she's tearing him apart, and I just might kill her for it. Not to mention I caught her stealing rens while she filled in for tax court.

—*Lo*

MY HANDS ARE SHAKING AS I OPEN *THE KING OF KINGS*, ignoring his gaze.

It's so late, and I'm so exhausted, I'm struggling to keep my eyes open.

Then I remember there's a solid fucking man playing with a giant-ass sword made of shadow in my room.

He flicks his hand, and it appears, then with another flick, it's gone.

I don't want him to leave, though. What is wrong with me?

Who am I kidding? I know what's wrong with me. It's that diary. I want to pull him into a hug with one hand and help Lo claw Kathreen's eyes out with the other.

He side-eyes me with a knowing grin, as if he can hear my desires for him to stay, to hug him, and even the one about eye-gouging Kathreen. Realms, I hope he's a spirit like Liha, who struggles to hear them, but thinking back over my conversations with him, I get the sinking impression he can read every damning desire I have.

"What is your obsession with that book?" he asks.

I run my finger along the frayed binding and shrug.

"So, you can ask brutal honesty of me, but I can't ask a simple question of you?"

"You can dig into my memories *and* my desires. I'd say that's more than fair."

He shakes a finger. "The ones you are actively thinking come into my mind whether I want them to or not. I've refrained from digging into your past ones."

I raise an accusatory eyebrow.

His hazel eyes turn dubious. "Fine, I mostly refrained. There was the night I almost ran you through with my sword near the dungeons, but that infringement on your memories happened to save your life."

"Thanks for showing such restraint."

He sits in my wingback chair looking too satisfied with himself. "You're welcome."

I begrudgingly return to my book, pointedly not looking at his chest.

"I've heard theories about the King's riddle," he says, eyeing my nearest stack of books with devout interest. "My sister mentioned it once."

"Did she solve it?" I think of mentioning Lo's diary, but I don't trust him. I decide to keep it to myself as a bargaining chip if it ever comes to that.

He shakes his head. "Not that I know of. Do you have any theories yet?"

"No, but I've noticed a lot of strange prophecies . . ."

"Like what?"

I yawn. Realms, I'm tired. "Some passages mention vessels, some mention Dark essences and Skeeves. Then, obviously, some passages about the king."

He glances at my face. "I'm keeping you awake, aren't I?"

"I'm fine."

His gaze falls to my dagger on my leg and he smirks. "Get some sleep."

"I can't sleep with you in here."

"Why not? You've done it before."

"That was before I knew you were an actual *man*."

He chuckles. "Very well. I'll leave."

He vanishes into the dark swirling air I've become so familiar with and leaves.

When I fall asleep, the nightmares find me.

CHAPTER 48

NIZZARA

Diary: Page 24

Dagen's been smuggling slaves out of the kingdoms. That's why Preysee and I spent the better part of the night underground—in what we've code-named "the linen room."

—Lo

PREYSEE WAKES ME FROM THE SIDE OF MY BED. I'M TO MEET Thaddeus before I begin my grueling three weeks of training.

Liha is not in my shield, and a fresh pang of hurt slices through my chest. A new layer of darkness accumulates inside. I feel it growing more and more each day. It's in my thoughts, my sight, my *soul*, and fighting to be myself takes monumental effort.

I dress, and Preysee is quick to pull my hair into a high, slick bun on top of my head. She lines my eyes with a casual smear of kohl and coats my lashes before I meet Brunar and his guards outside my door.

I'm trailing them to breakfast when Dagen feathers in beside me.

I look over to where his spirit keeps in step with me.

"*Did you dream of me?*" he purrs.

"*No*, I didn't," I mutter low enough for my guards not to hear. My nightmares had me in a cold sweat all night.

"*But you wish you had*," he says.

"I do not."

"Do you know how distracting it is . . ." He leans toward my ear. *"When I ask you a question like that, and your desires answer louder than your words?"* I hear the coy mischief in his voice when he adds, *"Desire to dream of Dagen . . . Desire to see Dagen shirtless . . . Desire to touch Dagen's bare chest . . ."*

I point my finger at him. "My desires were *not* saying that."

"They weren't," he says. "But they are now."

I huff. "I *desire* to punch your face."

Brunar turns over his shoulder. "What was that, Princess?"

"I said you're walking too close. Give me space." I glare at Dae. "Get lost or I'll start throwing shoes," I hiss.

"So feisty." Dae chuckles. "Don't you want me to come with—"

"No." I storm off, leaving him chuckling in the hall, making sure my desires do not include him. It must've worked because he doesn't follow.

When I enter the dining room a few minutes later, Father's hard gaze snaps to me from his seat at the head of the table. "Nizzara."

Tarella's in her seat, her hand trembling beside her plate as she keeps glancing at the doorway.

"Will Mother be joining us shortly?"

He runs a finger along the sharp dinner knife on the table. "No. She will not."

Tarella stiffens, her breathing suddenly seeming more careful.

"And why is that?"

"Your *mother*," he says, a corner of his lips twitching and his words slurring, "is not feeling well, I'm afraid."

A maid delivers my meal—sliced sausage on a gold disk, cart cow milk in a slim goblet, and a side of sauce in a boat.

I arrange my face to match his—cold and cruel. It's becoming easier to do.

"Where is she?"

Father wipes his mouth with his cloth napkin; his eyes, devoid of all warmth, bore through me. "Somewhere she belongs."

A nudge comes on my shield and Liha slips in.

"*Nizzara,*" she says, sounding drained of all zest. "*He doesn't have much control right now.*"

My sister has stopped eating, her gaze darting from Father to me.

I curl my hands into fists, trying to defuse this rising temper, and take my seat. I'm standing across from a sister who loathes my existence, beside a father who punishes my existence, and in front of a chair absent a mother. What fuels my dark rage the most is that I care more for them than they ever will for me. I *care* about Soriah.

Father leans forward over the top of his untouched plate. "Your little Awom friend is quite the diligent worker. She scrubbed half the dungeons clean last night. Maybe she'll take heed of my lesson and learn not to care for you either."

Nausea sweeps through me, every muscle in my sore body tense.

"*Think of your matches with Sorren,*" Liha whispers, anxiety simmering through her voice.

"*Why?*" I snap.

"*Because with the First-Made and the evil possessing him, your father is twice what Sorren is. Defuse the situation and submit.*"

"*I don't fucking submit, Liha.*"

"*But today, you have to. He won't start with you. He'll start with Yisabell.*"

I close my eyes, breathe through my nose, and think of Yisabell. It's enough to curb the storm inside.

I open my eyes and take my seat. "*Very well.*"

Father's jaw flexes before he asks, "Are you ready to face the higher-ranked competitors?" Something tells me he's fighting to have a normal conversation.

I nod.

Liha dissolves from my shield, and I reach for my milk.

A servant refills his goblet. "I'll be gone for the next few weeks. So I've called my . . . advisor to assist in affairs here."

I almost choke on my first sip of milk. "You have an advisor?"

He tents his fingers above his plate. "I do."

On cue, a figure detaches from the shadows of the room and glides forward. She's tall with powerful shoulders and cheekbones, with glowing, silver tattoos writhing up her arms beneath leather straps. Just like Lekk, but where Lekk has a brightness about him, she has darkness.

A Dark Jaxelli.

Her black, chin-length hair is slicked back behind her head. Was she there this whole time?

"This is Halix. She will manage things in my absence."

Halix studies me while Father swirls the remains of his wine, drains his cup, then rises from the table. "I'll be taking Sorren with me, but he'll return periodically to prepare you for your duels."

Striding over to me, he lowers himself until his face is beside my ear and whispers, "One step out of line, and the bondslave will pay dearly."

He evaporates into nothing as if he's been sucked away into an invisible hole.

Tarella pushes up from the table, wide-eyed and fixated on the spot Father just vacated. Halix reaches for the mighty gray blade glowing at her back, evaluating Tarella with the lethal calm of a large cat before surveying the black walls and gem-studded tableware. Her gray eyes flick to me, then my arms, as if looking for something.

Halix has a presence like my father. Powerful and dark. Tarella excuses herself and leaves the dining room. I follow.

My guards escort me down the hall toward Thaddeus's wing, and Dagen's cool presence encases me as I scorch a trail down the black hall.

"A Dark Jaxelli in Mazzar's court. Now I've seen everything."

I stop in front of Thaddeus's door but don't go in as Dae's spirit wraps around me. "If I asked you to do something for me, would you?" I whisper against the door, where only he can hear me.

"Brutal honesty and now favors?" His voice is a luxurious calming velvet against my ear. *"Violent and demanding."*

"Will you check on Yisabell?"

His presence somehow becomes heavier around me. *"I already have."*

I knock on Thaddeus's door. "And?"

"She's as okay as she can be."

CHAPTER 49

NIZZARA

DIARY: PAGE 25

While I'm debating whether or not the original *King of Kings* book is worth dying over, I'm focusing on my assassin problem. I'm starting with suspect number one, and it won't be pretty. I'd say I'm sorry for what I'm about to do to Kathreen. But I'm not.

—*Lo*

THADDEUS OPENS THE DOOR AND USHERS ME TOWARD THE desk. I plop the red book down and sigh.

He smiles. "Any theories yet, my pupil?"

"No." I rub my temples.

My months of nightmares catch up to me all at once, and a fatigue headache blossoms. Dae's cool presence brushes across my skin, easing the pressure.

Thaddeus takes the seat opposite me. "Tell me your findings," he says, folding a leg over the other and resting his hands on top of his knee.

My eyes wander to the carved figurines of Scientia perched on shelves while I mentally gather my notes.

"This book has typos. Whether or not that's relevant is debatable."

The corner of his mouth perks up. "Go on."

I flip the book open to page thirty. "Like here. It jumps from page thirty to page thirty-nine, then back to page thirty-one."

"What else?"

"I found a passage," I say.

He raises an eyebrow. "Well, read it, then."

I flip to where I've marked the page and read out loud:

"'Rebels rise and food is stone. What was reaped shall be sown. Men of kingdoms turn to monsters of night. Three families fight out of sight. The soil turns dark from blood and death. To deliver the king, she'll give her last breath.'"

Thaddeus nods along as I finish the passage. "Thoughts?"

"The words *deliver the king* remind me of childbirth," I say.

"Any other notable sections?"

I shake my head. "No, but I have a question," I say. "About energy gems."

His brows flatten. "I should've known you'd dive into that subject on your own. A mind spread too thin is called mush, you know."

"Just one question."

"Then you'll promise to focus on our subject matter?"

"Of course."

He waves his hand. "Ask your question."

"They amplify and siphon, right? I get how they work on *things*, but how do they work on people?"

He shakes his finger. "Come in with a *King of Kings* theory and I'll tell you."

I deflate in my chair. The gem book only mentioned their effect on technology. "But you agreed to answer a question."

He shakes his finger at me again. "I let you ask your question. I didn't agree to answer it."

"Fine."

Dae's cool air churns at my shoulder, sending goose bumps up into my hairline. *"You and that lip of yours."*

Heat flushes my system, and I stop biting my lip, not realizing I had been.

After forty minutes of studying, Thaddeus nudges *The King of*

Kings closer to me. "Your father shortened our study sessions to make time for your training. Our time is up."

Thaddeus stands and brushes his white robes. "I look forward to seeing you in the King's First Duel," he says. "Besides Kazem's victory, your headbutting tie against an infantry soldier is all the buzz."

If I'm being honest, *that* could also be the culprit of my headache.

My shoulders slump. I'm not in the mood to face Sorren again. I hope Father meant he was taking Sorren *today*.

Dae slides around me again, his cool, dark air soothing, as if he knows his presence eases my burdens.

CHAPTER 50

NIZZARA

UNFORTUNATELY, SORREN *IS* AVAILABLE TO WIPE THE floor with me. And he does. Over, and over, and over again.

As I keep getting back up, I swear I feel flickers of pride emanating from Dae. He wouldn't let me face Sorren alone, even though he can't help from outside my shield.

Having Dae at my side is like having a sturdy wall holding me up, especially when Sorren delivers a nasty kick to my jaw that blurs the room.

Dae's tension radiates around me as gashes appear down my leathers and small bones get broken, but I don't back down.

When I crawl into bed after Preysee's oils and salve have begun healing my wounds, Dae heads to my balcony to leave like yesterday. Last night's dreams play across my mind, as if promising a vengeful return tonight.

"Wait," I say, my voice small.

His presence halts, air swirling near the balcony doors.

As much as I'm trying to hold myself together, pretending my world isn't crumbling around me, I don't have it in me to watch him leave, don't want to face my nightmares alone.

Or the growing darkness creeping into my mind.

"Don't go," I whisper.

Without a word, his spirit hovers back to me and settles near my side of the bed, a cool wall of energy blocking out the rest of the world.

Not a single nightmare finds me.

PREYSEE BUSTLES IN BEFORE THE SUN'S RAYS ARE HIGH enough to shine through my balcony doors. "Your betrothed just arrived for you, my lady."

I sit up. "This early?"

She disappears into my closet and returns, a red dress with a plunging neckline in tow. "I don't pretend to know much about the other realms," she says. "But I wouldn't be surprised if their sense of time is a bit different from ours."

I groan and find the cold marble floor with my toes before trudging to the vanity, where she's currently preparing my makeup, uncapping lipsticks, blush, and eye palettes. "No time for a bath today, I'm afraid." She lifts a gown she picked out.

I take the dress from Preysee and put it on myself. Liha would be bouncing all around my room right now. My heart aches, missing her.

Preysee does my hair in a sleek updo and keeps my makeup simple but to my liking—black around my eyes and a matte red lip. If Lekk doesn't like it, he can take his betrothal somewhere else.

Preysee leads me to the full-length mirror inside my closet to approve her work. Just when the pit in my stomach from Liha's absence begins to gnaw deeper, Dagen's dark presence floats around me.

"*A second date,*" he says. "*Must be serious.*" His voice has an edge to it this morning that wasn't there last night.

When Preysee leaves for my perfumes, I mutter, "Jealous?"

"Brutal honesty?"

I shoot him a look that says *duh*.

He's standing behind me as I face my full-length mirror, and his velvet words caress my skin. *"Annoyingly so."*

"You're such a shameless flirt," I say, but warmth floods every part of me, and suddenly I'm remembering him in my bathing chamber, his hazel eyes burning for me. I brush a crease from my dress and remind myself he only looked at me like that because of the oil.

I'm trailing my guards to the throne room, Preysee in tow, when Dae fades away just before Liha slides into my shield.

"I will not stay long, just let me work on your protection from within your shield." She sounds exhausted.

"I didn't even know you could do that," I say, my tone harsh.

Her sadness breaks through our bond. *"I've always been protecting you from your monster or from your father's. But since I'm going with him while he's gone, I'm leaving a bigger part of my soul in it to protect you while I am away. It's not permanent but it will hold for a time."*

"You will not leave part of yourself." It sounds like something that will permanently weaken her.

"It will help you suppress the darkness inside."

"I don't want you to—"

I sense a tendril of her soul absorb into my shield, and she pales in the glo lights.

A loaded silence fills the air as we near the ballroom. Of course she would do it anyway. Her warm pocket of air nudges me, softer—weaker. *"When you're alone, go to the book Soriah left. Your father decided to leave it there for you in case he—"*

She takes a deep breath. *"In case he—"*

"Nizzara." My father's voice booms as we enter the ballroom through giant black doors. He's on his throne, eyeing the two Jaxelli Warriors—Solis, the redhead, and a woman with a spray of freckles on her cheeks—that are today's collateral. He must've made a quick trip back here just for this.

Lekk stands below the dais, appearing as comfortable as a man awaiting execution.

Halix stands behind Father, wearing Zarr infantry armor that hides the gray swirls on her skin.

Father's eyes are lucid as they find mine, not the hard things I'm so used to. The corner of his lip twitches, the only tell of strong emotion he's ever had. The last time I saw it was when I won my level-five-dueler ranking.

Lekk clears his throat and pointedly keeps his fiery gaze away from my plunging neckline.

"*Give him a chance,*" Liha whispers. Is she whispering? Or is her voice just softer? "*Your father is giving you a gift; you just might not see it yet.*"

Her presence is so familiar and safe, but she lied to me for ten years.

"*Are you done with my shield?*" I say. "*Because I want you to leave.*" The words are painful, but I need to stop surrounding myself with people who hurt me.

"*What about translating?*"

"*I'll figure it out on my own.*"

"*Nizzara—*"

"*I need space, Liha.*"

There's a long pause before she says, "*I'll go. Just be wary of who you are around. Learn from your father.*"

My attention snaps back to the throne and Father's entire face is different, harder. I realize I've been dealing with his condition for a long time.

"*I'll leave now,*" she says, and once she's gone, a bubbly piece of her energy remains, humming through my shield.

My father flicks his hand toward Lekk. "You are free to roam, but do not keep my daughter long. She has a tournament to train for."

The amount of normalcy in his voice is unsettling, and I think that's why it was so easy to delude myself for so long.

Preysee follows, as our chaperone, as I lead Lekk out to the grounds. The wind is mild, nothing but a small breeze, and it reminds me of Dae as it tickles past my cheeks. His teasing has been a reprieve from the constant heaviness I feel, and I find my lip curling upward when I replay my last conversation with him about my dreams.

We walk in silence to a black fountain with flowers and birds carved into the marble, marking the beginning of the stone gardens.

Lekk peers into the ice frozen at the bottom, spouting something off in his own language.

The only thing I can do is stand here like a mute idiot.

Dae's deep voice ghosts across my skin. "*He said you look pretty. Although, he's remembering how last time you had freckles . . .*"

Lekk's tired-looking eyes are distracted by the stone statues and mazes, so I use the opportunity to whisper, "Will you translate for me?"

"*I hate to break it to you, but whatever your little pink friend did to your caster's shield has silenced your desires. It's like she's inside it. I can't hear what you want to say unless you say it out loud.*" He pauses. "*You could just allow me into your shield, then we could have all sorts of secret conversations.*"

I fold my arms and shake my head. "Not happening."

Dae ghosts along my shoulder, chuckling. "*I will translate for you.*"

I wave Preysee over. "I'm going to say random things to you, and I need you to nod and play along, okay?"

She dips her chin, her gaze tracing the strange orange markings that glow on Lekk's chest as he continues to take in the castle grounds.

I utter what I wish to say to Preysee, so Lekk doesn't think I'm talking to myself, and Dae, with no small amount of smugness, translates.

"How do I know you won't embarrass me?" I say to Preysee's face.

"*Guess you'll just have to trust me, won't you?*"

"Don't you *dare* embarrass me." I glare at him as he swirls behind Preysee's dutifully neutral expression as she nods.

He laughs.

"We asked each other questions last time," I say to Lekk, using Dae's translations. "Do you mind if we do it again?"

Lekk shakes his head as if trying to keep himself awake then says, "Ask your questions, Daughter of Zarr," Dae interprets.

"Have you ever kissed anyone?" I ask, genuinely curious.

Lekk half laughs, half winces as he responds in his own language. Instead of translating it, Dae says, *"Don't tell me you have a thing for the Nightlight just because he has glowing muscles,"* Dae purrs beside me.

I shoot him a sideways glance and tell Preysee to shut up and translate Lekk's response.

He laughs then says, *"If you are into Nightlight, you're wearing the right dress."* His velvet voice brushes my neck. *"The Jaxelli women usually cover their bosom, and you have him squirming with the desire to stare."*

"Translate it, Dae."

"Lekk said, no, he hasn't kissed anyone."

I mutter my reply to Preysee, who's taking this very well. "You've never kissed anyone? In almost two hundred years?" I repeat Dae's translation.

I've read about their strange ways of mating, but not even kissing?

Lekk offers a tired smile. "Our first hundred years of life are spent mastering our gifts." He shrugs his wide, defined shoulders. "And our lifespans are so long, it's like you waiting until you're sixteen before the desire hits, and even then, kissing is usually reserved for a chosen mate."

I take a few steps to the opposite side of the fountain until I'm facing Lekk and bend over its edge a little more than necessary to wipe the snow off a carved lush flower. Maybe he'll break the engagement if I show more of my chest, since it goes against their customs.

Lekk's breath hitches.

"So, you *are* allowed to kiss outside of a matehood?" I ask, studying the stone petals.

"So cruel of you to make him squirm this way," Dae whispers behind me.

Lekk's throat bobs and his eyes dart away from my chest. "Technically, yes, but it's . . . frowned upon," Dae continues to translate.

"Tell me, Lekk," I say, going for my real question. The question that will decide whether I give this betrothal an ounce of consideration. "You are here because my father promised to help you reclaim your homeland in Xoshbesh," I say, walking back around the fountain until I'm face-to-face with Lekk, Preysee moving with me. "What if I ask for your help in my own war?"

His brows shoot up.

"Theoretically, of course."

"What kind of *theoretical* war?" Lekk asks.

I shrug. "None. I'm just asking. If there was a cause that was important to me, would you fight by my side?"

The muscles in his jaw flex. "We are a peaceful people who've been at war for longer than you've been alive. First against the Dwarf witches who pine for our gifts, and then a second war against our own Dark Jaxelli Warriors, who betrayed us. We lost half of our Light Warriors and our home nineteen years ago. We've been living as refugees ever since. If you were my mate, I would fight any threat that came against you to my death. I would fight to defend you." His entire body tenses. "But I would not start another war when my people are still trying to survive the last one."

I hide the pang of disappointment from showing on my face. Maybe if Lekk's answer was different, I'd give this union a chance. Because I *will* be freeing the bondslaves, and it *will* be messy.

"What is keeping you from accepting this union?" I finally ask. I need to know so I can exploit it—make the issue even bigger.

He shakes his head. "I—I'm unsure if that is polite for me to answer," he says, and I can't tell if the red around his eyes is from fatigue or the fire-like energy that runs over every inch of his rolling musculature.

"*Bite your lip,*" Dae says, pacing back and forth behind Lekk.

I tilt my head around Lekk's shoulder, shooting Dae a questioning look.

"*He wants to jump your bones, okay. Bite that bottom lip of yours.*" He folds his arms, a movement of swirling air with a grumpy tone. "*He'll talk.*"

I look at Lekk, touch his muscled arm, and bite my lip. "I want to get to know you more, that's all."

The swirling glyphs on his chest plunge from orange into a deep, deep red.

It *is* a nice chest.

CHAPTER 51

DAGEN

DO HIS DESIRES HAVE TO BE *THIS* STRONG?

It'd be one thing if he *knew* Nizzara, if this monstrosity of sexual desire was based on a relationship of any kind, but it is all—a thousand percent—his mating urge. Raw sexual tension built up for a hundred-some-odd years bursting out all at once.

If he compares Nizzara to the blond-haired Jaxelli with freckles one more time in his memories, I'll lay him out. There is no fucking comparison here.

And what idiot would *not* go to war for her?

I've seen her loyalty, seen her friendships. She'd bring down the three kingdoms for Yisabell, or Preysee, or even Liha, at the drop of a hat.

That is the kind of loyalty I'd burn worlds for. And yet, as my rage and jealousy flare, I remind myself that aside from his unwillingness to start a war, and his fetish for freckles, he's a *good* betrothal for her. And far more worthy of her affection than I am—the deathwalker who came to steal her soul.

Nizzara clears her throat, and I realize I am slacking in the translating department. I'm still behind Lekk because his memories keep jumping between his hatred for Mazzar (totally understandable) and Nizzara's perfect breasts.

And the breasts of the freckled woman and even some random brunette's breasts.

When he suddenly tenses, so do I, like a battle reflex. If he reaches for his sword . . . If he touches a hair on her head . . . I don't care if she can defend herself. I'll end him. The deathwalker in me tries to convince myself it's because if he harmed her, then I would not gain my freedom, but I know better.

"He said he will outlive you by nine hundred years, bearing his child might kill you, and he doesn't trust your father. That's why he hesitates to mate you."

Nizzara's look of death—my favorite expression—rounds Lekk's shoulder again, silently threatening to give me hell later for something. I don't know for what. But whatever she has in store, I am completely looking forward to it.

A chuckle escapes me, but it quickly dies as I allow the cold to reclaim me.

Hell. That's what this is. Having her so close I can *physically* touch her and yet completely, absolutely out of reach. Not to mention Nightlight's arm, which she still hasn't let go of.

Her eyes are still shooting daggers at me from around his biceps.

He glances over his shoulder, probably wondering what she's glaring at. "*Yes?*" I offer.

"Ask him what he means about childbirth."

I give her the answer instead of a translation: *"Jaxelli Warriors can't have children outside of their kind, not without losing both mother and child."*

"Never?"

I give her a translation asking more about Jaxelli childbirth.

Lekk gestures to his chest after she asks him. "The essences passing through us are too strong. It is hard even for our own women to give birth."

Nizzara lifts her chin. "I am not weak."

I smile at that and give her the translation for it, adding a word or two to help her get her point across.

Nightlight flinches, but recovers quickly. *"He says he doesn't doubt your strength."*

Nizzara's trying not to get angry. I can tell because she's too still and tense. I make a mental note to never tell her she can't do something, unless I want that look directed at me. Which, maybe I do.

"I want to ask him about his lifespan," she says. "I know there is a big difference in longevity, but he could mate again after I die."

Nightlight growls when she mentions it to him. "We mate for life. One time to one person. Forever."

Her eyes flare. "Even if I wanted you to find a mate after I die?"

"It is our way," Nightlight says, and I translate.

"Well, shit," she says in her own language.

"There's no translation for that," I say. *"The closest word would be* scanta, *but that's the equivalent of saying* bird doo-doo. *Probably not the effect you're going for."*

"Well, what should I say to that?"

"You could try puntaka. *It's the Jaxelli version of the F-word, but a lot worse."*

She gasps. "You told me to say that three sentences ago!"

"What sounds better? 'I am not weak' or 'I am not fucking weak, you swine'?"

Her mouth gapes open, but when Nightlight turns his gaze back to her, she washes her face of all emotion.

With the expression of a lethally cold ruler, she says in the calmest tone I've ever heard, "You will pay for that, Dagen."

Cruel little beast.

CHAPTER 52

NIZZARA

DIARY: PAGE 27

I'm packing to leave for Zem. Coco doesn't like this plan, but she doesn't like anything that doesn't have to do with copious amounts of blood. I get the feeling she was quite the conniving little blood barbarian in her past life.

—Lo

AFTER LEKK LEAVES, MY GUARDS LEAD ME TO THE TRAIN-ing room, where I'm supposed to meet Sorren, but he's not there. He's been absent more and more lately.

We pass Tarella's room, and her door is open. I catch her shoving clothes into a suitcase.

"Halt," I order Brunar before pushing Tarella's door open farther.

"Haven't you heard of knocking?" she says without glancing my way. She pulls dress after dress down from her closet and shoves them into her suitcase.

"What are you doing?"

She stiffens, her back still turned to me. "Leaving."

The pit in my stomach deepens. "Tarella—"

"Where's Mother?" She flips around and jabs her finger at me. "What did he do to her?"

Her eyes are red from crying.

"I don't know."

Her hand shakes with rage as she jabs her finger at me again. "Then get out."

"Tarella—" My voice cracks. "Please stay. I know we have our differences, but I care about you."

"You didn't seem to care all the years Father trained *you* for dueling and not me. You don't seem to care when you sit on a throne, and I stand off to the side like an outcast." Her jaw works. "You get fancier dresses, better dueling coaches, smarter tutors, a bigger room, and you've never cared enough to ask Father to do the same for me." Her cheeks glisten with tears. "What's more, I've seen your temper. I've seen when your control slips and the cold murder in your eyes when it does. You're not a killer yet, but you will be. You're exactly like Father, and I'm not safe around either one of you. Mother told me if anything ever happened to her, I should go back to Zo. That's what I'm doing." She balls her hands into fists. "And I won't miss you at all."

As she talks, my pain fissures deeper and deeper inside until some inner part of me cracks open, and the darkness trickles out. I can feel it. I can hear it . . .

Such a burden it is to feel, it whispers.

When my gaze meets Tarella's she takes a step backward, goose bumps washing over her arms. "Get out of my room."

"I hope you get all the things you deserve in Zo," I say. "Since *things* are all you seem to care about." I leave.

I spend the rest of the walk to the training room shoving down the pain.

And it's so much easier with the darkness webbing through me.

When I reach the training room, Sorren still isn't there. Brunar and his guards stand out in the hall as I enter, exchanging wary glances as if I might ask one of them to spar.

The door closes, and I amble over to the longswords resting on their perches. As I pluck the bottom one, I hear the slow draw of metal on metal.

"You and that lip will be the second death of me."

I turn around to find Dae in physical form, holding a sparring sword, his hazel eyes dancing behind the black blade. He saunters over until he's directly in front of me. If he stepped closer, my nose would be the perfect height to graze the little divot where his neck meets his well-defined pecs, visible thanks to his unbuttoned black tunic. He tilts his head and his dark hair glimmers with hints of bronze under the glo lights.

My throat goes dry, and all coherent responses evaporate from my mind. "What lip?"

His gaze turns dubious as his eyes find my mouth. "That one."

I remind myself that this man made a deal to steal my soul and has unlimited access to my memories.

"I'm going to lift weights," I say, turning around.

He tosses the sword over my head, reappears in front of me, and catches it. "Your first duel is in three weeks. You need to work on your longsword, not weights."

I sidestep him, but he blocks me, my face full of his chest and his scent, which smells like—

Realms. I don't even know. Tantalizing? Is that a scent? Why is he so much easier to be around when he's a ghost?

I back up and point my sword at him. "I'm not sparring with you. I don't trust you." Maybe I trust him not to kill me, but as my family has proved, there are other ways to hurt someone. I don't want to let him in any more than I have.

"You'll be slaughtered in your first duel if you don't practice the sword with someone."

"Why does that matter to you?" I snap.

"If you die, my soul will be shattered into nonexistence." He clutches his hand over his heart as if he's declaring his affection for me, when he adds, "Literally, Nil will shatter my soul if you die before I can deliver it."

He watches my face fall. Is that what it takes for someone to care? For their life to be tied to mine?

"Then maybe I should die just to spite you."

He slowly pushes my sword aside with the back of his hand and walks closer. He raises his hand toward my neck, and I flinch.

Pain flashes across his face, and his hand pauses midair, silently asking permission. When I don't back away or tell him no, he gently takes my chin and grazes his thumb across my cheek. "I've come to like you alive." Something about his touch chases the darkness away, and a trail of warmth spreads across my cheeks where he touched me—despite the chill surrounding him.

"I know you desire to win the King's Duel and the bestowment," he says. "But I also happen to know that you want to do it with minimal power. That only leaves one option." He nods toward my sword. "Let me help you."

He's right. I can't headbutt all my opponents, not if I want to retain brain cells anyway.

He's close enough that I feel it when his whole body stiffens. I look up. His eyes are on my mouth, and I realize I'm biting my lip again.

"Distractions," he mutters.

"What?"

His hand finds my waist, and his head dips toward mine, his burning gaze locked on my lips. "The first lesson of level-six duel rings . . ." he whispers, "is distractions."

I'm leaning closer when he smiles and pops the sword from my hand before turning to ghost.

"As in, don't fall for them."

CHAPTER 53

DAGEN

THAT COLD, SPITEFUL ANGER RISES IN NIZZARA'S EYES. "I don't think my opponents are going to be distracting me like *that*."

I chuckle. "I was only making a point."

She huffs and readies her sword with a widened stance and tight core. Couple that with the lethal glare she's pointing at me, and I'm glad she can't read *my* desires right now.

Not that I have any right to desire her.

She stabs her sword through my ghostly form just for spite. Having watched Nizzara's trainings with Sorren through her memories, I see he's all about brute, lethal skill, which is good. She'll need that, but she isn't going to achieve it before her next duel. She needs to utilize every advantage she already has.

I materialize and pluck my fallen sword from the ground. "How much do you know about the King's Duel contestants?"

She shrugs. "Kazem is the highest rank. The Zarr infantry soldiers are savage, and I hear the few Zos who made it into the championship this year are decent."

I lunge my sword toward her, and she blocks. Not weak, but not as strong as she needs to be. "Use your core, like Sorren taught you. Try again."

I swing the sword, and she blocks again.

"More," I say. "Ground your feet. Put your weight into your block and lock every muscle you have."

I swing again, and she blocks harder. "Good. Blocking will be your most important skill in level six."

"Tell me something I don't know." Her dark eyes solidify into the look I've watched a thousand times from hundreds of memories. Focused and resolved.

I swing again.

She blocks harder.

I swing faster, stronger.

She blocks at the last second, core engaged.

"The next important thing is to know your opponent. Like your little lover boy, Kazem. Do you know if he has a Mark?"

"I don't know," she pants. "No one does."

She swings at me, crossing our swords, pushing one against the other, and growls, "What about offense? And don't call him my lover boy."

The swords, still holding tension, lower between us.

"No headbutting for offense. And why not? You *did* try to kiss him, so he gets a nickname. I can't call your betrothed Lover Boy because his name is Nightlight."

She huffs, sliding her sword away to deliver another blow. I block and slam my pommel against her chest.

She stumbles backward, rage igniting in her eyes.

She swings.

I dodge.

She swipes.

I spin.

She lunges, and I evaporate.

Flailing toward open air, she catches her balance and spins to where I'm hovering behind her.

"That's cheating," she growls, and her frustrated voice is one of the sexiest sounds I've ever heard.

I materialize, trying not to imagine that frustration in a very different setting. "*Know* your opponent."

"What does that even mean?" Her chest huffs from exertion.

I step closer. "It means you know I can disappear. You know how I move. So use that knowledge when you fight me. Don't keep falling for my same tricks." I linger on the flush in her cheeks and find myself committing the moment to memory. "Get to know your opponent as quickly as you can in that ring. How they move, their favored side, their rhythm, and their tells."

I look down at her grip on her sword and reach out for her, running my finger along her hand, down to her wrist. "You also need to use spirit power to keep a permanent hold on your sword, or your opponent will jerk it out of your hands every time. Strength is not enough."

A knock sounds, and I disappear before the door swings open.

"A message has arrived for you," Brunar says, eyeing my dropped sword on the floor.

Nizzara waves him in. He marches toward her with a letter outstretched, his gaze repeatedly finding Nizzara's ass in her tight leathers. Thankfully his drooling desires are nowhere as strong as Nightlight's, which are forces of nature in mortal form.

She takes the letter and opens it.

Her body goes rigid. I'm trying to give her as much privacy as I can, so instead of looking into her memories, I ask, "*What is it?*"

She tilts the paper so I can see.

If you survive to see the Final Duel, I look forward to killing you.
—*Kazem*

Her hands curl into fists, crumpling the paper.

"*He has a childish flare, doesn't he?*" I say.

She sputters a laugh before going silent again, staring at the crumpled note while Brunar returns to the hall.

"*What's wrong?*" I ask. "*You already know he wants to kill you when you face him in the duel ring.*"

It takes her a moment, her face trying and failing to pull up that regal mask before she says, "I've seen him duel." She peers down at her sword, and a flash of doubt crosses her face. "I should've learned the sword a long time ago."

I move in behind her, not stopping until her caster's shield hums from proximity.

"*He wouldn't have bothered with a note,*" I say beside her ear, "*if the thought of you and your daggers didn't spark fear in him.*"

CHAPTER 54

NIZZARA

DIARY: PAGE 28

Shit. That's what I'm in. Deep shit. I infiltrated the Zem castle disguised as a guard, slipped Kathreen an illegal sleep potion, locked her in her ridiculously decorated room, and went about talking to people, using my Mark to disguise myself as her. I even mimicked her insufferable nasal tone. All according to plan. What wasn't part of the plan was when King Tigous showed up with his sons, who have the uncanny ability to sniff me out. Hence the roadblock I hit a month ago. When I sat next to one of the little brats at dinner, I couldn't shake the feeling he was seeing right through my mind. He kept trying to touch me. Oh, and there's the fact that the sleeping potion was wrongly labeled—the reason my father banned them in the first place—and Kathreen is dead.

—*Lo*

THE MEGADOME, DURING A LEVEL-SIX DUEL, IS SOMETHING to behold. But the Megadome during the King's Duel Tournament is utter chaos. Not a single person is in their seat, which is probably for the best, because there's way more bodies than seats.

The noise is almost painful.

"Are you ready?" Liha asks. It's the first we've spoken in weeks. My heart aches. It feels so familiar to have her in my shield, but we are not

the same as we were. I can't duel without a spirit in my shield, but honestly, I don't know how I feel about it. I love her as much as I'm mad at her, and I want her here as much as I don't. Either way, the dark, terrible power inside me is less noticeable—smaller—when she's in my shield. That, at least, is a welcome change.

I nod. *"Are you?"*

She feels different. Less vibrant; even her voice has lost that octave of excitement and sass.

"I will not fail you," she says, and that response is enough to make me worry.

"What's wrong?"

"He's getting worse, and he's losing time." She pauses.

From the competitors' tunnel, I look to the royal boxes that hug the duel ring. Father wasn't in my dueler suite. Halix was. But even I'm surprised at the piercing sadness I feel when I don't find him in the audience. He's never missed a duel.

As if Liha catches my train of thought, she says, *"He is trying his best to stay alive so he can keep you alive."*

"I don't care," I snap, but it's all hurt.

She nudges my cheek. *"He loves you."*

"Don't." I don't have the capacity right now, not when I'm in line to duel.

Both the infantry soldier from the preliminaries and I were given a rank of zero. That means we get the shittiest schedule, having to wait for all the other duels to finish, then it flips, and we'll be the first set of duelers to fight again—with only two days of rest between duels.

Kazem has the highest rank of four. He's dueling now, then he gets a full week off before re-entering the ring. A week while the lower-ranked duelers kill each other, the best healers in the tournament, the duel suite with the most attendants, and the advantage of watching all his future opponents fight before they can watch him.

The audience screams and cheers as Kazem's ridiculously showy sword—decked out in red gems—slices his opponent's head clean off in the first round.

Every duel after his ends in a similar fashion. Only one duel does not end in death, but that's because a Zo nobleman cut off his opponent's vessel hand, which is an immediate win, even if it's considered extremely tasteless. If a dueler uses this tactic more than once or twice, they get booted from the circuits. Regardless, the audience cheers for any bloodshed, esteemed or not.

My nerves feel like live wires buzzing beneath my skin as I wait my turn to enter the single duel ring centered on the floor of the Megadome. I'm dressed in a new pair of leathers with black spikes running down my forearms, each spike tipped with gold. I count them over and over again, just to occupy my mind while I wait.

When my time finally comes, I slide between lush black ropes to—annoyingly—face the same infantry soldier from the preliminaries.

"*I will not fail you*," Liha whispers again, but it sounds as if she's reassuring herself more than me. I was going to try Dagen's advice about using Liha's power to keep my sword in my hand, but not now. Using that much force for the entire duel would drain Liha.

The Zarr infantry soldier squares his shoulders and grins at me.

That golden spirit has been hovering nearby from the moment Kazem beheaded his own soldier.

Facing my opponent, I clutch my midnight-black sword. Training with Dae and Sorren the past three weeks has given me more confidence. Although here, squaring up against the soldier in front of me, that confidence is shriveling.

From up in the rafters, a cold, dark presence swirls, and I smile.

Dae.

When the siren blares, I snap Liha's power out of me like lightning, yanking the soldier's own sword from his hand and burying it into the mat between us. So deep that with a good casting power—or even his bulky arms—it will take him a second or two to pull it out.

Just enough to get a start on him.

Liha fades even more as soon as the power leaves us.

"*Nice work*," she says.

The infantry soldier resorts to throwing daggers from his belt as I charge him. Now, *this* I can handle.

I duck, spin, and slide, moving faster than I ever have. When I close in, he's reaching for his sword still buried in the mat. I throw all my body weight and momentum into a roundhouse kick to his jaw, shit-brawl style.

His head bounces off my boot.

On his flight backward, he calls his sword with a spray of red smoke, and after a buildup of his power, the bolt of steel jerks out of the mat and into his hand.

"Keep him on the defense!" Liha yells, but the sound is soft in my mind.

I drive my sword toward his. Steel hits steel. The clang reverberates through the lower bowl of the Megadome and I come alive, feeling the rush and flow of violence. Deep down, the darkness purrs.

His eyes widen before he strains, pushing his sword up against my own. He sidesteps, letting his sword go slack, and I stumble forward, but a stream of red smoke jets toward my feet—

Stuck. He's using his moving power to hold my boots to the mat.

I jerk. My toes wiggle. My boots don't.

He chuckles. "Haven't seen that one before, have you?" He swipes his sword for my neck.

I duck. Liha pools her power into me. A trail of pink unlatches my boot buckles, and she pales even more in my sense.

He thrusts for my chest this time, and I backbend out of my boots and jump back to my feet. I swing, duck, and thrust, meeting each of his attacks with a solid, engaged core.

He tries to barrel through my defenses with blunt manpower, but I hold my own. Hope blooms in my chest.

Until he shoots a pillar of red smoke for my sword hand and yanks it out of my grasp with power I'd never met in level-five duel rings.

When he smiles and uses my own sword to slice a deep gash up the inside of my thigh with more speed than I've seen from him, I realize this whole time he's been holding back, putting on a show for the audience. Taunting me. Because he can afford to.

He circles my sword back around and slices my abdomen, leaving a deadly gaping tear across my navel.

I lurch forward, grabbing my stomach. Blood spills from my gut. Blinding pain hits me the same time the shock does. My insides are slipping out, and my vision flickers.

My knees hit the mat.

"*Nizzara!*" Liha screams somewhere distant inside my head. Her power is weaker, but it's building as if she's pouring everything she has into me. "*Stand up. Kill him!*"

Gold light eclipses the stands, blinding me to anything else, calling to me as if to say *take from me . . . drain me.*

"*I will not!*" I growl through the pain, as warm, wet things slide against my hand at my abdomen. The amount of blood pouring down my leg is not a good sign.

The hulking soldier looming over me starts to disappear behind black spots. Blood is gushing out and, if I move my hand from my stomach, things will slide out.

He throws my bloodied sword down in front of my knees to mock me.

"*Use me.*" Liha's voice is a whisper. "*Take what's left. And end him.*"
"*I will not.*"

Something tells me if I use what Liha has pooled into me, it will end *her.* I tilt my head up to see the soldier's smug expression. If I touch that darkness, another restraint will break from it. I *know* it.

I will not break. I will not become my father. And if I am to die, I will not die on my knees. I clutch my sword, dig its tip into the mat, and use it to stand.

My opponent raises his sword to deliver the death blow—aimed right for my neck—when I hear *his* dark, velvet voice.

Dae is hovering behind the soldier. "*Move that sword again, and you die.*"

The soldier spins, looking for the invisible voice. *A distraction.*

The soldier spins back toward me, and Dae repeats it again, this time visible frost cracking across the mat.

When I swing my sword for the soldier's hand, it's anything but pretty. A scream breaks from my lungs, from the blinding pain, but I hit hard and true.

His right hand drops to the mat.

A spirit screeches out from around the infantry soldier, now visible without their caster's shield. When the victory siren shrieks from somewhere it sounds soft and distant as my vision blackens.

For a fleeting moment, my eyes open. My cheek is pressed against the mat, the Megadome tipped on its side, growing darker and darker. The monster rumbles deep inside.

Dae's voice comes at my ear, cracking as he says, *"Don't you dare fucking die."*

CHAPTER 55

DAGEN

I TAKE BACK WHAT I SAID IN THE STONE GARDENS. *THIS* IS hell. Hearing the thud of her knees hit the mat, her head bouncing when her arms don't catch her.

And so much blood.

Even if I were to materialize, even if I had all the strength in the world, I could not pull her away from death's door. I can't *heal* her.

Zarr healers swoop in. Brunar and his men fend off approaching refs and riotous fans. The whole Megadome chants her name as I'm screaming it.

The healers surrounding her apply pressure, trying to staunch her blood loss.

In this moment, when each rise of her chest could be her last, I know. There's nothing I won't do to keep her soul from leaving her body.

I fly off, hating that I have to leave her, but knowing she'll die if I don't find help.

I materialize in front of Jasper inside the Red Mask, and shock surges through his brown face when the entire hallway turns to ice.

I shove him against the wall with too much force. "I need a healing potion. *Now.*"

His jaw clenches and unclenches. "They're extremely rare." His breath is a cloud of air in my raging cold.

"*Drain him. We're hungry,*" the shadows hiss. "*Make him scream. They taste better when they scream.*"

"If you value your soul, you'll get one. Now."

A flash of fear crosses his face. "I know someone, but it'll cost a steep price and I'm not talking about ren."

"I'll pay it."

"You won't pay now. It will be at a time you least—"

I jerk his shoulders, slamming him into the wall again. "I don't care. Get it."

He dips his chin. "Give me an hour."

CHAPTER 56

NIZZARA

DIARY: PAGE 29

I had to tell Dagen about the accidental poison. He said
Kathreen had been stealing from his people, still cheating, and
apparently raising taxes without his consent. He's not condoning
my recklessness, but he'd already ordered annulment papers.
Kathreen was hurting his people in the lesser district. Our mother
came from the lesser district.

—Lo

※

IT'S AN UNSETTLING FEELING TO GO FROM DEATH'S DOOR
to fully functioning.

Thanks to Dae, who somehow smuggled an enchanted potion to
Preysee in the infirmary wing of the Megadome, I'm healed and standing on the outskirts of the after-party.

Liha left as soon as she knew I was okay, and Dae told me it's bad
luck not to attend the ball after the King's First Duel.

I guess it's a good thing the three kingdoms operate on a "don't
ask, don't tell" basis, since it's obvious I had illegal help.

Kazem's gaze keeps finding me from across the dance floor; he appears quite happy that he'll get a chance to kill me himself.

"*You should dance*," Dae whispers from all directions, his protective, dark velvet voice curling around me.

Competitors and rich noble families dance about the grand room, celebrating the start of the King's Duel. Vessel smoke of all colors floats around the dance floor.

"I don't want to dance," I hiss under my breath.

"Your desires say otherwise."

My chest tightens. "My desires are delusional from my almost dying."

"Have you ever seen the roof of the Megadome?"

I look up to the glass ceiling, toward the night sky. "No."

"There's something up there for you."

I scoff. "What? A windstorm?"

He chuckles. *"Maybe."*

CHAPTER 57

DAGEN

AFTER SLIPPING AWAY FROM BRUNAR AND HALIX, NIZZARA steps through the ward guarding a stairway reserved only for kings. It's powered by blare gems and sensitive to my bloodline. As long as I'm with her, she can enter. I take immense pleasure knowing I'm taking her somewhere she's never been.

When we've crossed through the buzzing energy field, the cheers and laughter of the ballroom fall away, enclosing me with Nizzara and her desires. The deepest ones, the quietest ones, are pure and heart-wrenching.

I'm beating myself up for not straining to hear them before now.

She climbs the stairs while I hover ahead of her, admiring her in that red dress. Its deep neckline and high-slit skirt show miles of honey skin. Every step she climbs, the slit in the dress opens to her hip, repeatedly robbing my mind of conscious thoughts.

When we reach the top of the stairway and step onto the glass rooftop, she gasps, tilting her gaze up to the night sky. I float beside her as she walks, her heels tapping across the crystal-clear floor while she watches the wind and fog churning against the ancient wards above, which keep the weather at bay.

Light and colors dance up through glass as she approaches the edge. She leans over, surveying the city lights, barely twinkling through the night fog below.

"What did you say is up here for—"

Her words die when she turns to find me in my human form.

A fiery song comes to life through boxes, stationed around the roof, enchanted to play when a soul passes them. I offer my hand. "You can't win the first duel without dancing at least once afterward."

Her brows furrow. "You're as bad as Liha," she says, but those desires . . .

"*. . . to be danced with . . .*"

"*. . . to be cared for . . .*"

"*. . . to be worthy of love . . .*"

"We're missing the song," I whisper, the beat growing faster.

Her desires are so raw, full of everything that makes her *her*.

"Fine." She takes my hand.

I fold her in my arms and dip her low to the ground, catching the fast, hot beat of the music just in time. Her leg hooks around my hip, pinning her against me. A buzzing current runs through me everywhere her smooth skin touches mine. I bring us upright. She unhooks her leg, turns away in sync with the quick beat, and presses her shoulders against my chest. My hands trail down her rolling hips. Tilting my head into her neck, I breathe in her soft floral scent, then spin her back around to face me.

Her hands find my chest, her gaze locking on mine before she shoves away in time with the song. I catch her hand and she circles me, her face as cold as steel. Her fingers trail up my arm and brush my shoulders all the way around until she's facing me again.

I lift her off the ground, hugging her tight against me as we spin. When her heels touch down again, her lips are slightly parted and right in front of me. Her desires whisper,

"*. . . see his smile again . . .*"

"*. . . get closer . . .*"

I pull her tight, stealing any space between us, and lead her across the rooftop. Each of her backward steps is powerful, precise, and timed perfectly with mine.

She tilts her head back, her leg wrapping around my hip again, anchoring her to me as we twirl. I hold her as we spin three, four, five times. When she rises to face me, her hand finds my chest again, and I swear there's a tremble to her fingers.

"... *to be touched by Dae* ..."

She rolls her hips in time with the beat. My hands can't help it. They find her hips and begin their way up her waist, then her arms as she raises them above her head. I twirl her away, then back. Her hips writhe against mine, sparking life into every inch of me.

As the song fades, I dip her one last time, and we stay there, catching our breath.

"Nightlight is a lucky bastard," I whisper in her ear.

Her big, black eyes find my lips.

"... *to kiss Dae* ..."

My head gravitates to hers until her sweet breath teases my lips, time seeming to fade away around us.

Her soul flickers at my touch, and the shadows choose now to start hissing.

"*Her soul*," they murmur. "*It changesss.*"

Since she nearly died on the mat, the shimmering onyx in her soul has grown. But the shadows lash at each other, hissing when they notice it for the first time as they claw their way to the surface of my thoughts. Stopping myself from kissing her feels criminal, but she deserves better than a deathwalker full of shadows.

I return us upright. The flash of hurt on her face nearly shatters me, but I've seen everyone hurt her. Keeping her away from me and my shadows—especially when my days are limited—is me *not* hurting her.

"I should take you back."

CHAPTER 58

NIZZARA

DIARY: PAGE 30

We attended the funeral, of course. Beautiful ceremony.

—*Lo*

∽♡

HOURS AFTER THE PARTY ENDS, I'M SITTING IN MY CLOSET, eyeing all my dresses, thinking about Liha, the duel, the dance . . .

Preysee bustled in an hour ago. After she fussed over the fact I'm still alive, and I thanked her for her help, I kindly excused her for the night.

It's not that I want to be alone. I just . . . I'm beginning to feel alone even when I'm with people, and the emptiness isn't quite so glaring when it's just me. Darkness swirls in my soul. Since my near brush with death in the duel ring, it's steadily growing closer to the surface. I feel flashes of it more and more. How it sees, how it feels. It even shares flashes of my memories—dark ones I could never remember before.

The scene of Tian's death is still shrouded—almost black—as I replay it, but it's as if my eyes have adjusted to the darkness. In the memory, I'm walking through the library in Zo after closing time, clutching my books. My Zo slippers make soft tapping noises on the white floor as I sneak deeper into the empty library to find Tian. I'm passing shelf after shelf when he jumps out from behind a pillar and yells, "Gotcha!"

The memory plummets into shadow until my father's muffled voice enters and my vision returns, just in time to see him summon a glowing red and black sword out of thin air and run it through Tian's chest.

Tears slide down my cheeks, and with a violent shiver, I shake myself out of the memory.

Enough, I decide. That's enough darkness for tonight.

I'm about to push off the floor and get ready for bed, when Dae's ghostly outline feathers in and sits beside me. Without thinking, I lean closer to him as if I'm being pulled by an invisible rope. He materializes and raises his hand to my cheek to wipe away the tears. His eyes are warmer, deeper than usual, just like they were on the roof, and the load bearing down on my chest—the one I didn't realize was so heavy—lightens for a moment.

The only person to ever touch my cheek like this was Tian. The Awoms believe that physical touch can heal souls, so Tian often brushed my hand or cheek when I was sad. I'd cry, and he'd wipe my tears with his thumb, telling me that the most beautiful and resilient souls grow in adversity; then he'd lead me into the library to find some book about a princess on a grand adventure. He was my best friend.

That was before my memories of him started to disappear.

"I do love your memories," Dae whispers.

"Will you try something for me?" I sniff. "If I think of a memory, will you tell me if you can see it?"

His brows furrow, but he nods.

I replay the memory of the library. Tian jumps out at me, and the scene goes dark. Dae's face remains patient and flat. "Did you see it?" I ask.

"No," he says. "Well, I felt like I was in a black room, with no sound or feeling." He leans back to look at me. "Are you blocking it?"

"No, it's a memory I lost a long time ago. I can't see it either." I huff a tired laugh. "The one time I actually *want* you to see my memories . . ."

Our eyes meet, and a moment of silence passes before he says, "I do try to leave your memories untouched."

"Why don't I believe you?" I stand up to grab a nightgown because my red ballgown has suddenly grown hot. I tug a silky purple one down, lay it on the ottoman, and crank my arm behind me to unfasten my dress. The moment I tug the tiny zipper, it gets stuck.

"Damn zipper," I mutter, tugging harder.

Dae draws a circle with his finger. "Turn." I drop my hand and do as he says.

With a whoosh of cool air, he's behind me. His fingers graze my skin as he zips it down to the lowest part of my back, and I catch the dress, holding it against my chest.

"When a memory is coursing through your current thoughts," he says near my shoulder, "I have no choice but to see it."

I turn to face him. His mouth is so close to mine. I want him to lean closer.

He *does* lean closer.

"Your desires are being . . . how'd you put it? Traitorous?"

Damning heat floods my cheeks. I push his chest away with a jab of my finger. "Like I said. You see everything I don't want you to."

"What if I shared a memory with you?" he says.

Heat is still stinging my cheeks. "It better be an embarrassing one."

His expression turns earnest for once. "The first time I saw you in your bathing chamber . . ." He closes his eyes. "I was flying through the rooms of this castle, angry at what was stolen from me."

Cool air stirs through my closet, brushing beneath the skirt of my dress.

"Spirits don't usually have to watch where we are going, you know, so when I smacked against your shield and saw you—"

I look up, and his hazel eyes are on me again. "You were . . ." He trails off.

"Wet and naked," I say.

Fire fills his gaze. "I was going to say stunning. But yes. You were wet"—he swallows—"and naked."

I tilt my head. "Now, look at whose desires are being traitorous." I wave my nightgown and point to the archway. "Shoo, while I change."

He bites his bottom lip, his satisfied smirk telling me he's hearing every damning desire surging through me. "I thought you don't mind spirits in your closet," he says.

"I don't mind dead ones."

"I am dead," he says flatly.

My gaze roams his chest. The same defined chest I was pressed against on the roof of the Megadome. "Not dead enough."

He grins, his expression proud and coy . . . and playful—every bit the young king portrayed in King's Hall.

The portrait I kissed once when no one was look—

I gasp, trying to bury that memory as soon as it plays but . . .

A devilish smile curls his lips. He folds his muscled arms and leans against the black pillar separating my sleepwear from my ballgowns. "*Definitely* my new favorite memory."

Damn him! I point to the open archway. "Out."

"Out of your closet?" He wiggles his brows. "Or just your memories?"

"Both," I snap.

He pushes off the pillar as if to leave, his face becoming more serious. "There is a way to block your mind if it truly bothers you. I meant it when I said I try to respect your privacy."

My face is still on fire. "I'm listening."

His gaze lingers on my cheeks and he swallows before glancing down at the robe in my hand. "It would require a different outfit."

I survey my racks of clothes. "What kind of outfit?"

He chuckles. "Not any outfit you own." He seems to think for a moment. "I'll place an order at this shop I know of. Have Preysee pick it up. If you want to go through with it, I'll take you tomorrow night."

"I will *definitely* be going through with it."

CHAPTER 59

NIZZARA

Diary: Page 31

Tonight is Dagen's twenty-sixth birthday. If I could give him a family with a wife and children, that's what I'd give him. All he has is me. So, I gave him a promise that he will always have me. And a pastry to share, of course. Oh, and a very illegally acquired glo-kar. I suggested he take us on a drive through the Barrens. He told me if I drop a crumb in his glo-kar, he'll slash every last party dress I own. I took no shame in reminding him who bought the glo-kar, and I devoured my half of the pastry without caution.

—*Lo*

"I AM *NOT* GOING THROUGH WITH IT."

Not in this outfit.

I peer down at the red tassels barely covering what needs to be covered. Red lacy straps wrap around my torso and thighs. I snap my robe tight over this atrocity. "I fail to see how wearing *this* will keep you out of my head."

Dae leans against the closet archway. He's in a deep red button-up shirt, so dark it's almost black. "I know someone who can teach you how to block your mind, but you'll have to blend in."

"Blend in where? A pleasure house?"

A dark brow raises, along with the corners of his lips. "It's a high-end establishment."

"So a pleasure house." I level a glare at him. "I'm not going in this outfit," I say, peeking inside my robe again.

Tassels... *Tassels.*

I peer into my closet full of tasteful dresses—none of which have tassels. "Why can't I wear one of my gowns?"

"Because you'll be recognized if you're not wearing a mask, and only dancers wear masks. Besides, the club is desperately in need of dancers. No one will think twice about me recruiting a new one."

I shuffle through the box Preysee discreetly delivered this afternoon. "Then you better hope there's something in here without tassels."

He leans over, peering into the box as I stir through flashy outfits. "So, your objection isn't the sneaking out, the pleasure house, or trusting a stranger to help with mind blocking... It's your *outfit.*"

"Precisely." Who wants to go into the city looking like a smut clown? I dig through red straps, red feathers, red sequins ... "It has to be a dancer's outfit? Do the bartenders not wear masks either?"

"The club is short on dancers not bartenders," he says. "You won't have to dance, and no one will touch you."

I raise a brow. "What if I want to be touched?"

His lips press together. "Not by these men, you don't. Besides, you're betrothed."

"I have not given myself to him in any way." I dig to the bottom of the box until I find it. Red leather—no tassels.

"What if you'd promised him your hand?" he says softly.

"Then I'd be his and only his, but I'm not." I examine the smooth leather outfit in my hand. "This will have to do." I shoo him out of my closet.

When I walk out of the closet a few minutes later, he's lying on my bed, arms pinned beneath his head. When he sits up, he goes still.

"Put the robe back on."

"Why?" I look down at the new outfit. Red leather scales writhe up and around my torso, jutting into sharp points.

His fingers curl into my black comforter. "For my sanity."

Half an hour later, Dae's guiding me past my unconscious guards after having slipped an enchanted sleeping potion into their dinners earlier. I hope for their sake the potion bottle was labeled correctly.

I tug my cloak tighter over the scarlet outfit as we approach King's Hall. "Where are we going?"

Dae's spirit walks beside me, and I swear his hand rests at the small of my back. *"Besides a visit to your favorite painting?"*

Before I can bite out a retort, footsteps pad toward us from farther up the hall.

Haren, my father's maid, hustles toward me with a sense of urgency until she's planted right in front of me.

"Where's Preysee? I mean"—she curtsies—"have you seen your handmaid, my lady?"

"No, I let her take the night off," I say, a layer of worry settling over me.

"Tell her she's in the linen room," Dae says beside me.

"I think she may be in the linen room."

Haren nods and hurries past, lifting her skirts to keep from tripping.

I'm about to ask if he saw her memories, but my mouth freezes as we approach my father's quarters, and every bad memory from his dungeon surfaces.

Dae turns to ice around me, and for the first time in his presence, a wave of fear sweeps through me.

He feels like death.

"Think of anything else," he growls.

I grasp for any other memory, but my mind only supplies bad ones. Whips, daggers, backhanded slaps, abandonment, darkness—

Dagen materializes, shoves us through the door, and pins me against the inside wall. He takes my face in his hands. His eyes are no longer hazel. They're black. Not black in the center, like mine. Entirely, lethally black.

"Nizzara," he breathes. "Happy. Memories."

I can't help it. With his face—his lips—so close to mine, my mind flashes to fourteen-year-old me, kissing his portrait in King's Hall.

The blackness lightens in his eyes. The deadly set of his lips loosens.

I become aware of his rock-hard body pressing me firmly against this wall, his gentle hands still on my cheeks, and those lips—

My head tilts up, just a fraction.

He stiffens, then pushes away. "I know I'm a tease," he says, voice thick, "but it can't go further than that."

I swallow the lump in my throat. "Because of who my father is?"

His jaw flexes, then releases. "Because of who *I* am."

I push off the wall. "I don't care that you're a spirit—"

"I'm a killer. Who isn't even alive. I'm a *monster*, Nizzara."

I flinch.

He clenches his hands. "Don't give me any part of you. Do you understand?"

Stinging builds behind my eyes. "Someone once told me we can choose not to be monsters."

He turns away. "If I didn't drain souls . . . I'd wither away. I've already made my choice." He opens the door that descends to the secret dungeons.

I halt beside my father's massive bed. "I'm not going down there."

"I know you don't want to go down there, but it's the quickest and safest way out of the castle."

"Then you go." I spin on my heel.

He vanishes and reappears directly in front of me, blocking the doorway. I glare at his solid chest, then his face.

"I'll never make you do anything," he says. "But I'm not the only being who can see parts of your mind. Do you really want to leave it unprotected?"

Why does he have to make sense? And why does my body want him to shove me back against that wall?

He has the audacity to give me the I-fucking-burn-for-you look as if he wants to shove me against that wall too. "I owe you the option of privacy," he says, his voice tight.

What he *owes* me is a hot, meaningless kiss and I want it against *that* fucking wall.

He smirks again. "That fucking wall, huh?"

Red-hot blood surges to my face as I step around him, but he blocks me again. I must be quite the spectacle because the black is gone from his eyes, and his smirk is now a full-fledged smile.

I sigh and give up trying to step around him. "Wouldn't you want *one* kiss that wasn't decided for you? Before you're married off to a stranger or run through with a Zem blade?"

He seems to fight against himself before his gaze falls to my lips. "A hot, meaningless kiss. That's all you want?" His breath is warm on my lips and his scent . . . realms, it's good. He steps closer, stealing all the space between us. "Tell me right now," he says. "That if I kissed you, it would be meaningless for you. Tell me that, and I will."

I swallow, my throat suddenly dry. Part of me goes weak in the knees, wanting to tell him exactly what he wants to hear, but something *stings* deep down. I tug him down by his shirt, a slow, deliberate motion, until my lips almost brush his. "I don't want one anymore."

I let go of his shirt and descend the stairs into silent darkness. The stinging sensation lingers, sharpens. *He only offered to kiss me because he feels sorry for me.*

I halt when my foot touches the bottom of the stairs, the door to Father's torture room directly to my right. I sense, rather than see, him swirl into his ghost form behind me. When I don't move, his cool pocket of air nudges against my back.

"*Keep going.*"

My father's whip cracks in my mind. Over and over. My mind lingers on each time, each crack of the whip.

"*Nizzara,*" Dae growls. But I can't move.

After a moment, he says, "*He's possessed, isn't he?*"

All I can do is nod when the tightness enters my throat. "He always had anger issues," I finally get out. "But he was a good father to me"—my voice breaks—"until he wasn't. I can't decide if that makes the whole thing better or worse, knowing it's not him who is hurting me."

For the first time in so long, I allow the good memories of him to come through. "He used to read to me." A tear falls down my cheek. "He hated books, but when he visited during his time as your father's infantry general, he read whatever atrociously sized book I laid in his lap." I smile. "Not all of it, but a chapter or so. He told me stories about the other six realms, of the Jaxelli Warriors in Xoshbesh, the Sand Gladiators in Heshena, and the lore of the Guardians, all in vivid detail, as if he'd been there himself. He made the stories come alive."

Dae swirls around me, listening. His presence soothing.

"I know he's done terrible things—"

"But he's your father," he says. *"And you're loyal."* His ghostly hand brushes my cheek as if to wipe the tear trailing down it. *"As much as I hate your father, I can't hate your heart. It's the most beautiful thing about you."*

I swat his presence and force my legs to move forward. "So, what you're saying is I have a nice *personality.*"

He materializes directly in front of me, glaring. "Do *not* twist my words. I've seen every type of woman. Elf, fairy, warrior, priestess, and dwarf. I've been to many realms and you"—he brushes his thumb across my cheek—"are the only one who returned some warmth to my chest."

His coy smirk breaks through. "Among other places."

I shove his chest without much force and continue down the tunnel. "You *are* a shameless flirt."

As we keep walking, my mind spirals back to my father, and inevitably Sorren's words come unbidden to the forefront of my mind, no matter how hard I try to shove them away.

"I know you don't want to hear this," Dae says softly, *"but Sorren's right. It's obvious you have more power than you let on. I've seen it. You may have to be the one to end him."*

I spin on him so fast it surprises even me. "I will *never* take a life."

"*Even to save lives?*"

My hands clench, anger rising.

"*I know you value life,*" he says, "*but sometimes a life has to be taken for the greater good.*"

"You don't get it! I was born with . . . *darkness* inside of me. It has no feeling, no remorse, and it's *part* of me. It *wants* me to kill. That's why I can't. I won't."

He's silent for so long that I wonder if his whole rose-colored view of me just shattered.

A stinging sensation rises in my throat. "What if I forget who I want to be?"

His dark tendrils surround me like an embrace. "*I'll remind you who you are.*"

After another stretch of silence, Dae lets the subject go. I force my feet to move again, down the corridor filled with black, wooden doors running along either side.

"What's behind these?"

"*I can't see. There's some sort of enchantment blocking them, even from me.*" After a moment he adds, "*When I ruled, I hid bondslaves in them until I could provide them safe passage home.*"

"That's—"

"*Reckless?*"

"Admirable," I whisper. "That's why you asked King Tigous and King Rajim for tunnel rights when you won the King's Duel, to smuggle slaves underground."

His presence darkens. "*I originally asked them to free their slaves—or offer them wages with proper living conditions,*" he says, "*but that's when I learned the kings only bestow what they want to bestow.*"

"They denied you?"

"*All three kings must be in agreement for the bestowment. That's why no champion has ever walked away with something as ridiculous as a kingdom. King Rajim and King Tigous both denied my request. Their economies would fall apart without bondslaves.*"

He materializes ahead of me, his jaw tight as he presses his palm into a stone in the wall. It sinks inward and part of the wall drops away, revealing another tunnel lit with red glo stones.

"This way."

I follow him, jumping at the grating sound of the stone wall sealing behind us. Before long, the air grows colder, as if there's an exterior opening close by. When we reach the end of the tunnel it widens to a big room with—

"A glo-kar?" I ask.

"This was originally an empty escape tunnel. My sister gave me that"—he waves at the glo-kar—"and stashed it down here, so I could get away from the castle for an hour or two when I wanted to."

"Where'd she find one like this?" I've never seen a glo-kar quite like it. Its red body is almost elegant. Not run-down and boxy like the rest.

He chuckles. "I've learned not to ask questions when it comes to Lo." He dusts off a metal box against the wall before tugging the lid open with a squeak and pulling out a glowing blare gem. He tosses it up and catches it before striding toward the glo-kar.

"Now, to see if it'll start." He opens the hood, removes a dull, cracked gem, and sticks the new one in its place. Red light ignites underneath its body, and a soft, rolling purr vibrates through the air.

His eyes light up. "It still works." He opens the door for me, and I slip into its slick, black interior lit with glo gems.

"There's no way this is from our realm," I mutter to myself. Maybe it's a contraption from the Tatum realm. I've read about their advanced technology. It far surpasses ours . . . But this glo-kar is similar enough to ours, with the same steering plate design. Perhaps this was one of the custom ones rumored to be lost in the destruction of the fourth kingdom. I study the luxury leather, the colorful glo gems sprinkled along black interior walls.

Dae evaporates into mist and in the same breath reappears in the operator's seat, his face alight with boyish excitement, so much so I can almost feel it myself.

He reaches his hand for the steering plate—a sheet of red-tinted glass mounted between our seats, then stops and changes course for me.

"Almost forgot your safety harness," he says, turning in his seat toward me.

"This thing has a *safety harness*?" I look around, and sure enough, thick, leather straps lay to the side of my seat. I pick one up.

"How fast does it go?" I ask, working up the courage to further trap myself in this thing with a harness. I hate glo-kars enough as it is. Let's just add suffocating restraints to them. That sounds fun.

"Faster than the ones you're used to."

Great. I've seen blare gems explode before. I can't imagine that going faster in a glo-kar reduces that likelihood. When I look back over to him, his expression is the definition of smug.

"I *will* wipe that smirk off your face one of these days," I mutter, fumbling with the straps.

"I hope you do."

I'm struggling with the harness, when he leans over and runs his hands along my bare shoulders until he finds the thick straps. His fingers brush my décolletage, eyes focused on the glowing gems set into the ends of the harness as he fastens it over my chest. The gems snap together as if they're enchanted to bind.

He stops and clears his throat. "It's a five-point harness."

I don't break eye contact as I bring the bottom strap up between my legs and snap it into place.

Dae places his hand on the illuminated steering plate and slides it in a backward half-circle. We roar into reverse, and I gasp, grabbing my harness with both hands. There's no way this thing isn't enchanted.

"What about *your* safety harness?" I say.

Spinning circles on the steering plate, he turns the Kar toward the exit tunnel and slides his hazel gaze to me. "I'm already dead, *Izzy.*"

He glides his hand forward on the plate, and the glo-kar picks up speed.

"*Izzy?*" I say.

"Yeah. Izzy." He taps the plate, and we surge toward the surface.

"Why? Do you not like the name?"

"I hate it."

"Good." He smiles in the red glow of gems. "That means it will stick."

I side-eye him and grip my harness tighter. "Fine. Then, I'll give you a nickname you hate."

"Don't make it dirty." He winks. "I'd absolutely loathe it."

"Insufferable," I mutter.

We drive through the underground tunnel for longer than I expect to. After a while, the stone walls of the exit tunnel fall away, and dark foggy sky appears through my red-tinted window. We must've driven under the wall, because as my eyes adjust, I can see we're in the Barrens. Black smears begin flying by outside. Boulders, I realize.

After a few minutes of watching the Barrens landscape zoom past my window, my gaze inevitably gravitates back to him. He's relaxed in his seat, leaned back, his legs casually spread. He glances over at me and smiles. It's the heart-stopping kind, and it sends my mind straight to his rejection of my kiss, first on the roof, then against the wall in my father's chambers. The sting flares through my chest and up my cheeks all over again. Offering to kiss me out of pity afterward somehow makes his initial rejections worse.

His brows furrow.

"Nizzara, I—"

"Stay out of my memories." I clench my fists and face the window.

The glo-kar slows. "Will you talk to me?"

"It's nothing."

Dae's voice is soft. "It's not nothing if it hurts you."

"I didn't need your pity then, and I don't need it now. Keep driving."

I grit my teeth and try to think of anything else, but the entire scene swirls through my mind over and over. The way his face hardened when I leaned in, and he pushed away. How he only offered to kiss me because he felt sorry for me, the poor heiress who doesn't get a say in who she marries. Heat climbs up my neck and cheeks.

He stops the glo-kar, materializes outside my door, and throws it open, wafting cold winter air in. He crouches at my side, bringing his intense gaze to my lips.

Knots instantly form in my stomach. I don't know what he's seeing in my memories, my desires, but something tells me he's seeing all of it. The embarrassment, shame, and the hurt.

"You think I didn't kiss you because I don't *want* you?" He runs a hand through his hair. "That I tried to kiss you out of *pity*?"

I don't answer, and he takes my silence as a yes.

"Fuck." His gaze locks on mine, no play, no smirk. Dead serious and nothing but pain. "I nearly reduced that Megadome to rubble yesterday. When your knees hit that mat—"

He closes his eyes, the wind turning sharper around us. "I didn't care that it was a duel—that it's illegal to interfere with one. It took *everything* I had to let that infantry soldier live. All because . . ." He trails off, his eyes going dark.

"Because you want my soul," I finish for him.

He grabs my face. "Because I want *you*. I want your death glare pointed at me. I want that damn lip to myself. I want your black eyes and menacing hands all over me. Your smile. Your anger. Your tears. All of it." He tucks a strand of my hair behind my ear, and I glimpse the self-loathing in his eyes. "I'm not . . . good for you," he says. "Besides the fact I drain souls . . ." His jaw flexes. "Nil *owns* my soul, Nizzara. If he wanted me to hurt you . . ." He shakes his head. "I can't have any part of you. No kiss, no touch, no soul."

"You're touching me now." His hand is still cupping my cheek. "And you *did* try to kiss me—the pity kiss—remember?"

"One, I don't do pity kisses. And two, these are relatively new rules." He smirks. "My hands are always the last to get the message." His gaze drops to my lips before he lets go of my cheek and closes my door, blocking out the frigid air. He doesn't materialize in the driver's seat right away.

I look out my window. We've skirted the outer walls of the city in a half-circle, the glo-kar idling among lifeless boulders, red dirt, and skiffs of snow. The Barrens territory. I've never been here before. I squint into the darkness past the first few boulders and swear I catch a patch of blackness moving. Chills crawl up my spine.

Dae finally reenters the glo-kar and places his hand back onto the glowing plate. "I'll go slower," he says.

"Why?"

He pointedly looks at my hands, which are still death-gripping my harness. "You're afraid."

I glare at him. "If you say those words to me again, I'll be the first person in history to dismember a ghost. I am not afraid. Don't go slower." When he raises a brow at me, I say, "Just keep your eyes on the road—dirt—whatever." I point forward. "Keep them pointed that way."

He grins. "That I can do."

CHAPTER 60

NIZZARA

Diary: Page 32

I'm dressed up as Rajim's mistress again. I'm going to look
through those ledgers, but this time I'll be looking for something
else.

—Lo

✌

WE RUMBLE TO A STOP OUTSIDE THE CITY WALL, AND I
can't unlatch the harness fast enough as Dae gets out and opens my
door.

"I didn't think this all the way through. Are you sure you'll be fine
climbing in *that*?" His eyes linger on the leather scales of my dancer's
outfit.

"Don't be coy." He thought this plan through *in detail*. That's why
he's grinning like a cat. I slide my heels off my feet and shove them in
his direction. "You're taking my shoes with you, and you're climbing
over ahead of me. And no, you can't *ghost* over. You get to climb like a
real person." There's no way he's climbing under me while I'm wearing
this outfit or ghosting around me while I'm climbing in it either.

He eyes my dancer's outfit again, takes my shoes, and offers a dramatic bow. "Yes, Your Highness."

I pull my cloak around me and step out to face the tall wall. "You
really can't ghost *me* over?"

"Nope. I can only carry things"—he lifts my heels—"when I'm solid."
I sigh. "You first, then."

After fifteen minutes and substantial cussing, I make it to the other side of the wall to see he's wearing a red mask.

He hands me my shoes and offers me a red silk mask from his pocket. "Last part of your outfit."

Liha would be in heaven right now: showy outfits, masks, a club . . . I miss her. She felt so fragile in our last duel, and another pang of grief hits me. I put my mask on and pull my hood over my head.

He tucks his hands in his pockets. "Ready?"

I nod and follow as he leads me through back alleyways toward the club. We pass tall, shimmering buildings polished to reflect the white glo gems mounted on elegant poles throughout the wealthiest part of the city. When we reach a cobblestoned road and turn left, a glo-kar passes by. It's almost as nice as the two royal ones in the castle. Steam-powered carriages decorated with red and blue glo gems chug by, and the few people we pass are dressed in fine clothes, with glo gems stitched around the collars.

I follow him past buildings tall and short, until we come to an immaculate red door. No scuffs, no scratches, no wear of any kind. Thumping music hammers from the other side. I shed my cloak and hand it to him. He reaches for the doorknob but stops and turns back to me.

"Two rules," he says. "Mask on at all times."

"And?"

"And"—his jaw flexes—"it wasn't my place to tell you what you can and can't do. If you wish to be with someone, fine." He grimaces. "But pay attention to your surroundings, okay?"

"Okay."

"We have to find Jasper. I told him I needed his help tonight." He reaches for the door again then stops one more time and turns to fully face me. "Remember, you'll have to pretend I recruited you as a new dancer."

I reach out, running my fingers along his muscled chest. "Like this?" Pressing my body up to his, I roll my hips against him in sync with the muffled music from the club, running my hands down, down, down his firm abdomen.

When I look up, his eyes are burning behind his mask.

He stops my hands with his and dips his head closer, whispering, "Yes, like that."

I swallow, wanting his hands to yank me closer, pin me against him—

"Nizzara," he groans, and lets go.

He turns the knob. When the door opens, a heady wave of perfumes, sounds, and red hues hit my senses. Red velvet benches, statues of naked women, and rosy abstract paintings against crimson walls.

He leads me in, and within seconds, two large men approach us. Everything about Dae shifts. "Jasper," he snaps at them. "Where is he?"

"Gone," one bouncer says. "Said he had business."

"Fuck," he mutters under his breath. "Well, what are you staring at? Get back to the door."

He slides his arm around my waist and tugs me toward the loud music.

Women—all dressed in red—dance on stages throughout the room. Other dancers are sitting on laps, tugging collars, and whispering in ears.

"So, you own a pleasure house."

His hand tightens around me, pulling me closer. It only intensifies the coiling sensation that began as soon as I touched him. "I'm only pretending to own one."

As soon as we reach the edge of the growing crowd, two more big men dressed in dark red shirts fall in beside us. He tightens his grip around my waist, his thumb brushing an open part of my outfit, against my skin.

The men tail us to a reserved table near the biggest stage.

Dagen sits at a table and gently guides me down onto his lap. His movements are suave but dripping with kingly power, so I match his attitude. His nose dips toward my neck, his breath leaving chills as he whispers, "I'm trying not to notice how every set of eyes keeps finding you."

One patron in a black suit winks at me as a drink is delivered to his table.

Dagen asks the men, "When did Jasper leave?"

"This afternoon," the leaner one says. "He didn't say where he was going or when he'd be back."

The thicker one plants his palms on the table and leans forward. "Seems like you and him have been gone a lot lately. Anything I should know about? Since I'm running security and all?"

"I've been recruiting more talent," he says.

The bouncer's eyes crawl over me. "It's taken you three days to recruit one dancer?"

Dagen lays a kiss below my ear. "That's Garret," he whispers. "I know I said you can do what you want but stay the fuck away from him." He lingers there, his lips at my ear, his breath raising chills along my neck. "Lift your arms," he says.

I lift them over my head. Dagen trails a finger from my elbow down to my waist, then rests his hand on my thigh. Dagen smiles against my ear and says to Garret, "This dancer is special."

Garret flares his nostrils. "Special enough to share?"

Dae turns to ice beneath me. "I told you. You must ask the dancers' permission, and they must say yes. But after your last incident, maybe you need a demonstration." He turns to me, removing his hands and holding them up. "Can I touch your thigh, miss?"

"Yes," I say over the music.

Dagen runs his hand along my thigh, leaving chills in his wake. His fingers stop at my hip.

"Can I touch your waist?"

"Yes," I breathe.

Both his hands lay on my hips and trail upward, brushing over open skin as they go. Heat floods my torso, and I can't help the writhe in my hips as his fingers tease me.

His whisper is a rasp in my ear. "Let's show him what no means."

"Can I touch your breasts?" His tone is cold and authoritative.

I lace my fingers through his and guide his hands up to my hard, swelling breasts. "Yes," I pant.

He goes rigid beneath me, which only sends my desire into over-drive. I'm not against putting on a show if it means more of him. "You said I could be with whoever I wanted," I whisper.

His breath hitches. "Cruel little beast."

The thinner bouncer clears his throat and nods toward the far wall, where a beautiful redheaded dancer beckons Dagen with her hand, curling her fingers in a come-hither sort of way.

Garret shoves away from the table with a growl and stalks off.

"Shit," Dagen says, gently removing me from his lap. "I'll be right back." He glances at the remaining bouncer then back at me. He straightens his cuffs. "Take care of her. Understood?"

The bouncer nods, pulls out a chair, and sits, folding his arms.

Dagen peers over at the redhead across the busy room then at me. "Surroundings, remember?"

I nod, my eyes trained on the half-naked goddess waiting for him.

He takes off through the crowd. When he reaches her, she takes his arm and leads him down the hall, out of view.

Dagen isn't gone more than two minutes before another gorgeous dancer, a brunette, coos toward our table, "Liam."

The bouncer cranes his neck to find the girl behind him. His en-tire demeanor softens. She drapes her arms around his neck and smiles down at him.

"Are you going to introduce me to your new friend?"

"New dancer," he says.

She dips to his ear, whispering something that makes his lip twitch upward. Then she rounds his chair and sits on his lap.

She sizes me up. "New dancer? Or Red's new plaything?"

Liam shrugs. "He just disappeared with Helina again, so who knows."

"Helina?" It's out of my mouth before I can stop it.

The dancer's grin turns feline. "Oh, he has favorites. Always has.

Helina has outlasted them all, though. He sneaks off with her every chance he gets."

Irrational anger and darkness sweep through me, and my entire body tenses until my teeth hurt from clenching so hard. Dagen is *Zarr*. I should've known how he is with other women. I mean, I have eyes. I almost sense the darkness saying, *You don't have to feel anything if you don't want to . . .*

"Don't worry," the dancer says, pulling me from my thoughts. She nods toward me. "With those eyes and that body, you'll do just fine here. Who knows, maybe you'll even dethrone Helina." She turns to Liam and whispers something that makes him squirm.

"I can't." He clears his throat and regains his stoic composure. "Red told me to watch her."

The dancer frowns.

"I'll watch her," Garret says, emerging from the grinding crowd with two glasses of dark liquid. Liam hesitates, but when the dancer tugs on his collar, he stands up.

Liam narrows his eyes at Garret. "I don't think—"

Garret nods in the direction Dae left. "Red sent me to take over." He points at Garret with one of his full cups. "He said you'd be useless as soon as your girlfriend's shift ended." He takes a drink from a glass before stamping it down on the marble tabletop. "So, here I am." His eyes creep over me. "I'll take care of her."

Liam grins at his girlfriend and quickly follows her down the same hall where Dagen disappeared with Helina.

Garret pushes one of the glasses toward me.

I shove the glass back even though I'm thirsty. "I don't drink spirits."

He shrugs. "It's juice. Dancers aren't allowed spirits on shift."

I reach for the glass and take a long drink, hoping he'll get the point that I don't want to talk. If I'm lucky, he'll try something, and I'll get to show him exactly why I don't need my vessel to win a fucking duel match.

"So," he says, taking the seat closest to mine and scooting it closer. "Are you going to let me touch those thighs?"

"Get lost. I don't need a babysitter."

He tilts his blond waves toward me, his eyes on my exposed legs. "What if I say please?"

"I said get loss . . ." My tongue slips. "Losst." I roll it in my mouth, but it moves slowly.

He grins. "What if I do all the work?"

I open my mouth to tell him no—again—but my tongue is numb. Really numb. I look down at the cup. Did I really drink that much? My heart starts pounding against my ribs.

He drapes an arm over the back of my chair, smiling. "I don't hear a no."

"What . . ." My mouth feels full of fluff. "What kind of juice is this?"

"The kind that makes everything consensual."

My fists curl, and I realize my mouth and tongue are numb, but the effects haven't reached the rest of my body yet. I jolt up from my chair and swing for him, but my arm misses by a foot. My vision is off.

"Whoa, blondie. I took you for a wild one. Good thing I doubled the dose."

I swing again, but my feet are not on the same page as the rest of me. My legs give out. He catches me against him. My fingers dig into his forearms as his big hands shackle around my upper arms, holding me there, my body failing to move on its own.

He rambles for a minute, saying something about my ass, but his words start to blend. The room blurs as he sweeps me off my feet.

"I don't mind doing all the work," he says, his voice watery, slipping and sliding through my ears. "Come on," he whispers. "I know a more private place."

I open my mouth to object again, but nothing comes out. I can't form words, can't see straight, can't distinguish what's real and what's not, as colors and shapes dance around me. Then suddenly, I'm somewhere dark, my back on something soft.

A warm heavy weight climbs on top of me, Garret's face going in and out of focus. Hands tear at my outfit.

I swing my arm for his jaw, but my arm is stuck under something. I look over to it, but nothing is holding it. I swing again, but the only movement I get is a twitch of my fingers.

A nip comes at my lips. Darkness fills my mind. I sense it, but when I try to reach for the cold, lethal essence inside me . . . it's as if the drug blocked it off.

Gold feathers in, like warm, delicate rivers flowing toward me. A tendril wraps around my finger, full of warmth, and life, and wonder. It drinks the haze away from me. Sound is the first sense to return.

Garret's voice comes from above. "I'll have to be quicker than I usually—"

The room plunges in temperature. Somewhere, I feel *him*, feel his rage.

With a sudden jerk and a loud crash, Garret is flung off me. Thuds and more crashes come from the floor and Dagen's lethal voice.

Thanks to the golden spirit, the effects of the drink are suddenly gone. I sit up to see Garret thrashing beneath Dagen's chokehold. Garret's face is a bloody, mangled mess. Dagen's eyes are the blackest I've ever seen. He's gritting his teeth, his monstrous sword poised under Garret's jaw.

Dagen pulls his shadowy sword away from Garret, appearing to be fighting against this version of himself.

Garret snarls, "She would've moaned for me."

The room nearly shatters with ice.

Ice that I can see, and a cold I've never experienced.

Dagen slams his sword into Garret's chest.

Garret's scream of pain dies before it's fully out. A brown-colored spirit leaves Garret's body. It makes a shattering sound as it disappears around Dagen, who's unnervingly still.

My breath hitches and his head snaps to me. In this state, veins popping from his neck and blackness consuming his eyes, he looks like a monster.

The black in his eyes slowly begins to recede as they crumple at the sight of me. My outfit is in shreds and there are bruises from Garret's grip around my arms.

Even though some warmth has returned to the room, my bones are still ice. "He spiked my drink."

"That's why he's dead," he says, not a stitch of remorse in his words. Dagen stands, his sword vanishing to mist as he steps toward me. Pain flashes across his face when his gaze lands on my torn outfit.

Two cataclysmic forces battle inside me.

He took a life.

To protect mine.

Part of me hates Dagen for it.

Part of me comes alive for him.

His hands slide to the buttons on his shirt, flicking each one in a smooth, quick motion until the red fabric parts and his tan, rippling chest, full of scars, cuts into view. He shrugs his shirt off and drapes it around my shoulders, wrapping me in his scent. That instant, calming scent.

I think some of the drink is still in my system after all because I can't move, can't talk.

Dropping to a knee in front of me, he begins buttoning it around my waist, my stomach, my breasts, closing it up. When he stands and offers his arm, the image of him walking away with Helina blares into my head, mixed with incredible rage and immense relief of what he just saved me from.

He tilts his head with that euphoric look he gets when he's watching my memories.

I don't want him to see them. I start purposefully remembering times spent with Yisabell.

Dae's brows furrow, but I continue my string of safe, neutral memories, like reading *The King of Kings*, or any book, for that matter. Suddenly, I have all I need to avoid his prying mind all night. I've read a lot of books.

Over my dead body will I allow him to see the hurt in my memory as he walked away with Helina, or how vulnerable I feel right now.

"Your memories are acting weird," he says, dropping his hand.

In my head, I move on to the book of gems, how much controversy they pose and the unpredictable things they do when cut incorrectly.

"Do you want to talk?" He steps toward me, a look of sympathy in his now hazel eyes.

I switch to learning the histories of the seven realms, reciting how intricately they are woven around our planet—like magical dimensions.

"No," I say. "I don't want to talk about any of it."

"Then I won't pry," he says quietly. "Jasper is gone for the night, but Helina has some experience with mind blocking. She's offered to help."

The stinging memory floods back in full force, and I curse out loud. As much as I don't want to face Helina, I would like to be able to block my mind when I choose to.

His brows furrow again, but he doesn't pry. He locks the door behind us when we leave so no patrons accidentally stumble upon Garret's body. We walk in silence.

My eyes don't leave his naked back, his muscles visible as he walks ahead of me. When he vanishes to spirit near the crowd, I begrudgingly mourn the view.

"*This way*," he says, keeping his distance even in spirit form. "*Behind the big stage.*"

After entering a secret door disguised as a painting, and multiple hallways, we arrive in a room more lavish than the one Garret dragged me into.

Waiting for me is Helina.

Beautiful, doe-eyed Helina.

CHAPTER 61

DAGEN

AFTER SHE'S DONE WITH HELINA, NIZZARA ENTERS THE hallway looking exhausted. Her eyes find mine, and I expect her memory to flash through their lessons, but nothing comes. Her mind is blank, and her desires are tragically silent.

"A master already?" I say.

She offers a half smile then gazes down the hallway, swaying on her feet. "Hardly," she breathes. "But I'm ready to go."

After what happened with Garret, I wouldn't be surprised if her body is still in shock. Cold, dark rage sinks through me all over again.

"Let's get you to bed," I say.

Her eyes fall on the new shirt I'm wearing, and she frowns before glancing back toward Helina, her mind and desires still blank.

The silence is too loud. I didn't realize how much I live for her bright snippets of memory. I foolishly hoped silencing her memories would suppress my desire to reach out and touch her all the time, but damn it all, my hands still yearn for her. When she pulled that hot little stunt on my lap—

"Yeah, let's go," she says, pointedly looking anywhere but me.

This is for the best, I remind myself. I'm not *good* for her.

I lead us back, returning to my spirit form through the massive, writhing crowd so I'm not tempted to reach for her.

Acting on this pent-up ball of sexual tension that only exists when she's around would be unfair to her. Especially when I'm still planning to kill her father. But as much as I *should* push her toward someone like

Nightlight, who despite his mating urge shows honor in his memories, I don't want to.

I stare at her through spirit eyes. Her hair is down, her jaw poised to slice anyone in her way, and she's still in my shirt. The thought of her wearing anyone else's shirt has my spirit swirling in frigid, angry whirlpools. Awful, selfish, and twisted, but it's true. Garret was an extreme case, but I know I won't be able to stand seeing anyone else's hands on her.

When we make it to the glo-kar, I open the door for her. This time, I don't miss the tremble in her hands. I materialize into the driver's seat.

"Fast or slow?"

"Fast," she says, buckling her harness.

I admire the hell out of that answer.

I drive fast but carefully. And the ride back is filled with utter silence.

No words. No memories.

Once we make it back to her room, she breaks for her closet and emerges in a long-sleeved nightgown that stops high above her knees.

"You should leave. Liha will be returning at dawn for our next duel."

I turn for her balcony, until her control slips and her desires whisper to me.

"*. . . to be comforted . . .*"

"*. . . to not feel alone . . .*"

"*. . . for Dae to stay . . .*"

I stop and face her. Her brows are pinched, her lips in a scowl, as if she's struggling to keep her guard up.

"I'll go if you wish. After I do this." I close the distance to where she stands, and hug her.

She stiffens at first but quickly melts, burying her face in my chest. We stand like that in silence, me stroking her hair until she pulls her head back and wipes at her eyes. Warm, fierce eyes. Any other time, they are like black daggers, but when tears glisten around them, they're infinitely more dangerous, because I'd do anything for those eyes.

I wipe a tear with my thumb. "What's wrong?"

Stupid question. I know what's wrong.

She was damn near raped and I—

She huffs but doesn't pull away.

Broken images of Garret on top of her—kissing her—flash from her. She grits her teeth as if trying to shut the memories down, but I catch another glimpse of me walking away from her with Helina on my arm.

"I shouldn't have left you." I cup her cheeks. Good hell, I really swore I wasn't going to do that, but I need her to know how sorry I am for leaving.

"I don't need a babysitter," she snaps up at me. "And you don't need me dragging you down at high-end establishments."

She shoves herself away, but I grab her hand and gently tug her back. Gentle enough for her to break away if she wants to. She allows me to guide her back.

I want to tell her how weak my knees are right now. I want to tell her how I've seen and heard the memories and desires of thousands. I've been married. I've even been in love before, but no one is *her*.

That's what I want to say, but instead, I find myself saying, "Will you talk to me?"

Her eyes search mine; those god-sent lips pinch into a firm line, then bend down. "It's not so much his attack," she whispers. "It's just—"

She stops and looks down at her hands so I can't see her eyes.

I gently tilt her chin up, a protective beast roaring to life in my chest. It takes effort to keep the ice to a minimum. "What is it, then?"

Her cheeks explode with a deep red. "Forget it. It's stupid."

I shake my head, wondering what in the world could cause such a flush in her cheeks. I swear I got there in time. He hadn't—

I breathe. "Nizzara. If it bothers you, it isn't stupid."

More red blossoms in her cheeks. Realms, she's gorgeous.

"It's just—it's not how I wished my first kiss to be," she whispers. And her neck goes crimson, crawling to her chest. "It's stupid, but I might not have a say in who I marry. This was the only thing that could be mine. He stole it from me."

My deathwalker heart thunders in my chest.

I dip my head toward her. My logical—honorable—mind begs me not to do it, but the words come out anyway. "What about your second kiss? I hear they are immensely better."

Her breath hitches and her still-wet eyes peer into mine beneath long, dark lashes.

"I don't want a pity kiss." Her words are sharp, but she's biting that full bottom lip of hers.

"I told you. I don't *do* pity kisses."

Meaningless. That's all she wants. I can give that to her.

Something in the back of my head warns me I can't—not with her—but it's quickly silenced when her eyes fall to my lips.

"What about Helina?" she says. "I'd never do that to another woman."

It hits me like a speeding glo-kar as her memory plays out, and I'm suddenly smiling.

"I am not with Helina."

My grin only gets wider when I feel her ravenous, blinding jealousy in her memories of working with Helina.

"But one of the dancers said you—"

I shake my head. "The owner before me had a sort of obsession with her. They all think I'm him. Besides, Helina is with Jasper."

Her eyes search mine. "You swear?"

"I swear."

I slowly guide her back to the wall and pin her firmly against it like her desires beg me to. A gasp escapes her lips as she tips them closer to mine.

My lips brush hers, and it's fucking fire. "Fast or slow?" I whisper.

She bites her lip, knowing *exactly* what it does to me, then says, "Both."

I grab her waist, and I kiss her. Her lips are silk moving against mine, her body pressing tight against me through her thin gown.

Utter. Blissful. Torture.

She wraps her arms around my neck, her fingers making pleading strokes through my hair.

Her lips demand mine.

Her desires demand *me*.

Without breaking the kiss, I scoop her up. She wraps her soft bare legs around my center, and I smother a curse. The feel of her . . .

That's all it takes. I'm rock, fucking hard.

I spin us for the bed and lay her back to the plush comforter as the kiss deepens, becoming urgent. She bites my lip and arches her back.

My hand trails her thigh, still wrapped around me. She moans softly. And fuck, if that sound won't be my undoing.

Her desires turn *very* traitorous, and one thought has my hands halting inches from her short nightgown. I'm breathless when I say, "You're betrothed."

"I do not choose him." Impenetrable steel enters her gaze. "I'll die in the duel ring before I'm married against my will."

I pin her arms to the bed. "No one will fucking touch you in the ring."

Her legs tighten around me. Red hot desire ignites in her gaze, and of course she bites that damn lip.

I groan. "I told you. I will not take any part of you."

"What if I want to give it?"

My head moves toward that pout of hers as if my lips belong there, but I stop at that tantalizing place where her breath mixes with mine. "No," I say.

Her brows pinch and hurt flashes. "You don't want me?"

"I told you. Wanting is not the problem here." I kiss her again, softly, pressing my hips into her thigh so she can *feel* just how much that's not the problem.

A ragged breath escapes her, and I almost give in, but one thought about her soul, her future, and the fact that I still plan on killing her father, who she loves, is enough to pull me back again.

"Brutal honesty?"

She nods, eyes wary.

"I don't want to ruin your opportunity with Nightlight."

She opens her mouth to argue, but before she can get a syllable out, I say, "One part of my plan hasn't changed, Nizzara." I do what my body is begging me not to, and I fully break away from her until I'm standing beside the bed. "I'm still going to kill your father before Nil takes my soul back."

The set of her lips harden as she sits up and scoots back. "He's my father."

I slide my hands into my pockets to keep them firmly to myself. "He's possessed."

Pain consumes her face. Her desires cry out, wishing he wasn't. She wraps her arms around her knees. "I hate him, but . . . I don't," she says.

"He is a danger to you and your kingdom."

Her eyes dart to me, her jaw flexing. "There has to be a scenario where we both make it out."

"There's not."

"Don't give up so easily." She folds her arms. "It's extremely annoying when people do that."

I smile, but it fades when I see the well of emotion behind her eyes, when her desires want me to live, even though I'm already dead.

"I will not let you give up your freedom or your soul," she grinds out. She's so *stubborn*.

I sit beside her and my hands—those traitorous bastards—leave my pockets, pulling her into another hug. "I won't let you give up your soul or ruin a future with the orange, glowing Nightlight."

She scoffs, silver in her eyes again. "Haven't you learned that I do what I want?"

Cold sweeps through the room. "Not this time." My arms drop away from her. "I better go." She has a duel tomorrow, and she needs rest. "I have something to check on in the morning." It's such a small chance, but I can't stop thinking about the tip Helina gave me on Lo.

Her brows furrow. "Check on what?"

I promised honesty. "I'm trying to find out what happened to my sister."

An understanding fills her eyes, then something like guilt. She opens her mouth to say something, but I stop her.

"I'd rather not talk about my sister tonight." I need to come to terms with the likely possibility that she may not be alive, or I may not find any closure. I need to prepare myself for that.

After a moment, Nizzara asks, "Will you stay the night . . . again?"

I could never tell her no when she is this vulnerable. Her expression is fortified, her body confident and unfazed, but her desires, the ones crying for my safety, my voice, and my closeness, give her away.

The irony is painful. This whole time, I've wanted her trust, and now with those warm, trusting eyes still holding me, I'd give anything for her not to trust or *care* for me. I've seen how her mind works when it comes to people she cares for.

I relent. "Only if you get some sleep."

A beautiful smile finds her lips before she lies back on her bed. I evaporate into my spirit form because the urge to touch her is unbearable, and in this form, I can pretend I'm not holding her.

She sighs when I lie beside her and closes her eyes.

"So," I say. "How was your second kiss?"

Her smile deepens and pink fills her cheeks. She replays the memory of us kissing, and it's so strong it startles me.

Her own hot pleasure rolls through me, eclipsing my senses.

Me holding her against the wall.

My hands trailing her.

Her fingers in my hair.

Then, the sudden fiery *need* she felt when I picked her up and took her to the bed.

"You know how it was," she whispers back.

She's still smiling when sleep finds her.

CHAPTER 62

NIZZARA

DIARY: PAGE 33

I broke into King Rajim's ledger room after slipping him a
sleeping elixir—and yes, it was labeled correctly. In his ledgers,
I found a letter from the king of Zo, informing Rajim that my
father and Dagen are responsible for the missing void gems. My
attacker is from Zo. They want me and my brother dead. But why?
—*Lo*

WHEN MY EYES OPEN, I ROLL TO THE SPOT WHERE DAGEN
had lain and run my fingers over the smooth, unruffled bedding.

Dawn is breaking outside my balcony doors, the black, wintry
gloom lightening to silver, when a knock comes from my door. White
hair and a set of ice-blue eyes peek around the black door.

I sit up. "Yisabell!"

She closes the door and hobbles in, wincing from the movement,
her back obviously sore. Her eyes have dark circles under them and
she's in the same garb she was whipped in. Dry blood and filth cover
the sack-shaped dress.

"I was just released from the dungeons, and I—my father was sent
away on an errand again." She looks down at her bloody rags then at me
in my clean bed and scoots herself a step back as if she doesn't want to
soil anything. "I just—I don't want to be alone any longer."

I hop out of bed, fresh anger building inside. "Come. Let's clean you up. I have a salve that will help with the pain too." I swallow. She's in pain because of me.

She shakes her head, tears forming. "No, I will be punished—"

Something snaps in me. "I will die before another whip touches you, I swear it. You will not be punished. Now, let's go." I don't know how, or *if* there's a way to control the darkness inside me, but seeing her like this . . . I'd try to control Evil itself if I thought I could protect her.

Tears stream from my own eyes. I want to crush her into a hug and never let go, but I don't want to hurt her back. I take her hand and squeeze it, and she curls into me, laying her head on my chest and sobbing.

I stroke her hair. "I'm so sorry," I cry, pressing my wet cheek into her dirty hair. "This is my fault."

She shakes her head. "Do not apologize for his actions, or *my* choice to take your punishment."

I want to tell her that it wasn't her choice, my father would've forced her anyway, but instead I say, "We need to be quick."

My next duel is in less than an hour. I tug her to the bath and start the water. "What did you tell my guards you are doing here?"

"Dusting," she says, eyeing the gleaming black tub.

I grab the enchanted salve that helps with pain. She shrugs off her rags and climbs into the tub. Her gaze keeps traveling to the door as if my father will burst in at any second and drag her out by her hair. When a knock does sound from the door to the hall, she jumps, splashing water.

"It's just Preysee," I say. This is the time she arrives each morning, but I silently pray that it *is* her.

My bedroom door creaks open and footsteps enter. "My lady?" Preysee calls from the foyer, and I slump with relief. "I managed to grab some biscuits from the kitchen before your duel."

She steps into the bathing chamber and freezes, the plate of biscuits poised in her hands.

My eyes find Preysee's. "Will you help me?"

She sets the plate down and immediately grabs a brush. Yisabell flinches and hisses as hot water and soap find each laceration, but she doesn't complain. When Yisabell is almost cleaned, I pick up her dress from the floor. There's absolutely no way she is putting this thing back on. I run to my closet and find a dress for her. It's black and plain, but it's not even close to her modest garb. It will have to do.

Yisabell's eyes go wide, and she shakes her head. "No. I couldn't—"

"You can." I hold the dress out to her. When I look at Preysee, a gold tendril touches my thoughts, and a vision of her forms behind my eyes—as if the golden spirit left a trace of power behind. I see Preysee smuggling people to the rebel camps. That's why she's been late some nights and where she's been on her afternoons off.

"Preysee," I say, and my tone has her freezing mid-movement.

She looks up at me. "Yes, my lady?"

"I need you to smuggle her out."

Both Preysee's and Yisabell's eyes go wide.

"The same way you're helping Haren."

She clears her throat. "Who?"

I point at her. "Now's not the time to play dumb. Haren, the maid. You're smuggling her daughter out to the rebels, and you're going to do the same for Yisabell."

Preysee's lips tighten, but she nods. "I can do this, my lady, but time is pressing. If we want to get her out with Haren's daughter, we need to move now."

"But my father—" Yisabell's voice cracks. "I can't leave him."

I bend down level with Yisabell. "I vow on my life. I will make sure your father follows you as soon as he returns from his errands."

I look across the tub to Preysee and she nods. "I can get him out."

A pounding sounds from my door. "It is time to depart for the Megadome," Brunar declares through the door.

Preysee stalks to the door and jerks it open, thoroughly scolding Brunar for rushing a princess. After shutting it, she turns to me. "You need to get your leathers on."

I nod and run to my closet. As soon as I'm facing my wall of fighting leathers, Liha's voice floats above, barely audible through the groans and whispers of lesser spirits. "*I will not fail,*" she mutters.

"*Fail what?*" I say.

"*I will not fail.*"

It's now I notice how pale she is in my sense, how she blends in with the fragments and wisps around us. I try not to panic as I pull a set of leathers down and Liha slides into my shield.

Brunar pounds on the door again. "Glo-kars are lit."

I call Liha's power to summon my leathers on, but only a small puff of smoke comes, leaving my nightgown on the floor and me undressed.

"*I will not fail you,*" Liha whispers in my mind.

I'm beginning to panic now. I grab the nightgown, which still smells like Dae, and tuck it away before yanking my leathers on and loading them with daggers.

My fingers wrap around the hilt of my last dagger as I slide it into the sheath at my thigh.

Then, I pluck one of my rings from my velvet tray beneath my evening gowns, and a few other pieces of jewelry.

When I emerge from my closet, Preysee is soothing Yisabell by walking her through how she will get her out, assuring her she'll be okay through the tunnels.

I bend down to Yisabell, who's now dressed in my gown, at least two sizes too big, and sitting on my chair.

"This is for you," I say, fighting back tears. This might be the last time I see her.

"A spider," she says, taking the gem-studded arachnid ring, and by the look in her eyes, I know she's remembering our first real conversation, when she told me her version of the mother spider tale.

"You can sell it if you ever get in a bind."

She shakes her head. "I don't sell symbols."

I smile and hand her my other handful of jewelry. "Good thing these aren't symbols." Tears form in her eyes, and I hug her.

She squeezes back hard for someone so small. After another impatient pounding at the door, I let her go and tell Preysee, "Wait till we're gone."

She nods.

I don't look back before I enter the hall. If I do, I won't be able to leave.

CHAPTER 63

DAGEN

I'M IN THE OUTERMOST REGION OF THE ZEM KINGDOM, past mines and quarries, about as far from the Megadome as I can be, waiting for a woman who happens to fit Lo's description, who *might* show.

Nizzara's duel has already begun, and that single thought has me restless to get going.

The meeting place on the flats beyond the hills of bedrock is devoid of life.

Every minute that ticks by heightens the feeling that Nizzara could be on the receiving end of a killing blow.

I perk up hopefully when a mining sled tugs into view, but it's pulled by a Zem miner. By the droop in their shoulders, I can already tell it isn't Lo. Even in her disguises, she's too proud to slouch.

I wait a little longer.

Lo could show at any minute.

But I can't shake the dread building minute by minute, knowing Nizzara won't land a killing blow or touch that power she's so afraid of.

I wait a little longer . . .

CHAPTER 64

NIZZARA

DIARY: PAGE 34

I can only leave the castle when Dagen is here to run things now that Kathreen is gone. That means I'm stuck here for another two weeks, stewing over what could possess the Zos to attempt assassination. I'm drawing blanks, so I'm rereading my unauthorized Zo books that keep mentioning two possibilities: the true King of Kings, or the heir of Zo wearing two First-Mades.
—Lo

THE MEGADOME WRAPS AROUND ME, A PIT OF MADNESS. Black and red flags wave from the sidelines, drinks splash over side rails, and a uniform stomping of feet spreads through the stands in a fight-or-die rhythm.

The siren is about to sound and my Zem opponent is smiling at me as if he's imagining all the painful ways he plans to kill me.

Liha is mumbling.

My father's not here.

Soriah and Tarella are still gone.

The only person in the royal box is Halix.

Dae is still looking for Lo.

The siren blares overhead. I call Liha's power, to rip my opponent's sword out of his hand, but the sword only wiggles—a polite tug.

He looks down at his sword, then up at me, nothing but a shit-eating smile on his face.

"*I'm fading,*" Liha says.

"*Don't you pull this shit on me. You are the Heshena elf princess of the largest continent in all seven realms. You fade for no one.*"

A nudge—so soft—comes beside my ear.

The Zem dueler in spiked red leather summons his vast, orange smoke. My long black sword, along with every dagger on me, is yanked from me. They sink through the mat in front of him.

"*It's the void gems,*" Liha says, as if there isn't a giant, bloodthirsty dueler waiting for me to retrieve my weapons at his feet. "*They weakened the shadows inside him, but they've nearly drained me.*"

"*Shadows,*" I pant. "*What shadows?*"

Liha's response is so quiet. "*That's how evil spreads—how Skeeves are made. Shadows . . . I will not fail you.*"

"*Liha!*"

My opponent curls his fingers, telling me to come get my weapons. I charge without a blade. "*His void gems are what's hurting you.*"

I dodge, bend, spin, barely avoiding his massive sword.

"*Yes.*" Liha's voice is nearly inaudible. "*They drain us.*"

"*Who is 'us'?*" I yell in my mind, jumping over a swipe for my legs.

"*Him . . . me . . . Gravera.*"

I spin away from a downward chop. "*Gravera—that's his other spirit?*"

Liha mumbles an incoherent answer.

I duck under a whooshing slice and roll, reaching for my sword, jutting out of the mat. My fingers graze the pommel—

The other dueler kicks his spiked boot into my gut, puncturing through black leather. He smiles at my blood dripping to the mat, and darkness ripples inside. I surge up, ignoring the searing pain under my rib cage, and roundhouse-kick his fist that grips his pommel.

I catch the ruby blade, spin to face him, and death-grip it.

One of his soaring daggers buries hilt-deep into my dominant shoulder.

The rest come in a rain of hellfire. I barely manage to chop them from the air, using my left hand to direct the sword, bracing the weight of it with my injured arm.

Liha pools power into me and I know if I release it, it will end her. "*Use it,*" she hisses.

"*No.*"

The darkness pulls on me as if to say *Drain her. She's willing.*

I grit my teeth as the Zem man yanks my black sword from the mat and advances toward me.

I block a downward swipe but miss his drive for my leg. I dodge a thrust for my chest but gain a slash down my arm.

I'm all defense and evasion. As my blocks and spins grow slower, my body catches more and more of his blows. I manage to block a slice to my neck, bringing our swords at a trembling cross in front of our faces.

"*Use it,*" Liha whispers.

My opponent is calm, composed, and in control.

Until I yield an inch, letting him closer, and ram my spiked boot between his legs—through his balls.

He howls, and I drive his sword through his shoulder.

A wave of orange smoke erupts from him like a dust storm washing through the ring. It grabs hold of my leathers. My clothes freeze me in place.

His blue eyes find mine.

My fingers move, my head moves, but my clothes are suddenly full-body restraints. Every movement of my arms feels like cutting through a hundred pounds of resistance.

He rises, dragging the tip of my black sword along the mat as he comes, then drops it at my feet.

"*Use my power!*" Liha's panic is palpable, but her voice is still quiet.

I raise my chin as he nears. I will face my death without fear.

He grabs the front of my leathers, his wild eyes not looking so calm now.

"I'll kill you slowly for that." He pries his red sword from my hand and drops it beside my black one.

A tendril of orange jerks a dagger to his hand. His smile is more teeth-gritting than anything. He peels open my clenched fist and drives the eight-inch blade clean through my palm.

I clench my teeth and pinch my lips together, denying him the satisfaction of hearing my scream. This only seems to deepen his sneer. I try to move against my clothes again, but his power holds.

You will use me eventually, the darkness whispers. *When you tire of the pain.*

A tear slips down my cheek. Another trail of orange and another dagger appears. He drags the tip up from my palm and sinks this one into my forearm.

Again, I hold back my scream.

Another trail of orange, another dagger, slammed into my biceps. I grit my teeth, holding back cries.

He sinks the next one into my injured shoulder. A sob breaks through, but I clamp down.

The next blade, he holds at my neck.

"*Nizzara!*" Liha begs, but I only lift my chin to give him an unobstructed view.

His hold on my entire body is too strong. I refuse to drain Liha, refuse to be a monster.

My opponent draws his dagger back, as if planning to stab it into my neck, when the Megadome creaks from sudden, depthless cold.

Black ice breaks across the red dagger aimed at my neck, down my opponent's arm, and up to his lips, giving them a black tinge. The Zem man stops, eyes darting around, and backs up a step.

Dae towers behind me, unperceivable to everyone but me. I allow him to see my memories of this duel, of Liha.

His dark, velvety touch brushes my shoulder. "*Do you trust me?*"

Without a second thought, I open my shield to him.

He enters my mind like a puzzle piece sliding into its assigned spot. Liha slumps with fatigue—and what feels like relief.

Dae's power surges through every vein, every pore of my body.

"*I will not kill him.*" I speak to Dae inside my mind and his velvet touch brushes my cheek.

"*I know.*"

He allows me to call his power. I release it, and every blade in the vicinity vanishes, including those in my hand and arm.

They reappear with fiery vengeance, the two swords surging through my opponent's shoulders, dropping him to the ground in a shriek of pain and pinning him there to the mat, sinking and twisting.

I use his own trick and pin his red, leather outfit to the ground, sprawling him out like a battle star.

I assess the extensive damage in my hand bones and shoulder. My darkness smiles.

I want him to pay.

"*Don't let me kill him,*" I whisper in my head, Dae's silky power building.

"*He deserves it . . . But I won't let you.*"

A battle cry erupts from my throat as his power releases from me, a raging sea of black smoke. Daggers sink through every limb in two-inch intervals. Another flick of my wrist has each blade cranking a ninety-degree turn, ripping through muscle and sinew.

A cry of agony tears from his lips and the audience is silent. Either that, or I can no longer hear them.

I stalk over to my opponent and find fear in his blue eyes.

I hate how I love that.

I crush his vesseled hand with my boot and rip out a blood-soaked dagger from his thigh.

"No!" he begs, but I'm already slicing through his finger bone.

CHAPTER 65

NIZZARA

DIARY: PAGE 35

Well, little diary, if I don't write again, I have most likely gotten myself killed in Zo territory.

—Lo

〜❦〜

KNOWING I'M PROTECTED BUT SILENTLY CRINGING AT Dae's presence, Liha leaves my shield, saying that wherever my father is (she wouldn't tell me) he's fighting off his spirit and the shadows on his own.

"*I can see her memories,*" Dae says once she's gone, "*now that she's weaker.*"

Halix is ordering my guards to get useful and load our glo-kars to go home. She plucks my black sword up from where I rested it against the wall in my duel suite.

"Keep that by you. Stupid woman," she hisses and shoves the blade toward me. I take it from her, and she stalks off.

"*So, you saw where my father is?*"

"*I saw a lot.*" His cold deepens.

"*Where is he?*" As much as I loathe him most days, he is my father and—

"*You desire to go to him.*"

"*No one deserves to be possessed! I could—*"

"*He's too far gone,*" Dae says softly. "*He has been for a while. He's staying away from you to protect you, and for once, I'm on your father's side.*" There's a pause before he adds, "*He'll be back.*"

"But—"

"*No. I'm weak from hunger, and you're leaving a fucking blood trail.*" Cold slithers around me.

His power is damn near bending the stone floor as I walk on it. My bandages, placed by the healers, are *not* dripping blood. "*This is weak?*"

He's silent for a long time before he says, "*You seem to forget that I'm the monster here, Nizzara.*"

AFTER I DRESS MYSELF FOR BED, SINCE PREYSEE STILL HASN'T returned, I pull up *The King of Kings* on my reading chair but instead of reading, I find myself studying my cuts and scrapes, which appear smaller than before—noticing a shimmer of gold in the skin around them. It's the glo lights, I tell myself. But my mind instantly goes to the book Soriah left.

"*Why haven't you returned for that book?*" Dae says, hovering overhead.

My mental walls are down, so I raise them. "*I haven't had time.*" Since the last time I tried to retrieve it, I've found myself piecing clues together and . . . I don't want to be right. There's only one piece of the puzzle that doesn't make sense, but I don't linger on it.

Either Dae believes me, or he knows I don't want to talk about it right now. Something tells me it's the latter. He hasn't left my side since the duel, but I've noticed he's grown quieter.

He descends into the wingback chair across from me and materializes, leaning forward to rest his forearms on his knees. He opens and closes his mouth twice, as if to say something. Finally, he sighs. "I was almost too late."

Why do I get the feeling that's not what he was originally going to say? I look up from my book. His brows are pinched in pain.

"It's fine, Dae."

He glares at me. Whether or not this is what he'd planned to bring up, it's obviously something he's angry about and determined to discuss. "You were two seconds away from dying—to protect *Liha*."

Such awe in those hazel eyes—and utter rage.

I turn the page. "I'm not afraid of death."

"You make no sense," he says. "You're the most fearless little shit I know when it comes to so many things, but you are the most terrified woman when it comes to you and your power." When I open my mouth, he points a finger at me. "Don't play dumb. I feel power in your shield—*yours*, not mine." His eyes bore into mine. "You are *good*, Nizzara. Why are you afraid of yourself?"

"I—" I swallow, my hands becoming clammy around the binding.

After a minute of silence, he sighs. "You don't have to answer if you don't want to."

I shake my head. "Just give me a second."

I clear my throat. "I don't fear death or pain." I look away from him. "Because they are better alternatives than living to be a monster. My power is dark like his, and I am so much like him." My voice cracks. "I don't want power ... because I *do* want it. I'm afraid if I touch it ..."

"You'll become like him."

I nod. "Possessed by it."

"You're not him, though. You were *born* with this power, not possessed by it. And the fact that you worry about this proves you are different."

"The only thing it proves is that I acknowledge my predisposition."

He runs his hand through his hair, clearly agitated with me. I suddenly remember Lo's journal entry, the one mentioning his tells and the reason why he does that ...

She's right. There's nothing but heat in his gaze, and seeing it directed at me ... it's as good as flipping a switch. Warmth pools inside me.

His body tenses. "Why are you looking at me like that?"

"Because *you* are looking at me like that." I close my book and drop my mental wall, allowing my desires to get creative.

His eyes darken. "No," he says.

I straighten. "You don't want—"

He shakes his head. "I already told you, *wanting* is not the problem."

"What, then? My betrothed?"

"There's a possibility that you win, and the kings won't grant you freedom from your betrothal. The betrothal law is written in the alliance, Nizzara. If that happens . . . Lekk is a good candidate for you. He can give you a future, and I don't want to take that choice from you."

"This again? I already told you I don't choose him."

He rises from the chair and scoops me up from mine in one smooth, easy motion, gently cradling me in his arms. His dark, beautiful scent wraps around me.

Nestling his nose to my ear, he turns us to the bed, pulls the sheets down, and lays my head on my pillow.

He disappears into a spray of black mist. "*I hear your desires. Hidden beneath all of those traitorous ones is one for sleep.*"

I glare up at him, despite how comfortable my bed is. "That one *is* the traitorous one," I say, a yawn stealing the end of my sentence.

He chuckles and sits on the bed beside me. "*Sleep, Izzy.*"

"*I hate that nickname.*" But the corners of my lips betray me.

A midnight laugh floats through our bond. "*Sure, you do.*"

CHAPTER 66

DAGEN

NIZZARA IS HEALING FAST—UNNATURALLY FAST. THAT'S the only reason we're in the training room—and the only reason I'm not completely losing my shit. Her next duel is in two days. She has to fight whether she's injured or not—and her next opponent is even higher ranked than her last.

Her healing is not a Mark forming in our bond—I'd know if that were the case—yet I have wondered what Mark *will* form. With the amount of power flowing between us, there's no way we won't share one. Her power feels depthless, like a hole about to swallow me into it. It grows daily, and it's far from the first time I've wondered what essence she's bonded to, but her memories don't hold the answer. Being in her shield, I feel more of her soul, and it's the strongest, brightest soul I've ever seen. But glimpsing how quickly the darkness is growing throughout her, I find myself wondering for the first time if she's strong enough to wield it or even hold it at bay.

She yells out, swinging her sword for my torso with more speed and ferocity than I've ever seen from her. But it's still not enough. She's advancing in her skill, but so are the opponents she's facing.

"Quit avoiding the death blows," I say. "Your opponents can fend them off."

Her only answer is another frustrated scream and a kick for my head. I catch her boot and toss her off-balance. She falls backward with a thud onto the mat.

I point at her. "If you don't make your opponents fear for their lives every second you're in that ring, you've already lost."

"No more lectures on *knowing* your opponent?" she hisses up at me before jumping back to her feet.

I want to smile at her sass, but the thought of who she's facing next has me plotting ways to cheat the system on her behalf. "Your next opponent is from Zo. He's fast, and his aim is better than anyone's I've ever seen—even yours. But don't change the subject. Killing blows—"

She punches for my face, but I turn to mist and rematerialize to the side.

"You have to use them."

"No. I don't." She punches again.

I catch her fist in my hand, and I feel the force through my arm. Definitely stronger, but winning will take more than muscle. I keep hold of her hand, and my traitorous fingers slowly weave between hers. Her statue-like mask cracks as her hand softens for me. I run my other hand along her thigh until my fingers find her favorite black dagger. I slide it out and place it in her hand.

"You can't hurt me."

She bows her head toward me. "What if it hurts *me*?"

I tuck a white strand that's loosened from her braid behind her ear and tilt her chin up. "You aren't afraid of pain, remember?"

Her fingers wrap around the hilt, a war of emotion raging in her eyes.

I meet her gaze. "You'll always be afraid of the dark part of yourself if you never face it." Even if it's stronger than her, there's no removing it from her soul—it's part of her. Being bonded to her vessel, I realize how intricately woven the dark onyx spots are throughout her brilliant golden soul. I see her conversations with Sorren in her memories, and I agree that cowering from it only gives it more room inside her.

Her throat bobs.

"I'm not saying you have to kill anyone. But your opponents have to believe you will kill them. You have to face this fear, so it won't hold you back in the ring?"

A moment passes before she nods.

I take a step back, giving her an unobstructed view of my chest for her to strike.

Her stone-cold mask dissolves, and undiluted fear rises in those eyes. Her tan face loses color, and her knuckles turn white around the dagger.

I guide her hand, inching the blade toward my chest until its sharp point pinches my black tunic. Her breathing picks up, chest heaving.

"I'm dead, Nizzara. You can't kill me."

She deepens the pressure of the blade until it pricks the skin of my chest. She pauses before she shakes her head and drops the dagger to the training mat. "I can't."

I turn to my spirit form. *"I'll never force you to do anything, but I will challenge you."* I caress her cheek with shadow. *"Because you have to live. I'll accept nothing else."*

She nods, closing her eyes when I wrap myself around her. *"I don't want to be afraid,"* she whispers. *"But today I am."*

I swallow the dread rising inside. Even though she's come a long way in her training, I know she's not ready to face the rest of the tournament. But I meant what I said. I won't force her.

When she collapses in bed hours later, her red nightgown accentuates her toned thighs . . .

And her breasts . . .

And her hips . . .

She glares at me as we lie facing each other on her bed; her desires about kissing and running her hands down my chest have every inch of me burning. That's why she's glaring—because I'm in my spirit form keeping my hands to myself.

"You're ghosting me?"

"If I human you, I will ruin your betrothal." As much as I want to rip that nightgown off and worship every inch of her, I'll be gone in a few weeks, and Nightlight won't take her if she's been with another.

"I'm willing to risk it."

"I'm not risking a damned thing when it comes to you. Now, go to sleep."

She gets up on her elbow and locks those lethal black eyes on me with vengeance.

". . . desire to punch Dae in the face . . ."

". . . desire to trace his lips with my tongue and—"

"Nizzara," I growl.

Her smug smile is more than infuriating. But I love it all the same.

My only saving grace is that sleep pulls her away from me before I can give in to her very explicit desires.

When she's deep asleep, Liha's pink spirit falls from above, so pale and weak. Even more so than in Nizzara's memory of her.

"I can leave," I say.

As much as Liha's betrayal stung Nizzara, she still loves the little, pink spirit. It angers me as much as it fills my chest with warmth. Such unwavering loyalty.

"She doesn't have nightmares anymore," Liha whispers.

Or maybe her voice is so weak it sounds like a whisper.

Liha shapes herself into an ancient princess with her crown and pointy ears instead of her usual ball of light. Her image flickers from pink to nonexistent. When her gaze falls on Nizzara, there is such undying love in it. Liha touches Nizzara's sleeping forehead.

"She suspects what she is. That's why she hasn't gone to the coves for that book." She smiles, her eyes still on Nizzara. *"She's smarter than she wishes to be, but knowledge runs in her blood."* Her smile fades. *"Among other things."*

I catch a glimpse of Liha's memory of Mazzar, and I see who her mother is. The knowledge . . . The healing . . . *"Wala is her mother,"* I say.

"Yes. Daughter of a Guardian—a pure soul." She nods, and a stretch of silence extends between us before she says, *"Mazzar is past the point of return, and her darkness is growing . . . I can't protect them anymore."* Her face crumples with pain and longing and regret. *"Very few souls can withstand what lurks inside her—what she is."*

My mind circles back to my conversation with Helina. *"Which of the dark essences lives inside her?"*

Liha's gaze cuts to me. *"That is her truth to tell. But if she can't overcome it . . ."* She shakes her head and sighs. *"She won't use me in the ring or outside it, so I'll offer what's left of me to her father."*

I stiffen. *"You're going to leave her? In the hands of a deathwalker?"*

Liha glares at me as if she can feel my judgment and hurt on Nizzara's behalf. *"I can only sense strong desires, but I've known yours for a while, Dagen. I know you'll protect her and I have little choice. My final death is nearing whether I choose it or not."*

She peers down at Nizzara as if this might be the last time she'll see her. *"I've seen her next opponent duel before."* Her eyes rise to mine, dread pooling in them. *"She won't use very much of you in the ring."* Her throat bobs. *"Don't let her die. She needs more time in this life."*

"She's not dying."

She dips her chin, satisfied with my answer. *"Will you tell her something for me? When she needs to hear it?"*

After a minute, I nod.

"Tell her I've seen the greatest warriors to ever walk these realms, be it men, women, or creatures. Tell her . . . that the greatest heroes have a touch of darkness inside."

She returns to a ball of light and disappears through the door.

CHAPTER 67

NIZZARA

DIARY: PAGE 36

I pulled it off. Not without a lot of blood, mind you. I not only have the original *King of Kings*, but also *The Book of Wala*. If the Zos didn't want us dead already, they will if they realize I replaced their precious treasures with enormous books on war tactics. They really should thank me for them. They'll need all the help they can get if they're going to war with me.

—*Lo*

THE MEGADOME VIBRATES. SPECTATORS POUND THEIR FISTS onto railings, their chants shaking the foundations:

"To the death! To the death!"

Dae floats beside me as I stalk toward the duel ring centered in the pit of madness, fans cheering and jeering above. As I slide in between velvet ropes to face my opponent, Dae dissolves into my shield.

My opponent's dark features starkly contrast against his white leathers, fit with matching daggers on his belt and a longsword at his back. He assesses me with a calm but lethal air as if taking note of which side I favor when I move.

"*You're going to use me,*" Dae says, nothing but cool stubbornness in his voice.

"*Maybe it's my turn to ghost you.*" I raise my sword.

"Nizzara."

Goose bumps trail my neck at the way he growls my name. I really hope I get to hear that again.

Dae pools his power into me, and unfathomable energy arises at my fingertips. I hold all of it at bay, as if I'm holding my breath underwater—the darkness inside yearning for me to drink Dae's power in.

The siren blares overhead.

I allow some of Dae's power through, and black smoke explodes from my hand. I use it to grab my opponent's white leathers like two invisible fists and throw him across the ring with more force than I mean to. His back hits a duel post, and he drops to the mat, wheezing. Darkness skirts my vision and a whole section of the audience nearby slumps at my release of power—as if I pulled from—

No. I'm imagining it, but the darkness inside *smiles.*

My opponent recovers fast, jumps to his feet, and shoots daggers at me as he charges from across the ring. I zigzag out of his line of fire, snatch the last speeding dagger from the air, and hurtle it back at him, using a tiny bit of Dae's moving power to overpower my opponent's control over the blade.

He roundhouse-kicks to block it. The dagger strikes his armored boot and ricochets to the mat.

I swing my blade for his leg.

He jumps over my sword, yanking his own from his back strap and swiping it at my neck midair. I dive away but it scratches a shallow cut across my throat.

Dae snarls inside my shield, and darkness bleeds through my vision, spraying little black spots across my view. My opponent raises his sword again, circling me.

"It's just a scratch," I pant, panic rising as the black spots grow bigger.

Dae grumbles, but it's distant, my darkness eclipsing him too. I feel its desire to drain everything and everyone, *including him.*

Breathe.

I stand my ground as my opponent stalks around me—taunting.

Calculating. I think back to every moment of training, every moment I fought against what I am, and shrouded by the darkness, I raise my sword.

I *will* lose myself to it eventually—I feel it—but today is not that day. Not while Dae is inside my shield. Some tiny part of Dagen's soul is enough for me to latch on to—anchor myself—and the darkness slows.

My opponent lunges.

I twirl away and slice through the back of his thigh.

He yells in pain, staggers a step, then throws his own blade through the air with a jet of silver smoke.

I dodge, but that calculating glint in his eye—

The sword alters course at the last second and carves a deep, bleeding gash across my belly.

Dae goes rigid.

"*I'm fine*," I hiss. It's not nearly as bad as the last time it was slashed.

I clutch my wound with one hand and swing my sword with the other. My opponent kicks my wielding hand on my downswing, knocking my sword from my grasp. He flicks it away with his vessel power then thrusts for my heart. I jump back, barely escaping his lunge, and rip a dagger from the sheath on my thigh. He fakes a swing left and catches me with a slice to my ribs on my right when I dodge the wrong way.

"*Did Liha get this frustrated watching you ignore your power?*" Dae growls.

I duck another swing and stab the inside of my opponent's thigh. He cries out again and slams his pommel against my jaw. My head jerks back, and the spots flare bigger, my control wavering.

The darkness doesn't *speak* to me. It simply exists in me like *I* exist in me.

Drain him. He wouldn't mourn your death. Why should you mourn his? I let out a cry of fury—because I *want* to kill him. I catch the Zo's free arm, slam my dagger through his elbow, and yank the blade up to his shoulder.

The Zo man screams and jerks away, his deep brown eyes coming alive with rage. Gray smoke explodes from him, picking up all his daggers—

They sink through me, milliseconds apart. I stumble back, jerking with the impact as each blade buries hilt-deep into my flesh. I can't breathe, can't think, as blood blossoms to the surface. Five blades. Three in my legs, two in my lower abdomen.

Dae's answering battle cry comes with an explosion of power through my veins.

Screams of excitement rain down from the stands.

The silent, gold spirit trickles in.

And darkness purrs through me.

It takes everything I have to hold back the cataclysmic power building and building.

At its peak—when the Zo nobleman is driving a killing swipe for my neck—I feel the twinge of a Mark rippling out.

My knees tremble, blood spilling down my front. Blackness and gold and *power* swarm me from all directions.

It explodes from me, and time *stops*.

My opponent freezes mid-strike. His white blade—smeared with my crimson blood—two inches from my neck. Beyond him a raging crowd halts, mouths open and fingers pointing.

"What did you do!" I pant. The power is still flowing through me, spending more and more energy every second, and the dark spots . . .

"I don't know." He's clenching his teeth. I hear it when he says, *"But if you ever try dying on me like that again, I will materialize—I don't give a fuck who sees—and I'll start tearing souls. Do you hear me?"*

My knees cave in, and I drop to the mat beneath my enemy's bloody sword, my vision too dark to see the daggers protruding from me.

Gold continues to trickle down from the sky-high dome, glinting through my darkness, until it takes the form of a woman-like figure in front of me.

"*Nizzara*," she says, her voice like a song, and my vision slowly returns. Her white hair flows over her shoulders. Her black eyes are wide and knowing. "*My daughter.*"

I recognize her with sudden clarity. *Wala.* The Guardian of life.

I open my mouth, but nothing comes out. She kneels and cups my cheek with a ghostly hand, and the darkness in me shrivels at her touch—a surge of light coursing through my soul. I feel every part of her. Infinite knowledge, life, healing, and, *realms*, such beauty.

Dae's energy slowly drains—coursing through me—holding time at bay.

"*I don't have much more time with you.*" She smiles at me, but it's full of deep sadness. "*I'm being selfish stealing your time like this, but I wished to speak to you once before I leave this life. It takes so much energy to project my voice.*"

My voice cracks. "You're dying?"

Her gaze deepens. "*Even I cannot bear a child like you and live.*"

"*Don't cry.*" She wipes my cheek with a warm, almost solid, hand. "*Death always steals life, Nizzara. That does not mean life isn't worth living—worth fighting for.*"

She removes the daggers still protruding from me and touches my abdomen, pulling the pain away. Every scratch, bruise, and sore muscle washes away in a trail of her warmth.

Her gold light dims around her as her hand grasps me. "*I'm already dying, but I've been saving what life I have left for when you need it most.*"

Her gold soul slowly seeps into me, letting my darkness siphon her. I jolt away. "No. You can't—" My voice breaks.

Her touch holds me in place—her power making it impossible to move—and her soul emits a cracking sound. The darkness swirls with triumph as it drinks her in.

I sob, unable to stop her from giving herself over to the darkness. "Please don't do this . . ."

Her gaze deepens. "*I've never left you, and I never will.*" She grazes her thumb along my cheek. "*Remember that when you feel alone. No matter what anyone tells you . . . no matter the darkness you feel, you are the last ray of hope in a dying world."*

"Why are you doing this?" I ask as she pours her life into me, her soul audibly cracking, *shattering.*

"Nexia is your father's enemy." She bows her head. *"But what bonded to your soul is mine."*

Dae slumps in my shield, his soul steadily draining. I know he's holding out, letting me have this time.

My mother's gold light fades more and more. *"It is a heavy burden, to be made of life and carry death in your veins."*

"Don't do this." My voice cracks as her soul does, Dae slumping more and more behind me. I'm the cause of both.

"Nizzara. Look at me," she says. *"I was already dying. You are not my end."* Her eyes behold me as if I am the center of her world. *"I will live on through you. I'll always be with you. Never forget that. You are worth dying for."*

A final, piercing *crack* emits from her soul, the sound like glass shattering around me, my veins filling with her golden power.

In a blurry blink of tears, she's gone, and I lurch forward.

"Nizzara," Dae whispers, bent over behind me, draining out too. *"Let go."*

Heart-stopping panic hits me. His voice is so shallow.

I cut the flow of our power and time resumes.

My body moves like it never has. I surge up from under my opponent's sword after he swipes through where my neck just was. I stab through his biceps and dodge his redirected swing back for me. I duck and bury my dagger into his flank. He cries out and grits his teeth as he swings again and again—visibly thrown by my new rhythm. His sword swooshes down, up, sideways, chopping for my torso. I duck and spin, missing his blade easily, tears still running down my face.

I move faster, *different*, as if a sliver of my mother's soul is guiding me.

Dae is fading still, and it sends my muscles into overdrive. Before my opponent's next upswing, I punch his face, shattering his nose. I rip his sword from his hand and turn full circle, smashing his pommel against his temple with more strength than I've ever known. He crumples, boneless and unconscious to the mat.

HALIX SAUNTERS INTO THE DUELER SUITE AN HOUR LATER with a thick sheet of parchment. "Looks like the next dueler you were supposed to fight died from her injuries a few hours ago, and the next one after her has gone missing." Her lips tug up, and her gray eyes twinkle in a way that makes me wonder if she had something to do with that. "So," she says. "That moves your final duel, against Kazem, to next week. It's time to load up." She spins on her heals and orders my guards to ready the royal glo-kars.

"*The King's Final Duel*," Dae says, his voice weak.

"*You need to feed*," I whisper through our bond, still staring at the marbled wall, not really seeing it as the healers finish wiping blood from my already healed wounds.

"*Later*," he says.

After I'm cleaned up, the healers leave and my guards station themselves outside the door, allowing me privacy to change. Dae materializes and wraps his arms around my waist, hugging me from behind.

I close my eyes and lean into him.

"So," he says, burying his head into my neck. "Are we going to discuss the fact that as a Guardian, with a pure soul, you're way out of my league?"

I sniff and wipe a stray tear running down my cheek. His closeness—his light teasing—distracts me from the anguish swirling in the pit of my stomach like it always does. And I welcome the moment of reprieve.

"Don't tell me who's in my league, lowly deathwalker."

He lays a gentle kiss on my neck. "Lucky for me you have a thing for lowly deathwalkers."

"That depends . . . Do deathwalkers have glowing muscles?"

He nips my neck. "Little beast."

CHAPTER 68

NIZZARA

DIARY: PAGE 37

I've been locked in my room for ten days, with a headache
courtesy of Wala and her pathways. I've been reading her book of
possible futures. There's one future that never changes.

I've concluded two terrible things.

The King of Kings is alive.

But he won't be for long.

—*Lo*

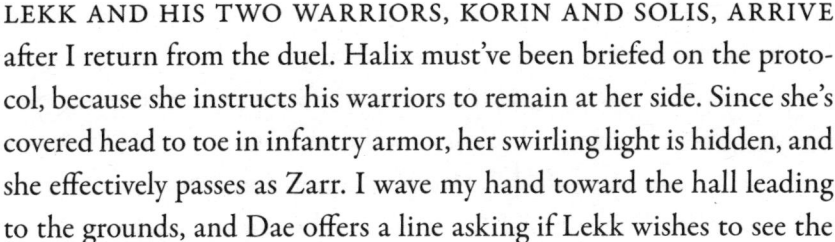

LEKK AND HIS TWO WARRIORS, KORIN AND SOLIS, ARRIVE
after I return from the duel. Halix must've been briefed on the proto-
col, because she instructs his warriors to remain at her side. Since she's
covered head to toe in infantry armor, her swirling light is hidden, and
she effectively passes as Zarr. I wave my hand toward the hall leading
to the grounds, and Dae offers a line asking if Lekk wishes to see the
grounds again.

I speak it softly, and Lekk nods.

Dae is cool inside my shield, but when Lekk falls in step beside me
and Preysee, a pang of despair flows from him.

I lean my head into his dark velvet presence. "*I do not belong to him.*"

He runs a dark tendril along my cheek. "*In that dress, with your
hair down, he wants you to.*"

Lekk speaks and Dae translates.

"I've come to accept your offer of a betrothal." Dae's voice is stiff inside my mind.

I freeze mid-step in the hall, and Lekk stops too. Everyone stops. His face is a mash of longing and torture and duty, but his eyes fall to my lips and stay there.

No.

I was supposed to have time to win the tournament and terminate the betrothal before he decided.

Lekk tilts his head, taking in my span of emotions.

Dae's heartbreak seeps through our bond, but he isn't leaving. He stays in my shield, where I know he'll stay until he's dragged back to Baratrum.

Baratrum, because he won't take my soul. Even if I were to hand it to him, I know he'd choose Baratrum.

"I decline."

"Nizzara. I am not translating that for you."

"Yes. You will."

"He is good. I see his soul, his memories, his desires. He can give you a life—" His voice breaks. *"A future. He'd be a good ruler, a fair mate—an equal."*

"I decline. Translate it." I know who I choose, and I allow Dae to hear it in my desires.

"Nizzara, I am a damned soul full of shadows—I have nothing to give you, not even time." He clears his throat. *"I won't let you throw the opportunity away so quickly."* Dae gives me a translation that means something along the lines of *I will consider,* but I don't say it.

I straighten my shoulders and speak directly to Lekk with the only word of their language I remember. "No."

Lekk's face softens, as if he understands how this situation is hard for both of us, and says, "Nizzara, I offer my matehood to you. I offer my sword, my loyalty, and my future. I will be at your side until the day my energy returns to the earth. I will protect you, comfort you, and stand beside you through every hardship and trial you face. I promise to serve you, respect you, and behold you as my equal."

Tears prick my eyes as I back away from him, suddenly feeling trapped, like the walls are moving in.

"*Nizzara*," Dae whispers. His spirit is at my back, nudging me toward Lekk.

"No," I say softly, meeting Lekk's gaze, hoping he can sense my apology when I turn my back to him, leaving him there with a look of shock, but also relief, on his face.

My steps grow faster and faster, until I'm *running*. I need to get away from the prying eyes of my guards, away from Lekk's beautiful proposal that I just declined.

My father will punish me if he returns, but I don't care. When I turn the corner, escaping my guards and Preysee, who are scrambling to catch up, Dae materializes. Faster than I can react, he shoves me into a dark room, locks the door, and pins me against the wall.

"What are you *doing*?" he growls. "He is the best betrothal you could ask for."

"I can't accept it," I say.

His emotions drown me through our bond. Frustration, relief, anger, relief. "Why? Are you so spiteful you'd decline a future—"

"I belong to someone else." My eyes begin to adjust, and I make out those hazel irises in front of me as I touch his face. "And I will not betray him."

He bends his head down to rest on mine. "Nizzara," he pleads, squeezing his eyes shut. "I have no future to give you. You cannot choose me." His anguish and longing rush through my shield, an all-consuming flood.

I take his face in both hands. "You cannot tell me who I choose, lowly deathwalker."

His hands sink into my hair and I watch his restraint shatter in his gaze. He kisses me, deep and urgent. Waves of his power—his emotions—crash into me. I crash right back into him, taking every second I have with him.

He hoists me up, and I wrap my legs around him.

He groans and pins me harder against the wall, kissing me like there will be no tomorrow.

His hand finds my leg and runs beneath my dress, setting me on fire—the icy, zapping kind that always comes with him.

I want him here.

I want him now.

When I flick open the top button on his tunic, he breaks the kiss, pain on his face. "Nizzara—"

A commotion of yelling comes from the hall, and Dae jets back into my shield.

I straighten my dress and step out to a fight that broke out in my absence between Lekk and Brunar.

I inform Brunar that Lekk did nothing wrong, even though Lekk is the one holding Brunar by the chest of his uniform.

"What if you change your mind after I'm gone?" Dae whispers. I feel his fear and regret over our kiss.

"I won't."

CHAPTER 69

NIZZARA

I have read, and read, and read. I refuse to believe what I'm forced
to believe at this point. I've memorized every single pathway.

I know who it is.

The only thing I can do to help is run.

—*Lo*

I PAUSE AT THE EDGE OF MY CLOSET AND LOOK AT DAE LY-
ing on my bed, his brows pinched as he stares up at the ceiling, lost in
thought.

He says his days are limited. But as the darkness infuses deeper
and sharper throughout my soul, my days are numbered too, and I
don't have the heart to tell him. I feel the vast emptiness of the castle
beneath my feet. Liha, Yisabell, my family . . . all gone. My world so
full of pain.

My heart bleeds for what my mother forced me to do, even if she
did it out of love . . . She *broke* me.

Even though she willingly gave it . . . I took her life, and I will never
be the same.

I look at Dae. He's the last shred of good inside my world. I want
to curl up in that good place next to him, savor what time I have left
with him.

For tonight, I will shut out the hurt and hide in the sliver of peace his soul brings me.

I crawl into bed wearing my favorite nightgown. It's black, it's silky, and it hugs me in all the right places.

Dae rolls his head toward me, and I memorize every plane of his face. I even note how each dark wave lies on his head, how his hair fades shorter and shorter down the sides.

His throat bobs when I curl up next to him, and his arms pull me in like that's where I belong.

"No disappearing tonight?" I ask inside his mind, my head on his shoulder.

He buries his nose in my hair. *"I thought you were going to die today, and then I thought you were going to belong to someone else. So no, I'm selfishly taking what you'll give me."*

"Whatever I give you?"

He stiffens; a concoction of his drowning desires and sharp anxiety go to war inside our shield. *"Nizzara—"*

When I lift myself up to glare down at those eyes, he sighs and reaches up to brush my cheek. *"Nil will come for me after the King's Final Duel, Nizzara. You know that."*

His words sink into me like daggers. I shield my mind and desires, hoping it's enough to hide my devastation.

"And when I'm gone, I'm sure there'll be a long line of deathwalkers to take my place." His jaw feathers. *"I won't take your soul, but others will try."*

I narrow my eyes. *"I'd like to see them try."*

He smiles. *"I love that expression on you."*

"I'm serious."

"I know." His eyes fall to my lips.

I lean down until his scent is the only thing between us and let my desires run away with thoughts of his lips on mine. His body against mine. His hands trailing up my nightgown, finishing the journey they started earlier.

His eyes darken as he guides my chin closer until his lips tickle mine. "So cruel."

I smile against his lips.

In a smooth, effortless motion, he rolls on top of me and pins my back to the bed. His eyes beg for me, just as his long, hard length digging into my thigh begs for me too. I bite my lip. How I long to touch him.

His nostrils flare. "I'll make you a deal."

I rock my hips into him, comfortably pinned beneath every firm inch of him. "What deal?" I graze my hands up his thighs.

He nearly groans—nearly gives in—but he takes my arms and pulls them above my head. "If you can beat me in a spar," he says, laying a kiss beneath my jaw, "I'll give you whatever you wish of me."

He kisses his way up to my ear, his sultry voice pooling heat into every part of me. "I will kiss you until tomorrow. I will hold you until your nightmares are gone. I will give you my crown and my kingdom, Nizzara, as soon as you prove you'll survive after I'm gone."

He pulls back and chuckles. "There's that face again."

"You want me to kick your ass?" I say, peering up into warm, sweet eyes.

He returns to my ear, drawing a tantalizing line with his nose down my neck, catching my breath. "Yep. So I know you can fend off any deathwalker who comes after the King's Final Duel."

"That's ridiculous," I breathe.

"I know you are capable of it, but I need to see it."

He continues grazing down my shoulder to my thin nightgown strap and takes it in his teeth before releasing it with a flick. My pulse pounds through me.

"I'm not doing it."

He shrugs. "Then no—"

I buck my hips up, flinging him forward. He catches my headboard as I slide out from under him.

He chuckles. Damn that coy grin of his.

"Now?" He smirks, raising that devious brow.

I slide my dagger from my leg sheath and take my stance. "*Now.*"

He points a look to my door, where my night guards are just outside in the hall. "We'll have to be quiet."

"Why are you telling me? *You'll* be the one begging for mercy," I whisper.

His eyes smolder. "Oh, I sincerely hope that's the case." He slides off the bed and summons his menacing blade.

I call his power, and it comes to me even though he's not in my shield, as if I can pull power from anywhere. Its icy-hot lightning snaps through my entire body as I suck his sword into another dimension, but his power doesn't leave my veins, as if I moved it on my own.

"That's *so* cheating," he says, but he's biting his lip, his gaze trailing my bare thighs as he says it.

"It is not," I hiss. "It's smart."

His power zaps inside, taut as a bowstring throughout my system.

I'd be more terrified of it if it wasn't coiling things into pleasurable, racy aches through my center. I need him. Judging by the smolder on Dae's face, he needs me too. He runs his hand through those soft waves.

"Fine. You'll bond another spirit after I'm gone, so I'll allow it."

I keep my mind shields nice and tight as I circle him, twirling my dagger.

"Don't you want to change out of your nightgown?"

I smile at the way his throat bobs while his eyes continue to roam over me. "Someone told me distractions can be useful."

He smirks. "I won't go easy."

"Good."

He kicks my torso. I fly back, but, before I hit the wall, he materializes behind me, catching me with impossibly strong arms.

I throw my head back, headbutting him in the chin, and stab an elbow into his abs. The same moment he doubles forward, I surge my head back again, smacking him square in the face. I spin out, swiping my dagger across his chest.

He vanishes, his ghostly outline circling, his power still coiling and tightening through me.

He materializes to my left. As soon as he's solid, my fist lands center on his chest. I throw everything I have into that single contact, reaching down inside and brushing my mother's golden gift—because her gift is *not* the darkness swirling inside, and I know I can't hurt Dae. It fills my arm as naturally as breath fills my lungs. Gold light sparks out from where my knuckles meet him, and his solid slab of muscle ricochets off my fist.

He flies backward, crashing into the stone wall, knocking books from my shelves. He's on his ass, beaming up at me with worship and pride in his gaze.

A pounding comes from my door. "Everything okay, Your Highness?" Brunar yells from the hall.

"I'm fine," I call back as I stride over, dagger out. "Get back to work."

Brunar offers a relenting mumble through the door as I straddle Dae and wedge my blade up under the smooth, short beard on his jaw, his power still wrecking me, his eyes still worshipping me.

"Ass. Kicked."

His expression melts. "You're fucking beautiful when you're pointing a dagger at me."

I can't stop the smile on my lips. "Does that mean I get those promises?"

His hand finds mine, weaving our fingers and tugging them to his lips, while his other hand trails my thigh. "They were already yours."

His eyes darken, and my dagger goes slack in my other hand. I recall his blade of shadow, letting it clink somewhere behind me.

But the deep, coiling sensation doesn't leave. Not even close.

Maybe because his hands are sliding up my nightgown toward my hips.

"Are you sure you want this?" he says in my mind.

"I choose you, Dagen. I want every moment I have left with you."

A flash of pain and sadness sweeps through our bond. I lean back.

"*Unless you don't want the same,*" I say.

He leans his forehead against mine, his fingers knotting in my nightgown. "*I've wanted you since the first time I laid eyes on you, Nizzara.*" His hands begin to move again, trailing the rest of the way up until they find the sensitive divot of my hips. A deep groan sounds in my mind. "*You just fought me without underwear?*"

His scent surrounds me, his breath on my lips. "I did."

"*Cruel, cruel little beast,*" he says, his fingers pausing. His eyes are on me, watching every flicker of emotion as his hand slowly moves again, finding my aching center. Dagen glides a single finger inside me. His arousal crashes through our bond as if the dam holding it back just exploded, so intense I can hardly breathe. He closes his eyes. "*Fuck, you're wet.*"

In a swift motion, he has me on my back against the floor. His hips settle between my legs as he kisses my jaw. "Your desires," he breathes against my neck, "are naughty little things." He moves to my ear and bites. "But I am very good at following directions, Nizzara."

I gasp. My hands sink into his hair, knotting from the unbearable tension. Slowly, he slides my nightgown straps off my shoulders, kissing me along my neck as he goes. My hands find his broad shoulders, needing to touch him everywhere. A low rumble vibrates through our bond before he pulls himself upright and tugs his shirt over those soft, dark waves on his head.

Scars web along his skin like that of any seasoned dueler, and I commit each one to memory. I run my hands over him, memorizing every muscled hill and valley on his tan chest, wondering—not for the first time—how he likes to be touched.

"*If you keep looking at me that way, I will beg for mercy,*" he says.

I drink him in with my eyes as he lowers himself over me, bringing a muscled arm on either side of my head. He kisses me exactly like I want. Hot and demanding. "*You want to know how I like to be touched?*" he asks through our bond as his tongue skillfully plays with mine.

When he moves his kisses down to my neck, I rasp, "Yes." It's all I can get out as his lips bring electric currents to my skin.

He growls inside my mind, *"Any way you want to."*

Suddenly, he scoops me up and strides for the bed, my legs wrapped around his waist. Every inch of him is rock hard beneath me. I bite off a whimper when he pins my back to silk sheets, his hips biting into my thighs as he stands at the edge of the bed. I reach down, yanking his button open, and he slides his pants down before climbing over me. My hands roam down his torso until I find his long, hard length. He groans and pushes into my touch, his eyes closing, and unbearable pleasure rolls through our bond as if it's my own. That coy smile finds his lips. I feel it against my jaw before he flips us over, pulling me on top of him. His hands guide my hips in rocking motions beneath my nightgown as I slide along his length. He closes his eyes, his hands squeezing my thighs tighter and tighter as I tease him. I pause only to remove my nightgown.

When he realizes it's gone, he takes hold of my waist and throws me back onto the sheets, his gaze taking its time rolling over me. When it finds my neck, where faded bruises linger, he brushes his fingers over them and lays a gentle kiss there.

His emotions surge through our bond as his lips brush that spot— such rage and overwhelmingly tender heartache. His lips continue to my shoulder, which has taken countless blades, before trailing all the way down to my abdomen, where the infantry's blade tore me open.

A tangle of fear and drowning affection weaves through the air around him. Heat pricks my eyes.

He moves back up to my mouth, kissing me until I am to the point of begging.

"Dae."

His hands grip my waist, bringing me to the tip of his hard length.

"Nizzara," he groans, sliding in slowly, filling and stretching me. A quick slice of pain comes before melting into a pleasurable, needing ache. He doesn't move, his hand caressing my cheek as his lips quiver against mine.

"Are you okay?" His forehead rests against mine, his breath mingling with mine.

I bite his lip. *"I'm not weak."*

His lips smile against mine, and he begins moving.

I've been on the cusp of explosion since I straddled him on the floor, and every pull and thrust has me hurtling toward oblivion. His hand slides down to where he's moving inside of me, his thumb stroking a deliciously tender spot.

My whimper is out loud this time, and I'm biting my lip to keep from screaming.

His eyes darken as he pools his power into me. He tosses a pillow into the air behind him, and I stop time before it hits the ground.

"As much as I love to see you bite your lip, don't. I need to hear you scream for me, Nizzara."

He continues. His pace, his hands, even my name on his lips spirals me toward the edge. His power explodes through me, time stopped as I come undone for him, shaking and screaming his name in a pocket of time meant only for us, where only we can hear. Every muscle inside me quakes with waves of pleasure as I melt around him.

"Beautiful," he whispers.

I'm breathless, my voice shaking in the aftermath of intense pleasure when I say, *"That's all you've got?"*

His dark, menacing voice purrs, *"Such a little beast."* He bites my lip and adds down our bond, *"I'm nowhere near done with you."*

He slides out and moves me higher on the bed, kissing his way down from my lips, to my breasts, to my stomach, until his tongue finds that same exact spot his thumb just had.

"Dae," I gasp, already near the brink again from his slow, sensual strokes. But as soon as I'm close to another oblivion, he pauses, holding me on that sharp edge for what seems like eternity, until I'm whimpering. Over and over again, he brings me to the edge, until I'm crying his name, pleading for release. Until it doesn't matter how slow he goes. I break at the softest, torturously long movement from his tongue.

I scream, this wave deeper, longer, and more intense than the last.

He growls and slides back in, his pace building and intensifying every lingering shudder as I turn into a boneless, hot mass around him.

Something flickers in our bond, and he stops moving. *"I'm sterile,"* he says, *"but if you want protection—"*

I shake my head, running my hand down his chest. *"You're perfect exactly as you are, Dae."*

Such deep, heart-throbbing emotion pools through our bond at my words and he slams into me with such wonderful, aching depth. His muscled forearms flex on either side of my head as he finds a rhythm that has me building until I'm riding the edge again. He pauses to take my nipple between those sinful lips. He bites, and nips, and sucks until I'm begging for another release.

Finally, he shows me mercy and starts moving, harder and faster, until I cry out. His body tenses, finding his own release as mine continues through me. He drops on top of me.

"Nizzara," he says, then kisses me, hot and breathless, before he rolls over and pulls me into his arms. Our Mark fizzles away, and time resumes around us. The pillow he threw drops to the floor.

The depth and intensity of his emotions wrap around me as if tucking me into a safe and guarded place beside his heart.

He presses another kiss to my head and whispers in my mind, *"I'm going to miss you."*

"I'll miss you more."

He nips my ear. *"Don't pull that shit. I'll miss you most."*

I turn over so my nose is touching his and his smile puts the one in King's Hall to shame. This one is happy. His eyes are bright, full of caramels and emeralds, until a shadow passes over them. *"Promise me you will wipe the floor with Kazem."*

I hear what he's really saying. *Promise you will not be afraid, that you will live, no matter what.*

"I promise."

He nuzzles closer, content with my answer. *"I won't be here for our training session tomorrow."*

I take the opportunity to touch those luscious dark waves on his head, cursing myself for not touching them every day since he materialized in my bathing chamber.

"Why?"

A crease forms between his brows. *"I need to find out what happened to my sister before the King's Final Duel."*

My eyes search his. "Your sister," I say, feeling the guilt for hiding her diary rise again, especially because I just read her last entry.

He nods, his throat tightening. *"I don't think she's alive, but I have to know for sure."*

"I have to show you something," I say, rolling out of the blankets. My feet pad the stone floor as I go to the chair and retrieve the diary using gloves. *"It belonged to your sister."*

He sits up and reaches out for it, but I yank it back. *"It has poison on it."*

"It can't hurt me."

"If you get sick because you didn't listen—"

"I'm already dead. I think I'll be fine." He takes the little black book in his hands with such reverence. *"It's a diary."*

"Read the last page."

He sighs and opens to the last page, his brows furrowing as he reads.

"She got out," he breathes.

I nod. *"I'll be fine tomorrow. Go. Find her."*

CHAPTER 70

DAGEN

I PULL NIZZARA'S BLANKET OVER HER SHOULDER, CAREFUL not to wake her. Her smell on my skin has me reliving every second of last night. I kept my promise and kissed her until damn near sunrise. The first rays of sun bleed into the horizon outside her balcony windows, and as much as I don't want to leave her, I need to find Lo. I gently roll her head off my shoulder and onto her pillow before turning back into spirit. I hover above her, in awe of how happy she looks right now—even in her sleep. Her hair is a sexy mess of white waves sprawled over her black pillows and blankets. Her lips have a slight smile to them, and the crease that usually pinches between her brows when she sleeps is gone. The view has me aching to crawl back into bed with her, but as the sky lightens, I sigh and float toward her balcony.

I'm about to dissolve through the doors when an open book, resting on an ottoman, catches my eye. Pages of her scrawly notes lie around it, and one passage is highlighted from a glo dust pen. I lean down to read it.

The soil shall turn red from blood and death.
To deliver the king she'll give her last living breath.
The king is near. This is the year.
The king belongs to her golden light.
He'll take the throne to make things right.

I pick up the book and reread the passage. The golden light has to be Nizzara—her soul . . . who'll die in childbirth?

It couldn't possibly be my child . . .

I gaze over to her sleeping form, and a heaviness sinks through me. Could it be Lekk's child? She's born of high power. Could she successfully bear his child? Is her future son the King of Kings?

I replace the book on the ottoman and back away, fearing for her, for my kingdom . . . I take a breath, forcing myself to let the anguish go, and take flight to find Lo.

I STOP AT THE RED MASK TO CHANGE CLOTHES. AS I WALK through the empty halls past closed bedroom doors, I hear raised voices coming from inside a room.

Jasper and Helina.

I continue past, giving them privacy.

After changing into a fresh set of clothes, I materialize at the bar and imagine my mother beside me, imagine what she'd say if I could truly speak to her.

"I told you." The figment of my imagination appears on the barstool beside me, a glass of chocolate rum beside her. "You've fallen for that girl."

"Even in my imagination, you're smug." My throat tightens. I've longed to meet my mother's spirit since my death, but I never have.

I grab the bottle of rum and pour a glass, my mind drifting toward Nizzara. She slept so soundly, not a single nightmare. I stare into the amber liquid. "Why does the universe also have to be so cruel?" I was murdered but not allowed to pass on. Given power but no freedom. Sent to kill the woman I wish to be with . . .

My mother's imaginary form tilts her head, looking me up and down. "Don't turn your back on your heart, Dae." That's what she'd say.

"There's no happy ending here. Either she dies or I do."

"Everyone dies, Dae. The happy ones are those who choose to live in the meantime."

Jasper clears his throat from the doorway. "Talking to yourself?"

Helina stands behind him with a scorned expression.

I peer at the stool next to me. The wonderful figment of my imagination is gone. "You could say that." I stand, tossing my glass of rum back in a quick shot.

Jasper takes the stool next to me with a grave expression. "The rebel camps were hit by Skeeves last night. They need supplies now. Many are injured and dying. They don't have enough to save—"

"Then, let's go."

"I have some medical supplies gathered here," he says, "but they'll need more. Someone needs to take what's here while I travel to Zem for more."

"I'll take it," I say. "You go fetch the next shipment."

Jasper clasps my shoulder. "You'll need to move fast."

I nod. I'll miss my chance to find Lo, but people are dying. She'd understand. My heart twinges, and I hope wherever she is, she's safe— happy.

Jasper leads me to the back alleyway, where he's assembled a mining sled full of medical supplies boxed in crates. Jasper wishes me luck and Helina, still teary-eyed from their spat, offers a goodbye before she follows Jasper to fetch the remaining sleds.

The sled is heavy, most of the boxes containing mineral rocks and water. I pull it through the narrow passage until I reach the wall.

The nearest perimeter gate is five miles down the wall, guarded by infantry soldiers. It would cost too much time to drag it that far off course. I resort to climbing the wall. Unable to spirit the boxes over, I hoist a box onto my shoulder and climb over before going back for the next one.

I move as fast as my human form can go, scaling up the stone wall with one hand, descending the other side, piling crates on the blood-orange dirt.

After twenty-six trips, only the sled remains. I tie the sled's pulling ropes around my shoulders and waist, creating a makeshift harness before beginning my final climb.

It thunks and scrapes below me. Once I reach the top, I straddle the wall and muscle the sled up, tugging and pulling the ropes until its nose peeks over the wall. I grab hold and pivot, yanking it up and over, before lowering it down to the other side.

Once it's loaded, I run. The first few miles are smooth terrain with few boulders. I pass through the glo-kar tracks I made with Nizzara the other night.

Boulders start to get thicker and bigger, reminding me why this journey must be made on foot. Even the narrow sled is barely squeezing through the open crags, and I'm forced to slow down to maneuver it.

I haven't consumed a soul since Garret's, and this is a particularly draining trek. Anything done in my human form simply requires more energy. I feel the last sliver of the soul snuffing out from within me.

It makes me think of Nizzara in the training room, lifting the weight out of spite. I smile.

And keep going.

CHAPTER 71

NIZZARA

PREYSEE FLIES INTO MY ROOM IN A PANIC. "ROACHY BAS-
tards," she mumbles as she hurls my covers off me.

The brisk air bites my exposed skin.

"Good morning?" I say, trying to organize my schedule in my
mind. Breakfast, training, tutor session—which I'm excited about because I have a theory for Thaddeus—

Preysee shakes her head and tugs me off the bed. "Not a good
morning, my lady. Your final duel has been moved to now. Decreed by
King Rajim and King Tigous."

My feet stop moving as Preysee's still tugging. "What? Why?"

"Because they can." She lets go of my arm to draw a quick bath—no
fancy oils, just soap. She yanks out a towel and hairbrush as the water
fills the giant tub, then she leaves for my closet.

"To catch me off guard?"

A muffled reply comes from the depths of my closet: "I'd bet gold
ren on it."

She emerges with my favorite set of duel leathers. Black with metal
spikes down each arm and an X belt down the front that holds more
daggers than any other suit.

"They only need two kings in favor of a schedule change," she
says, pointing me to the bath. "Zem is still bitter about your stunt
at the Winter Rave, and Zo is resentful their fighter died outside of
the ring, losing them the tournament again, so I imagine they want
to get it over with."

I climb into the water and freeze.

"What time is my duel?"

Preysee dips the loofah in the water and begins scrubbing me. "The glo-kars leave in thirty minutes."

Dae.

He's still gone.

CHAPTER 72

DAGEN

BY THE TIME I REACH THE EXPANSE OF PILED STONE, I AM drained. The guards recognize me and emerge from their rocky hiding places.

"I brought supplies," I say, catching my breath.

Hoack steps forward, eyeing the sled. "There's a lot more supplies than usual." He scratches his chin and mumbles, "I'll have to check the storage caverns to see if we can fit it."

I straighten. "You don't need to use them now?"

That's when I notice the guards are at ease, smiling and laughing with each other.

"No, Your Majesty. There may be a few in the cave who might need a bandage or disinfectant, but the rest is surplus." He tilts his head, thinking. "The purified water will be nice to have. Our supply has been waning."

Baratrum cold sinks through me and the guards around me stiffen as if they feel the change in the air. "There was no Skeeve attack?"

Hoack's thick brown brows bunch together, and his breath is visible. "Skeeves? No, Your Majesty." He taps his finger in the air. "Actually, there was one attack. We just stumbled upon it this morning."

He waves for me to follow, and my feet drag from exhaustion as I do. He leads me and another guard down a rocky trail a few hundred yards away to a bloody mess.

A dead woman, one eye wide open in an expression of fear and agony. The other eye is nonexistent, smoothed over by onyx skin.

Black spots span her face, neck, and hands. It's as if the Skeeves thought about changing her into one of their own, but devoured her soul instead,

"See that blood trail?" Hoack points to a long bloody mess that stretches as far as the eye can see. The blood turns more black and less red as it nears the body. "Looks like she was dragged from Zarr city."

My gaze returns to her face. I've seen her before. Not in person, but from a memory. Nizzara's memory.

It's Palko's wife.

"This is the Skeeve attack?" I ask, fists curling.

He nods. "The only one I know about."

Why would Jasper lie?

Why would he send me here?

Ice cracks along the ground. No answer I can think of is a good one. I point at Hoack. "Double the guards around camp. Don't let anyone pass."

His grip tightens on his axe. "Is there a threat, sir?"

"I don't think the threat is here but be ready. Just in case."

He dips his chin. "I will, Your Majesty."

I turn toward the horizon, and that's when I see them.

An army of Skeeves.

CHAPTER 73

NIZZARA

I WALK DOWN THE POLISHED-STONE TUNNEL TOWARD THE duel ring. The Megadome above me sounds deserted. I tilt my head up, peering at the spotless ceiling, where my reflection in the black stone follows me. No shouts or cheers seep through the walls. No stomping of feet. No vibrating hum thumping through the massive building. As I continue up the tunnel, I don't pass anyone. No officials, no healers, no weapon servants. I emerge through the tunnel opening and continue to the duel ring. Kazem waits, a promise of death on his face and not a single scratch on him from his duel two nights ago. The Megadome *is empty*, filled only with two rows of Zo and Zem noblemen along with the King's Duel officials; no one else was notified of the schedule change, it seems.

Kazem's burgundy dueling leathers showcase every broad muscle. Under these glo lights, his outfit shimmers. Glistening red studs cover his forearms, one stud for each opponent he's killed in the ring—or so people say—and too many to count.

I climb up and duck between the luxury ropes. He smiles and takes hold of the dueling swords at his waist. "Nice of you to come on such short notice."

I death-grip my sword and shrug. "Today. Next week. I'll kick your ass any day." Even if I was the type to back down, the law requires all duelers to fight to the end of King's Duel.

His smile turns lethal. "Except *today* your spirit is busy, isn't he?"

Blood freezes in my veins. He shouldn't know Dae is gone . . . or that he's a *he*.

My knuckles strangle the black hilt. "That's why it will be even more embarrassing when you lose."

Nodding toward the gold vessel on my hand, he adds, "You can't win if you don't use your vessel at least once."

A duel ref, whose light features and blue eyes tell me he's from Zem, takes his podium beside the ring, and I'd bet my life that he's in Kazem's pocket. The bell blares overhead, sounding louder in the nearly empty dome.

A blinding spray of red smoke from Kazem's hand sends his gleaming sword surging for my chest.

I bend backward. His sword grazes the leathers over my abdomen, slicing through my suit.

Before my feet firmly land, his second sword swipes my flank, slicing with faster-moving power than I've ever seen. Searing pain races up the gash.

I death-grip my sword with every ounce of golden strength I have, but his red smoke snaps it from my hand as if I wasn't even holding it, faster than my eyes can register.

His vessel strength and speed are powerful. *Too powerful.*

He drills my sword down through the mat, past the hilt until it disappears, sinking down through the stone floor beneath us.

That's when I notice the red studs on his shoulder. They're not just glinting in the lights. They're *glowing* on his shoulders. Blare gems.

Fuck.

I don't have time to glance at the official, but if I did, I bet I'd see gold ren filling up his pockets for overlooking *that* little detail.

I hurl a dagger at Kazem's leg, but a puff of red smoke stops it midflight, and it doesn't move again. I palm two more daggers and run toward him.

Another puff of red steals every dagger on me except the one hiding in my boot, sending them in line with my first.

Fuck, fuck fuck.

By the way he's neatly arranging each dagger in the air with his red smoke, turning their points toward me, I know he's going to drag out my humiliation as long as possible.

With his attention on my plethora of floating blades, I charge at him. I yank my last dagger from my boot and jump. My knife carves a gash down his face, deep enough to scar.

I land, turn to admire my work, and—

Dread sweeps through me. The sliced edges of his cheek begin mending together with tendrils of his red smoke.

His *Mark*.

He can heal himself. Not just accelerated healing like me.

Instant. Healing.

Kazem laughs at my expression. "Ready to join the Awom from the Winter Rave? After I ruin your reputation as a skilled dueler, that is."

Darkness rolls through me, and golden light breaks out with it— *fighting against it.*

A scream tunnels from me as I charge him.

Kazem hurls his sword at me and it pierces my torso so hard and fast, it blows me off my feet like a piece of shrapnel. I hit the mat. Kazem's smiling face appears above me through the black haze climbing through my vision as he drives the sword deeper with his vessel power.

My scream eclipses the sickening crack of the blade running clean through my body and into the mat below. Blood pools at the surface, bringing a gold light with it, shimmering among the shades of scarlet. It's Wala's gift running through my blood, healing around the blade lodged in me.

But it's not enough.

Not for the wound. Not for the rising darkness.

Kazem bends over me as if admiring his work. I kick my spiked boot as hard as I can, driving it into his face.

He crumples to a knee, growling from pain before mending the gash on his cheek.

"You're a dead bitch," he snarls, taking his second sword and driving it through my gut with the same wet kiss of blood and flesh.

Stars explode on the ceiling of the Megadome only to be snuffed by building darkness.

Another scream escapes my lips, but it's quiet. Air is barely coming, wheezing in and out.

For the first time in my life, I *reach* for that darkness. I want to kill him—I *will* kill him—but the golden light flares inside, shoving the abyss back like a moving wall, keeping it from my grasp.

Kazem rips his first blade out of me and raises it, its bloody point aimed for my heart. He grips it with both hands over his head—a death blow about to land.

I grab the blade of the sword still pinning my abdomen to the mat. Its edges cut through my palm like butter, but I don't let go. I scream as I pull, slicing new flesh as I yank the blade free. With every grunt and cry of pain, the darkness beats against that golden wall inside.

Kazem's eyes widen with a flash of disbelief before he thrusts his blade for my heart again. I roll out of his line of fire.

Barely.

My arms shake, my breath wheezes, and my muscles seize as I pull myself onto my elbows, crawling away.

Kazem must like the sight of me crawling, because from my peripheral, I see him raise his arms. Noblemen cheer as blood spills from my face and body, and noblewomen scream his name from his royal box, which is completely full.

My eyes find my royal box.

It's empty.

Silent.

Not a soul is here for me.

Kazem saunters around to face me and kicks my jaw. My head rebounds with a spray of blood. Darkness slams against that golden wall, cracking it.

I push myself up, but my arms give out, dropping me back to the mat.

Kazem stomps on my hand and bends down to me. "I'm not supposed to say anything," he whispers by my ear, "but your bonded spirit is dying a final death as we speak."

Dae.

There's no hesitation. No one nearby to get hurt. I mentally punch through that golden wall—that final layer of protection from the monster inside—the forbidden essence bonded to my soul. Its darkness sweeps in.

And I welcome it.

It peers out of my own eyes with me, gazing up at Kazem as a black hole of power forms inside. For the first time, I acknowledge what I am and what my power does.

I'm a Guardian, and I siphon.

I steal power and it becomes mine.

The Megadome goes black in my vision like a night sky with no moon—black like my nightmares. This time, I *can* see through the darkness, see every life-form and soul twinkling in the distance, tempting me to steal their power as easily as taking a breath.

Inside, I find shreds of power I've accidentally siphoned over the years, begging for release, I find a tendril of my father's Jaxelli blood gift—stolen from him when he whipped Yisabell. As my father's power fills my veins, I understand it like it's my own. A piece of the puzzle clicks into place. His control over others wasn't his Mark. It was the power of a Dark Jaxelli with the gift of blood.

Get up. We do not lay at the feet of others, the darkness hisses.

Or maybe it's me who hisses. The distinction between it and myself blurs.

I push from my elbows up to my knees, my mother's soul slowly healing me from the inside.

Kazem's eyes glint with false victory as he points his sword at my neck, its tip centered in front of my throat.

Kazem goes to surge the blade forward when my father's power explodes from me. I take control over his body, and Kazem freezes like a statue, his blood *bending* to my will, his sword unmoving at my neck.

He grunts, veins popping as he tries to move, his reddish-brown soul flaring in the darkness around me.

I gaze at the sword in his hand—or perhaps the monster does—and force Kazem to snap it up, until the bloody blade pinches his carotid artery. I sense his blood pulsing beneath his skin. I could halt it, and it would obey me.

Kazem's eyes are wide, a lucid puppet full of fear.

A shudder of pleasure washes through me, the monster loving that sight.

"I will enjoy this," I growl, not recognizing my own voice.

I force him to step away from me and he does, his boots jerking backward on the mat. I command his blood and raise his blade up, up, up, until his red smoke falls from his vesseled hand. All my daggers still floating above fly for me.

I flick my wrist, and he surges the sword through his own jaw before his daggers reach me. Blood sprays from his neck as he crumples to his knees and crashes in front of me, his fallen daggers beneath him.

The monster growls inside of me, forcing me to turn and look at all the innocent souls twinkling in my solitary darkness.

Drain them all, it thinks inside my mind, and the monster jerks my hand up, calling all their power and life into me. The audience sags.

A golden thread of light thrums inside me, and light returns to my eyes, more of my mother's gift absorbing into me, healing and giving me control once more.

The darkness smiles at me before receding into the depths of my soul.

I look down at my hands, swaying on my feet.

My pulse weakens, the Megadome spins, and pain stings my—

I look down. One of Kazem's daggers did hit me.

Right through the center of my chest.

I sink to my knees, a golden buzz humming through me.

The last of my mother's gift.

CHAPTER 74

DAGEN

I NEVER CONSIDERED WHAT WOULD HAPPEN TO A DEATH-walker who is starved for souls, but as my weakness gnaws from expending so much energy on this wildly rushed trip in my human form, I wonder if I could wither away from existence.

A final death.

The Skeeves are bigger than humans, with hard, onyx skin and no faces. Only a mouth with razor-like teeth, which shadows drip from.

The whispering kind.

"Ready a defense!" I yell over my shoulder to Hoack, who yells orders to his second.

Thirty Skeeves glide toward us.

Thirteen guards fall in behind me, where we protect the cave entrance.

"This is it?" I hiss to Hoack. "I thought we had at least fifty."

Hoack's face pales. "I sent half to retrieve a supply train this morning."

From within the cave, a baby cries.

I call my sword of shadow to my hand. Its long, black blade flickers, my weakened power fighting to sustain it.

"Fall into two lines," I yell behind me. "One in front, one in back! Guard the entrance!"

"Remember," Hoack calls out. "Chop their heads off or they'll keep moving!"

Skeeves jump onto our lines. An axe sinks through the shoulder of one, while my blade slices the head off another. The one with an axe in its shoulder removes the blade from itself, yanks the weapon forward, and sinks its rabid jaws around the neck of the man who held it.

The body of the one missing an arm and a leg begins crawling impossibly fast for the man next to me, claws thrashing. The man beside me chops it with his axe, and its head rolls before it drops like a rock, ceasing to move.

They move so fast, and our lines dissolve in bloody screams. We're outnumbered. I reach through a Skeeve chest with my fist, and I realize they have no souls left for me to feed on.

With every thrust of my sword, I'm draining. A Skeeve jumps and lands on Hoack.

I pivot, slice, and the head drops.

Another one jumps onto Hoack's second. I spin and drop it too.

One clears the wall of guards and takes off for the tunnel. I spirit to it and catch my blade around its neck as it thrashes, and saw through until its body hits the ground in two pieces. Fuck, it takes so much time and energy to behead every single one.

My short absence from the front is noticed. Cries of pain and death erupt as the Skeeves begin attacking in twos and threes.

I jet back to the front.

Skeeves are falling, but our lines are falling faster.

It doesn't matter how skilled I am. I can't save the man twenty feet away while I'm saving the man behind me.

My blade is beginning to shorten, flickering. My movements are slowing.

Our lines shrink to five men, who are barely standing, and we have roughly twenty Skeeves left.

That's when more appear on the horizon.

CHAPTER 75

NIZZARA

I HAVE NO IDEA WHERE TO BEGIN LOOKING FOR DAE, SO I return to the castle. My only thought is to try the Red Mask. When I run up my steps, prepared to change clothes and find a way to sneak out the tunnels, there's a new set of guards at my door. A dark-haired giant with walnut-colored skin and brown eyes blocks my doorway when I try to move past.

"Infantries do not belong in the castle," Brunar spits.

The handsome infantry grins. "King's orders. You've been relieved."

Brunar stiffens at my side, his face turning a mottled red. "I take my orders directly from the king—"

The brown-eyed infantry soldier pulls a gem gun out from under his dark winter cloak and holds it against Brunar's temple, pushing the barrel until Brunar is leaning his head all the way to the side.

"The king has business to attend to and told me that if you put up a fight, well . . ." He rubs the gem gun alongside Brunar's temple, and it hums with energy, ready to fire. "I think you get the idea."

"The code," Brunar grits out. "What's the code for me to stand down?"

"The code," the soldier says with a wild grin, "is death."

Brunar's eyes flash to mine. It only takes one tiny shake of his head for me to understand—and for him to die.

The sound of gunfire rings throughout my corridor.

Brunar's red soul rises as his body falls. Infantry soldiers surround my personal guard.

Another round of gem gun fire, and my guards all drop dead. I hurl my dagger for the center of the leader's forehead.

He stops it midair with a wave of silver smoke and tsks. "I don't think you want to do that."

The Dark essence curls inside, and I reach for it, no golden thread to keep it in check as the monster grows. It fills my limbs, takes control.

Blackness slides into my vision as the leader's soul flickers green and black—a halo of light surrounding him. I begin to drain it.

The leader clutches at his throat. "The collar," he chokes out to his men. "Get the collar."

Giant hands fight me to the ground and strap a collar around my neck with a black gem the size of my fist. The moment it latches, the connection between me and my power is severed. Instant, burning agony shatters through me, pulsing throughout my body.

The darkness is still here in my soul but inaccessible. It claws for control over me again—hissing and thrashing—but it can't reach me either. I feel its cataclysmic hatred and fear of restraint—of being locked away. It screeches with fury as I shove and kick the men off me, trying to drain the leader again, but nothing happens. Just intense waves of pain that make my knees shake.

I claw at the collar, the monster hissing at me to get it off.

The brown-eyed leader holds a key in front of me. "Locked."

I swipe for the key, but his silver vessel smoke yanks it from view.

I jump for a kick to his jaw. He snatches my ankle with a crushing fist and slams my body to the cold stone floor.

Crouching down as agony courses through me, he says, "If you annoy me, little princess, your Awom friend will die."

Yisabell.

The leader plucks my daggers from their sheaths and hands them off to his men. "Now, get up and walk," he snarls.

I climb to my feet, and he takes a position close behind me.

Tilting his head beside my ear, he says, "Don't draw any attention to yourself, and we won't have a problem."

They lead me back down the stairs, down the next two floors, through King's Hall.

We're halfway through the hall when Halix materializes in front of us, blocking the men with a look that could kill. "Let her go," she orders, bearing her sharp Jaxelli canines.

"Kill the animal," the leader barks, and his men raise their gem guns.

Halix throws her arm out and a violent wind sweeps through the hall, knocking giant portraits from the wall. The gust changes direction and pulls the cloaks of the infantry soldiers over their heads, blinding them, before the wind slams us all to the ground and sends their guns sliding across the floor behind her. I quickly rise to my hands and scramble toward Halix, but a man grabs hold of my leg and drags me backward. I kick for his face, but he doesn't let go.

Two men jump up and run at Halix while the leader crawls closer. She moves fast, whipping out a gray wavy sword, and kills the two infantrymen.

"Halix!" I scream the moment the leader reaches her. He snatches her ankle and yanks her off her feet. Her head makes a sickening thud when she hits the floor, but she still fights as the leader crawls on top of her and slams one of my daggers through her side.

The man fighting me catches my other leg and pins me to the ground.

Halix's gray eyes find mine, pain and panic swirling in them, before she disappears into a trail of mist.

The leader drops to the floor from the sudden absence of her body beneath his. He climbs to his feet, shaking off the surprise. "You know our orders," he barks to his men. "Let's go."

The one pinning me down jerks me to my feet and shoves me forward. They step over their fallen comrades and lead me into my father's chambers. I'm manhandled down the steps, led under the castle by my own infantries, who are obviously *not* ours. Somehow, despite their silver vessels, they are spies, but who do they work for? Unless— the awful thought occurs to me—they're carrying out my father's orders. But if that were true, why would they not know the code to make Brunar stand down? Why would Halix be fighting them?

It can't be my father.

The leader shoves me unnecessarily hard, and my rage snaps through me. I turn, winding up for a punch to his jugular, but he says, "Yisabell would pay dearly for that."

My fist halts midair before lowering back to my side.

"Good little princess," he says before kicking me in the back— which is still healing—and I fall down the stone steps.

They lead me through the passage to where a white glo-kar, beaming with red gem light underneath, sits idling beside Dagen's red one.

A man with bronze skin and a white eyebrow piercing opens the back door of the glo-kar for me. "I don't think we've officially met." His smile darkens. "I'm Jasper, heir to the Zo kingdom—the rightful owner of the First-Made vessels."

CHAPTER 76

DAGEN

HOACK AND I ARE THE ONLY TWO LEFT STANDING WHEN my sword severs the head off the last Skeeve. We slump to the ground in sync with the Skeeve as it falls lifelessly off my blade.

"Please tell me there aren't any more," he gasps, clutching one of his nastier gashes along his side.

"There aren't."

"I've never seen them attack in numbers like that," he says, out of breath. "They usually hunt on their own, or in no more than groups of three."

Hoack's memories flash of the Skeeve attacks he has witnessed and he's right. This was much more organized—not the hungry frenzy of one or two rogues.

My body tenses as rage fills every inch of me.

Jasper told me there was a rogue attack *before* it happened. Why?

I think back to the fight I overheard before he sent me here. Something about the King's Duel schedule—

I jump to my feet. There's no hiding the sway in my legs. I am starved.

"What's wrong, Your Majesty?"

"Hoack, I have to go. Are you—"

"I'm okay. Go."

I point to the Skeeves littering the ground, remembering Jasper's warning. "Separate the heads from the bodies. Round up what help you can, and take these remains far from the cave, as far away as you can get." I glance at one of Hoack's fallen men, just as a lingering shadow disappears into his lifeless body, and the skin on his neck turns a shiny black color as it slowly spreads toward the man's face. "Take the fallen soldiers with them. They will rise again."

He dips his chin, exhausted and full of dread. "Yes, Your Majesty."

I disappear into spirit, and it lessens the fatigue, but as I fly toward my castle, I can't help the feeling that I'm too late.

And my flight is too slow.

CHAPTER 77

NIZZARA

JASPER MOTIONS FOR ME TO CLIMB INTO THE GLO-KAR. "Has your ghost king returned to you yet?" Tilting his head down to mine, he reads the look on my face. "I didn't think so. Come on, now. We have places to be, and time is pressing, I'm afraid."

Dae. My insides twist. Where is he?

When I don't jump into the glowing glo-kar, he brushes a gloved hand against my cheek before grabbing my jaw and yanking my face closer. "My guards did mention the bondslave, didn't they?"

I scowl.

"Ah, they did. Good, so I don't have to. Get. In."

I slide onto the white leather seat next to the woman who helped me with mind blocking. Helina.

"I'm sorry," she says.

I release the full force of my father's glare, and she shrinks in her seat. A moment later, she whispers, "He threatened my daughter. You don't understand a parent's love for their child."

"You're right." My teeth clench. "I don't."

She flinches.

Jasper slides in with a smile, sitting on the opposite bench from me and Helina.

I hide the shake in my hands by clenching my fists, and despite the fatigue in my body and the collar chipping away at my sanity, I focus out the window, on the Barrens flats as we drive over the tracks Dae and I left behind. The glo-kar slows to a stop when we reach the Zarr city gate, and the soldiers stationed there allow us through. The glo-kar rumbles as it hits the cobbled streets and continues through the city of black towering buildings toward the Zo kingdom.

"The Zo heir is Hollom," I say, my mind working.

Jasper rolls his eyes. "Decoy."

"Why?"

He flicks a speck of dust from his white suit. "If you're half as smart as Dagen thinks you are, you'll figure it out."

"You know about the prophecy regarding the blood of the Zo heir," I say. "There are two possible futures—two heirs who could wield the First-Mades."

His grin becomes lethal. "I know all there is to know. About prophecies, about Dagen, about you . . . All through his cold, tortured mind. *You cruel little beast.*"

My heartbeat races in my chest. *Through Dae's mind . . .* I slam my mental walls down, wondering what he's already seen inside my head.

Jasper leans forward, glaring at Helina, and tugs a small box out of his suit jacket. He opens it to reveal a white, gleaming First-Made vessel. "The Zems really are prideful to a fault, aren't they? Kazem gave me the location of *this* in exchange for my father's vote for a duel change, and a window of time where Dagen wouldn't be with you. I will admit," he says, "waging your life on that schedule arrangement certainly was stressful. I wasn't sure that you could beat Kazem." His eyes slide back to me. "But here you are, alive and primed for my next arrangement."

"What arrangement?" I grind out.

"The First-Mades can only be worn together if they are placed at the same time," he says. "The ancient ones did like to complicate things, but no matter. I've made a deal with someone who wants you very badly. I'll hand you and your possessed father over to her, when he inevitably comes to save you, and she'll remove his vessel for me."

"My father won't come," I snarl.

"Ooh. Touchy subject." He grins.

We pull under the white arches of the Zo palace and a fleet of Zo guards in white uniforms surround the glo-kar holding gem guns. I'm

yanked out of the glo-kar by one guard. Just as he moves to clasp man-
acles around my wrists, a gray, wavy sword sinks through his chest, red
blood soaking his pristine uniform. He drops to the ground, revealing
Halix behind him, my father standing next to her.

His eyes are *lucid*. When they land on the collar around my neck,
they fill with rage. He raises his hands. No black smoke falls when his
power of blood seizes every surrounding guard. One by one, the Zo
guards lift their own guns and end themselves at my father's hand.

"I only have minutes," he grunts to Halix.

Even Jasper is frozen by my father's gift—standing halfway out of
the white glo-kar. His eyes wide, as if he didn't expect my father so
soon.

My father's neck vein pops as he holds the fifty guards surrounding
us. Halix speeds the process along with her sword, ending them with
swift, deep stabs through their chests.

"How did they take you?" Father growls at me as another gunshot
rings out. "I trained you better than—"

An oily spirit falls in from above, shadows swirling through it.

"*So clever you are, prolonging the inevitable. If you'd give in to her
shadows, the pain would be over quickly.*" His spirit disappears into his
shield, where my mind's eye can no longer sense her. And veins of onyx
spread across his face.

His eyes flicker, the cold stones I've become so used to, and his
body falls under her control.

With a jerk of his hand, all the gun barrels point to Halix, and at
least six bullets fire through her torso. She collapses. Her sword loses its
gray glow. So do her eyes, as she bleeds out.

When my father opens his mouth again, his voice barely sounds different. "*Ah,*" his spirit says. "*What a prize indeed. Nexia has grown bored
torturing your daughter this way. She's excited to see how long your soul will
hold out when she kills Nizzara in front of you like you did her mate.*"

"*Nizzara!*" Liha's voice screams through the air, and relief floods
through me. She's still alive. "*His soul can't hold out anymore. You have
to kill him now or else he'll turn—*"

Father's arm surges toward me as the shiny onyx climbs farther up his face. My body bows to his command. It's the first time he's ever used his power on me, but—

His eyes.

He's dying inside them, the hardness snuffing him out. As the blackness slowly crawls over his skin, it hits me with sudden clarity. He's turning into a Skeeve.

My gaze is the only thing that can move. It lands on Halix's bloody sword near my feet.

"*I'll buy you time*," Liha says, her voice fast and panicked. "*But only seconds. You must end him.*"

I'm unable to argue; my mouth is frozen. She's not inside my shield to hear, but I'm screaming at her mentally not to.

She disappears inside his shield, and a pink wave of smoke blows out in every direction, the sound of shattering glass ringing throughout the air—Liha's soul shattering.

I'm released. I scoop up the wavy sword and snap it to my father's chest. But he's *here*. His eyes are warm like they were when I was little, full of love for me. I sense it raining down and drowning me in its intensity. He forces Jasper forward with his power and makes him unlock the collar around my neck. It drops to the white cobblestones. Jasper immediately stumbles backward as my father's power shoves him away from me again.

"Do it, my Nizzara," Father whispers. "You don't have time to hesitate. Do not let your heart blind you."

My arm shakes. "You can fight the possession," I yell at him, tears streaming.

I should be ramming this blade through my father's chest, but I'm paralyzed. Liha is gone.

My father is about to be.

He shakes his head. "I cannot. I've already been fighting my bonded spirit, and I have been fighting her shadows too long. To have more time with you.." The hard, stony presence creeps back into his eyes, and the onyx spreads over his face. "Her Skeeves will be here soon. Finish me and run." His eyes gaze into mine. "Your soul is strong enough to control what lurks in it—far stronger than mine." He stiffens, his eyes darting past me as if sensing something I can't. "You must do it *now*."

The collar's effects linger. I feel my power slowly trickling toward me instead of in an instant rush. "I can't—"

He grabs my sword as if to do it himself, but he's not fast enough. His arms jolt to a stop. When I look up from his grip on my sword, half of his face is a shiny jet black. I shove the tip toward his heart, but it stops at the point of puncture, not breaking through his black uniform.

My father's hand jerks up and releases a force so much greater than the possessed caster I fought in the ring. It takes hold of my neck, lifting my feet from the ground. All around me, the same is happening to Jasper, and Helina, and the fleet of guards.

That's when the world turns to ice around me.

"*Dae*," I whisper as he sinks in my shield. I instantly feel how drained he is. "*What happened?*"

"*I'm fine. No time*," Dae says, pouring what power he has into my veins. It explodes through my body.

Time stops, and the Dark essence unfurls inside me—furious at being locked away.

Its anger surpasses any I've ever experienced. Its power builds and builds . . . my terror building with it. I feel it about to—

"*Focus, Nizzara. You've got to move her power off of you.*"

I breathe through the surmounting darkness, my arms trembling from it. I feel my father's invisible power like a fist around me, and I drink it in—the sensation toxic, *addictive*, like breathing air for the first time—

I stop the moment I'm free, but the monster demands *more*.

When my feet hit the ground, I jerk Halix's sword up to my father's frozen chest. Blackness builds behind my eyes. The last of its restraints are snapping. It will drain everyone here, including Dae. I feel its mind. I try to placate it, force it down, but its anger is ancient, vast, and insatiable. And I just fed it.

I cry out as it claws through my mind—my soul—yearning for the surface. My legs shake from the pain and fury coursing through me. The nose of my blade starts to lower. The darkness digs its claws into me, climbing up, up, up . . .

Black, thick ice cracks up the sword in my hand, and the world sinks into a cold I've never known, infinitely colder than Dae. Infinitely colder than anything.

Dry ice climbs through my veins, freezing as it goes, until a dark figure is towering at my side. No shape, no eyes. And more power than I've ever witnessed.

"Dagen," it says in a voice that sounds like many. "Your time is at an end. Deliver her to me."

"Nil," Dae wheezes. I feel him draining to the point of fading. Draining from *my power* as I use him to suck time from existence. "I will not deliver her." His voice is weak, hollow.

"Then you shall face your bargain." He begins to pull Dae from me.

"Wait!" I shout. A small *crack* comes from deep within. The monster is clawing its way out, yearning for pain and destruction. As it drinks the sands of time, it grows. It tastes the life and magic in the air, and it wants—

"I will bargain."

If there's any chance of saving Dae, of saving everything . . . it's me that has to go.

Nil's clouds of darkness stir. "I'm listening."

"I will go with you—"

"*You will not!*" Dae's dark spirit encases me like a blanket, trying to hide me. It only makes me long to save him more. Even from myself.

I stagger toward Nil, my knees threatening to give out as I internally battle the monster about to take control of my soul. There's no time left. No pushing it down. No hiding. It's manifesting, and I can't stop it. "I will give my soul in exchange for Dagen, the King of Kings." A foolish part of me still hopes I'm not what I think I am, but—

"*Nizzara!*"

"*It is you, Dae. You are the king who will bring peace to this realm, not me. Find Yisabell when I am gone. Save her.*"

I speak to Nil as the world remains frozen in time. "You will give him complete freedom. You will not call upon him."

The frigid air gusts around me, taking my breath away—halting the dark monster inside as if it recognizes Nil.

"Your father was right, Pure One. It is your heart that weakens you."

I grit my teeth. "Do we have a bargain or not?"

"*You do NOT!*" Dae flickers in my shield, fading fast.

"I cannot return him to life," Nil says. "He will still have shadows in his soul. He will still be half dead."

"Complete. Freedom," I hiss.

Nil's power hums across my skin without him even touching me. Somehow, I feel his satisfaction . . . as if he'd planned this exact outcome.

There's no contemplation, no pause. "We have a bargain, Pure One."

I waste no more time and do what I should've done minutes ago. I ram my sword through my father's frozen chest. Tears slide down my cheeks, but I land true through his heart.

Dae slumps as time resumes.

My father stumbles back, hissing and thrashing before he disappears. Gone in a trail of dark mist.

Jasper is still frozen, but out of obvious fear as he eyes the giant, visible, dark god now looming in front of him.

"It is time." The god speaks like an earthquake through the air.

"*Try not to miss me,*" I say to Dae.

Such anguish leaks from him. I hear his tears when he chokes out, "*You cruel beast.*"

Nil wraps himself around me. A scream rips from my lungs as my soul is torn from my flesh, but the worst part is the bond shattering between Dae and me.

He disappears from my senses.

No more cool nudges at my shoulder.

No more velvet voice.

No more coy jokes.

The golden vessel ring drops from my finger, clinking to the cobblestones with a metallic clarity.

It rolls until it hits Dae's black boot.

He picks it up and squeezes it in his hand, tears in his eyes.

Clutching my vessel ring with one hand, he sinks his other through Jasper, dropping him where he stands as it tears and cracks Jasper's soul.

Helina screams, but Dae's gritting back tears as he finishes shredding Jasper's soul with no reverence.

No remorse.

Just cold ruthlessness.

Dae fades from view as I'm sucked from my lifeless body, lying at his feet. That's when the darkness sinks in.

The soul-burning cold.

And the shadows.

CHAPTER 78

DAGEN

IT'S BEEN THREE DAYS.

I think.

My castle is empty because her room is empty.

But I haven't left it. Her sheets still smell like her. Her books are still where she left them, full of notes scribbled in her awful scholar's script, and her favorite black dagger is in my hand.

My eyes glisten in its reflective sheen, puffy and red around the edges.

I should've known she'd pull something like this.

I've been in the same spot on the floor, against her bed, for a while, replaying her end with the sinking feeling I missed something—something she blocked in her mind. I replay it all, how I killed Jasper, the hidden heir of Zo, for what he did. If there wasn't already a war, there is one now. Especially since I took the First-Made off his dead body.

A knock comes on her door.

I don't answer. I don't care. Her *funeral* is tomorrow. She's no longer brimming with heat and life. I know exactly what she's facing, and I'm powerless to stop it.

After I ignore another demanding knock, it opens to a man in white robes. I jump to my feet, Nizzara's dagger clutched in my fist.

Thaddeus steps in. I'm starved and incapable of reining in the shadows. They claw to the surface.

"All the ways we could kill him."

Before I can take a step in his direction, dark purple smoke washes his face and it's—

"You're in my room." Her voice is just as menacing as I remember.

My hand falls slack at my side, my voice splintering. "Lo."

She runs to me and buries her face in my chest.

I squeeze her hard. Her chest is heaving, or maybe it's mine. She's the same height, her arms wrapping the same spot around my chest, her hair the same dark brown. Her presence the same, my fiercely protective older sister.

Finally, she looks up at my face. Her teary green eyes, now ten years older, search mine. "You loved her."

The unbearable sting burns behind my eyes, down my throat, and lodges in my chest. All I can do is nod.

CHAPTER 79

DAGEN

I TAKE ANOTHER STEP AGAINST THE ICY BARATRUM WIND, searching the dark glaciers and plains of ice for her white hair and honey skin. My tether to Nil is cut. I no longer feel the tug to where he is, and I don't expect him to appear anytime soon, so I wander aimlessly through the crags and shadows looking for her.

I don't care if I'm the King of Kings. She cannot take my place in this realm. So, every night I come here.

Shadows slither around me, taunting me with *her* voice, beckoning me into the glacier's deep crevasses. Such evil things, they are.

My hands go from icy blue to black. That's how I know it's time to go. When I give the horizon another desperate sweep and find nothing, I return home, loathing the heat of my castle as soon as it hits me.

"You're not going to find her unless Nil wants you to," Lo says from the wingback chair in Nizzara's room. She moved her belongings from the small scholar's quarters into my former chambers, letting me stay here in her old room.

"I will find her," I growl. The shadows slither inside, trying to slip through any restraint I place on them—barely contained.

She crosses her legs and leans back into the chair. "Nil has his prize. He won't let you near her. You have nothing he wants."

Ice breaks across the floor like black webs. "Then I will find something he wants."

Her green eyes soften like they always have for me. "*We* will find something he wants."

I close my eyes, fists clenching. "While we fight a war from all sides."

"We need funds to secure our infantry," Lo says, her thin eyebrows pinching down. "I've seen Mazzar's ledgers. There isn't much." She taps the armrest, her agitated tell. "As much as I hate to admit it, we need the Zo libraries. They have lore on Skeeves."

"We can ask Rajim for money, but we cannot go to Tigous after what I did to his heir."

The lines on her face tighten. "I don't think we can go to either of them at this point."

"So, what are we going to do, Lo?"

She smiles that conniving smile of hers, the one that tells me we have a lot to discuss, as she pulls Jasper's First-Made vessel from her pocket.

"We will show them why you are the King of Kings."

ACKNOWLEDGMENTS

I want to thank my husband, Mason, for supporting this wild dream of mine, and my two boys for loving me even when my head is in the clouds. A special thank-you to my agents, Alex and Brenna, for believing in this story. A big thank-you to my editor, Nate, who not only championed this story but gave me all the creative freedom, fully trusting my chaotic brainstorming and writing process. Thank you to each and every reader, bookstagrammer, and author who has encouraged me, accepted me, and helped me in this journey. A special thank-you to Kim, Courtney, Amber, and Katie (aka the Marketing Gorls) for brainstorming marketing ideas and helping me get this story into the world. Thank you to my tough but loving beta reader, Sarah Kaake, for shaping *Vesselless* into what it is today. Thank you to Torri, Bodie, and Kharyssa, who nurtured my dream of writing books and were my first fans. Thank you to all my author friends on Instagram, the Beta Fish group from Twitter, my beta readers, and every person who has believed in me. Last, but not least, thank you to my amazing Secret Street Team. Your support will stick with me throughout my life. A special thanks goes to Hollie, Heather, Kate, Amanda, Alex, Keri, Nickesha, Alex G., Aspen, Skye, Kayla, and so many others who helped spread the word for *Vesselless* and believed in its earliest version.

ROYAL LINEAGES

ZARR
GLINDELLA RULE

MAZZAR GLINDELLA
KING

SORIAH AMBROSE GLINDELLA
QUEEN

**TARELLA
GLINDELLA**
DAUGHTER

**NIZZARA
GLINDELLA**
DAUGHTER
CHOSEN HEIRESS OF
ZARR

ZARR
CORVONNA RULE

GORRIK CORVONNA
KING
(DECEASED)

MAVEN CORVONNA
QUEEN
(DECEASED)

**LOLA
CORVONNA**
DAUGHTER
(DECEASED)

**DAGEN
CORVONNA**
SON
CHOSEN HEIR OF
ZARR
(DECEASED)

**AARIK
CORVONNA**
SON
(DECEASED)

ZEM

RAJIM VALENCIA
KING

LORNA VALENCIA
QUEEN

SEBASTIAN VALENCIA
SON

KORINA HAANS VALENCIA
WIFE

DAGEN CORVANNA
HUSBAND
(DECEASED)

KATHREEN VALENCIA CORVANNA
DAUGHTER
(DECEASED)

KAZEM VALENCIA
SON
CHOSEN HEIR
OF ZEM

HARPER VALENCIA
NEPHEW

ZO

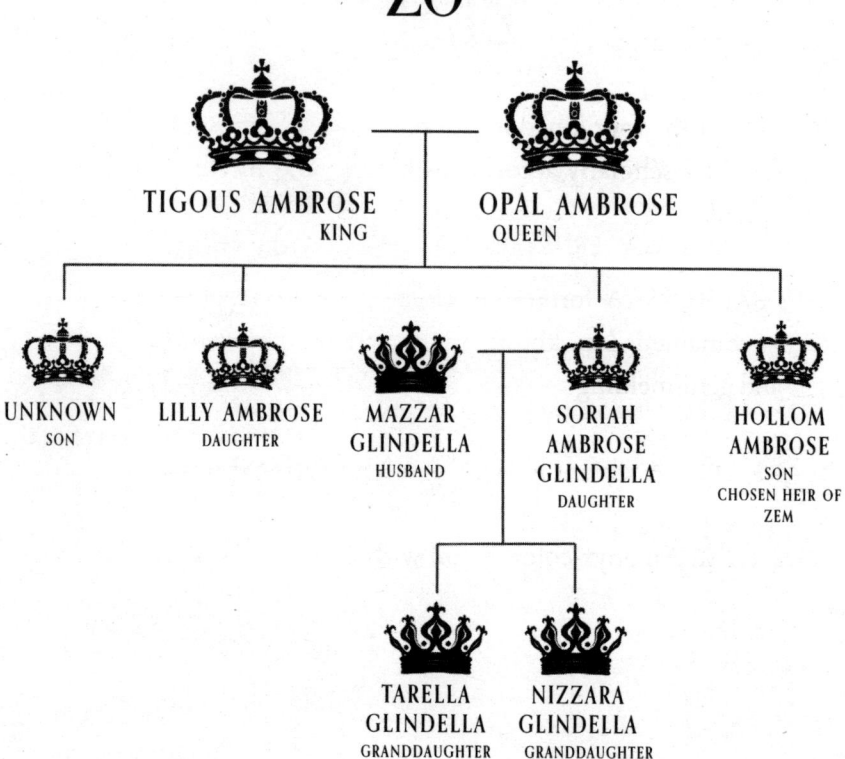

TIGOUS AMBROSE
KING

OPAL AMBROSE
QUEEN

UNKNOWN
SON

LILLY AMBROSE
DAUGHTER

MAZZAR GLINDELLA
HUSBAND

SORIAH AMBROSE GLINDELLA
DAUGHTER

HOLLOM AMBROSE
SON
CHOSEN HEIR OF ZEM

TARELLA GLINDELLA
GRANDDAUGHTER

NIZZARA GLINDELLA
GRANDDAUGHTER
CHOSEN HEIRESS OF ZARR

GLOSSARY

ZARR: One of the four kingdoms in the Bond of Kings Alliance, known for their ruthless military, border control, and law enforcement

ZEM: One of the four kingdoms in the Bond of Kings Alliance, known for their economic savvy, financial resources, and mining of special gems

ZO: One of the four kingdoms in the Bond of Kings Alliance, known for their scholarly accolades, libraries, and intelligence-gathering abilities

THE BARRENS: A former kingdom in the Bond of Kings Alliance, once named Zap, known for their advances in both technology and gem-melding

BLARE GEM: A vibrant red gem that has the power to amplify

VOID GEM: An onyx-colored gem with the power to siphon or drain

ABOUT THE AUTHOR

CORTNEY L. WINN is the author of *Vesselless*. She's also a mom, wife, business marketer, wedding cake artist, and self-proclaimed Diet Coke enthusiast. Born, raised, and still living in Utah, Cortney writes in the early mornings, starting her day at 4 a.m. with her laptop and a giant coffee in hand.